"Shh… Tracy, it's okay." He hugged her tighter and ran his hand down her red hair.

A tenderness he hadn't felt since his wife was still alive kindled inside him. David wanted to release Tracy. He needed to release her, but *she* needed *him* right now.

She shook her head, her face still pressed into his shoulder. "No, it's not going to be okay."

David eased her from him and gripped her shoulders to look into her tear-reddened but still beautiful silver-blue eyes. "I'm so sorry about what you came across today, but Jay is going to be all right. And the police are searching for the guy who did this."

"You don't understand." Shaking her head, she moved away from him.

"Why don't you tell me, then? Is it the man who shoved Jay over today that has you upset and scared? Or is there something more?" The question sounded too personal, but he couldn't think of any other way to say it.

"Yes, there's more." Tracy stared into the fire.

"I'm listening. Tell me."

"I was the key witness in a murder trial. The killer on the mountain might be here for me."

Elizabeth Goddard
and

USA TODAY Bestselling Author

Margaret Daley

Lethal Rescue

Previously published as *Backfire* and *To Save Her Child*

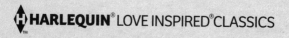

H HARLEQUIN® LOVE INSPIRED® CLASSICS

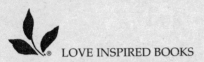

LOVE INSPIRED BOOKS

Recycling programs
for this product may
not exist in your area.

ISBN-13: 978-1-335-08186-5

Lethal Rescue

Copyright © 2018 by Harlequin Books S.A.

First published as Backfire by Harlequin Books in 2015
and To Save Her Child by Harlequin Books in 2015.

The publisher acknowledges the copyright holders
of the individual works as follows:

Backfire
Copyright © 2015 by Elizabeth Goddard

To Save Her Child
Copyright © 2015 by Margaret Daley

www.Harlequin.com

Printed in U.S.A.

CONTENTS

Elizabeth Goddard is the award-winning author of more than thirty novels and novellas. A 2011 Carol Award winner, she was a double finalist in the 2016 Daphne du Maurier Award for Excellence in Mystery/Suspense, and a 2016 Carol Award finalist. Elizabeth graduated with a computer science degree and worked in high-level software sales before retiring to write full-time.

Visit the Author Profile page at Harlequin.com.

BACKFIRE

Elizabeth Goddard

And we know that in all things God
works for the good of those who love him,
who have been called according to his purpose.
—*Romans* 8:28

This story is dedicated to my Lord and Savior
Jesus Christ, who gave the ultimate sacrifice
when He laid down His life to save us. And to all the
first responders, search-and-rescue volunteers and
firefighters who give their time and energy and face
dangers of the worst kind to help others. I pray for
God's grace and many blessings for you. Last, but
never least, I dedicate all my stories to my husband
and children, who give me the time and space I need
to create stories, with a special dedication
to my daughter, Rachel, a real princess.

Acknowledgments

Many thanks to all my writing friends
who have encouraged me along the way, and a
special thank-you to Teresa Haugh for providing me
with the important details to keep this story true to
the southeast Alaska setting. I can't thank my agent,
Steve Laube, enough for believing in my work
early on, and to my editor, Elizabeth Mazer—
thank you for making each story the best it can be!

ONE

Mountain Cove, Alaska

Tracy Murray knew she had little time. A storm brewed in the distance.

But Solomon's urgent bark pulled her up the rising trail, indicating that there was someone in danger.

She sucked more air into her lungs that were already screaming from her workout.

Any other season on this trail—spring, winter, fall— she'd have to be concerned about the avalanche danger. But not during the summer, and because the season was so brief in Alaska, Tracy had every intention of enjoying the outdoors. Out for a run with her search-and-rescue golden retriever, summer abounded around her in the form of wildflowers and sundry small wildlife scurrying in and out of the flora.

Tracy had been heading for Keller Falls, four miles up the trail, until Solomon had taken off. She'd let him run free and hoped to practice a few commands. Up until a moment ago he'd run beside Tracy, surprisingly ignoring his natural instinct to chase forest animals, but then he'd taken off. With his continued excited and ur-

gent barks, she knew that he had caught a human scent
and was sending his vocal cue to alert Tracy that something was wrong.

Dread replaced the serenity she'd found on the trail.

Solomon was an air-scent search dog, wilderness
search-and-rescue certified, and Tracy was still training him for both cadaver and avalanche certification.
They'd already participated in several searches in the
region as part of the North Face Mountain Rescue team.
But Tracy hadn't taken her dog out looking for trouble
today. No. She'd been looking for peace.

Instead her much-loved pet had likely found something. Or rather, someone.

Avoiding the steep and hazardous drop on the right
side of the trail, Tracy kept running toward Solomon's
sound-off. It surprised Tracy how far Solomon had gone
on his own in the wilderness, but he'd obviously picked
up a human scent that he intended to follow.

Though certified, Solomon was often eager to con-
duct a search even when he wasn't tasked with one,
which frequently ended in false alarms—finding someone who wasn't lost. But if this was something more
this time, at least she wasn't alone if she needed to call
for help. She wasn't the only one who enjoyed an early
morning run on this trail. Another runner had taken
off on the trail ahead of her, and she'd run into David
Warren heading the opposite direction on the trail, too.

He'd nodded and she'd nodded and they'd both
given each other wide berth. Kind of funny now that
she considered it. Living in Mountain Cove for two
years, Tracy had worked with the firefighter on several
search-and-rescue missions, but he seemed aloof. A
few years older than Tracy in his late thirties, the man

still attracted plenty of female attention with his rugged appearance and strong, lean body. His smile was the kind that turned heads and could make a woman weak in the knees.

Despite all that, he wasn't married, didn't have a girlfriend, and Tracy knew why—he was too cold on the inside. Even if he wasn't, she'd have kept her distance because of his profession. Tracy wanted to avoid any reminders of the night that had changed her life forever. Any reminders of what had sent her into hiding.

Make that who.

And that was one reason she'd chosen to live in Mountain Cove. Surrounded by temperate rain forest in Southeast Alaska, the chances of seeing a wildfire were next to zero.

She shook off the unwelcome thoughts and focused in on Solomon's alerts. His barks came from the area to her right, which was nothing but a steep ridge. Her heart sank. She'd purposefully avoided that ledge. How had Solomon found his way down? Or had he fallen?

God, please, no.

"Solomon!" Tracy crept to the edge and peered out over the rocky, jagged escarpment, part of the gorge that originated at Keller Falls. Where was he?

The drop was steep, terraced with granite or bedrock in places, and it was on one of those natural terraces that Solomon stood barking. Fear gripped Tracy. How could she bring Solomon back up?

"Solomon! Come," she called.

The position of his ears and tail signaled that he'd found someone who was injured or scared. Solomon peered up, his brown eyes somber, and when he saw her, he lay on the small space—a signal to mark the spot. But where was the injured person?

Then, just beyond a bush growing from the ridge, she spotted a body. Tracy's pulse thundered in her ears. The breath rushed from her—it was the man who'd run ahead of her. But Solomon hadn't signaled that he was dead.

And then the man lifted a hand and called out to her. He wasn't dead after all, but he'd taken a fall. How had he survived?

Tracy could barely hear his cry for help.

"I'm calling for assistance," she yelled down to him. "Just hang in there!"

A chill slid down her spine. The sense that someone watched crawled over her. Phone in hand, she called for help for the fallen jogger while she scanned the woods behind and around her.

A man stepped out of nowhere and Tracy gasped—then let out a sigh of relief when she saw it was David.

But the sense of unease didn't disappear.

And she still had a feeling she was being watched.

Breathing hard, David bent over his thighs before gasping out, "I heard the dog, wanted to see if there was a problem." David wiped the sweat from his eyes, sucked in a few breaths to slow his breathing after he'd sprinted up the trail then cut through the woods.

Phone to her ear, Tracy stared at him with those big silvery-blue eyes of hers, the terror slowly fading away to shock and concern. What was going on?

Scrunching her freckled nose, she glared at her phone. "Lost the signal. Oh, I don't have time for this."

"What's wrong?"

A deep frown crossed her features as she shoved the thick red hair from her face. "I'm so glad you're here. A runner fell. He's down there." Urgency in her voice, Tracy paced as she pointed to the steep, rocky drop. "He needs our help."

David peered over the edge and spotted Solomon—how had the dog made it down there?—and just beyond he saw the hiker. The man was still alive? Apprehension lodged in David's gut. How long had he been there?

Pulling his own phone out, he looked for the bars. "Got 'em. Use my phone to call for help. I'll climb down to him." David was assistant chief of the Mountain Cove Fire Department and a paramedic. He spent most of his time as a firefighter answering EMS calls rather than fires, and he had too many SAR certifications to count. He was well qualified—he just wished he was better inventoried. Out on his morning run, he had no medical equipment or emergency supplies. All he could do was assess the man's injuries and reassure him while they waited for help to arrive.

Reaching over, Tracy pressed her hand against his arm, uncertainty in her eyes. "Be careful. You don't even have your climbing gear."

He'd gone on enough free-soloing climbs—free climbing with no ropes—to know this ridge wouldn't be a problem for him. "Don't worry. When you reach someone, tell them we'll need a helicopter to hoist this man out. That fall had to have severely banged him up." If he wasn't mortally wounded.

David suspected the latter but wouldn't voice his concerns because Tracy was already on edge. She'd seemed unusually distressed. In their previous interactions, the experienced search-and-rescue volunteer was always in control of her emotions. Was there more to this than she'd admitted?

Before he climbed down to the injured jogger, he needed to know. "Did you see what happened?"

She shook her head. "Like you, I followed Solomon's bark. He took off ahead of me."

David eyed the dangerous ledge, deciding on the safest and quickest path to the man. He started down, with one last glance up to Tracy, and noticed her looking behind her as though she expected someone to jump out of the woods.

Gripping the rocks, he paused and called up. "Tracy."

His short, snappy tone got her attention.

She peered down at him. "What?"

"Did you reach anyone?"

"I'm on hold."

"Figures. Are you going to be okay?" He should be more concerned about the fallen runner, but he couldn't shake the sense that something had scared Tracy. Or was he just being an idiot?

"Of course. Why wouldn't I be?"

He shrugged and continued down.

Tracy had caught his attention the first time he'd met her a couple of years ago. She'd just moved to Mountain Cove, she'd explained after he'd run into her coming out of his brother Adam's bicycle shop. Collided, more like, and he'd had to assist her off the ground—her and the new bike she'd purchased. He should have offered to buy her coffee or something. Any normal red-blooded male would have. With her thick, red mane and deep, striking eyes, he hadn't stopped thinking about her for weeks after running into her.

Maybe he was just lonely. Starved for female companionship. But he didn't think that was it. There was just something about Tracy. But getting involved wasn't for him anymore. Yeah, he saw how happy two of his siblings—Heidi and Cade—were now that they had each finally gotten married. Cade and his wife, Leah, had had their first child two months ago, naming him after their late father, Scott Daniel Warren. And Heidi had married Isaiah, a family friend, SAR volunteer and a coworker at the avalanche center that their father had founded. David's siblings had done well for themselves.

He'd known that kind of happiness once. But he'd lost it; let it slip through his fingers. He didn't deserve it again. His wife had died in a fire when he, a decorated firefighting hero, had failed to save her. How could he have let that happen?

He didn't deserve happiness. Not after that. And after Tracy had snagged his thoughts with one run-in, he knew to keep his distance from her on their search-and-rescue missions and training events. And even when he saw her in town.

He reached Solomon and petted the dog, giving him plenty of reassuring verbal rewards.

"I'm on my way down," he called to the injured man. "Hold on."

The trim man looked to be about average height, healthy except for the way he lay twisted at an angle a few feet below the narrow ledge where David and Solomon now stood. He likely had a few if not many broken bones and possibly had internal injuries, as well. David was astounded he had survived, and if the rescue helicopter didn't arrive soon, he might not make it.

Carefully gripping the rocks, David inched his way down.

Finally he reached the narrow terrace and looked

down into dark gray eyes filled with pain and fear. "My name's David. I'm a firefighter and paramedic. Lie perfectly still. Help is on the way."

Kneeling beside him, David assessed the fallen man's wounds the best he could, but with a possible spinal injury, David avoided moving any part of his body. Blood oozed from a gash in the man's head, coagulating in his light brown hair. David removed his own jacket and then his T-shirt, using it to apply pressure to stanch the flow. He could do at least that much. He cringed to think of what was going on inside the injured man's body.

"It's pretty bad, isn't it?"

"You're going to make it."

God, let my words be true. Save this man, help him. The man closed his eyes.

"What's your name?" David had to keep him awake, keep him talking, if he could.

"Jay Woodall."

Maybe David couldn't offer much physical assistance, but emotional and mental encouragement was just as important.

Clouds brewed in the distance, forecasted to bring a torrent, and David could already smell the rain. Lightning flashed and thunder rolled, warning of the storm's imminent approach and leaving David unsettled. They didn't usually get thunderstorms. He sure hoped that helicopter got here soon. He didn't want to see Jay suffer any more by getting soaked and chilled on top of his injuries.

"Why?" Jay's croak resounded with the shock of his trauma.

Recognizing the man's emotional distress over his

predicament, David frowned. Was he asking why God would allow him to fall? David had enough of those questions himself. Questions he'd never resolved since he'd lost Natalie. He feared it might take a lifetime to find the answers, or worse, that he never would. He fought to keep from railing at God on some days. But he shoved his inner turmoil aside to focus on the here and now and the man who needed his help.

David might not be able to answer those kinds of questions, but maybe he could help in other ways if he knew more. "Can you tell me what happened?"

"Someone…pushed me over. Tried to kill me."

The news stunned David. Did Jay know the person who'd done this?

David glanced up the rock-faced cliff and spotted Solomon watching. From here, David couldn't see Tracy. He wished Solomon would find his way back up to her.

Was Jay's attacker still up there? If so, Tracy was up there alone with a dangerous man—a man who'd attempted murder.

TWO

Tracy ended the call.

Help was on the way, but would it get here before the storm? Wind whipped around her and the trees swayed. A sound caught her attention from the thick woods behind her. Woods she'd enjoyed only moments before. But now the dense tangle of trees had turned dark and sinister, as though hiding a secret.

Or a killer.

She rubbed her arms to chase away the chill that crawled over her. She was being ridiculous. If only David hadn't sprung from the woods like that and startled her. Her heart still pounded from the scare he'd given her. That was all this was about. There wasn't a bogeyman standing in the shadows. She didn't have to be afraid anymore. The only people who had any reason to want to harm her were thousands of miles away and had no idea where to find her.

She peered down the ledge. David was with the injured man, holding his hand and offering gentle reassurances. She couldn't hear what they said from there, but could tell the man, broken as he was, had relaxed somewhat.

Maybe David wasn't as cold as she'd thought. From here, she could barely make out his chuckle. Probably telling the man a funny story or joke to get his mind off his injuries. Glancing up at the sky, she tried to gauge whether help would arrive before the storm. She knew how difficult it could be to execute rescues in stormy conditions, but this man would die without immediate help. As the sky grew darker, so did the woods.

Again that sense that someone was watching slinked over her and kept her on edge. Tracy hated her paranoia, but she had good reason.

Tracy looked behind her again, watching her surroundings to reassure herself no one was there. Normally she had the comfort of knowing that Solomon could protect her if there was anything to worry about. But how to get the dog back from where he'd traveled down the ledge? She called him, using the command he should quickly respond to, but he wouldn't move from his perch. She had no idea if he simply wasn't able to make the climb—though she hadn't seen him try—or if he was committed to the fall victim.

There was nothing for it. Tracy would have to climb down to him. She was an experienced climber herself and had paid attention to David's path down, but she couldn't see herself going all the way to the fallen jogger without climbing gear. Again she searched for the path Solomon had taken, but saw nothing, at least from this angle.

She eased herself down and, her feet and hands gripping the rock face, pressed herself into the granite, taking in quick breaths. She hadn't ever done this solo—without the ropes in case she fell. But it wasn't that difficult. Solomon had picked his way down without climbing somehow, so she knew she could, too.

She sent up a quick prayer and continued to make her way until Solomon was only a few yards below her. When fear crept in, she imagined she had the necessary ropes and gear to keep from falling and continued on.

The next thing she knew, hands gripped her waist. "You're almost there," David said. Relief flooded her as David assisted her the rest of the way. She could have done it without him, but it was a comfort to know he was—literally—watching her back. But why had he felt it necessary to leave the fallen runner?

When she turned her back to the rock face she'd just scaled, David stood mere inches from her.

Much too close.

"What…what are you doing? Why did you leave him down there alone?"

"I needed to check on you, too."

"I'm a big girl. I know how to take care of myself." His nearness and concern confused her. Putting space between them, Tracy knelt next to Solomon and hugged him to her. "Good boy."

"The man's name is Jay Woodall, by the way."

David studied the ledge above as if looking for that same bogeyman she had feared moments before. Or maybe more help.

"Oh, now I can see how Solomon found his way, David." Tracy pointed to a place a few yards to the right that connected with the trail farther down. There were enough rocks and outcroppings for the dog to stair-step his way. "Solomon and I could go back up and wait for the SAR team coming on foot. We can show them the easier way down, while you wait with Jay for the helicopter."

"No. You and Solomon should stay here, where I can see you."

"David." Tracy stood as he turned to face her. "What's going on?"

"Somebody pushed Jay over."

The news punched her gut. Tracy gasped and cupped her mouth, stepping back.

"Watch it." David caught her and pulled her away from the ledge. He gripped her arms. "I don't know why someone would do that, but we can't know if they're still lurking in the woods somewhere and waiting for their chance to finish the job."

"You have a gun, right?" Tracy expected he carried some form of protection with him when in the woods in Alaska, as did most people. Bears were the main threat. Tracy had her bear spray, but somehow it didn't make her feel secure if she had to face off with a killer of the human variety.

His features twisted into a half frown, half smile. "Yeah, even when I'm jogging. But don't worry. I can't believe anyone would do something like this and hang around for long. We'd see him for sure."

Tracy nodded. Solomon could warn them, as well. Jay was fortunate that she and Solomon had been on the trail when they were. People often told her Solomon's breed didn't make for a good guard dog, but he'd saved her life once. She'd trust him again.

"I want you to go down and wait with Jay," David said a moment later. "I'm going to check the trail and make sure it's safe for the incoming SAR team."

"I'm not as good a climber as you. I don't think I could make that."

"It's not that far. I'll go down first and if you can ease down a few inches I can almost reach you."

When David moved to scale the cliff the rest of the way to Jay, Tracy grabbed his arm. "David."

"Yeah?"

"Thanks for coming back to check on me."

"Of course."

His gaze lingered on hers longer than necessary. She wasn't sure why, but unfortunately, she liked it. What was it about him?

Then he turned his attention to the climb down. She couldn't have known when she woke up this morning that the day would end with her taking refuge on a small terrace in a cliff face with Solomon, a fallen jogger and David Warren, hiding from a would-be killer.

Tracy waited with Jay while David climbed up to make sure it was safe by the trail for the incoming SAR team. The guy had courage and was all about protecting others.

He leaned over the ledge and looked down at her now to let her know he had finally returned. The clouds chose to release their burden at that moment, lashing them with a relentless fury and forcing her to drag her eyes away from the ledge.

At least the rain woud keep her from looking up every other minute, terrified that the next person she saw would be the man who'd shoved Jay over the ledge.

How was it that she had to face off with a killer twice in her life? She wanted to question God about the insanity in this world. Wanted to condemn David for leaving her. Solomon, too.

As it was, she feared Jay was quickly losing his battle with death. But she was thankful David had returned. She never thought she'd ever be so glad to see him—a man she'd avoided.

She looked up again and saw David. His gaze held hers as the rain pounded all of them and he shouted, "I'm coming down."

"What about the rocks? Won't it be too slippery? Maybe you should wait," she called up.

"I have gear this time. SAR is here." He shot her a smile and gestured with the climbing ropes before he started setting an anchor. But then he frowned. Called down to her. "How's Jay?"

Tracy's heart lurched. "Not doing very well, I'm afraid."

He made it about halfway then called down to her again. "You pray, Tracy?"

She'd prefer he paid more attention to rappelling in the rain than trying to reassure her.

She wished she had a hood. Something. Rain splattered her face when she called up. "Yes, of course."

"Well, good, then. Because we have that, if we have nothing else. And it's what truly matters."

Tracy had seen the Warren family in church; heard they were heroes and Christians. But she hadn't known the depth of that conviction until now, when David gave her a glimpse of the man he really was on the inside.

And then he was right next to her, holding her steady in the pouring rain.

He pulled the pack from his back and took out a big

sheet of plastic. "Here, take this for a minute. I'm going to hold this over you and Jay to cover you."

He also tugged out a thermal blanket. "Now, cover Jay. At least we can keep him from getting any wetter. Keep him warm."

Tracy nodded and did as David asked.

Jay's eyes blinked open. "Why did this happen?"

"I'm sorry… I don't know. But there is a helicopter coming. It'll be here soon, Jay. You're going to be just fine." She didn't want to ask if he was in pain because she knew he was. "As soon as the helicopter gets here, the SAR team will position you in the rescue basket and the medics will take care of you."

God, please let the rain stop, just long enough for us to get Jay to safety. Airlifting someone injured could be treacherous on a good day, much less in a rare thunderstorm.

Why had this kind of weather unleashed now, with Jay straddling this world and the next?

"What happened, Jay? Why'd someone push you off a cliff?" Tracy cringed. Should she really be asking him? It wasn't her business. Those questions were for the authorities.

Still, it creeped her out to think that Jay's would-be killer had been lurking in the woods. Maybe if she understood what had happened, she wouldn't be so scared.

"Saw him on the trail. Stopped to catch my breath. Just making conversation. Then he tried to kill me." Jay coughed. "Probably thought he succeeded. That's what I get for being too friendly."

Tracy had nothing else to say but that she was sorry, and she didn't want to say that repeatedly. Nor did she like the sound of his cough. Maybe he shouldn't even be talking. She opened her mouth to tell him that he should rest now when he spoke again.

"He had an interesting tattoo. I've been thinking about getting one...and I asked him about it. Maybe that's what sent him into a fit. How crazy is that?" He squeezed her hand.

But it was as if he squeezed her heart. Tracy couldn't breathe. Images of the worst night of her life filled with flames and smoke and death accosted her. Somewhere outside her memories, David asked if she was okay, but she couldn't escape the images.

"Tattoo?" she finally managed to ask. "What...kind of tattoo?"

Jay closed his eyes. Was he unconscious again?

"Jay, please, I need to know. It could help us identify the man who did this."

She held her breath, afraid she would never get the answer. Fearing what the answer might be all the same.

The pounding rain slowed to a trickle, giving them a reprieve. In the distance she heard the whir of the rescue helicopter.

The plastic David held shifted. "Tracy," he said. "I need you to climb back up to give us room to get Jay on the rescue basket and into the helicopter."

Still reeling over what Jay had said, she couldn't respond.

"It's safe, Tracy. Others are up there. The Mountain Cove PD is on the way, too."

He lowered the plastic. "Tracy? Are you okay?"

"Sure. Give me a sec." She squeezed Jay's hand, trying one last time. "What kind of tattoo, Jay? Please, it's important."

He looked at her then, the pain in his face almost intolerable. "Numbers and a scorpion with flames on the wrist. I should have known better, but I thought it was cool. Asked what the numbers—"

Tracy didn't hear more, having already gone into a shock of her own.

No, it couldn't be...

How had he found her?

THREE

The helicopter hovered above them.

David stood underneath the rescue basket that was used like a medical stretcher, watching as Jay was hoisted up and into the chopper. The rain was beginning to lash them again. Carefully securing Jay in the basket without complicating his injuries had been a difficult task and had required the SAR team and the expertise of the flight paramedics working together. David was also a paramedic, but he was tired and drained and had stepped back to let the fresh crew on duty do their jobs. However, Jay had wanted him there, holding his hand, making it a tight fit on the rocky terraced outcropping.

David said a silent prayer that Jay would fully recover. All things were possible with God. Like Jay being found to begin with. The helicopter swayed unsteadily in the wind, and lightning flashed. This was one of the most hazardous rescues he'd participated in.

And he hadn't even been on call. He'd just happened upon the situation, or rather, Tracy had happened upon it. Her search-and-rescue dog had been the one to alert her, and David had heard the dog's bark in the distance.

He hadn't even thought twice before he'd turned around and run back up the trail to find Tracy and Solomon.

Despite his severe and potentially lethal injuries, Jay would live—that much David believed to his core. The guy was a survivor and had a strong will to live. Once he had been lifted and secured, the helicopter carried him away on the flight of his life.

The adrenaline rush that had kept David going bled out of him, and he realized he was chilled to the bone in his rain-soaked running clothes, minus his T-shirt, of course. But there was one more mission David needed to complete. One more person he needed to see to. Tracy had never left his thoughts.

The SAR members that had helped with the extraction—David's brothers, Cade and Adam, and their brother-in-law, Isaiah—had already climbed back to the trail. David followed them up, making his way slowly and meticulously in the rain, bringing the climbing ropes with him. When he'd come here for a quick run before the storm he could never have imagined this day would turn out this way.

When he finally reached the trail, David discovered Tracy had already gone. But what had he expected? For her to wait in the rain for him? Not to mention there was a would-be killer out there. Unless the police had caught the guy, no one was safe on the trail. Besides, why would she wait for David? It wasn't as if they had ever been anything beyond acquaintances until today. And even now, David wasn't sure they'd inched any closer to an actual friendship. That was why his disappointment surprised him. But on the other hand, he was glad she had gone.

The torrent had begun again. David didn't bother to

make conversation with Isaiah, Cade and his younger brother Adam. Instead they trudged their way toward the trailhead.

David tried to process everything they'd just been through, including Tracy's reactions, which unsettled him in some way he couldn't quite define. They just didn't make sense. It was normal that she'd been shaken by the idea of an attempted murder, but there was more to it than that. David hadn't been able to hear her conversation with Jay over the noise of the rain beating down on the tarp he'd held, but he was sure that whatever it was Jay had said had shaken Tracy. But what could it have been? David shrugged the question off. He wouldn't be getting any answers to it out here.

Finally the rain let up again. David hoped it would stay that way until he was inside his truck with the heat on.

Isaiah stepped up next to him. "The police showed up and escorted Tracy and Heidi back. They were going to take Tracy's statement about the fallen jogger and what she'd seen."

"Are you saying they didn't search the woods?" David asked. "Just took a statement?"

"I'll talk to Terry and see what I find out," Cade said.

Terry served on the Mountain Cove PD. He and Cade had been close since grade school, though Terry was a friend to all the Warren siblings. David would ask Tracy what she'd told the police, as well.

They made the trailhead where their vehicles were parked. Isaiah and Cade scrambled into Cade's truck, Adam into his own vehicle, and David climbed into his shiny, brand-new, blue Ford Super Duty F-250 FX4 4x4. He loved his truck and was glad he'd special-ordered it, though that had required a wait. But if he'd been trying to fill the empty space inside with material goods, he knew he'd failed. For whatever reason, the incident this morning seemed to drive home his loneliness.

He waved at his brothers then turned on the ignition and the heat. Dripping wet, he shivered and stared out the window, recalling what had happened.

The fear he remembered from Tracy's expression told him that something was terribly wrong.

Considering the way their brief encounter had affected him the first time he'd met her, David had made it his policy to steer clear, never involve himself with her. He shouldn't get involved now, but he couldn't stop thinking about her reaction. Couldn't stop thinking about her. He wanted her to be safe, but he knew it went much deeper than that.

He was more confused than ever.

Finally at home, Tracy gave Solomon a much-needed bath and fed him. Then she took a hot shower to wash away the events of the day as well as the chill from her body, then put on a pot of coffee to brew. She needed to stop her shivering limbs. But as she slipped into her comfortable, warm sweats, she was still shaking. The real source of her trembling had nothing at all to do with getting chilled on the mountain.

No. Her trembling had everything to do with the strong possibility that Carlos Santino had somehow found her.

The tattoo that Jay had described was the tattoo worn by Santino and his gang members.

Fear crept over her again as she recalled Jay's words.

"Numbers and a scorpion with flames on the wrist...

I thought it was cool. Asked what the numbers—" Tracy knew what those numbers meant. She knew more about that particular tattoo than she'd ever wanted to. Every kind of gang—ethnic or otherwise, street gangs or prison gangs—had their coded tattoo system and tattoos symbolizing membership.

The scorpion and flames identified Santino's gang, and the numbers identified how many kills. As that number grew, other tattoos would tell the story elsewhere on the body.

But Santino was supposed to be in a prison in California—over a thousand miles away. As far as she knew, no one in this region of Alaska had even heard of Carlos Santino or his gang…except for her.

How could that be a coincidence, especially when you threw in Jay's attempted murder? Had he finally found her so he could pay her back for her testimony against him? He'd threatened her, warning that he would find her and kill her with his own hands. And that had sent her running.

Hiding.

There was only one thing to do next. Find out if Santino had escaped. Tracy dug through the drawers in the old rolltop desk that came with the cottage, her nervous fingers creating a mess of the contents and making it more difficult to find the card she needed. She should have memorized the number. But she'd wanted to put that part of her life as far behind her as possible. Find some normalcy.

Lord, why did this happen?

She huffed a laugh. She was asking Jay's question now. She hoped they would both get answers.

There. She gripped the corner of the card at the very

back of the drawer. Of course. Tracy slid it to the front and lifted it from the drawer. The insignia at the corner was a marshal's badge similar to those worn in the Old West movies, only this one had an eagle embossed over the top of the badge. It read "US Department of Justice, United States Marshals Service." Then "Jennifer Hanes, Deputy US Marshal" was printed beneath those words.

Jennifer would have handled Tracy's transfer into the WITSEC program if Tracy had chosen to go that way. She had told Tracy to call her if she ever needed her.

Tracy's hand shook so much, she couldn't read the number. She placed the card on the desk. Though she dreaded the call she had to make, Jennifer would be able to give her answers. The problem was Tracy wasn't sure she wanted to hear what the woman had to say. Still, she needed to know if Santino was still in prison or if he had escaped.

She moved around the cottage until she found a good signal and made the call. It went to voice mail and Tracy left a quick message. She didn't detail what had happened; only asked if Santino was still in prison.

"Please call me back," she said. "Something's…happened."

Tracy ended the call. She had thought she'd never talk to Jennifer again. She hadn't imagined she would ever have to. Setting the phone on the desk, she admitted that she'd really just hoped and prayed she would never have to contact Jennifer again.

The call made, there wasn't anything more Tracy could do until she heard back. She'd told the Mountain Cove police everything that had happened today. Everything except about her past and why she'd come to Mountain Cove. Telling them a killer could have followed her here when she was still considered relatively new to the community might make her look like a troublemaker. She'd been afraid to take that risk.

Though she'd lived here only a couple of years, Tracy loved Mountain Cove, and up until today, she had thought she'd found a place she could finally call home. She could never go back to live in Missouri, where her family lived, or Sacramento, where she'd worked as a newspaper editor and where she'd met Derrick. Where all her troubles had begun.

Of course, if Santino had actually come after her here, then she needed to tell the police everything so they would understand what they were up against. She wondered if other law-enforcement entities would get involved, too, swarming down on Mountain Cove. Then the community would wish they had never seen Tracy Murray.

At the moment all she needed was time to think things through. Then if she confirmed it really was Santino she would proceed according to plan, whatever that was. Unfortunately, she didn't know where else she could go.

How could anyone have found her here?

In the old comfy chair by the fireplace, Tracy tugged her knees up to her chin and watched the flames. Even though it was summer, the evenings were cold enough in Mountain Cove, Alaska, to justify lighting the fire. Soaking in the warmth, she tried to calm her nerves. Until she received a return call from Jennifer she would be on edge, trying to figure out what to do next.

She lived rent-free with Solomon in a small cabin as part of her pay for working at Jewel of the Mountain Bed and Breakfast. The job and her living situation had fallen into place so easily after her arrival and had made her feel as though she was exactly where she was supposed to be. Finding Mountain Cove in the first place had been providential. It was the perfect place where she could hide as well as train Solomon for search and rescue. And it was so far off the beaten path, so distant from the world she'd known before, that she'd felt completely hidden and totally secure. But after the events of today, it didn't appear to be far enough away to keep her safe. There was still a chance that her testimony, given years before, would get her killed.

She hadn't been the only witness to Santino's crimes, but the other guy had taken the get-a-new-life card and run with it straight into witness protection. He'd left everything behind to escape having to live his life in fear that Santino would come for him one day.

A knot grew in Tracy's throat and lodged there. Had she made a mistake by choosing to stay out of the program, trying to keep from losing everyone else she loved? Hadn't losing Derrick been enough? Had her decision backfired on her?

Though Tracy had feared for her life during Santino's trial, and the potential retaliation should he be convicted, her biggest fear had been losing her family. Her father had refused to change his name and move the family to start a new life with her. He'd refused to be forced away from the life he loved, surrounded by lifelong friends and extended family. He'd refused to leave behind the oil business he'd built. That wasn't something he could easily build up again elsewhere.

And Tracy had refused to leave her family behind— never seeing them again. Never making contact. That kind of price was too high for the added security of witness protection. It was as though she was the one being punished for doing the right thing.

Instead, Tracy had moved to Alaska, to a place that couldn't even be approached by car. A person could reach Mountain Cove—in the Inside Passage of Southeast Alaska—only via floatplane or boat. Hiking in was out of the question.

And this way, she could still go see her family anytime she wanted, while protecting herself by being almost completely isolated from the rest of the world. Yes, in a way she had in fact run from her life and was in hiding after a fashion, but it wasn't quite as severe as the other choice.

And it wasn't quite as secure, either. As today had proved, there was still the chance that she could be found and her life could be put in danger again.

Tracy paced the room, rubbing her arms, forcing down the bile rising in her throat.

When would Jennifer call back? Tracy wanted to know Santino's status. If she had internet she could search the news feeds and find out. Maybe. But she didn't. Part of the allure of the Jewel of the Mountain Bed and Breakfast was that people were forced to enjoy nature—there wasn't anything else to do, and that, according to Jewel Caraway, the owner and Tracy's boss, made the place the perfect getaway.

Solomon rested by the fire, and Tracy crouched next to him, ran her fingers through his thick, golden fur. "You did well today."

She leaned closer to him. He wasn't a trained attack or guard dog, but she knew that Solomon would protect her better than just about anything else. Or anyone. He'd already proved that once, the night that Santino had burned down her house. The same night he'd burned Derrick's house to silence him forever. Solomon had been able to save Tracy.

A growl erupted from Solomon and his ears perked up. In that moment he wasn't the typical overfriendly golden retriever. No. Solomon was protective of Tracy and he sensed a possible threat. Tracy stood, her gaze flickering to the windows and the door. Fear corded around her throat.

But when she heard the telltale sound of someone approaching the front door, she ran her hand down Solomon's back to reassure him. "Bad guys don't knock."

No. Bad guys push people off ledges. Burn down their homes while they're sleeping. Find good people where they hide in order to kill them.

FOUR

David stood at the cottage door, his knuckles ready to knock. He took in a breath. What was he doing here? Tracy probably wouldn't appreciate the intrusion. And David was conflicted about whether he wanted to be here, too. He'd set his boundaries and now he was taking a step outside that imaginary line.

But Tracy's welfare was much more important than David's need to protect his heart. That was it, then. He wouldn't stand on the sidelines and do nothing. If there was a way he could help he would.

He knocked on the door.

Behind it, he heard Solomon's bark. He couldn't tell if it was a friendly bark or not.

Better identify himself. With a potential killer on the loose out there, he might have startled Tracy. But she wouldn't expect Jay's attacker to knock.

"Tracy, it's David Warren."

He heard the lock disengage and then the door opened. Tracy stood on the other side and eyed him, a tenuous smile on her lips. He could see the questions in her eyes. And along with the questions, that same fear in her gaze that he'd seen on the mountain today.

"Hello, David. What are you doing here?" She held on to the doorknob.

A short laugh escaped him when he realized he didn't really have an answer for her. He'd thought this through so well. *Way to go, David.* "Checking on you."

Solomon pushed through from behind her and came up to sniff David. He leaned to run his fingers through the dog's fur, rub him down. "Hey, boy," he said softly.

With everything that had happened today, he wondered if anyone had told Jay about the dog finding him. Or if Jay had been coherent enough to hear the dog's barks and know how he'd been discovered.

"Why do you think you need to check on me?" Her free hand trembled.

Why indeed? He pulled away from the dog and stood tall, scraping his hand around the back of his neck. He turned to the side and peered through the trees toward the house at the front of the property, noticing the lights were on at the main building of the bed-and-breakfast. He turned his gaze back to Tracy. Might as well be transparent.

"I can see something's wrong, that's why." With each second, he felt more like an idiot. Of course there was something wrong. They'd helped a man today who had nearly been murdered. David should just turn and go. She didn't want him here. Even though he could easily see something was wrong—she was scared to death— he wasn't the one to help.

Just as David opened his mouth to apologize for disturbing her evening, Tracy opened the door wider. "Please come in. I have coffee brewing, if you'd like a cup."

"Thanks, I'd like that." He stepped inside the warm and comfy cottage.

Her simple invitation and the offer of coffee made him happier than it should. He wasn't here to explore a relationship with Tracy. In fact, he wanted to avoid one at nearly all costs. But Tracy's safety was not one of the costs he was willing to pay.

She moved to the small kitchen area against the wall and grabbed two cups. David stood in the middle of the cozy main room and took it all in. She'd made the cabin her own, with quilts hanging on the walls. On the rocking chair hung a partially completed rainbow afghan. A fire glowed in the fireplace, chasing away the chill brought on by this afternoon's storm and the approaching evening. But as comfortable as the room was, David felt awkward and wasn't sure how to proceed.

Tracy moved to the kitchen table that sat only two and set the cups there. She poured coffee into both. "Cream or sugar?"

"Black is fine, thanks."

She appeared to feel as awkward as David. What was it between the two of them? He didn't have this much trouble feeling comfortable with any other person in town.

"Sit down. Make yourself comfortable."

He did as she asked while she went back to the fridge for half-and-half. She poured it from a glass container and again he noticed how shaky she seemed. Then she dropped the glass.

It shattered on the floor, the crashing sound slicing through the awkward silence.

Tracy just stood there and stared, her whole body shaking.

David was up and next to her in a second. "Don't worry about this. I'll clean it up."

His gaze shot around the room, searching for where she might keep her broom and cleaning supplies. What he really wanted to do was just take her in his arms. He'd do that for anyone else who was as obviously upset as she was. Why couldn't he do that for Tracy? What was the matter with him?

Then she covered her face and her shoulders shook. *Oh, boy.*

David pulled her away from the glass on the floor and into his arms. Of course, he knew this breakdown had nothing at all to do with the fact she'd dropped the cream container. That event was simply the catalyst to shred her poised veneer, which David knew had been shaken already.

She sobbed into his shoulder, igniting all those protective instincts inside his heart for her. Having her in his arms this way, her tears accosted the wall around his heart. If he wanted to protect himself, he'd leave before her vulnerability had the chance to obliterate his defenses altogether. But what could David do? He was here now. He had to see this through.

"Shh... Tracy, it's okay." He hugged her tighter and ran his hand down her red hair against her back, trying to stay focused on just reassuring her and nothing more.

But a tenderness he hadn't felt since his wife was still alive kindled inside him. David wanted to release Tracy. He needed to release her, but *she* needed *him* right now.

Her sobbing finally spent, she shook her head, her face still pressed into his shoulder. "No, it's not going to be okay."

A shudder ran over her. What in the world?

David eased her from him and gripped her shoulders to look into her tear-reddened but still beautiful silver-blue eyes. "I'm so sorry about what you came across today, but Jay is going to be all right. And the police are searching for the guy who did this."

She sniffled and pulled away from him to grab a tissue from the counter. He knew he should be glad to have some distance between them again. It was crazy that he wanted her back in his arms. They burned, his chest burned now, where she'd been pressed against him. The girl was more caustic to protecting his emotions than he realized.

"You don't understand." Shaking her head, she moved farther away from him and grabbed a broom and dustpan from a small closet.

David went ahead and picked up the bigger pieces, careful he didn't cut himself handling the glass.

"Why don't you tell me, then?"

Tracy swept the glass into the dustpan and disposed of it. Then she pushed her hair away from her face and behind her ears and turned her big eyes on him. "All right. I'll tell you."

He didn't know why, but her willingness to talk startled him. The fact she trusted him with whatever it was made him happy, though it shouldn't.

"I was surprised to see you at the door, honestly." She grabbed her cup of coffee and instead of sitting at the table moved to the small sofa, curling her legs under her.

He was surprised he'd come himself, but he wouldn't tell her about his inner struggles.

Not wanting to sit too close to her, David took the kitty-corner chair. He also took a sip of the black coffee, still trying to regain his composure. She'd been upset and she'd transferred all that to him, it seemed.

"Is it the man who shoved Jay over today that has you upset and scared? Or is there something more?" The question sounded too personal, but he couldn't think of any other way to say it.

"Yes, there's more." Tracy stared into the fire.

David had suspected there could be more going on from the beginning, but hearing her say the words unsettled him.

"I'm listening."

She dragged her eyes from the fire and studied him. "And that's why I'm going to tell you. I never thought I'd be talking to you like this. Or telling David Warren, of all people, my troubles."

What was that supposed to mean? But he swallowed his pride and kept quiet.

"But you showed up at my door, and there is no one else for me to talk to. I'm waiting for a phone call from the only other person I can talk to about this, and she hasn't come through yet. My family… I can't tell them what happened today. I don't want to scare them, worry them."

"Tell me."

"I was the key witness in a murder trial."

David set his cup down on the side table. "You have my attention."

"Jay's attacker might be here for me. He might have come to Mountain Cove to kill me."

Tracy couldn't stand to see the stricken look on David's face. He shoved himself up from the chair and paced the homemade rug in front of the hearth. His sturdy form seemed to further diminish the size of her small cottage.

She rubbed her eyes, hating that she'd lost it with him. For all practical purposes, he might as well have been a stranger. But, no, that wasn't right, either. She'd known him, just from a distance. And that had all changed today. Why of all people had David Warren come into her life here and now? During this crisis?

"I can't believe this." His voice was gruff. "How do you know? How can you be sure? If that's true, why did he shove Jay and not wait for you to come up the trail? Or why didn't he shove you when you found Jay?"

David stopped pacing and stared at Tracy. She had a question, too. Why did David care so much? The urgency in his tone made it sound as if he cared like someone deeply connected to Tracy. A father. A brother... A husband. She shook off the thoughts. This was crazy. She needed an ally, but at the same time, David was risking his life by getting involved with her. Maybe she should just refuse his help, his friendship.

Tracy frowned. "I don't know if I should answer any of your questions. In fact, I don't think it's a good idea that you're here. Being with me only makes you a target. I need to be alone." If only she wasn't so desperate. If only she didn't need someone.

Tracy had moved here to be more isolated, and she'd been wary of making friends until enough time had passed. She had only started growing closer to Jewel, her boss. That had been a mistake. David being here was a mistake, too.

He stalked over and sat next to her on the sofa, too close for comfort. "You're kidding, right? If there really is a killer after you, you can't go through this alone. I assume you told the police what you told me?"

She shook her head. "Not…yet."

He stiffened. "We need to call them."

"I've put a call in to my contact at the US Marshals office. She'll know if Carlos Santino has escaped prison. That will tell me what I need to know—that he's out and after me."

Oh, no. Tracy grabbed her head, fisted her hair. She'd been so focused on Santino's threat—that he would kill her with his own hands—she hadn't realized what should have been obvious. Santino's long arms could reach her from prison via the gang network.

Santino didn't have to be out of prison to be after her. Still, she had to know if Jennifer knew if something was going on; had to know if Santino had escaped.

"Tell me what Jay said to you that made you think his attacker is after you."

David's nearness, the protectiveness pouring off him, was difficult to resist. More than anything, Tracy wanted to feel his arms around her again. She would never forget that moment, but the problem was, she couldn't afford to dwell on that. To wish for something more with him.

"Carlos Santino is the head of a far-reaching gang and Jay told me the guy who pushed him over had a specific tattoo—it is the tattoo worn by those gang members."

There. She'd told him everything. Almost. Tracy stood to put space between them and went to the fireplace.

Behind her, she heard nothing at all from David. Maybe he was absorbing it all, which she understood.

That could take some time. Or maybe he was contemplating the quickest escape from her and her problems. She wouldn't blame him for that. She wouldn't blame him if she heard the door shutting behind her, but she realized that probably wouldn't happen. If she knew anything about David, it was that he was a solid, trustworthy sort of guy.

Tracy turned to face him then. He was right behind her and she hadn't realized he'd moved from the sofa.

"Listen," she said, "I didn't mean to drag you into this. I won't hold it against you if you bail."

"Are you in the witness protection program, Tracy? Is that even your real name?"

A sardonic laugh escaped. "No, I'm not. And, yes, Tracy Murray is my real name. What does it matter? Did you hear anything I just said?"

"Why aren't you in WITSEC?"

"I chose not to run and hide—well, other than to Alaska."

"If this guy is so dangerous I think you need to get help and disappear. Let the Marshals office assist you with that."

Seeing the concern in his eyes, Tracy couldn't help but smile. "You know, we're only just getting to know each other and you're already trying to get rid of me."

Oh, please, she did not just say that.

He cracked a smile, though only half his face responded.

She liked that look on him.

"I'll be up-front with you," he said. "I'd like to get to know you better, but not at the risk of your life. I'm sorry it took me this long to say more than two words to you, but that doesn't matter anymore. You need to disappear. Where's the number? I'll call them and tell them what happened and how important it is to keep you safe."

David was definitely a take-charge kind of guy, thinking his words would move Jennifer to take action. And his words confirmed to her why she loved Mountain Cove so much. The sense of community here. People cared. She couldn't afford for them to care for her, but still, she didn't want to leave. Didn't want to run again.

"I've called my contact. Left a message. Until she calls me back there's nothing more that I can do." There was nothing he could do, either.

"Sure there is. You can get out of here."

"And go where?" She almost yelled the question at him. She moved away from him, which was increasingly difficult to do in this cottage that seemed to grow smaller by the minute.

At the kitchen sink, Tracy washed out the cups and the coffeepot. She doubted either of them would drink the rest.

"Anywhere would be safer than staying here."

"I'm in the middle of nowhere, practically, David. People can't even drive here. You know that. If someone can find me here, they can find me anywhere. So…no." Well, that was it, then. She had made up her mind, thanks to David. "I'm not leaving. I refuse to have someone else control my life anymore. I won't be forced out of a life I love, a town I love. I'm just like my father after all."

David took the cup from her and placed it in the cabinet. "Your father?"

"Yeah, when I first agreed to testify, I told my family that we could all go into WITSEC. He refused to go into the program with me. He has a successful business he doesn't want to leave behind. He can't start his life over. I couldn't leave my family behind like that, never to see them again. I'd already lost so much." Lost someone she loved. "So instead of entering the program, I dropped off the map on my own. And I love my home now. I'm staying here."

"Okay, then, it sounds like you've made up your mind and I can't convince you otherwise." Something in David's tone pulled her attention from washing out the sink and up to his earthy green eyes. "And believe me when I say that I don't want you to leave."

Tracy wanted to go into his arms. The oddest of things—she'd spent half a day with the man and here she was, wanting to feel his arms around her. She shook off the foolishness his proximity brought on and took a step back.

"I'm not really sure what to say to that."

He laughed. "At least sleep in the house with Jewel and her guests until they catch this guy, okay? And if you don't already have a weapon, then get one."

Stay in the main house and put Jewel and the others at risk? No, she couldn't. "I have Solomon to protect me, to warn me. He saved me before, so I trust him to do that again." And she had the big can of bear spray and the smaller pepper spray she carried in her purse. But her excuses sounded weak, even to her own ears.

David didn't appear convinced, but it wasn't his decision. And yet Tracy cared about his opinion and she wished that she didn't.

"You really think Solomon can protect you from a killer? Maybe he saved you before—I don't know the circumstances. And maybe he can warn you, but, Tracy, even if Solomon was a real guard dog, he couldn't protect you from this guy. And what about the danger to *Solomon*? What if the man has a gun next time? Solomon doesn't wear armor. What if he gets hurt trying to protect you?"

Tracy hadn't thought of it that way, and the accusation in David's tone choked her. But she didn't get a chance to respond. Her cell phone chirped. Tracy rushed to the end of the counter and stared at the caller ID. The number on the screen belonged to Marshal Jennifer Hanes.

FIVE

The next day Tracy was still thinking about her phone conversation with Jennifer as she bought a few groceries and necessary items. She couldn't stay holed up in her cabin, turning it into a self-made prison because of what had happened. After her shift at Jewel's this evening, she'd needed fresh air. Besides, she would soon run out of the basics, such as shampoo, toothpaste and soap—not to mention food. She could eat up at Jewel's but she didn't like to overstep.

And now it was nearing ten o'clock at night and the sun had set about half an hour ago. She had another half hour of twilight or so, at least, but the sour expression on the store clerk's face made it clear that she wanted Tracy to leave so she could close out her register and lock up the store.

She reached for the half-and-half to replace what she'd dropped last night right in front of David. That had been the catalyst that had sent her into his arms. Wonderful, strong arms. And from there she'd ended up telling him nearly everything.

Her hands weren't shaking now, but the danger was

still there. She could feel it closing in on her, despite what Jennifer had told her.

The woman's words drifted back to her now.

"Santino is still incarcerated, Tracy. I haven't heard any chatter on my end to lead me to believe members of his gang have any intention of looking for you to exact revenge. They're busy focusing on running guns and drugs and fighting the law down here in the Lower 48. Honestly, there isn't enough information to go on from what you've told me. Other than WITSEC, there aren't many options for you, if you're concerned about your safety. But I'll tell you what I will do. I'll contact the local police chief in Mountain Cove to bring him up to speed with your particular situation. But let's not escalate things unless it's warranted. You could still be safe there. Please call me if you need me. And, Tracy, remember, per our agreement, the door is still open for you to enter WITSEC."

Though relieved that Santino was still in prison, and the fact that Jennifer sounded unconvinced his gang had come for Tracy, she felt a little let down by the conversation. She wasn't sure what she'd expected Jennifer to say or to do. But if Jennifer believed Tracy was in danger, at the very least Jennifer should try again to convince Tracy to let the Marshals office assist her into a new life. Maybe this time Tracy would listen. She'd mostly wanted Jennifer's reassurance and she'd gotten that, but for some reason it didn't make her feel any better.

Admittedly, Tracy's story didn't sound all that credible, even to her own ears. But she couldn't shake the feeling that Jay's attacker—whoever he was—had come to Mountain Cove for her.

She'd give Jennifer enough time to speak to Mountain Cove's police chief before she went in to talk to him, too. That way, they'd take her seriously.

She finished paying for her few groceries and toiletries and gave Veronica, the store clerk, a big smile, hoping to defuse any hard feelings because she'd shopped beyond the ten o'clock closing time. She hated shopping so late and then having to drive back out to the B and B, but Jewel had kept her late tonight.

Tracy hadn't found a way to tell Jewel her story yet. She wasn't sure how she would react to the news, and Tracy needed more time to figure things out. What if Jewel fired her, fearing Tracy had brought danger to her door? Then she really would have no options. And yet it wasn't fair to keep her boss and friend in the dark, either.

God, what do I do?

Her thoughts went immediately to David and his concern for her. She had a feeling that he would throw a fit if he knew she was here alone at the grocery store at this hour, though it wasn't his business. He knew everything now—well, almost everything—and the previous day, he'd acted as if he might stand guard over her cottage until the end of time if she hadn't run him off. He'd been so concerned about her, and she'd wanted to shake what that did to her insides.

She was still much too raw to put herself in that kind of heart-risking, vulnerable position again. Now that she knew him a little better, there was no doubt that she could fall for a guy like him hard, but caring about him would put him in danger. Caring about him would also be a liability to her heart.

She couldn't afford to get involved with him. Still,

she admitted that, deep inside, David Warren gave her just another reason to want to stay in Mountain Cove.

A noise like cans being knocked over sounded at the back of the store. The clerk looked up from assisting Tracy with her groceries.

"What in the world?" Veronica said. She shook her head. "And I wanted to get out of here early. I have to work tomorrow, too."

"I'll help you stack whatever it is back up. After all, it's my fault you're here so late." Tracy smiled.

"You'd do that?" Veronica eyed her.

"Sure. Why not?" Tracy waited for Veronica to lock the front door. Then, leaving her groceries at the counter, she followed the clerk to the back.

Cans of green beans that had been on the endcap for a promotional sale were scattered everywhere. Veronica blew out a breath. "Can't imagine how this happened."

The look she gave Tracy was a little accusing. "Don't look at me. I didn't buy any green beans. Didn't even touch them."

Another sound—garbage cans tumbling—resounded from outside the back exit. Tracy stiffened. She headed to the back of the store and immediately felt a rush of cold air. The back door wasn't closed completely. She and Veronica had been alone in the store. But it looked as though someone had entered through the back, accidentally knocked the cans over and then sneaked back out. Or maybe Tracy's imagination was getting the best of her. Still, she didn't want to risk it. "Veronica, you should call the police."

Veronica stooped over to grab a few cans and stack them. "Look, that would mean I'd get out of here after midnight and I sort of had plans. It's nothing. A cat or something. The wind. Could even be a bear messing with the garbage."

"What about the cans?"

"Someone didn't stack them right to begin with."

"Are you sure?"

"I'm positive. Wouldn't be the first time. I appreciate your help with the cans."

Tracy went to the back door to secure it. Hands against the panic bar, she considered opening the door to look outside into the alley. But that could be inviting trouble if there had been a bear messing with the garbage or if a creature of the two-legged variety was out there.

No. Tracy wouldn't open the door. She tugged it closed completely, which should automatically lock this kind of door. Then she helped Veronica with the cans. When they'd finished, Tracy grabbed her two bags of groceries and Veronica let her out the front door so she could close out her register. Tracy didn't like the situation at all, but maybe she was being paranoid. Veronica hadn't thought anything of the cans or the noise.

But Veronica didn't know what Tracy knew.

Outside a lone fluorescent light in the parking lot flickered on and off as darkness tried to settle on the short Alaska night. Her old junker Corolla was parked at the far corner. It had been the only spot left in the small parking lot when she'd first arrived. The place had been full of people making that last run for a quart of milk before it was too late. And Tracy had hung around too long, too lost in thought to concentrate on her shopping. But she hadn't thought this part through.

She didn't relish walking the parking lot alone even if it hadn't grown completely dark yet. She wished Solomon had come with her, but folks didn't usually like to see a dog in the grocery store unless it was a service animal. Tracy needed assistance of another kind.

There was nothing for it—she had to get to her car. She couldn't stand here all night. She started off across the parking lot, but that sense that someone watched her crawled over her. Just like on the mountain. If someone had come here to kill her, why didn't they just get it over with? Why toy with her or play games?

Juggling her groceries, Tracy pulled out the small can of pepper spray she kept in her purse, just to be safe and prepared.

And after tonight, she'd take David's advice and get a weapon. Learn to use it to protect herself. He was right. Solomon couldn't fight off all threats, especially if he wasn't even with her. And the dog wasn't bulletproof, even though it had seemed as though he'd been fireproof the night he'd saved her.

The sounds of boxes overturning erupted from the shadows in the alley next to the store. Tracy took off, running to her car. She'd rather the attacker just come out in the light so she could face off with him. But what she really wanted was to not face him at all.

Terror coursed through her.

Her car was only a few feet farther but might as well have been a mile away.

She looked back and saw a shadowy figure standing in the alleyway. Jay's attacker? She couldn't be sure. But she was nearly certain she saw the glint of a knife in his hand. When he saw her, he started running toward her. Tracy put on an extra burst of speed and hoped it would be enough.

Car lights shone from another direction, closing in

on her. The attacker's accomplice? Was he going to run her down?

Her heart in her throat, she heard the vehicle screech to a halt behind her and someone exit just as she reached her car door. She wouldn't have time to unlock it. Not with her hands full of groceries. Not with her hands shaking. She dropped the bags.

And now he was breathing down her neck. She thought she heard him say something, but her heart was beating too loudly for her to make out the words.

Tracy whirled to face her enemy and squeezed the button on the pepper spray.

Pain erupted in and around his eyes, which he squeezed shut reflexively. David coughed profusely, backing away from Tracy and into his truck. He couldn't see where he was going, but he had to get fresh air. He blinked a hundred times, despite the pain, as his eyes filled with tears, the body's natural defensive response—all while Tracy apologized profusely.

Coughing to clear his lungs, he held his hand out for her to keep her distance, though he didn't know why. He just wanted her to back off.

He bent over his knees, coughing again, blinking some more. He wouldn't be driving home anytime soon.

Then Tracy grabbed his arm. "I'm so sorry, David. I thought…I thought…"

"Just give me a minute," he said, sounding gruffer than he'd like. But he couldn't help it.

Next to his truck, David dropped to the ground and sat there, leaning his head back against the tire.

"What can I do to help?" she asked. "Please tell me.

Let me take you to the ER. They can give you something to flush out the pepper spray."

"No." He would be the laughingstock of this town if anyone found out what had happened.

"Oh, David, at least say you'll let me drive you home, then. I owe you that much. And we probably shouldn't stay out here."

Blinking a few more times, David got up. Coughing, he cleared his throat. "I'd appreciate that, because I can't see enough to drive myself. And you're right that we shouldn't stay out here. But please stop apologizing. This was all my fault. I should never have rushed up behind you like that. But, Tracy—" David wished he could look her in the eyes "—did you see what I saw? Was that why you were running scared?"

He ignored the pain to listen intently to her reply.

She inhaled a long breath. "W-what did you see?" she stammered.

"I saw you first, sprinting toward your car. When I pulled into the parking lot to see if you were okay, I thought I saw a man running toward you. But when he saw me, he took off for the alley."

When she didn't respond he imagined her frowning, contemplating how to answer. David reached for her, found her shoulders and squeezed. He hoped he was wrong—that there hadn't really been a man trying to attack her—because they were vulnerable out here, and he wasn't able to see what he was doing if the man came back.

"I...I only caught a glimpse. Not even enough to give a good description to the police. When he caught sight of me, I just freaked out and ran. And the rest... you already know. But why didn't you call out to me?"

"I did, Tracy. I saw you were upset and I was trying to reach you to make sure you were all right."

"Well, all I can say is at least it was pepper spray instead of a gun."

David huffed a laugh. That was for sure. Still, Tracy needed protection, and he'd try to talk her into getting that weapon. Teach her how to shoot. He'd try to protect her, watch over her, but he couldn't do that 24/7. Maybe he could talk to the police and see what was going on. If the man was following her closely enough to know when to attack her in the parking lot, then she needed someone to keep an eye on her and make sure she stayed safe.

"Why don't you park my truck and shut it off. Lock up and grab the keys. Then you can drive me back to my apartment."

Heidi always teased him about his bachelor pad— the place he'd lived for ten years since his wife's death. There hadn't been a house to go back to anyway after the fire.

He tried as best he could to help Tracy retrieve the groceries she'd dropped, but he was more trouble than he was help. Once he was seated in the passenger seat of her Corolla, he leaned his head back, keeping his eyes shut. When she steered from the parking lot, David gave her the address. She headed toward town and he felt guilty that she had to drive him then drive herself all the way back home.

"Listen, maybe I should call Cade to escort you home. I don't like you driving back to the cottage this late at night, after that creep tried to come after you in the parking lot. Until they catch this guy, you aren't safe. I know what you said about not wanting to give up your life here, but you should go into WITSEC. Change your name. Get out of town. Something. Have you even told the police since we talked last night?"

"Look, I already have a guard dog. I don't need a personal guard. We've been over this."

Yeah, they had—and he still wasn't satisfied with her answers. "If it's within my power to help, to do good, then that's what I have to do."

"You act like you have a choice," she said. "You don't get to insert yourself into my life without my permission."

Ouch. That hurt. Maybe she really didn't like him.

"That sounded harsh," she said, "and I don't mean to be, but someone has already forced me to change my life once, and I'm just overly sensitive about the thought of that happening again." She sighed.

David wasn't sure how to respond. Maybe he was coming on too strong, too controlling, in his simple effort to watch out for her. She hadn't asked for his help, in so many words. But David had felt her need for reassurance, for protection, for a friend—someone to talk to—last night in the cottage. And she'd shared her past with him. Something she hadn't shared with others in Mountain Cove, or so she'd said.

David sensed when Tracy turned right.

"Okay, this is Main Street. Where to now?"

"Go all the way through town to Crescent then take a left. You'll see the complex on the right." David felt like more of an idiot by the minute. She didn't want him involving himself. "I'm sorry if I overstepped."

The thing was, David wasn't about to go away until this was over, regardless of what Tracy said.

"Look, David. It's not that. Not really. I don't want you to put yourself in danger for me, that's all."

"How about you let that be my choice."

When she didn't answer, he hoped she was at least thinking about it. David could tell when she turned into the parking lot of his apartment complex. "It's all the way down, then the first building on the left. I'm upstairs. Number 201."

She parked the car and turned it off. "I'll assist you up, but I won't be coming in. And I'm not going to let you call your brother and force him to come out here to follow me back. I'll be fine getting home, and Solomon will be with me once I'm there."

"But what if that really was Jay's attacker tonight? What if he really is someone from Santino's gang after you? Seriously, you could have been in real danger. If you're going to go somewhere alone, take Solomon with you. I know what I said about him, but he's better than nothing."

David got out of the vehicle and Tracy assisted him up the stairs. He allowed it, wanting to keep her by his side longer, or at least until he figured out how to persuade her that she needed to leave town. Do something besides wait in that poorly protected cottage.

Once they were at his door, he turned to face her. He blinked hard and could see her better now.

"Your eyes are swollen. I wouldn't look in the mirror tonight if I were you." A teasing grin sneaked into her frown.

"I have some milk. I think that's supposed to wash away the pepper spray as opposed to water."

"I would offer to help, since I did this to you, but I don't think you need me."

No, David didn't need her help for this, and even though he wanted to keep her safe, he wasn't quite ready to invite her into his life. Besides, she'd spent the better part of the ride over rejecting him, putting him in his place.

David dug in his pocket for his apartment key and fumbled with the keyhole.

She laughed softly. "Here, let me."

After she unlocked and opened the door for him, she followed him inside. "You know what? Maybe you do need some help. I'll get the milk." She led him to the sink.

David could probably do this himself, though he might have to feel his way and stumble around. Still, he couldn't turn Tracy's offer down. After he washed his face and eyes with the milk, the burning sensation diminished, but he knew he must look a wreck. He eased onto the sofa of his sparsely decorated apartment.

His sister had tried to help brighten the place up, but he didn't want a woman's touch. It brought back too many memories.

Tracy watched him from the kitchen. "Are you going to be okay now?"

"No, because now you have to drive home down that lonely road that curves through the mountains to the B and B, and that's all my fault. If I hadn't spooked you into spraying me, I could have followed you home." David blew out a breath and reached for the phone next to the sofa. "I'm calling Cade to drive you back." He should have called Cade to pick him up at the store, but he hadn't been about to turn Tracy's offer of help away.

She snatched the phone from him. "You're overstepping again. Sure, I got scared tonight and ran to my car, but the guy didn't get anywhere near me. And if he had, he would be the one with the face full of pepper spray. I'm fine, David. Marshal Hanes, Jennifer, said she would speak to the Mountain Cove police, and I gave her time to do that. I'll talk to them tomorrow, tell them what happened tonight, but they're already looking for Jay's attacker. You know that. I'm done running and hiding."

"Yeah, what I saw tonight convinced me of that." He pursed his lips, wishing he could retract the words.

"I need you to stop worrying about me. Just…leave me alone."

Then she left his apartment.

Wow.

That was downright cantankerous, to use one of his grandmother's words.

He couldn't remember anyone ever being so adamant that he stay away, and it cut through his pride. He hadn't realized he had such a big ego, but he wasn't used to having a woman reject him for any reason. It was always David Warren who did the rejecting. There hadn't been anyone since his wife, Natalie. No one had ever caught his attention.

That was, until Tracy Murray. Why her? Especially since she clearly didn't want him around. But there was something in her adamancy that made David believe it went much deeper and had nothing at all to do with disliking David.

He couldn't get out of his head the way she felt in his arms. There was more to his comfort and reassurance, more between them. An attraction; a connection that was dangerous to his well-being. So what was really going on? Why didn't Tracy want his help?

Regardless, he wouldn't stalk the woman.

Somehow he'd find a way to help a woman in need. That was all this was about; David helping to keep a woman safe—a woman who had a dangerous man after her.

SIX

Tracy exited the small but modern building at the edge of downtown that housed the Mountain Cove Police Department. She shouldn't worry too much about coming to harm in the middle of the day in front of the police department building, but she couldn't help but search her surroundings, glancing at every vehicle, every person who approached her. Or who walked across the street from her.

She hadn't gotten any sleep last night for jumping at every sound. Or the night before. The way Solomon watched her, as if he wished she would go to sleep so he could, too, settled her enough that she'd at least closed her eyes. But sleep had not come.

That was, until early morning, when she was too exhausted to care if her past had caught up with her. Except she'd had to get up and go to work at the B and B, cooking and serving breakfast. And then she'd cleaned the bedrooms. Jewel had given her the rest of the day off to take care of "this killer business" after Tracy had told her everything. Tracy had taken comfort in Jewel's concern for her safety that she'd heard in her friend's tone. Seen in her expression.

Throwing her bag over her shoulder, Tracy walked
away from the building and headed down the sidewalk
to her car, tension knotting her shoulders. She'd had
to sit there waiting to see Colin Winters, the Mountain Cove police chief, for more than an hour, which
had made no sense. Talking to her should have been
his priority. The police didn't seem to have a lot of op-
portunities to fight crime in this town, and the one big
thing everyone was talking about was the fallen hiker.
Oddly enough, the police weren't calling it an attempted
murder. According to Chief Winters, they didn't want
to incite panic by saying there was a would-be killer
on the loose.

Tracy figured they should worry more about protecting the citizens of Mountain Cove, warning them so
they could be on the lookout for a man with a specific
tattoo, than about inciting a panic. Good grief.

She'd said as much, too. But he'd assured her that
when they had verified the facts based on the information Jay and Tracy had given them, along with what
Chief Winters had learned from Marshal Hanes, then
he would decide what action to take for public safety.

In the meantime, they were conducting an investigation.

He'd said the words with all seriousness, but then
proceeded to tell her that the kind of violent gang member Tracy described when she shared some of her past
couldn't hide for long in Mountain Cove. He would be
found out sooner, rather than later.

"The good folks of Mountain Cove will push him
up and out of here like the body pushes a splinter out,"
he'd said.

Tracy wanted to tell him that might be true, but the

splinter could fester. There could be swelling and irritation and even infection before it was expelled. Who knew how much damage one of Santino's men could do before he was caught?

In front of her vehicle, she stepped off the sidewalk and kicked the tire, then slung her homemade blue-jean bag onto the hood, glad she'd bought a junker car so she wouldn't feel guilty for using it to vent her bad mood. She unlocked the door the old-fashioned way—with a key instead of a fob. Before she grabbed her bag off the hood her cell went off.

Maybe it was Jennifer calling again to give her some good news.

David Warren.

Tracy sighed. She still felt so bad for her last words. *Just...leave me alone.* And then she'd walked out.

He was only trying to help and any sane person would have accepted the offer. But David didn't fully understand what he was getting himself into. And Tracy couldn't risk his life by bringing him into her dangerous world. Besides, she liked him too much, and she sensed that he liked her, too.

For the best part of the two years she'd lived in Mountain Cove, he and Tracy had steered clear of each other, or so it had seemed, each having their own reasons. Now that they'd spent more than a few minutes together alone, Tracy knew there was something more between them, just under the skin. Maybe David hadn't realized that yet, but a woman knew these things.

Tracy was in no place to go down that road with him now. If ever.

But she knew instinctively that if she ignored his call, he'd just drive out to see her and make sure she was okay. She had to answer the phone—but she silently resolved to keep it brief and to discourage him from putting himself out any further on her account. She answered, forcing a smile into her tone.

"Hey, David."

"Hey." An awkward pause hung between them.

"I'm so sorry about what I did last night." What was she doing? He hadn't called her so that she could tell him she was sorry again, had he? Regardless, the words needed saying.

"Which part? You mean the pepper spray? Or the complete and utter rejection of my help?"

David's question left her searching for words. Frowning, she leaned against her car, watching the hustle and bustle of Mountain Cove, enjoying its small-town charm. Yeah, this was home. Nobody was going to run her off this time.

He huffed a laugh. "Listen, I shouldn't have said that. Besides, I blame myself for getting sprayed. And…can we keep that just between us?"

Her turn to laugh. She stared down at her secondhand boots, the scuffs visible just beneath the hem of her jeans. "Sure. It'll be our little secret. I wouldn't want the whole town afraid to approach me."

"Maybe not the whole town but…"

He hadn't said "Santino" or "Jay's attacker," but she knew that was what he was thinking. "And I'm sorry about all of it, if that makes a difference. I deserved the words." But this conversation with him was taking too long, going too deep, getting too personal. She could feel the pull between them over the cell phone.

"Why did you call?"

She wished she could tell him she wanted his help,

but she had a feeling that once she'd said yes to that one offer of help last night, he'd glue himself to her side until her stalker was caught. David Warren had "fierce protector" written all over him. He might think he could protect her.

But it would never work.

What would he do, sit on her porch all night? Follow her around? He would die if he tried to protect her. She already knew from experience.

"It's Jay," he said.

She sucked in a breath. "What's happened?"

"Nothing happened. He's doing well, considering his injuries. He wants to talk to us both at the hospital."

What could that be about? "When?"

"Whenever we can get there. Where are you now? I can come get you."

Tracy eyed the police building. "No, I'll meet you at the hospital."

"Um, Tracy. You do realize he's in Juneau, right?"

She released a pent-up breath. "I didn't even think about that."

"His injuries were too severe, so they had to transport him to a regional hospital. Juneau was it."

Tracy was surprised he hadn't gone on to Seattle, but he'd probably needed the quickest care he could get. "What did you have in mind, then?"

"We can take a floatplane to Juneau together. I have a bush-pilot friend, Billy, who can be ready in an hour. I can come get you and we can grab a bite before then."

Oh, David was good. Really good. She smiled to herself. "I'll meet you at the floatplane dock in an hour."

"See you there." Disappointment cut across the line before he ended the call.

She'd just successfully rejected David again. She was getting far too good at this. What would it hurt to eat with him? Her stomach rumbled and she called him right back, but the call went to voice mail. Just as well.

On the flight from Mountain Cove to Juneau, David listened to Billy fill the time and otherwise silent flight with small talk about his adventures in the bush. At first David had wanted to focus on Tracy and get her to talk, but he realized that Billy offered Tracy a much-needed reprieve from thinking about her problems. A person could carry around that kind of burden for only so long. And she seemed to be listening intently to Billy's stories. Of course, she was sitting next to the pilot, so it wasn't as if she had much choice.

For his part, David only half listened. Sure, he laughed and smiled at the appropriate moments, but he wasn't giving Billy his full attention. They were friends. Billy would understand. David scratched his head and watched out the window as the seaplane flew over one of the many channels of the Inside Passage, the Tongass National Forest and the mountains—always an awe-inspiring sight.

But the beauty couldn't drag his thoughts from the seriousness of Tracy's situation. If what Tracy had said was true and Santino or one of his gang members was after her, then why hurt Jay and not Tracy? There could be only one reason for that and it fell in line with Tracy's fears that anyone involved with her would be in danger. In Jay's case, he'd been at the wrong place at the wrong time. But her explanation for rejecting David's help, that she didn't want to see David get hurt, made more sense. David was glad he understood. But understanding didn't mean he agreed. He was willing to face some danger to himself if it meant keeping Tracy safe.

David wanted to know what had happened, what Tracy had witnessed to put Santino away. But he wouldn't push her. It was enough that she was with him on the plane to see Jay.

They arrived at Juneau International Airport and caught a cab to the hospital. Unsure of what they would see when they walked into Jay's hospital room, David led the way, giving a light rap on the door as he pushed it open. He'd already called Jay to let him know they had arrived in Juneau and were on their way.

The guy's face looked as though it had been used as a punching bag. His left leg was in a cast and traction, his arms were in casts, and he wore a neck and back brace. He cracked a smile when he saw David and Tracy. Yeah. He was a trouper.

David watched Tracy's reaction and noticed she paled, though she kept her smile in place. "Oh…Jay." Compassion filled her voice. "I'm so sorry this happened to you."

"Don't be. It's not your fault." Jay had no idea what he was saying, but David hoped Tracy would hold it together. "The good news is I'm alive. After a fall like that, I should have died. But I have nothing more than broken bones."

"You look good," David teased. Somehow he knew Jay would take it in the right spirit. "What's broken?" Though he could see plenty.

Jay's chuckle was good-natured. "Nine fractures in my arms and legs. Broken ribs." Jay blinked his eyes. Even that looked painful. "Thanks for coming." His voice sounded weaker than it had on the phone. They couldn't stay too long; he needed to rest.

David noticed Jay studying Tracy. Her face still pale, she moved to the side of the bed. David had a feeling she would have taken Jay's hand—much as she had on the side of the mountain—but due to the casts there wasn't much of his hands exposed. How had either of them been able to hold his hand on the mountain without causing more pain? Maybe Jay had been in *that* much shock.

Man. David gave a subtle shake of his head, thanking God that Solomon had found the man and praying for his eventual full recovery.

His mind went back to that moment when Tracy had leaned closer to Jay to listen. Then she'd freaked out. He understood the reason for her reaction now and wondered if Jay's request to see them again had to do with the man who had tried to kill him.

"Thanks for coming," Jay said. "I wanted to thank the two people who saved me. If you hadn't found me I would have died on the mountain."

"There's no need to thanks us." Tracy glanced at David for his agreement.

He nodded. "No, the real hero isn't here. We knew the hospital wouldn't let Solomon, Tracy's search-and-rescue golden retriever, come inside, so we left him at home."

Jay coughed a laugh. "Is that right? Well, maybe after I get out of here, I'll meet Solomon. Tell him thanks for me, Tracy."

"I will." She looked to David as if unsure what to do or say next. "We should probably go now and let you rest."

"No." Jay blinked at her. Studied her. What was the man thinking? "I asked you here for a reason. I need to know that you believe me, Tracy."

"What…what are you talking about?" She edged closer.

"You believe me about the man who pushed me over."

"Of course I believe you. Why would you ask? What's going on?"

"The police questioned me. They say they haven't found anyone who fits that description. But when I told you about the tattoo, you had a strong reaction—like you'd seen it before. So I'm hoping you believe me and you can help me make sure they get this guy."

"Yes, I reacted the way I did because I've seen that tattoo before."

She stopped and appeared uncertain if telling Jay everything would benefit him or if he'd be better off not knowing. David wasn't sure about that himself.

Walking around the bed to where she stood, he placed his hand on her shoulder, hoping to reassure her, and then he addressed Jay. "Can I ask if there's any reason the police would doubt you, besides the one they've given?"

Jay grimaced, releasing a painful sigh. David wondered if that was from his physical pain or something else.

"Two years ago I tried to commit suicide," he said.

Ah. That made sense, then. They thought this was another attempt, or at least were considering the possibility. Except why would Jay make up a story like that? And how could he have described the Santino gang tattoo so accurately if he hadn't seen it? David didn't think the police would discount the tattoo or Tracy's history with the gang. He had the highest respect for the police officers he knew, and he wasn't sure why Winters wasn't acting quickly on this. Then again, he could see where the hesitation came from.

But what about Tracy's history with this gang? Was Winters seriously going to discount that?

"I'm sorry to hear that." Tracy placed her hand gently on the cast encasing Jay's arm. "I want you to know that I believe you. I talked to the police this morning and told them how I know about the tattoo. I think they'll believe you now, too, if they didn't before. I had a bad experience with members of a gang. That tattoo symbolizes their membership. I'll do everything I can to make sure this guy is caught. Now, do you believe *me*?"

"Yes." Jay blew out a ragged breath. "It's hard being stuck here. A friend came with me to see this part of Alaska. It had been a childhood dream. We'd already been here a week when he had to go home a day early. I decided to stay. It's so beautiful here I didn't want to leave. I had just gotten my life back together, too, after my suicide attempt. Have a great job back in Texas and now I'm not sure I can even go back to work there when I'm finally recovered. My family is on their way to see me, but they can't stay here as long as it'll take for me to get stable enough to move." Jay closed his eyes.

"Let us know what we can do to help," David said. "I don't live in Juneau, but I have a lot of friends and family in the region, and I'll make sure they know you're here. We'll be your family while you're in Alaska. Whatever you need."

"Thank you."

David thought he might have heard tears in Jay's voice.

Tracy turned to him then, a soft smile edging into her lips. The look in her eyes stirred his heart, the intensity there surprising him.

Not wanting to overtire Jay, they said goodbye and headed back to the seaplane dock.

"Your chariot awaits," Billy said with a flourish, winking at Tracy.

"Seriously? You're flirting with her?" Jealousy stabbed through David. It wasn't his place to be jealous. He couldn't believe he'd scolded Billy in front of Tracy like that. Thankfully, Billy seemed to shrug it off, holding up his hands in a "no offense" gesture.

David didn't think Tracy had noticed his reaction or Billy's attention and, for that, he was grateful.

On the short flight back to Mountain Cove, David could feel the tension coming off her. In the short time he'd spent with her, he'd gotten to know her better and knew he couldn't push her to tell him what she was thinking. She didn't like to be controlled or manipulated.

David had decided to sit up front with Billy to let Tracy have some time to herself, as much as one could have in a small seaplane. He was the one to pay attention to Billy's stories and this time Tracy was the one who barely listened.

"Had a fire up north in the Kenai Peninsula again. They called in extra crews."

Billy'd had to bring that up.

David rubbed his jaw. "You know I don't do that anymore." Not since Natalie had died. If he had quit earlier, stopped traveling to fight the wildland fires, she'd still be alive today. He believed that to his bones. So he'd quit fighting wildland fires for the Forest Service and joined the Mountain Cove Fire Department, and he'd never seen a wildfire again. It had been too little, too late.

But he wouldn't go back to doing something he loved. The guilt wouldn't let him.

"I need your help." Tracy's words pulled David from his self-recriminations.

After her persistent rejection, David wasn't sure he believed her. But he wasn't about to turn down this opportunity. "Whatever I can do. Name it."

"We have to convince the police that there is a potential killer out there. I cannot believe any of this is happening. I need to find Jay's attacker myself. Draw him out."

That wasn't the kind of help he could give her. And he wouldn't even if he could. "I know you're frustrated, and I'll do whatever I can to help, but you have to let the police do their job. You don't need to go looking for trouble."

"If he's here, we have to find him before it's too late. Before someone else gets hurt." She stared out the window. "Because of me."

David couldn't help himself. He reached behind him and grabbed her hand. Held it. Squeezed. And Tracy didn't throw up her wall and pull away. "I know I already told you to go into WITSEC. It's not that I want you to go. Believe me, I don't. But maybe it's for the best."

"I can't leave now. I won't. But I didn't think I'd have to convince the police like this."

"Guys. You need to see this." Billy's voice called David's attention forward.

Smoke billowed in the distance.

"You don't think that could be a wildfire, do you?" Tracy asked.

"No."

David's pulse jumped and he pulled out his cell. He was assistant fire chief, but still worked shifts—twenty-four hours on, two days off—and should have been on today, but he'd taken it off to see Jay, so he shouldn't expect a call. But still, a text about what was going on would have been appreciated.

The fire crews responded to a couple of thousand incidents every year, most of which were EMS calls, and only a few were fires. House fires, apartment fires. Buildings in town. A few brush fires. No blazing wildfires like what they showed on the news in different regions of the country. The Tongass National Forest was a temperate rain forest and it was simply too wet here. The fires they did see usually involved the thick underbrush burning beneath the surface, smoking mostly. No tree crowns. So, no, this couldn't be a wildfire.

"Fly closer, Billy. Let's see what's burning."

David sent a text to his chief asking about the fire. When they got close enough to Mountain Cove, Billy circled around for a closer look.

"The grocery store. Oh, no!" Tracy sucked in a breath. "Veronica... She said she was working today. It's happening..."

"What's happening, Tracy? What are you talking about?"

She pressed her face into her palms. "It's happening all over again."

SEVEN

Tracy couldn't believe the devastation she saw as David parked his truck at the curb across the street from the grocery store to keep out of the way.

When Billy had landed the plane, Tracy had climbed into David's truck without even questioning what she was doing. Her car was parked at the dock, as well. But she knew as a firefighter, David would get into the middle of things, and she had to be there, too. Had to find out what had happened. If anyone had been injured.

If they had, Tracy would take it as proof that she had brought more trouble to Mountain Cove. And if that was the case, how could she live with herself? On the plane, David had demanded to know what she'd meant when she'd said it was happening again. So she'd told him about the fires Santino and his gang had started to target the people he viewed as his enemies, and the murders. Santino was a pyromaniac. But the details of her own personal trauma she'd kept to herself. The details of Derrick's death. It was too hard to talk about any of that.

David had listened, frown lines growing deeper. They hadn't left his face. Nor had he said much to her, but to be fair, he'd spent most of the time on the phone trying to reach someone for details. She didn't want this to be all about her, but she would still like to know what was going on. What he was thinking.

She climbed out of his truck and followed him across the street, sticking close; though she wasn't sure he even remembered she was there. Emergency vehicles had taken over the parking lot of the small grocery store. Fire crews had already put out the fire, and the acrid smell of recently doused flames lingered in the air.

An ambulance was parked there, too, its lights flashing, but there did not appear to be the usual urgency of emergency personnel rushing to save someone. That could mean one of two things. No one had been inside who needed medical attention. Or they were already dead. Dread soured in her stomach. She followed David past a fire truck and then he turned to face her. He seemed torn about what to say or do.

Tracy didn't know what to say, either, her own fear curdling with the hurt and pain of this loss in her stomach.

"Come on." He took her hand.

She thought he would lead her over to where some officers and firemen were talking. Instead he positioned her near a couple of cruisers, out of the way of the chaos.

"What are you doing?" she asked.

"I need to go, and you need to stay here."

"I want to go with you."

"It's not a good idea. Just let me find out what is going on—what happened. If this looks like arson or an accident. Find out if anyone was hurt." He grimaced and then his gaze pierced hers. "Trust me on this—you need to stay here. You should be safe. Plus, I can find you when I'm done. Okay?"

Tracy nodded. Her need to argue would only keep him from where he needed to be. She watched him trudge over to the authorities and hoped he could find out what she wanted to know, too. From here she could see what she hadn't been able to earlier: the store had been so damaged by the fire, it would likely have to be completely rebuilt.

There wasn't anything that could be salvaged.

Too many unbidden memories surged to life in her mind and heart, but Tracy didn't want to lose it here and now, in front of the onlookers across the street. She'd already done that in front of David twice now.

No more. She had to keep it together.

Across the street the crowd watched in dismay. Tracy scanned it for familiar faces and she saw a few but didn't know their names. Medics came around from the other side of one of the three fire trucks and into her view, heading for the ambulance with a body bag. And it wasn't empty.

Tracy rushed forward to meet them. "Who is it? Please, I need to know."

"Ma'am, step out of the way," one of the medics said.

A police officer grabbed her arm. "You shouldn't be here. Please leave the premises."

The burn of tears singed her eyes. "Who died?"

"Ma'am, we won't know anything until there's an investigation. Please cross the street and stand with the others or get in your vehicle and leave."

Oh, Lord, if it's possible, please let this be an accident. Please let this have nothing at all to do with me or with Santino's gang.

The officer assisted her to the edge of the parking lot, after which Tracy crossed the street and stood with the crowd. Some of them asked her questions. But she had no answers other than she knew that someone had died in the fire, though she kept that to herself. The community was small enough there was likely at least distant family or friends of the grocery store's employees or customers, whoever had died, in this crowd. Sharing that news wasn't Tracy's place, but surely they all had eyes and could see for themselves.

Finally she saw David emerge from around the charred walls of the building, shaking his head. The serious look on his face told her the fire had hit him as hard as if the attack had been personally aimed at him. Maybe all fires were personal to David since he was a firefighter. Or perhaps the fact that someone had died because of a fire put that odd mixture of anger and pain on his face.

She rubbed her arms, feeling those emotions herself. But what she couldn't know, and desperately wanted to find out, was if David blamed her.

Still watching David, she wanted to go to him, to cross the street and find out what he knew. He turned his attention from the burned-out shell of a grocery store to the emergency vehicles and then searched the parking lot.

He had to be looking for her. His eyes scanned the crowd and found her. He put his hands on his hips and she gave a little wave. When he started toward her, she decided that was her invitation, and after letting a couple of rubbernecking cars go by, Tracy crossed the street to meet David.

"You scared me half to death," he said. "I told you to stay put."

"A police officer told me differently and practically hauled me across the street himself."

Another frown from David. "Sorry about that."

Tracy didn't care. "Who was in the body bag?"

"Veronica was in the back of the store and succumbed to smoke inhalation. The fire didn't get her, but the smoke did."

The shaking moved from her knees up her body. She couldn't do this in front of everyone.

"Tracy, are you okay?"

"Of course not. Someone is dead." *Oh, God, please let it not be because of me. Because I'm in Mountain Cove. Please don't let this be a message to me.*

David ran both hands through his hair. What she saw in his eyes nearly did her in. He didn't even have to say it. Nausea swirled in her stomach and she bent over.

Hold it together. Hold it together. Veronica wasn't even family.

"What else can you tell me?" After everything she'd told him, he had to understand what she was asking.

"I don't have any answers for you. I don't know anything yet."

"But will the police believe me now?"

"If this was arson, I think Winters will have to listen now, speed up his investigation. Mountain Cove will have to be put on alert."

"Of course this was arson. What else could it be?"

"Tracy, you're jumping to conclusions. We don't know that yet." He gently squeezed her shoulder.

Even David didn't believe her. All Tracy wanted was to be alone. To process the fear and pain and sorrow by herself. But before she did, she needed to ask him the question burning inside.

"If it's arson, will you blame me? Because if I'd gone into WITSEC, then Veronica would still be alive."

David gripped her arms. He needed to make sure she heard him loud and clear. "Of course I won't blame you. You shouldn't blame yourself, either. No matter how this happened, it isn't your fault. Nobody else blames you, either, Tracy. Or will blame you, that is, if it's arson that's related to this Santino guy."

When he knew she'd heard him, he released his grip.

He could see in her eyes she didn't believe him. But they needed to have this conversation elsewhere. He had a feeling that Winters would come for her now, to ask the questions he hadn't been willing to ask before. David didn't want her to answer him when she was in this frame of mind.

"Let's get you back to your car. I'll follow you home and you can move your stuff in with Jewel." He'd decided to take a more direct approach and insist she move out of the cottage. How could she disagree with him now? Maybe he was being presumptuous, but he couldn't imagine Jewel would have it any other way.

"I'll think about it. But this is Jewel's busy season. She might not have extra rooms."

If Tracy couldn't stay in the B and B with Jewel then she could stay with his grandmother. Both Cade and Heidi had gotten married and moved out of the family home, wanting a place of their own. David had even considered moving back in with his grandmother because he hated that she lived alone. Or was it more that he hated that *he* lived alone?

As he studied Tracy, she once again stirred that forbidden longing in him. He didn't want to live alone anymore. Except he couldn't afford those kinds of thoughts, especially when Tracy was in danger. Especially when there had already been an attempted murder and possibly an actual murder, if the fire was declared arson and Veronica's death was classified as a homicide. He was certain Chief Winters couldn't keep this to himself much longer.

David was ready to get her out of here and back to her vehicle. "Let's talk about it on the way."

When she didn't follow he reached for her, but she shrank away from his touch and looked at the charred remains of what had been the grocery store. "It's because I was there last night. Was with her. That's why he did this."

On second thought, David would drive her to the cottage. She didn't need to drive herself just yet.

She finally allowed him to usher her around the edge of the parking lot and away from the dispersing crowd. Finding his truck, he opened the door for her, and because she appeared so shaken, he assisted her up onto the running board and into the seat.

"I need to check on Solomon," she said. Her eyes were more blue than silver today and held his gaze. He could look at them for an eternity if ever given the chance.

In that moment he knew…

Nobody was going to get to Tracy.

They'd have to go through him first.

That sense of protectiveness burned inside him as never before, and he didn't know why. Even as someone who saved people on a regular basis, he had never felt this kind of sheer, blind determination.

What was it about this woman?

With the surge of emotion, David had the need to reach out and caress her cheek, to reassure her, to somehow convey the depth of his commitment to her well-being. He certainly didn't deserve her trust, but he wanted to let her know that he would protect her.

Something stirred deep inside—warm and unexpected, unwelcome and yet undeniable. He wanted to kiss her. Kiss the pain and hurt and fear away, if he could. And he had a feeling that kissing Tracy Murray could chase away his own pain, too.

Regardless, this was the wrong time and place. And not something David should even be thinking about.

Ever.

He didn't deserve it.

And the awful truth of it hit him—he hadn't protected his wife; he'd failed on that count. Who was he to think he could protect Tracy? But he had to try. He had no choice.

"My car is at the seaplane dock, which is pretty far from this side of town. Do you mind if we head to the cottage first?"

"Of course not." That was his thinking, too. He shut the door and marched around the front of his truck, trying to shove away his errant thoughts until only one thought remained.

Protect Tracy.

Inside his truck, he started the ignition and then left the grisly scene behind them. Instead of going down the street in front of the store that was clogged with traffic and onlookers from town, he headed down a back country road that was little more than an overgrown trail but would cut across and connect him with the road again closer to the Jewel of the Mountain.

David quietly stared at the road, listening as Tracy tried to hide that she was crying. It was something he'd learned to do with his wife—he'd known when she was crying without even looking. And he'd also known when to give his wife space. Or when he needed to speak up.

But this time he didn't have a clue. Of course, Tracy wasn't his wife. Far from it. But he knew that sometimes a woman just had to cry. David didn't want to interfere with Tracy's process. He had enough anger and hurt inside for the both of them.

Veronica Stemson was thirty-four and had gotten divorced a couple of years ago. He thought she might have been seeing someone. Her mother was still alive, but her father had passed five years ago. She had one sibling still in the area. Funny how he knew so much about her. Come to think of it, maybe Cade had dated her in high school. That was what life was like in a small town—everyone was connected. A death like this was a huge loss for the community. A complete waste.

He squeezed the steering wheel until his knuckles grew white and then composed himself, if for no other reason than to keep it together while he was with Tracy. She had enough to deal with. Both of them lost in their grueling thoughts, silence hung between them, except for the noise his truck made as it bounded over the occasional pothole on the back road.

Because he knew how caring the community was, he didn't doubt that Jewel would let Tracy stay at the main house. She was considerate that way. He might have had a thing for Jewel, even though she was a few years older, if he hadn't met Natalie first and fallen madly in love with her.

If only he could let go of his own guilt for his wife's death and move on with his life. Then he would be free to love again. But David was a loyal man, loyal to his guilt, and he had no intention of letting go of that. No intention of falling in love again.

He steered down the bumpy excuse for a driveway past the B and B to the cottage out back. Yes, she definitely needed to leave this cottage, which was too far from the house for comfort, especially with a dangerous man out there somewhere. And now a possible arsonist. That was, if the fire truly was about someone from Tracy's past coming to Mountain Cove to seek revenge.

God, please let her be wrong about that.

They wouldn't know a thing until the fire marshal conducted his investigation. In the meantime, people could die. David needed to make sure that Tracy was safe and secure, tucked away in the main house before he could head back to find out more.

At least it was still daylight. It was nearing seven in the evening. The sun wouldn't even set for another two and a half hours and twilight lingered forever this time of year. Sometimes he thought the summer hours in Alaska were much too long. Sure, he could get a lot done, but it seemed the day would never end.

He'd barely parked when Tracy climbed out of his truck.

"Hey!" he called after her.

Her frantic rush to the cottage clued him in that something was wrong. And looking up ahead, he saw that the door was open.

David hopped out and ran after her, beating her to the door. "Just hold on," he said. "You can't just waltz in there. Let me check things out first. We should probably call the police." He wished Winters would get a grip on this investigation and finally decide Mountain Cove had a real situation going on.

"Solomon!" she called. "Come, Solomon!"

Dead silence was their only answer.

EIGHT

"Go ahead and call them. What are you going to tell them? Someone lost her dog?"

Cell to his ear, he frowned, then dropped the phone. "You're right. That's not going to work, and any explanation would take too long." David called the dog, too.

After hiking up to the B and B and asking Jewel if she'd seen Solomon, Tracy and David searched the surrounding area and called out using the command Solomon should have down by now. He wasn't perfect, but he was a good dog. He wouldn't have just run off like this, not when Tracy was gone. Besides, the door had been closed, securing him inside until she got home.

David called the dog, pressing deeper into the woods behind the cottage. He was here with her, after everything that had happened today. After the fire. She would have thought he'd want to be back at the fire station with the boys and in the middle of things to discuss the fire, and maybe even bring up a suspect to the police, if Chief Winters hadn't already thought of it. But she had to admit, she was comforted by the way he'd stayed by her side.

"Solomon, come on, boy," David called again. That

he was here searching for Solomon with her kindled something in her heart.

One day she'd have to tell David about the night Solomon had saved her life. It would help explain what the dog meant to her, though she suspected he already knew.

And maybe David was beginning to mean a little too much to her, considering she wanted to share that with him.

She'd told him she didn't want or need his help. That had definitely been a mistake. When she'd seen the door to the cottage hanging open, she was more than glad David was here with her. What if someone had been inside waiting for her?

But if there had been someone there, David could have gotten hurt. If the burning today was part of Santino's retaliation—bringing back the terror he'd rained down before—then David or anyone near her was in danger. Something she already knew, but she hadn't realized how far that danger could reach.

"David, wait." Tracy rushed through the thick and lush forest of Sitka ash, maple, cedars and a host of other trees and undergrowth she couldn't name. A person could easily get lost.

He paused and turned to face her, pushing a leafy branch out of the way.

"Be careful, please. I don't want you to get hurt. What if *he's* out there? What if we run into him?" What if Solomon had caught his scent and gone chasing him?

He frowned. "Don't worry about me, Tracy. Stay close to me and let's find Solomon." Letting the huge leaf pop back up, he pushed on, and Tracy shoved through the greenery to keep up.

"I appreciate your help, I really do, and I'm not going to stop today until I find Solomon, but I want you to face the facts. You could be in danger, just by being with me. Talking to me. Being my friend. Look what happened to Veronica."

"You don't know that fire was related to your situation." Hands on hips, David stopped again, searching the woods.

"Of course I do. And you do, too. What we need is for Chief Winters to see that, if he hasn't already. But if I've learned anything about that man, it's that he will get the facts before he makes any decisions. I can't actually blame him for that, though. Can you?"

"Not really. No. It's part of police procedure. And it takes time." David still studied the woods.

They'd gotten off topic. Tracy wanted to make it clear to David that being with her might cost him. Was she worth it to him? Either way, she couldn't ask him to pay that price. Nor could she *want* him to pay it.

David turned his forest green gaze on her, the lush vegetation behind and around him emphasizing the intensity in his eyes. Taking her hand, he squeezed. Reassurance? Her heart jumped. He'd encouraged her and much more. It was the "much more" that she was worried about. She should pull her hand away, but her heart refused to reject him again. This man was out here helping her find her dog. Inside, she smiled—helping her find Solomon was only a small thing, but sometimes the small things were what meant the most.

"Don't worry. We'll find him," he said with a wink and then flashed that grin she'd seen him use on other women around town. But now she knew it wasn't manipulation on his part. His charming smile was simply part of who David was. And he'd found a way to smile at her like that with all that was going on. After the fire that had them both on edge.

Reining in her thoughts, she focused on the task at hand. "We should probably split up," she said. "You can call me on your cell if you find him."

"Are you crazy? We're sticking together."

She'd figured he would say that, but she was trying to be practical.

"So I take it this isn't a usual thing? Solomon doesn't usually run off?"

"No. Not like this. This isn't right." Tracy was afraid to voice her worst fear—that Solomon didn't run off on his own, but that someone had done something to him. Was she being paranoid? She felt alone in all this—except for David. Even the police were not taking any of this seriously. At least not yet.

"See, even Solomon isn't safe." Tracy paused, swatted at the mosquitoes and rubbed her arms against the chill as the woods grew darker. "Jay might be home with his family in Texas tonight, Veronica home with her family if I had gone into WITSEC. Oh, David, what have I done?"

David tugged her to him. Did he realize how he held her up, kept her from collapsing on her trembling legs? She hated that she'd shown him how weak she really was, been this vulnerable in front of him, and not just once. Finally he held her at arm's length and kept his gaze fixed on hers.

"I want you to listen to me," he said. "I know I urged you to get a new identity, so you could be safe, but you were right when you said you shouldn't run or hide. Anyone who could find you *here* could find you anywhere, even with a new name and identity. But this time we're one step ahead. We know someone is after you, and we'll be prepared. I don't intend to leave you until the police nab this guy."

His words bolstered her courage even as they made her realize she was crazy to think she could stand her ground—stay in Mountain Cove—without someone by her side. But she never would have pictured David in that role.

"Is that okay with you?"

"Oh, so *now* you're asking my permission?" She couldn't help but give him half a smile, even in the face of all that was wrong in the world. "It's too much to ask."

"You're not asking. I'm insisting."

"You always get your way?"

His smile slowly flattened. "Not always, no."

Tracy waited for him to say more.

David dropped his gaze. "I…"

"What is it? What were you going to say?"

"I failed someone before. I don't want to fail you, Tracy, but maybe…maybe you should count on more than me and more than the dog."

"Who should I count on, then? God?"

David's silence on the matter chilled her to the bone.

David wanted to reassure her and be there for her, but he reminded himself of his colossal failure that had come at the cost of a life. He'd said too much, and realized it when he saw the look of hope in her eyes.

David hadn't meant for her to believe in him—if that was what he'd seen flashing in her beautiful gaze. He'd only meant for her to know she wouldn't have to go through this alone. He definitely wasn't a hero—not like his father. Not like his siblings. And he wasn't sure that he was the person Tracy should count on. Of course, he believed in prayer and that God listened to his prayers. Answered them, too. But David couldn't reconcile why God would let him fail his wife. Why Natalie had died in a fire, instead of David, who'd spent his life fighting them. It made no sense.

Aware that Tracy waited for his reply, he searched for the answer to her question. Deep inside, he knew what it was, and despite his own struggles, he couldn't withhold it from her. "Of course you can count on God. So pray hard."

He sent a teasing grin her way to lighten the moment and started off again. "The sun's going to set before we find that dog of yours if we don't get busy. Dusk in the forest is dark."

He caught Tracy's frown; saw her shoulder sag a little. Since they hadn't found Solomon yet, he knew she had reason to be worried.

Even as they searched deeper in the woods David started to think this might be some sort of trap. Was the Santino gang member using the dog as bait to draw them away from safety? David was glad he carried a gun. As always, his weapon was tucked safely in the waistband holster clipped to his belt. Besides, he was equally concerned about coming across a bear as he was a two-legged killer.

Finally, after they'd searched long and hard, calling for the dog without receiving the hoped-for response, David pulled out his cell and prayed for a decent signal. To Tracy, he said, "I'm calling in the family. The more the merrier."

He didn't want to incite more fear than Tracy already carried, but he wanted reinforcements. This was taking much longer than it should. There could be no doubt that something was wrong. Something had happened to Solomon.

Before the call went through, he heard barking in the distance. Solomon? He gazed in the direction from which the sound came. A glance at his phone told him he'd lost the signal, so he tucked it away.

"It's faint, but it's Solomon!" Tracy took off as fast as she could make it through the undergrowth. Good thing she had on jeans, he thought absently. But he should lead the way in case this was a trap.

He caught up then pushed past her. He pressed his hand against the gun in his holster. "Listen, in case this is something more than your dog simply running off, let me go first. I have the means to protect us."

She frowned. "Don't shoot my dog."

"I'm an expert marksman, okay?"

He led the way, but at the edge of the trees he paused and put his hand out for Tracy to stop, too.

"What is it?"

David listened and his heart sank as memories of his childhood rushed back, confirming what he thought he heard.

"I think Solomon's barks are coming from there." He gestured ahead of them where the trees opened up to an adit—an entrance to what remained of an old mine—driven into the side of a mountain.

"What's that?"

"A shaft to an old gold mine. It's not a working operation, abandoned long ago. There's none of the buildings you might expect, though some of the area's old mines

have been renewed in recent decades. Gold is what built
the town of Mountain Cove, remember?" Or maybe
she'd never known that to remember in the first place.

"I can't believe it's not boarded up."

"It was."

From the cover of the trees, David peered at the shaft.
It looked as if someone had broken through the old
boards put in place years before after it had been discovered that David and his friends had been exploring
the mine. Probably, more should have been done to
close it off for good.

"Let's go get him."

"Not that simple."

Tracy pushed past him out into the open.

"Wait! What are you doing?" David snatched her
back. "This could be a trap."

"This isn't exactly the modus operandi of Santino's
gang. Luring a dog into a mine?" She shook her head.

"No. Luring *you* into a mine."

"Like I said, this isn't the way they have worked in
the past."

"Was pushing someone over a ledge something
they've done before?"

Tracy's silence was answer enough.

Chambering a round into his gun, David led the way.
If nothing else, they could disturb a bear. Either way,
David was prepared. "Doesn't matter if it's their MO
or not—we can't go in. It's not safe."

"Then how do we get Solomon out? Since he hasn't
already come out on his own, something's wrong."

"Maybe he found someone who is injured inside the
mine, just like he found Jay."

Except Solomon sounded different than he had that

day on the trail. Uncertainty crawled over David. They stood at the yawning opening of the old mine, listening to Solomon's barks echo inside.

"I can't take this anymore." Tracy moved past David to enter the shaft, knocking a board over.

"No you don't." David grabbed her arm and held fast. "It's too dangerous."

Solomon yelped as if he was in pain.

David wasn't sure what to do. He couldn't let Solomon suffer. What had the dog gotten into? Had he found someone? Or worse, had someone taken the dog to lure Tracy inside? *Lord, what do I do?*

Tracy put her hands on her head. "We can't just leave him down there, David. But how are we going to get him out? We don't even have flashlights."

"I don't know."

"Solomon! Come, boy, come," she called, desperation in her cries.

"All right. I used to play in this mine when I was a kid—that is, until Dad found out. After that, it was boarded up to prevent anyone from getting hurt, but obviously someone wanted inside."

"What are you saying?"

"I know my way, if memory serves me."

"Didn't you just tell me it's too dangerous? And…I can't let you do that for me."

Tracy stared up at the sky as if she could find a way to Solomon there. David figured it was more about hiding the raw emotions pouring from her face, but he had already seen and his heart twisted.

"Solomon… He saved my life." She lowered her gaze to meet his. "I have to do something to help him."

At the look in her eyes, David saw the depth of her

devotion to the animal and it left him with more questions about what had happened that sent her into hiding in Mountain Cove.

"I know that he's important to you, but the mine itself is dangerous enough, even if there's no one lying in wait to attack you. Maybe this isn't how a Santino gang member would normally operate, but you can't be sure, and what if Jay's attacker took Solomon into the mine to draw you in? What if he just wants to get you alone? Think about it. On the trail, he wanted you alone, but that plan was foiled when Jay ran ahead of you. And last night at the grocery store, he was ready to attack before I drove up. Today's fire was only a warning."

"But I've been alone at the cottage all along."

David scratched his chin. Good point. "Except he obviously doesn't know you're staying there. Maybe if he's followed you at all, he's seen you drive up that way and thought you were staying at the actual main house. Maybe he didn't even know about the cottage." Except Solomon had been taken from the cottage. "That is, until now," he added.

David was jumping to a lot of conclusions. He wasn't a detective, but he cared about keeping Tracy safe. And he hadn't wanted to scare her, but maybe she needed to open her eyes.

He'd make some demands from Chief Winters as soon as he could. Find out what the police knew about what was going on and if they were actually searching for this guy. But in the meantime, Solomon was their main concern. And if the dog had found someone else, they'd deal with that, too.

There was nothing for it. He pulled his cell phone out, grateful for the signal, and called Cade. To Tracy, he said, "I need someone to know where we are, in case something happens."

Her eyes widened. "We're going in?"

He pursed his lips, then said, "We're going in."

Still, he didn't intend to go too far. Without flashlights they couldn't anyway. They would see what they could and get out. And then they'd know more about what was needed. Once the appropriate help arrived, bringing the right equipment, they would proceed with taking the proper precautions in extricating Solomon and whoever else they could retrieve.

But what else would they find? Another victim?

Or was the man who wanted to kill Tracy waiting for them inside the mine?

NINE

Tracy stayed right behind David as he crept into the opening of the mine.

This had "bad idea" written all over it, but for the life of her, Tracy didn't know what else to do. At least they could take a look.

David had called his brother Cade to let him know what was going on and had received a stern warning in reply as though David was a child instead of the eldest brother. But Cade didn't have to listen to Solomon's barks turn into whining pleas, the sound of which broke Tracy's heart.

She couldn't think with clarity.

And then his whines turned to a low growl… What was going on?

Could there be a bear down there?

Or maybe David was right—this was a ploy to lure them inside.

"We're just going until the light from the opening no longer guides us, right?" Tracy asked.

"Right."

God, please keep us safe. Please let us find Solomon, or let him come to us before we have to go too deep.

"And then what? Solomon sounds like he's much deeper in the mine than we can go."

"I don't know. I'm making this up as I go."

She wished he would have kept that to himself, though she sort of already knew. Anyway, this was her fault, not his. She'd talked him into something he didn't want to do. Something she didn't want him to do for her, but she'd had no choice. She'd needed his help.

"We're coming, Solomon. Just hold on," she called into the shaft. She wasn't sure if calling out to him was a good idea, but it was too late to worry about that now.

As they crept forward, darkness slowly swallowed them.

"Hold on to me," David said.

"Why?"

"Just in case. I don't want to lose you."

Tracy hesitated.

He sighed. "Don't worry. I won't bite."

"You *won't* bite not you *don't* bite? Are you saying that sometimes you do?"

"Maybe." His reply held laughter behind it; much-needed levity for the moment.

Though she barely saw it, she liked that he could elicit a small smile even during an intense situation such as this.

Unsure exactly how he wanted her to hold on to him, she pressed her hand against his shoulder and felt a zap of an electric current. She instantly snatched her hand back. Entirely inappropriate.

She'd already been in his arms and let him comfort her through her tears, but this was different.

Instead she wrapped a finger around his belt loop. Clinging to safety at the moment was more important than her self-consciousness. And David Warren was the definition of *safety*.

"I'm sorry. I can't see much farther," he said. "This isn't going to work. I should have known to grab a flashlight from my truck, but I didn't think we'd be attempting to navigate an old mine."

David turned around, and with Tracy's finger entangled in his belt loop, her arm wrapped around him so that she was pressed against him. That seemed to take him by surprise as much as it did her. Using his free hand, he grabbed her arm but didn't push it away. He held his gun in his other hand.

"Are you okay?" He was so close his warm peppermint-scented breath fanned her cheeks.

Her heart pounded in a way that had nothing at all to do with the desperate barks of her poor dog. No, she wasn't okay. She was entirely too close to David, feeling his sturdy form against hers.

"Sure. Let me just unravel my finger." She was glad for the dim light so he couldn't see the heat crawling up her neck and slapping her cheeks.

David turned away from her and Tracy was able to free her caught finger. Needing to put some space between them, she faced the opening of the mine and saw something.

Or someone.

Just a quick glimpse—but she knew she'd seen someone brush past the opening.

"Hello? Who's out there?"

"What is it? Did you see someone?" David walked toward the entrance.

Tracy trailed him. "I don't think it was your brother."

"I don't, either. No one could get here that fast." He paused. "Unless they were already here."

"Then stay here with me." Fear coiled around her neck. "Don't go out there."

A pebble fell from above. Then a few more trickled down with dirt.

"Watch out!" David pushed her deeper into the shaft and covered her body with his as the ceiling of dirt and rocks caved in.

David coughed in the settling dust, taking care not to crush Tracy but to protect her. He'd shoved her out of the collapse zone in the nick of time or else they'd both have been crushed under the tonnage. He should have paid more attention and looked for warning signs as he was trained to do when fighting fires. But when they'd entered the mine, he'd taken note of the rectangle timber supports lining the shaft to keep unstable rock in place and they'd looked to be intact and stable.

Had someone tampered with the lining?

Time enough to figure that out later. They'd survived, but now they faced another problem. Complete and utter darkness surrounded them. David needed an action plan. He'd been a complete idiot. For whatever reason, he couldn't think straight to save his life—or rather, save their lives and keep them safe—when he was around Tracy. And that didn't bode well for either of them.

David wished he could remain covering Tracy, protecting her, and that it would make a difference. But it wouldn't. He eased off carefully, dirt and pebbles falling away.

She hacked in the dust, as did he, until the air cleared enough they could breathe freely.

"Are you hurt?" he asked.

"No. How about you?"

He wished he could look her over to make sure that was true. "A few rocks to the back, but thankfully nothing big and deadly."

"What do we do now?" Her voice shook. "I can't see my hand in front of my face."

"The mine is deep, of course, but I'm not sure about the quality or quantity of our air supply."

Solomon's barking had subsided to only a few whines now and then. David's prognosis for their situation was not good. Somehow he had to turn this around. Increase their odds of surviving the mine. Or find a way out. He swallowed his fear. He didn't want Tracy to hear or sense his panic, adding to her own.

This should never have happened, and there was no one to blame but himself. But he could beat himself up later.

He grabbed her hand, glad for her strong and steady grip, and kept himself directionally oriented so he could find the wall. He placed her hand against the cold rock surface. "Here, stay right here. I'm going to edge over and start digging us out."

"Are you sure that's safe?"

"What other choice do we have?"

"We could wait for the others to get here."

"Can't waste any time. This could take a while. It's better if I get started." They needed light and fresh air. He didn't know if he could provide that for them, but he had to try.

"Then I can help you."

"No, please, don't move." One of them stumbling around in the dark was one too many.

"David, you can't dig us out on your own. I'm coming, too."

"Let me make sure it's safe, okay? Please. I need you to be out of harm's way in case I get in a predicament."

"As if we're not already in one of those."

"You know what I mean."

She coughed again. "Okay, okay. I'll stay here."

"Good. I don't want anything more to happen to you." David squeezed her hand and for some unknown reason pressed it against his chest so she could feel his beating heart. Why, he couldn't say. He wasn't exactly making sense to himself. Maybe he wanted her to know how deeply he cared, if something happened to him. And yet he continued to prove to himself just how much he didn't deserve another chance.

"Please, be careful." Her voice was soft, tender.

David closed his eyes, though in the dark it didn't matter, and prayed silently he could get her out of this.

"What do you think happened?" Her question broke the silence. "Do you think whoever we saw at the cave opening is responsible for trapping us in here like this?"

He swallowed the rising panic again. "I hope not."

But what else could it be? If this didn't convince Winters, David didn't know what would. He wasn't sure how the entrance had been destabilized, but Tracy definitely had someone after her. Was it connected to the man from her past who wanted payback? He didn't know.

He turned his focus to digging them out and hoped help would arrive on the other side soon. But would his brother think to be on the lookout for someone with ne-

farious intentions? Cade would try to call him in a few
minutes, and when he didn't get a response, he'd come
looking, though cell reception was iffy this far out of
Mountain Cove. He hoped Cade wouldn't come alone.
Now David wished he had gone into more detail when
telling his brother about their search for Solomon.

*God, please, let Cade bring reinforcements. Isaiah
and Adam.* Chief Winters would be a nice addition,
too, except he would be all over David for entering the
mine. He wasn't alone there.

David hit the wall of dirt and rock and felt his way to
the top, figuring there might be an end to the pile, something he could dig his way through. Even if he made a
small hole through to the other side, that would encour-
age him. And right now he definitely needed a boost.

He pressed his palms against the rubble to find traction and made sure it was solid. The last thing he needed
was to create a rockslide that would bury him and take
Tracy down, too.

"You okay back there?" he asked.

"I'm fine. What are you doing?"

"I'm climbing to the top of this pile and then I'll start
digging, removing rocks and dirt. If this turns out to
be a mistake and it slides, please back out of the way
but don't lose contact with the wall. I can find you that
way. Understand?"

"Yes." Tracy's voice was barely a whisper. "Please
be careful, David."

"I will." *I promise.* The words zinged back to him
from the past—the same words he'd said to his wife
when he'd left for the Kenai Peninsula to fight a wildfire. He'd promised Natalie that he'd come back and he
had, but she was dead before he got there.

David started up the pile of rubble, finding his way by feeling and gripping the larger boulders. He and Tracy were fortunate they hadn't been completely crushed. Regardless, he didn't know if he could forgive himself for making such a stupid mistake as coming in here without backup or proper equipment.

Again, he pulled his thoughts back to the task at hand.

He'd equate this experience to rock climbing with a blindfold. He wouldn't be surprised if there was already such a sport, something extreme-sports addicts participated in. He had about ten feet or so to climb, with only a few more to go. Tucking his foot against a secure boulder, he reached up and felt his way for his next hold.

Then everything shifted and collapsed beneath him.

Somewhere in the chaos, Tracy's scream broke through.

TEN

Both hands against the wall and eyes squeezed shut, Tracy turned her face away, pressed her forehead down and against her shoulder, even as she flattened herself against the wall. Screaming, hoping and praying through the rockslide. Or had the ceiling caved in even more?

Her bottom lip trembled. *Oh, God. Oh, God. Oh, God...please help us! Keep David safe. Please, please...*

Before the dust settled, Tracy called out for him. "David, you okay?"

Nothing but silence answered. She was grateful he'd told her to cling to the wall because that was her only anchor. From deep within the mine, Solomon's intermittent whines broke through the trickle of pebbles, but she wasn't as concerned for him as for David. Now she realized what an idiot she'd been to pressure him into going inside—even a short distance—for her dog. They should have waited for help. Her stomach twisted at what she'd done.

She kept her eyes shut until she knew the air was clear so she wouldn't get dirt in her eyes. Though it didn't matter—she couldn't see anything anyway. "David, please answer me. Are you okay?"

Tracy opened her eyes, expecting to see pitch black. But she could see the slightest outline of the wall. What was going on? Where was the light coming from? She felt her way forward, unable to see well enough to trust her eyes yet.

"David!" she called again.

When he still didn't answer, panic kicked in, her heart thudding against her ribs. She sucked in rapid breaths. *Lord, where is he? Please let him be okay.*

Then she saw a gap between the pile of rocks and what was left of the ceiling of the mine shaft—a hole that allowed light inside.

"David!" someone called from outside the entrance to the mine, the sound filtering through the small opening. It sounded like Cade. Relief whooshed through her that help had come.

"In here," Tracy cried. "We need help!"

He didn't respond, but she heard another voice outside. Heidi? Tracy tore her gaze from the hole and allowed her eyes to adjust to the darkness around her so that she could search for David.

"You guys, please hurry. David is hurt," she called, unsure if anyone could hear her.

And then she saw him. His body appeared lifeless. *Oh, Lord, please no...*

Hot tears burned down her cheeks. Tracy dropped to her knees next to where David lay and assessed his injuries. No boulders or rocks had crushed him, and she thanked God that he wasn't pinned or buried.

But he must have hit his head. That was the only explanation for how he'd been knocked out. She wouldn't think the worst, but that he'd simply been knocked unconscious. As the clatter of digging erupted from the other side of the rocks and fallen earth, she edged closer to David and, with limited lighting and equipment, did her best to assess David's injuries. There didn't seem to be any broken bones. She ran her fingers gently through his dirt-filled hair, around his head, searching for a knot. There. She found it, along with sticky moisture.

Blood.

He'd hit his head. She prayed he would wake up soon with nothing more than a concussion, if that.

"You hear that, David? Help is on the way. They're digging us out of this. We're going to be fine. And you're going to be good as new. Thank you for protecting me, for pushing me out of the way. I didn't think I needed protecting." Tracy lowered her voice to a mere whisper. "But I needed your protection after all. Thank you for watching out for me, for being stubborn about my safety. You're a special man, David Warren. And I wish you weren't so good-looking."

Dirt and pebbles trickled from the top.

Her pulse jumped.

She hoped by digging her and David out, they wouldn't disturb the pile even more.

If there was a chance of another rockslide, she needed to move David. But first, Tracy did her best to carefully climb closer to the hole. She needed to let them know what was going on.

Anchored against the wall and a boulder wedged near the top, she called through the break in the debris. "Hello out there."

"Tracy? Is that you?" Cade asked.

"Yes. David's hurt. I'm scared that if you dig us out, the rocks will fall on him and crush him."

"There isn't time to come in any other way. This whole thing could collapse in on you both, Tracy. You'll have to move him."

"But I'm scared I'll hurt him."

"Did you assess his injuries?"

Tracy had some medical training, but she was far from any kind of certification. "I did, and I think he has a head injury." Man, she hated how the words sounded.

Cade's hesitation said volumes. "Okay, then. No back or neck injury that you can ascertain?"

Oh, God, why do I have to do this? Apprehension pressed against her chest. What if she made a mistake?

"Tracy, there's no time to waste, please…"

"I can't be sure. What if I'm wrong?"

"In order for me to climb through to check him myself, I have to move rocks, and that could put him in danger. I need your best assessment."

"No, I don't think he has a neck or back injury."

"Then do your best to gently move him away."

"But can't you call others to help? I've seen how they rescue people who get stuck in old mines or caves."

"That kind of expertise would take hours to get here, and we don't have time to wait. The shaft is unstable. We have to get you out *now*." Though he was patient, frustration edged into Cade's tone.

"Okay, okay. I'll let you know once I have him positioned out of the way. But be careful." Tracy hoped no one else would get hurt because she'd insisted on an ill-equipped rescue of Solomon.

She climbed back down to David and gently tugged him by the shoulders. Though she was strong, David was pure muscle weight and she struggled every inch of the way. Finally, after she'd managed to tug him several yards from the collapsed debris, she cradled his head in her lap.

"Everything okay, Tracy?" Cade again.

"Yes, David's at a safe distance, I hope." But as she said the words, pebbles trickled from above her. "Please hurry!"

If this truly had been planned, the goal must have been for Tracy to be buried alive, and Santino would have exacted his revenge. As it was, this could still end badly, and in that case, he would have the pleasure of knowing he'd killed her along with someone she cared about deeply.

Someone she cared about deeply…

When had she started caring about David in that way that would lead to deeper feelings—feelings that were supposed to be reserved for that one special man? Especially when she'd made sure to guard against caring like that. Tracy needed to harden her heart, but right now she had to focus on getting David the help he needed. Getting them both out of this mine was far more important than issues of the heart.

"David, please wake up." She couldn't take this anymore. A knot grew in her throat. "Why is it that every time I care about someone, they get hurt?"

Saying the words out loud, she heard her own desperation. She couldn't let this happen again. She couldn't care about him. Tracy stiffened, her heart and mind warring with wanting to move away from him and wanting to hold on to him. She only wanted to protect him from further injury. But the urge to hold on to him was more than that. For far deeper reasons, she wanted to be close to him.

When she shifted to reposition his head so she could pull away, David's hand reached up, catching her wrist.

"Where do you think you're going?" David stared up at her, a half grin on his face.

She started. "You're okay. Thank You, God."

She tried to move away again.

He held fast to her wrist. "I asked you a question."

Even in the dim lighting, she could see a glimmer in his eyes.

He acted as though he'd been enjoying their proximity a little too much. Was he teasing her? But he'd been unconscious, hadn't he? Given their predicament, her pulse really shouldn't be racing at that look in his eyes.

"I need to find out what's taking so long." Tracy still held his head in her lap. Awkward. She eased away.

Was that disappointment in his eyes? Releasing her, David sat up slowly, gripping his head. He groaned.

"Just how long were you awake?" she asked.

"What?"

"I was…talking to you." She shoved thoughts of his reaction to her when he'd opened his eyes just now out of her mind. No point in dwelling on it. "Have you been awake and listening, just letting me…?"

"No. Not long. I heard a voice and I don't know… I wanted to wake up and find who it belonged to." His voice was husky. "And I found her."

Tracy couldn't breathe.

David winced. "My head is killing me."

"You're lucky you weren't killed."

When he pushed all the way to his feet, Tracy grabbed his arm to steady him. "Take it easy."

Had he forgotten where they were? What had happened?

Though he appeared disoriented, David found the wall, leaned against it and rubbed the back of his head. He'd found the knot. Then he gazed at her. "We *both* could have been killed."

Guilt washed over her.

Dirt and pebbles trickled from the wall of debris as Cade worked to clear a path. The ceiling shifted above them. David pulled her into his arms and shielded her against the wall, protecting her and trapping her at the same time. She was scared they were going to die. But there was no other place she'd rather die than in his arms.

She was in trouble.

A small rock tumbled. Scraping sounds coupled with more shifting and moving from the front of the mine caught David's attention.

Cade stuck his head through a hole he'd been widening at the top of the pile. "Okay, boys and girls. Sorry to interrupt your fun, but we need to get out of here."

He tossed a flashlight in.

"I couldn't agree more." David reined in his emotions and tried to ignore his pounding head. Tried to ignore the feel of Tracy's soft form in his arms.

She had power over him just as he'd feared that first moment he'd met her. It was the whole reason he'd intended to stay away from her. Even this dangerous situation hadn't prevented her effect on him. When Tracy had held David, spoken softly to him, he'd heard both her desperation and something more in her tone that had warmed him, drawn him out of his unconscious state. And he couldn't seem to shake this…whatever it was between them.

Nor could he be open with her about it, especially when he hadn't figured things out himself. He knew well enough he shouldn't connect with her on an emotional level, and here he was. It was too late. David slowly released her.

Dizziness swam over him.

She shifted under his arm, bolstering him. "I told you to take it easy."

Anyone else would have done the same thing, but it wouldn't have had the same effect on him as Tracy. He had to shake off these emotions.

"I'm all right." He untangled himself from her. He could stand on his own. "We need to get out of here."

"But what about Solomon?" Tracy's distress rushed over David.

From deeper in the mine, the dog's barks grew stronger and his form became visible as he emerged into the dim light from the opening of the mine shaft. Solomon nearly knocked Tracy over in his exuberance.

She hugged him to her, rubbing his head and body. "What happened to you, boy? Why'd you go so far into the mine?"

David should remind her that he'd likely been taken to lure them in. The trap would have worked perfectly if he hadn't called his brother to let him know where they'd gone.

Solomon started in on David then, jumping up to lick his face. He didn't want to push the dog away, but they needed to get out while they still had the chance. "Come on, Solomon. Let's get you out of this mine." He projected his voice toward their small exit. "Cade…"

"Yeah?" His brother stuck his head into view.

"A little help, please? Call the dog."

Cade called Solomon, pulling him up and out through the hole.

Then David assisted Tracy, positioning her as carefully as he could.

God, please keep things stable until we can make an escape.

Tracy climbed up ahead of him. The debris appeared to have settled and was packed enough that they could climb it without causing another shift. Once Tracy climbed through the opening, Cade and Heidi assisted her the rest of the way and David followed.

He was grateful that if this had to happen, it had happened during summer in Alaska. The sun wouldn't completely set until late, and even then, they could expect twilight until well after eleven. Not that he was afraid of the dark, but they weren't safe here and every bit of added visibility helped. "You guys came alone? You didn't bring Isaiah or Adam?"

"They were on their way," Cade said. "Terry, too. But I just texted them you're out."

"What happened in there?" Heidi rubbed her hand over the back of David's head.

He winced. It could take him days to get over this headache. He'd stop by the hospital and get his head checked out as soon as he could.

Heidi peered at him, concerned.

"We went into the mine after Solomon." David crouched down. "Solomon, come here, boy."

The dog wagged his tail and came willingly, then licked David all over his face again. Not something he'd normally prefer, but he allowed it for Tracy's benefit. When he looked up and saw her beaming at him, it was worth all the dog slobber in the world. But his chest tightened. He shouldn't be thinking along those lines.

She crouched next to him to pet her dog and wrestle him from David's face. "I think he likes you."

Cade and Heidi laughed.

"You think?" Heidi said.

"I'm sorry," Tracy said. This time she pulled Solomon off David, but she had to use so much force that she overbalanced and fell on her backside. Laughter erupted.

He liked her laugh and he liked her voice. A soft, compelling voice that had pulled him from an unconscious state. He couldn't seem to grab hold of her exact words—they hung at the edges of his mind, just out of reach—but there'd been something inviting in them, that much he knew.

Then he noticed the thick marine rope around Solomon's neck. "This yours, Tracy?"

"No." She shook her head. "I don't tie him up. But someone must have tied him up in the mine, just as you said—to lure me inside. Solomon obviously chewed his way out. Good thing it wasn't a galvanized steel tie-out or he'd still be down there." She ran her hand over the dog's forehead and down his neck and back. "What would we have done if he hadn't escaped?"

Cade pulled out a pocketknife and cut the remains of the rope from Solomon's neck.

Tracy crouched to get in the dog's face. "What would I do without you, Solomon?"

She tugged him close.

"Tell me," Cade said.

David glanced around. "It's not safe to stay. We need

to hike out of here. There's someone bent on harming Tracy."

"We don't have to hike far. My truck's just over there."

"You drove up here on these overgrown roads?"

"Yeah. I figured you'd done something stupid and I didn't want to waste time."

David wanted to glare at Cade. After all, David was his older brother and deserved some respect. He should be the one dishing out advice. Instead he tugged his brother to him. "Thanks, bro."

"You're welcome."

Together they hiked along the overrun trail toward the truck.

"So who is this guy, Tracy?" Cade asked. "Any ideas?"

"Someone connected to my past. You could all be in danger now because of me." Tracy sighed.

David eyed the woods. Tracy had caught a glimpse of someone just before the mine collapsed. Someone could be hiding in the trees. He put his hand on his weapon in his holster.

A twig snapped somewhere in the shadows of the forest.

Cade's truck was only fifty yards away, but it wasn't close enough. David shook off a wave of dizziness, retrieved his weapon from the holster and grabbed Tracy's hand. He picked up his pace. Cade and Heidi followed his lead. The person after Tracy—a killer, an arsonist from her past—could be watching them now. He shuddered to think what a person like that could do to the small town of Mountain Cove.

He feared Jay wouldn't be the last person attacked, that Veronica wouldn't be the last person to die. He feared in the end, he would fail Tracy.

ELEVEN

"I don't know if I can do this to you, Jewel." Tracy peeked between the curtains to see Cade and David talking to Terry, Cade's police friend, who stood next to his cruiser. "You need this room for your income. Bad enough I was taking up space in your cottage."

"There's nothing I wouldn't do for someone I care about."

Tracy pulled her gaze from the three men and looked at Jewel, who leaned, arms folded, against the door-jamb. In her midforties, Jewel was beautiful, with a quiet and elegant grace about her. Her ash-blond hair, long and straight, hung down past her shoulders. Tracy pictured her as the kind of woman who would wear it the same way even into her sixties and seventies and look just as beautiful.

Moving to Mountain Cove, Tracy had tried at first to avoid any close friendships, but Jewel had refused to be pushed away. "Thanks. I care about you, too. That's why I'm not sure this is a good idea. What if—?"

"You don't need to worry." Jewel closed the bedroom door and came all the way into the room. "The boys down there are going to switch out watching the house while the police track this guy down. We stick together here in Mountain Cove. Nobody is going to do this to one of our own."

"But he already did. His fire at the grocery store killed Veronica."

Jewel frowned and sat on the bed. It was covered with a gorgeous mariner quilt, and Jewel spread her hand over the design. "Veronica's grandmother quilted this. The woman lives in Massachusetts. She sent it to me a few years back. This along with two more in the other guest rooms. She stayed here once years ago when she came to visit Veronica."

How could Tracy ever make up for any of this? "It's my fault. She'd still be alive if it wasn't for me. And by letting me stay here, you're putting yourself in danger. And what about your guests?" Tracy rubbed her arms and stared at the window again. The woods surrounding the B and B made for a beautiful natural setting, but a killer could hide there and make a plan to attack them, undetected. "I should contact Jennifer, Marshal Hanes, and go into WITSEC. I shouldn't stay here for even one night."

Jewel was at her side and hugged her. Then she held her at arm's length. "Now, you listen to me. None of this is your fault. You didn't kill anyone. This guy who's after you is the guilty party. And he's just a man, nothing more. He's flesh and blood. My guess is that he's out of his element in Alaska. We'll get him before he takes someone else down."

"You can't promise that, Jewel."

"No, I can't. But there are no promises in life. People die every day, people who don't have a killer after them." Jewel released Tracy and adjusted the earth-colored drapes. "I lost my husband a few years back. He was a firefighter—he mentored David Warren, in fact. But he didn't die fighting a fire. No. He had to get struck by lightning when he was out hiking in the mountains. A lightning strike killed my husband."

"I'm so sorry," Tracy said.

"Do you hear me? Lightning killed him. We never get lightning here. He put his life at risk all the time for his work, and the thing that killed him was literally a bolt out of the blue. There are no guarantees. We have to live each moment as if it was our last. Treasure the time we're here. Cherish our loved ones. So if you don't want to run and hide, if you want to stay here with your friends, we'll stand with you in this."

The depth of Jewel's conviction touched a place equally as deep inside Tracy. How could she leave people who were that committed and loyal? And yet how could she stay?

"David thinks that if the guy could find you here, he could find you anywhere, even if you had a new identity," Jewel added.

Tracy wasn't as sure about that and wondered if David was only trying to justify a reason for Tracy to stay. That thought zinged through her—why would he care so much? She smiled inside. After the way he'd acted in the mine, she had no doubt as to the reasons. There was a strong pull between them, but Tracy knew better than to succumb to her attraction or any feeling she might have for him.

Plopping on the bed, she pressed her hands to her face. "I don't know about this."

Jewel lightly squeezed her shoulder. "You need to rest and then you'll see things more clearly. This is one of the rooms with a private bath. If you don't feel like joining us for dinner, I can bring up a tray."

"No, Jewel. I should help you serve. It's my job."

"Piffle. I'd say you need a day or two off. I have more than enough friends in town that can help when I need it."

The way Jewel eyed her, Tracy was reminded that she'd given Tracy a job because she'd felt sorry for her. She'd been her charity project—in the nicest possible way. Tracy hadn't come to town begging, but somehow Jewel had known she'd needed a refuge. She smiled at the woman.

"Thank you." The words creaked out. She could never fully express the debt of her gratitude.

Jewel gave her an easy, knowing smile then exited through the door, shutting it with a soft click. Tracy needed a shower or maybe a long, hot bath. They'd already brought most of her things up to the room—easy to do, since she didn't have much.

Solomon had been sleeping in the corner on a mat. He lifted his head and whined, but he didn't come to her for attention. Today's experience had worn him out. Tracy stole one more glance out the window. The men were still there talking, the deep grays of dusk dwindling behind the mountain silhouettes.

She was about to let the curtains drop when David glanced up at the window. He caught her watching and his gaze lingered. Was that smile suddenly lifting his lips for her, or something one of the other two men had said? Her heart skipped all the same. She was grateful they didn't seem to notice David's attention on the window. She let the curtains drop and sucked in oxygen. She really couldn't afford her reaction to that man.

David Warren.

Somehow this nightmare had given rise to him entangling himself with her, something that should never have happened. She would have been better off leaving town as soon as she'd heard Jay's story. But she didn't know where to go. Coming here in the first place, finding a place to stay and a job, had been a monumental task. She couldn't imagine moving again, and if she did, would she find a group of people who cared enough about her to stand with her, as Jewel had said? Would she find another protector like David?

Bone-tired, she headed for the bathroom and started filling the tub with hot water. In the bathroom, she noticed a cross-stitch on the wall. "Thy word is a lamp unto my feet, and a light unto my path. Psalm 119:105."

God, what do I do?

"You don't get to order my officers around." Chief Colin Winters worked his jaw back and forth.

David stood on the other side of the man's desk. When they'd started this conversation this morning, they'd both been sitting, but as tensions had escalated, both men had gotten to their feet. "Terry wasn't on duty last night. He chose to watch over the Jewel of the Mountain on his own time."

"In police property!"

Winters had already had words with Terry, and that was why David was in his office to face off with the police chief. "To let the killer know we're onto him. To scare him off."

"First off, we don't know there is a killer. Nobody's been murdered, that we know of. And even so, scare him off? We want to catch him, Warren."

"I thought we wanted to protect the town."

Chief Winters crossed his arms and eyed David. "You want to run the police department, then you can get a job and work your way up. You'll have to go through me every step of the way."

David ground his molars. "Why are we arguing? We both want the same thing. To catch this guy and protect the town. There's a killer out there, whether you know it yet or not. We know Tracy is in danger. Others, as well. Why are you being so stubborn? Let's protect Tracy and catch this guy."

Winters relaxed his jaw.

David saw that as his chance to press the man. "I want to know what you've found in your investigation. Why is it taking so long?"

Maybe he shouldn't have made those demands or added that last part. He'd probably sent the man over the edge and would get kicked out of his office. But they'd known each other long enough that Winters respected David as much as David respected him, though tempers were too high to really demonstrate that respect right now.

To David's surprise, Winters dropped his arms and took a seat. He blew out a breath, obviously regaining his composure. "Sit down."

David did as he was asked and welcomed the chance at a civil conversation.

"I know what this is. I know what you're trying to do."

David stiffened, not liking where he suspected this was going.

"You're turning this into a way for you to make up for the past."

Was he that obvious to others? He hoped not. But his throat grew thick all the same. "What are you talking about?"

Tapping his fingers on his desk, Chief Winters studied him. "Never mind. Look, Warren, it *is* summer, and we've got lots of visitors coming through town with the cruises or to hunt and fish, using the cabins spread out in the woods and on the nearby islands. I'm in a precarious position here. I can't incite panic and scare all the tourists off until I have solid evidence. That said, there's only a couple of ways in and out of this town, and my department is on full alert. We're all looking for this guy who fits Jay's description. According to Tracy, this man might be after her, but she can't give a description."

"The tattoo. That's description enough. And there is no 'might' about it. Someone tried to get at her from the alley at the grocery store."

Winters arched a brow. David realized he might not have been informed of that incident. They hadn't called the police then.

"Then it burned down the next day." David knew they were still waiting to hear back from the fire marshal's investigation to find out if it was arson. "And then she saw someone at the mine last night before it collapsed."

Was Winters even listening?

"Again, circumstantial. Seeing someone there just before the collapse doesn't mean they caused it. Though I'll admit, it does look suspicious. We're investigating how it collapsed, and then we can tell you if it was intentional. But it could just as easily have been an accident. The mine was clearly marked as dangerous." He sent David an accusing look.

David had no response to that and shifted in his seat.

Winters deepened his frown. "By the way, how's your head?"

"It hurts, but I'll live."

"I hope you're not driving around town. You need to rest. That'll give you clarity, too, so you can be sure you're really thinking this through and not just reacting emotionally."

Frustration boiled in David's gut. "You know me better than that. And Tracy is not some paranoid woman."

"But do you admit she has a reason to be distrustful? Maybe even fixated on the idea that someone is trying to kill her?"

Standing again, David pressed his knuckles into the desk and leaned forward. "You go too far, Winters."

Winters held his palms up. "I don't blame her. If I'd lived through her experience in California, I would probably be looking over my shoulder, too. But I can't ask every person coming in and out of Mountain Cove to show their tattoos, and some of them have many."

"Then what *can* you do?"

"We can look for this man like we're doing, even though we don't have much to go on."

"And what about Tracy's protection? And Jewel and her guests?"

"I only have twelve officers, which isn't enough when the population explodes in the summer months. But…I'll concede on that point. Jewel and her guests at the B and B need a police presence if Tracy is staying there."

David wasn't 100 percent sure he liked the way Winters had worded that, as though Tracy wasn't his first concern. David had always trusted the man to do his job well before. But he couldn't help but think he was conceding because he had a thing for Jewel. Everyone knew that except Winters and Jewel.

"The Warren brothers will help you keep watch, then, too."

"No deadly use of force. Got it? Call the police if you see anything suspicious. And be careful. I understand how you think. You'd rather die trying to save someone than lose them, but the citizens of Mountain Cove don't want to lose *you*." Winters pinned him with his glare and David saw the truth in his eyes.

Satisfied that he was getting the police response he wanted, he said, "Then let's get this guy."

Winters stood and thrust out his hand. "You should have applied to the police force instead of becoming a fireman."

David took Winters's strong grip and shook, feeling better about their conversation by the minute. "You're a good man, Colin."

Winters offered him an amused smile. "You had your doubts?"

"I knew you'd come through with some prodding."

David left the chief's office and exited the building.

Mountain Cove was small enough that most of the locals knew each other. Add to that the residents were made up of rugged men and women who could live through a harsh winter environment and who mostly packed weapons. Knew how to handle themselves. The threat came when someone was off their guard because they didn't know they were in danger. Someone like an innocent store clerk working at the grocery store.

But word had spread fast enough and people knew now to keep an eye out. He just hoped they didn't blame Tracy for Veronica's death. He hoped no one suggested she leave town. Most people he knew here would quickly come to her defense, but there was always one or two who stood apart.

What David had to do was figure out how to do his own job and keep Tracy safe at the same time. He had taken too much time off as it was.

David approached his truck, thinking back to the moment when it had arrived in Juneau. His shiny new truck had been meant to somehow fill that emptiness inside, and it had worked temporarily. Or at least he'd lied to himself that he was happy. Somehow when facing life and death, when trying to protect a woman he cared too deeply about, he wondered why he'd bothered spending the money on a new toy with all the bells and whistles, when there were plenty of other more important places to put his money. He already gave to plenty of charities and missionaries abroad. Local needs, as well. All more important and less selfish. But maybe he could give more and spend less on himself. He could have bought a used and older-model vehicle and it would have done the job. Still, as he climbed inside and ran his hand over the newness of the leather interior and started the ignition, he smiled. He was only human, after all, and though he hated his shallowness, he couldn't help but take joy in this small pleasure.

His cell rang and David dug it out of his pocket. It was the fire chief. They'd heard from the fire marshal. He'd determined the origin and cause of the fire. That had gone much quicker than David had expected.

"I'm on my way." David headed over to the burned-out hull of a grocery store. He'd already made up his mind—based on Tracy's reaction and what she'd told him—that this had been arson, though he hadn't wanted to admit that to Tracy. The fire marshal had sent debris to be analyzed for chemical accelerants, but ultimately it would be Winters's responsibility to investigate criminal activity if the fire marshal determined evidence of that.

Had he found something?

Or had David jumped to a lot of conclusions without any facts based on Tracy's story? What if he'd been wrong?

TWELVE

"Where is it?" Tracy grumbled to herself.

There wasn't anyone in the cottage to hear her complaining besides her. On her knees, she fumbled under the desk, searching for Jennifer's business card. It had been a couple of days since the grocery store burned down and the mine had collapsed, nearly killing her and David. And even two days since she'd seen David last. He had a job, after all, and had to work his twenty-four-hour shift at the fire station.

At least there hadn't been another fire in town.

For some crazy reason she'd almost started to believe he would never leave her side. She'd almost started to count on that when she knew good and well she shouldn't. And her heart ached a little, when it shouldn't. But between the Warren brothers and the police department standing guard at the B and B, Tracy was almost convinced she was safe.

And she was all the more confused. How long could they go on like this? Certainly not indefinitely. Tracy was trapped between someone who wanted to kill her and people who wanted to protect her, and she couldn't breathe. She needed to talk to Jennifer.

Behind her, Solomon barked, startling Tracy.

She bumped her head on the desk. "Ouch."

At least she recognized it as a friendly bark.

"What. Are. You. Doing?"

And the familiar masculine voice.

David.

Even the sound of his voice sent warm tingles through her. She crawled out of the confining space under the desk where the chair had been and rested on her knees. "I'm looking for something."

"You shouldn't be in the cottage. You shouldn't be alone. What's so important?"

"I'm not alone. Officer What's-His-Name is out there."

"No, he's not."

"What? He was sitting in his cruiser not five minutes ago."

His rugged face shifted into a deep scowl. "He must have gotten called away. Glad I showed up when I did."

"And you didn't pass him on your way in?" Tracy frowned. That meant that he'd been gone awhile and that Tracy had been here longer than she'd intended. Alone.

So much for having guard dogs of the human variety—they weren't reliable.

David held his hand out to her. Tracy took it and allowed him to assist her up. On her feet, she stood and realized she was in his personal space. Or he was in hers? Either way, his masculine scent wrapped around her and she took a step back.

Into the desk.

He was close. Much too close. And she'd missed him

more than she wanted to admit. Her heart pounded, and unfortunately, her breathing gave her away.

The smallest of grins broke through his frown. Did he realize the effect he had on her? Not good. Still, he kept her pinned and stared down at her, his hands at his sides. "What am I going to do with you?"

Excuse me? You don't own me.

Tracy thought of a few more unpleasant retorts, but she calmed herself. David meant well. "I'm sorry. I can't find my cell phone anywhere. I think I lost it in the chaos in the mine. So I don't have my contact list or numbers. And now I can't find her card."

"Whose card?"

"Marshal Hanes."

"Don't tell me you're thinking of going into WIT-SEC."

Tracy slipped around him, putting space between them. He looked too good for his own good. Or rather, for Tracy's good. Tongue hanging out, Solomon lumbered toward David as if taking Tracy's place and wagged his tail. David reached down and rubbed the dog behind the ears.

"I'm not sure what to do." She needed some advice and had hoped that the marshal could give her that. She was still mulling over Jewel's words, as well.

If she thought he was going to try to talk her into staying, though, she was disappointed. David said nothing. Instead he studied her long and hard until she grew uncomfortable. She shouldn't care if David wanted her to stay or not. That shouldn't matter.

She finally averted her gaze. "So…um…I'm sure you didn't come here for idle chitchat." Oh, man. She could have said something much nicer.

It's good to see you. How are you doing? Something. Why couldn't she tell him that? Instead she sounded rude, and she hadn't meant it that way. She lifted her hand to reach out, squeeze his arm—she was far too demonstrative—and apologize for her tone.

"You're right. I didn't."

Tracy dropped her hand before making contact. So much for good intentions. Not wanting to meet his eyes, she searched the cottage for anything else she might have left inside.

"We've finished investigating the grocery-store fire."

That got her attention. She jerked her eyes back to him. "And?"

"The fire marshal and Chief Winters agree that it was arson. To tell you the truth, I was hoping for something else. I was hoping that you were wrong."

Tracy sagged where she stood. "You were hoping I was delusional, that's what you hoped."

"No. Not that. But I'm having a hard time wrapping my mind around any of this. As I'm sure you are. You already told me about Santino and his gang and the fires. But is there anything, any details that would help us, that you left out?"

His question knocked the wind from her. Tracy reached for the sofa and made her way around, easing down into the soft cushion. Yes, there were details that she'd left out. She'd told him that she'd witnessed Santino burning a house, but she hadn't shared she'd been a target long before she'd been a witness. And she should tell him everything now, but she wasn't sure she could talk about it. Not yet.

David looked stricken at her reaction. "Maybe I shouldn't have asked you. Maybe I can get that information from the police if they're willing to share. I didn't think… I thought you'd be able to talk about it by now."

David approached her then sat on the edge of the sofa at the opposite end. Why did he keep getting closer to her?

"No, it's okay. It's just that when you asked me, I realized that I was running from that night in more ways than one. I wanted to forget everything that happened. I can't believe it followed me here. That he found me here."

"Then let's end this here and now. Let's catch this guy in Mountain Cove so he can never harm you again."

She shook her head. "Santino is still in jail. It's only one of his minions in his gang following his orders from inside prison. It will never end. There will always be the next guy until Santino moves on to another target."

"There has to be something we can do." David jumped up and paced the cottage, his presence and sturdy form once again making the cozy place seem much smaller.

"Santino would have to die first, and even then I don't know if his gang would stop targeting me. And that's why I can't know if staying here is the right thing to do. Jewel had a lot of brave words to say, and I'm privileged to know a community filled with such loyal people who have welcomed me as if I'm one of their own."

"But…"

"But I don't know, David." Tracy stood and blocked his path. She knew she should steer clear of him, but when he was this close, protectiveness and concern pouring off him, she couldn't help herself. She wanted to be near him.

In his arms.

Maybe she wanted him to convince her to stay in this hopeless situation. He made her think crazy thoughts, unreasonable thoughts. She shouldn't stay here.

Oh, God, please don't let him read my mind. Please don't let him see what has to be obvious.

But when he stopped and looked at her, his eyes were warm and soft, and she knew he'd done just that.

"I'm not usually so indecisive," she whispered.

He took one slow step forward and then another, forcing her breath to hitch again.

"I don't want to run again. I don't want to hide anymore. But I can't stay here knowing I'm putting everyone in danger."

David stood close again, and this time his hands didn't stay at his sides. He lifted his fingers and wrapped them in the tendril that had fallen into her face. She heard him swallow and understood he felt the attraction, too. But this thing with David that she couldn't let herself have went so much deeper than attraction. How had some gorgeous woman not snagged this man already? He was a prize worth fighting for.

She didn't want to leave Mountain Cove or the friends she'd made here, but David had quickly become her biggest reason to stay.

And he couldn't be.

"Then don't," he finally said. "Don't run and hide. Let your friends in Mountain Cove protect you, and at the same time the police can take this guy down, and then everyone will be safe. Including you."

Did David really believe what he was saying? "I don't think you truly know what you're up against."

He twirled her hair and stepped even closer. "Maybe

not. But you're worth whatever the cost, Tracy. Don't go."

Then his lips made contact with hers and lingered, igniting something deep inside both her body and soul. Tracy breathed in the essence that was David and lost herself in his sweet, tender kiss that conveyed how much he cared, more than words ever could.

She didn't want this to end—this feeling of being cherished that David's simple kiss had ignited. But Tracy stepped away, breaking the spell. "I'm no good for you. I can't do this."

Anguish spread over his expression, regret in his eyes. "I'm sorry. I shouldn't have done that."

"Look, it's okay. I felt it, too. I kissed you back. But this can't go anywhere, so maybe we should keep our distance."

"You're right. It can't go anywhere."

The look of complete resolution on his face wasn't what she'd expected, and for a brief, selfish second she wished she could take her own words back.

Tracy frowned and looked at the floor. It needed sweeping. "I should get back to help Jewel."

Solomon nudged her and whined, sensing it was time to go, too.

"I won't kiss you again, Tracy, but I'm going to stick around until I know you're safe, once and for all. I promise." David gestured to the door. "So if you're ready, I'll escort you back to the main house."

"Come on, Solomon."

Tracy walked with her dog and David strolled behind, keeping his distance.

When she caught a glimpse of him over her shoulder, she saw that he'd taken out his weapon and was scan-

ning the woods edging the property. She didn't bother
to protest. If she wasn't going to get a new identity—
run and hide—then yes, she needed David's help. She
needed his protection, but he brought his own brand of
danger with him. He was a threat to her heart.

David watched Tracy hesitate at the back door to
the main house. She glanced back at him but didn't
smile or wave.

Fine with him.

Keeping their distance it was. As far as he was concerned, this was close enough.

Yeah, right.

He'd been a complete idiot to kiss her, but he'd been
swept away by her crazy red hair and eyes with those
flecks of silver on blue, and her soft-spoken personal-
ity, determined nature, courage—the list went on, including something innate he couldn't define. All of it
drew him to her like nothing before. Well, since his
wife. The thought of Tracy leaving, walking out of his
life, had sent him over the edge.

Something about Tracy made it hard for the man in
him to ignore.

But he had to try.

Careful not to scratch it, he leaned against his truck.
So he'd start his shift watching the B and B and occu-
pants a little early. He had two days before he was due
back to the station. And then he'd worry about Tracy the
whole twenty-four hours that he couldn't be with her or
watch out for her as he'd just done. That had driven him
absolutely insane. In fact, it had driven his firefighting
buddies crazy, too. But at least they hadn't been called

out to another fire started by this arsonist murderer. That was one positive in this whole mess.

Another was that he'd convinced Winters to participate in protecting her.

He'd parked at the edge of the property near the woods and mostly out of sight of the guests. He didn't want to scare them. He'd already tucked his gun into his holster and out of sight, as well, but that was more in keeping with Winters's request. David didn't have the authority of the law behind him, technically speaking.

Fortunately, Jewel had agreed to this setup and knew it was important to keep someone watching the place. And true to her word, she'd informed her guests of the situation, as well. He would have thought that news—that a killer was after one of her employees—would have scared her guests off, but that hadn't happened at all.

Jewel told him that an older man and his wife enjoying their anniversary on a dream Alaska vacation had left the morning after Tracy moved in, but the other guests dug in deeper. Some had even tried to reserve another week, except Jewel was already booked for the summer. Were they hanging around to catch some action or watch the drama unfold? He thought it more likely they wanted their part in keeping Tracy safe. Though they hadn't known her for long, the guests interacted with Tracy every day and he could understand why they'd feel protective of her. David approved. Just as well to have the whole town, and then some, on guard and protecting Tracy since he was sure that he, himself, wouldn't be enough.

He shifted against his truck. This would be a long evening. He texted Cade to talk. Called Chief Winters to find out if they'd learned anything more. Jewel brought him some dinner—baked salmon in a puff pastry—and tried to coax him into the house at least to eat, but he refused, thinking Tracy wouldn't want to see him there after he'd crossed the line. Besides, he needed to watch from outside. Inside and near Tracy, and he would grow weak and stupid.

She was his kryptonite.

The symphony of insects harmonized around him, and though he'd plastered himself with repellent, the mosquitoes were relentless in accosting him. He especially hated the whining buzz in his ears. Dusk would descend soon enough and Terry should arrive around midnight, when it was finally dark, to watch over the B and B through the night.

David yawned, rubbed his neck and watched, waiting for the last light in the house to go out. Tracy's room. He knew because he'd seen her looking out the window that first night.

He fiddled with his cell, wanting to call her then remembering she'd lost her phone. Disappointment surged. He was like a stupid schoolboy who didn't know when to let go. But he had the urge to throw pebbles up to her window to see her open it and smile down.

Time crept slowly by and no one stepped from the woods to set the B and B on fire or attack Tracy, and for that he was grateful. On the other hand, if this guy was still out there, David would rather get the confrontation over with while everyone was still on full alert, rather than have the guy show up when they had let their guard down after too much time passed.

Finally car lights flashed in the long drive. David

could tell it was the cruiser. The lights went off and out stepped Terry.

"Any news?" David asked.

Terry shook his head. "If he left town, he didn't leave by any of the usual routes, which leaves me to think he's still here."

David followed Terry's look to the darkened woods. "There are a lot of places someone could hide out there. He'd have to know how to survive in the Alaskan wilderness."

"If he knows what he's doing. Whether he does or he doesn't, don't worry. We'll get him."

"Hopefully before anyone else comes to harm." At the look Terry gave him, David wished he'd kept those words to himself. He almost sounded as if he thought the Mountain Cove PD wasn't doing its job. "I should get going."

Terry nodded his agreement.

David climbed into his truck, started it up and then rolled down the window. "Don't let the mosquitoes eat you alive."

He tossed Terry his bottle of repellent. The man scowled at David, but beneath his frown hid the hint of a smile.

Though David hated leaving, he'd grown tired and someone fresh would be better watching the house. If only he could have called Tracy just to say good-night before he left. He steered down the drive off the property and turned onto the main road. That was when he heard it.

That warbled sound that told him he had a flat tire. "Of all the…"

David pulled over to the side of the road and hopped

out. Sure enough, his left back tire was flat. He must
have hit something on the drive from Jewel's. He raked
his hands through his hair, so not in the mood to change
a tire. Not on the dark road in the middle of a short
Alaska night when he was exhausted and emotionally
drained and there was a murderer out there somewhere.

He got out the jack, lug wrench and retrieved the
spare tire. After jacking up the truck, he glanced around
and behind him. Pulling his gun out, he set it within
easy reach, then bent over and started removing the
lugs. He was on the last one when a footfall crunched,
alerting him to someone behind him.

Before he could react, pain split his skull and everything went black.

THIRTEEN

David had had the most exhausting week, deployed to a wildfire in the Kenai Peninsula. He'd been trained as a wildland firefighter, but 99 percent of the time, he was fighting fires away from home. He loved his job, but it was hard on his marriage and all he could think about was getting home to Natalie. Climbing into bed to lie on the best mattress in the world next to the best woman in the world. But as he steered his truck home in the early hours of morning, something didn't feel right. Warning signals pounded in his head.

The smell of smoke filled the air and the fireman in him kicked into gear, stiffened and searched for the source. His phone alerted him to a text at the same moment he heard the blare of fire-truck sirens.

His house came into view, flames shooting out the windows and roof.

Oh, dear God, save her!

David wasn't sure how he made it into the house, but he hadn't waited on the trucks. All he could think about was Natalie.

He called her name. Shouted it. Kicked in the bedroom door but the room was already in flames... The

heat singed him, burned his lungs. Without his equip-
ment, he couldn't survive. And neither could she.

Strong arms pulled him out of his house. He'd wres-
tled on the gear he needed to go back inside, but it was
too late.

And now she was gone forever. And he was alone.

The fire had caught him off guard—somehow he
should have prevented it.

David coughed, smoke filling his lungs. Heat crawled
all over him.

His eyes blinked open. Where was he?

He was inside his truck…and it was on fire. David
tried the door handle, but it was too hot. He leaned
back, pulled his knees to his chest and kicked the door.
Again, again and again.

He was going to die. He deserved it. He should never
have lost his wife to a fire. He should have seen the
signs. Paid more attention.

But, no, he couldn't die. Not when Tracy was still
in danger. He had to live to make sure she was safe.

God, help me!

"David!" Cade's shout penetrated the flames. Then
the door popped open. Cade tossed in a wet blanket and
David wrapped himself then jumped from the burning
truck. Hitting the ground hard, he rolled.

A hacking cough overwhelmed him. Cade handed
him water. "Let's get you to the hospital."

Anger at the situation coursed through David. "I'm
fine. The fire truck will have what I need." Except his
head was killing him, from the smoke inhalation and
from the blow that had knocked him out. He wasn't sure
he could take another hit in the head.

But at least he wasn't burned. He'd made it out in the nick of time. "How'd you find me?"

"I needed to get out of the house. Get some fresh air. Leah's crying. The baby's crying. And I'm doing everything wrong. I knew Terry was relieving you at midnight and I headed that way to intercept you on your way home. I had nothing better to do, so I came looking. Good thing I found you when I did. What happened?"

David stood, anchoring himself over his thighs, dragging in more fresh air.

"We should move back." Cade tugged David a good distance from his truck.

Now a blazing bonfire. What a complete waste.

Then his truck exploded. Dizziness swept over him. The world tilted. Cade assisted him to the ground. He gripped his aching head in his hands. He had a million other worries, but that…that was his truck. His new truck!

He felt Cade's squeeze on his shoulder. "I'm sorry, man. I know you loved it."

"It was only a truck." That was what he got for loving it. "Did you call for help?"

"First thing. I saw the flames and made the call."

Pulse racing, head pounding, David got to his feet again. That was too close.

"You scared me to death," Cade said.

Tracy hadn't been kidding when she'd said the people around her were in danger. Now David questioned the sanity of having her stay at Jewel's with so many other people who would be in danger. What had any of them been thinking? "Can you call Winters for me?"

"Sure, but do you think this is related to Tracy? To the grocery-store fire?"

"Absolutely."

Sirens erupted in the night. That sound happened too frequently of late for David's comfort, even though he was a fireman and should be accustomed to it. Lights flashed in the distance down the road as flames devoured David's truck, illuminating the surrounding area in a bright ring of light. Shadows danced in the forest around them. David peered into the woods. Was *he* still out there?

"Tell me," Cade said.

The words reminded David of their dad, who'd founded the Mountain Cove Avalanche Center. Ironically, he'd died in an avalanche.

"I was changing a flat tire and heard someone behind me. They struck me before I could react. I woke up in the burning truck."

The tanker truck arrived. Using the water in the two-thousand-pound tank, firefighters doused David's truck. Though it would have eventually burned out on its own, they wouldn't risk the fire spreading.

His firemen coworkers treated him with oxygen. Strange to be on this side of things, but he'd been here once before—the night his wife had died.

This event reminded him of all he'd lost. Little wonder he'd been dreaming about that night when he'd woken surrounded by flames. His body or mind had tried to warn him, bring him out of his unconscious state. That was the second time he'd been knocked out in a week. At this rate, he would end up with a traumatic brain injury like some jock professional football player.

Another vehicle turned onto the road. David recognized the cruiser. He would let Terry have it if he'd left Tracy unguarded. But then he saw Terry had a passenger. The police officer steered the cruiser over to the far side of the road, and Tracy jumped out of the vehicle before it had even come to a complete stop. She ran all the way to David and threw herself into his arms.

That stunned him. Filled him with pure joy he was too shocked to suppress. He savored it instead. After their conversation about keeping their distance, David was surprised at her action, but then he understood. That same force drove him to wrap his arms around her, pull her against him hard and breathe in the scent of her freshly washed hair. Try to soak in the goodness that was Tracy.

"Oh, David, I'm so sorry this happened." She sobbed into his shirt. "I couldn't stay away."

This was getting to be a habit with her. To be fair, she'd cried on him only twice now, but if she was going to cry into anyone's shoulders, it had better be his. His gut twisted. He'd become far more possessive than he had a right to be.

She pushed away, though not too far. "See, David? See what happens when you get involved with me? This is all my fault."

He held her face in his hands, weaving his fingers through the soft, wild hair behind her ears, and pulled her close so he could look her in the eyes.

"It's not your fault. It's this crazy man's fault. With every move he makes, he only makes it harder on himself. There isn't a person in town that won't be looking for him now, once they've heard what happened."

If only he could convince her that she shouldn't blame herself. Though he completely understood her thought process—he blamed himself for his wife's death.

Her eyes brimmed with concern, telling him things she felt about him that he knew she could never say, and stirred him to the bone. He wanted to kiss her again but instead he tugged her to him, wrapped his arms around her and held her soft, warm body tight against him. Funny, he was the victim this time, but here he was, reassuring her. No. He had that wrong. She *was* comforting him. The fact that she'd come to find him and run right into his arms made him crazy inside.

Crazy for her.

Another police vehicle pulled up. Winters.

David released Tracy, but held her hand, and she didn't resist. They were both crazy.

Chief Winters stepped out of his vehicle and made his way to David. He put his hands on his hips and surveyed the situation.

"What happened?" Winters asked.

David told him everything, except the dream, of course. But Winters had to know this sent David right back to the night Natalie had died.

"A close call. But not as close as it could have been." He eyed David.

David got his meaning, all right. He could have died. He was that close.

Winters took off his hat and adjusted the rim. "Looks like our assailant caught you off guard."

David understood what Winters wasn't saying. The man hadn't wanted David involved to begin with. Said it was police business, but David had insisted he needed to be part of protecting Tracy. Finally, Winters had relented, and look where that had gotten him?

How could David protect her when he couldn't even take care of himself?

* * *

Tracy had already caused Jewel enough trouble, so the next morning she decided to be up early and help Jewel serve breakfast. Maybe work would get her mind off the fact that David had almost died. She left Solomon in the room, promising to return after breakfast and take him on a long walk. Of course, she couldn't go alone, if at all. Still, he needed time to run off his energy after being cooped up in the room to avoid setting off Jewel's allergies. At least the woman had let Solomon stay as long as he kept to this room.

Jewel liked to serve a big breakfast around a table so folks could get to know one another before they headed their separate ways for their activities. Tracy had already made up a batch of wild-blueberry muffins and they baked in the oven, filling the kitchen and dining room with a wonderful aroma. She helped Jewel prepare her specialty dish, salmon quiche and reindeer sausage. Too robust a breakfast for Tracy, she snacked on fresh blueberries and began serving coffee and juice to the guests settled in at the large table.

A pass-through, a windowed counter in the wall separating the kitchen and dining room, allowed them to see and hear the guests. One place setting remained unattended, but breakfast was served at seven o'clock, regardless. Jewel pulled the muffins out and stuck more in, and together, Tracy and Jewel placed the serving dishes on the table.

Jewel winked at Tracy. "Let's say grace."

The ten guests present—believers or not—bowed their heads.

Though Jewel smiled when she finished, Tracy could tell she was on edge today. What had happened to David had them all jumpy. Tracy tried to talk to Jewel about moving out and away, but the woman shushed her and said they would talk later.

Maybe Tracy should leave without saying anything, but she couldn't do that to Jewel, either.

The final guest moseyed down the stairs and took the empty seat. Tracy hadn't seen him here before. Something about his appearance and demeanor made her feel uneasy. She needed to get a grip and calm her nerves. She was seeing bad guys everywhere she looked. Tracy made sure he got coffee, juice and the full meal deal, then moved on, her thoughts on everything except her task.

She needed a new cell. Using Jewel's phone, she'd made some calls to find Jennifer's number and finally left a voice mail for the marshal. Tracy hadn't heard back, which frustrated her beyond words. But what had she expected? The woman had a job to do and other witnesses to protect. Tracy had passed up her chance, and her indecision had to be driving the woman crazy, as well. Too much was happening. Tracy was too frazzled to think straight.

While the guests talked about their experiences so far and what was on their agendas for the day, Tracy served. Jewel mostly stayed in the kitchen, busy with food preparation. When Tracy poured more coffee into the new man's cup, she felt his dark eyes on her. She blinked up then back to her task when she realized she was missing the cup, pouring hot coffee on the table.

"Oh, I'm so sorry." She quickly wiped up the liquid from around his plate.

The man replied in an understanding tone, but she didn't register his words.

She went into the kitchen and came out with more muffins. Through her peripheral vision she could see him watching. Again.

"Are you finished? Can I get your plates?" she asked the twentysomething couple at the end of the table, clearly caught up in a world of their own.

They were in love. Anyone could see that. They simply nodded to Tracy. She scraped the plates away then dropped one of them on the tiled floor. It shattered.

Silence hung in the air.

Jewel quickly moved to her side and helped clean up the mess. Together, they carried the pieces of shattered glass along with the dishes Tracy hadn't broken to the kitchen and dumped them in the sink with a clank. Fortunately, the conversation in the dining room revived.

But now they had moved to discussing the killer. Someone brought up the car fire last night. It had happened where the B and B drive met the road, so she wasn't surprised they already knew. Or maybe they'd heard her talking with Jewel. Either way, news traveled fast.

Tracy stared at her shaking hands.

Taking Tracy's hand, Jewel pulled her to the far corner of the kitchen where no one else could see or hear. "What's the matter? Other than what we already know, of course."

"That man…the new guy," Tracy whispered. "What's his name?"

Jewel straightened. "Clarence Mercado. Why?"

"I don't know if it's anything, but… He was…watching me."

Jewel pursed her lips. "Do you think he's the one?"

Tracy covered her face. "I don't know. That sounds crazy."

Dropping her hands, she looked at Jewel's pale face. "Forget it. It can't be." Tracy had to sound crazy. She was being paranoid to think Jewel's new guest was after her.

"He's had this reservation for weeks now but, still, we should call the police." Jewel put her hand on the mounted wall phone. "Or better yet, I'll march out to the cruiser outside. Tell the officer we need him in here."

"No." Tracy pressed her hand over Jewel's. "I've caused you enough trouble. You'll never hear the end of this if this guy is just a guest and nothing more. Let's wait."

The thing was, most members in Santino's gang were covered with tattoos, including their faces—at least in the pictures Derrick had shown her. But not the guy sitting at the dining table. Yet Jay hadn't mentioned more than the one tattoo he'd seen on the wrist of the guy who had pushed him. She really was losing it.

"Wait?" Jewel lifted a brow. "For what?"

"Give me a few minutes." Tracy took a few calming breaths. "There's one way for me to know."

Jewel frowned, tilted her head. "How?"

"The tattoo. I need to see if it's there." Tracy kept her voice low.

Crossing her arms, Jewel leaned against the counter. "Could it be that the tattoo guy is onto the fact that you know to look for tattoos and he sent someone else to do his dirty work?"

Now, *that* made Tracy grin. "You've been reading too many mystery novels."

But the levity didn't last long, especially when Jewel eyed her. "This isn't a game."

"I know that." Better than Jewel did.

"Where is the tattoo and how do you intend to look for it? Tell me that, and I might give you two minutes before I call for help."

"I'm making it up as I go."

Without waiting for Jewel's reply, Tracy shoved through the swinging door connecting the two rooms. She didn't have a plan and she had to hurry.

God, please, let this guy just be ogling me because he's a creep, not because he's come to kill me or to hurt these people or to burn down this house.

When she put her prayer like that, she could see why Jewel wanted to call the police immediately. But it could be nothing.

Taking in a breath to steady her nerves, she approached the man. "More coffee?"

"Please," he said. He never took his eyes off her. If he wasn't a killer, he was downright rude. A jerk. And even if he was the guy sent to taunt her and kill her, why would he be so blatant about staring? Why didn't he just get on with the reason he was here?

Tracy decided she might enjoy this too much. She answered his stare with one of her own, feeling the flames from her past flashing in her eyes as she deliberately missed the coffee cup and poured hot coffee on his sleeve. "Do I know you, sir?"

He yelped and jerked out of the chair so fast, Tracy fell against the wall as she gasped.

Jewel broke through the kitchen door. "What's going on in here?"

Clarence Mercado released a string of what had to

be profanity in Spanish, then glared at Tracy. She could swear he was about to take a step toward her, but everyone in the room had stopped to watch. This incident wouldn't look good in the online reviews of Jewel of the Mountain Bed and Breakfast.

The room was quiet as everyone watched and waited for something more to happen.

A fork clinked.

Clarence grabbed a napkin and wiped his arm off.

And Tracy held her breath.

The tattoo… She could see it on his wrist, just under the cuff of his sleeve. Her pulse rocketed.

Breathe. Just breathe.

She dared to look him in the eyes. In his dark gaze, she saw the thrill of his game. He *knew* she'd seen his tattoo.

FOURTEEN

David floored the gas pedal of the truck he'd borrowed from Cade. The truck rocked and bounced along the drive to the Jewel of the Mountain until the house came into view. He hadn't expected to see this many police vehicles lining the path.

David slammed the brakes.

The truck skidded, leaving marks in the grass, he was sure. But he didn't care. He jumped out and banged the door closed behind him. Running to the house, he hopped up the steps to the porch and barreled through the door.

"Tracy!"

Jewel appeared in the foyer. "She's upstairs."

He pressed by her.

She grabbed his arm. "Just calm down. She's fine. The police are here, as you can see. They're searching the woods."

David inhaled a long breath. Then another. Tracy didn't need to see him this upset. "You're sure she's okay?"

"Yes. She's on the phone...I think."

David's spirits sank. Jewel had been the one to call

him, not Tracy herself. But what did he expect? "What happened?"

"He was here. The killer. Right here in my house. He was here at breakfast. Kept looking at Tracy." Jewel's voice clogged with tears. "She's a bold one, that girl. She poured hot coffee on his arm to see if he had the tattoo."

David ground his molars. "That was a dangerous move. What about the other guests? Who was on duty to watch the house today? Why didn't you just call him or the police, Jewel?"

If David hadn't been at home nursing his concussion, he would have insisted on staying to guard the house himself.

"I wanted to get help, but what she said made sense. We had to know if the guy had the tattoo. He was wearing a long-sleeved shirt."

Wanting to go up to question Tracy himself, he glanced at the stairs, but thought better of it. "Then what happened?"

"He spouted off a few choice words in Spanish, and then a couple of the guys who'd left earlier in the morning came back for some gear. They were more burly than the other guests still at breakfast. I don't know if he would have done something different had they not showed up, but as soon as he saw them, he ran. He was out the door before we could stop him. Tracy…" Jewel shook her head. "I thought she'd collapse right there. We went into the kitchen and called the police. Then I went outside to find the officer in the cruiser and told him everything. He'd been instructed to watch for intruders. Not guests already staying."

Jewel pressed her face in her hands. Then, finally, she looked at David. "I'm so sorry this happened."

"It wasn't your fault. You couldn't have known or suspected your guest." But they were all to blame for this fiasco.

"I've never been so terrified, David. He could have burned down my house." She grabbed David's arm. "But what am I saying? It's just a house. You could have died last night. Others would have died today. This old house can be rebuilt."

David understood what she'd meant. He'd lost his truck last night, but he could have lost his life. Or the killer could have chosen to target the B and B instead of David and his truck. Tracy, Jewel and all the other guests could have been killed.

"I appreciate you calling me to let me know."

Her concerned expression eased into a smile. "I knew you'd want to know. You should go up and see her."

Boots clomped on the front porch. Had they found the killer? David stiffened. Winters pushed through the screen door and into the foyer. He nodded to Jewel, his eyes lingering.

"Tell me," David said.

Winters frowned at David. Then his gaze traveled to the stairs, where Tracy took the last step down. "Chief Winters. What's going on? Did you get him?"

"Not yet. But we're closing in on him. He won't get away this time."

"Are you sure?" David asked. "Do you need more help in the search?"

"He's on foot. He can't go far. And he won't be leaving Mountain Cove by any other route. But just in case he decides to backtrack and come for you, I want you out of here." Winters's gaze flicked to Jewel and warmed. "You, too. Just for the rest of the day. I see this thing ending over the next few hours."

David didn't want to tell the man he was being far too hopeful, but maybe David would do better to cling to hope himself. He kept wondering about Tracy's phone call. Had she called the marshal? Was she going to leave Mountain Cove after all? Leave David?

Inside, his gut twisted. She wasn't his and he didn't deserve her or anyone. Didn't deserve a second chance. He couldn't protect himself, much less Tracy.

It was time to go. He shouldn't have come. He should let the police handle things.

"Well, then, it all sounds like things might get back to normal." David nodded at Jewel and turned to leave. He eyed Tracy, but she looked at the floor.

"Warren," Winters said. "Where do you think you're going?"

David hesitated at the door and turned. "What can I do for you?"

"Can you please escort these ladies to town? Keep them under your watchful eye? This isn't over yet. I don't have enough officers to search the region and guard Tracy, too."

"Of course." David should have offered, and he would have, but he was too busy protecting his own hide. His heart. Cad. But he wouldn't waste more time calling himself names. He turned to Jewel and Tracy. "Is there anything you want to grab before we leave?"

"Oh, no," Jewel said. "I can't leave yet. I need to keep the house open in case any of my guests return. Chief Winters, you can stay with me, can't you? And, Tracy, you gather what you need for the day and go with David."

Tracy hesitated. "I can't leave, either. I need to take Solomon out of the room for some fresh air."

"Oh, piffle. Let Solomon out of the room now. With this new development, he's free to wander the house." She winked at Tracy. "I'll take an allergy pill and then I can take him outside myself, or Chief Winters can help me. He's no problem."

Tracy didn't look convinced. "Are...you sure?"

"Of course. Solomon will be fine here with me. I can't leave, and there are too many police vehicles sitting outside. I doubt he'll come back."

"She's right." Winters maintained a serious demeanor but David didn't miss the twinkle in his eye.

"What about you, David?" Tracy asked. "You were set to leave. Am I keeping you from something?"

Funny they were both acting distant when just last night she'd run into his arms. And before that, they'd even shared a kiss. Then again, Tracy had her reasons for pushing him away, and he had his own, so he knew to keep his distance.

Still, he took a few steps closer and held out his hand. "Nothing that can't wait."

He bit back the urge to tell her the truth—that there was nothing he wanted to do more than be with her now. Slowly, as if measuring him, she placed her hand in his. He wanted to bring it to his lips and kiss it. But he resisted. She didn't need that from him, and he didn't deserve it.

David squeezed her hand and she felt the strength and warmth there. Took the reassurance that he offered.

"This will be over soon," he said. "You're going to be okay."

The words reminded her of their reassurances to Jay when he was hanging on to his life on the ridge. Was this David's training talking, trying to keep her calm, or did he really believe what he'd said? She studied him, searching the depths behind his forest green eyes, wanting his words to mean more to him. But even if they did, Tracy had been the one to close that door.

Dark shadows outlined his eyes. That had to be from his close call last night. But his haggard look didn't detract from his strong, handsome features. Myriad emotions swelled in her chest, and Tracy wanted to run to him, to pull him to her, much as she'd done last night when he'd nearly died. She wanted to rest her head against his chest and hear the steady beat of his strong heart inside. Her own heart grateful for his survival.

God, thank You for saving him.

The outcome could have been much different. How could he stand there and offer his help when she'd brought so much trouble to this town? And to David personally?

"Let me just grab my pack." She bounded up the stairs to her room and hugged Solomon, offering reassurance that she would return. When she opened the door to let him out, he just sat there and stared at her.

Tracy threw a few items into her backpack. No telling how this day would play out. She might need an extra set of clothes. She wasn't as certain as Winters they would catch the killer today, but she wholeheartedly agreed she shouldn't stay here.

Solomon's sad brown eyes tugged at her heartstrings. She rubbed him behind the ears. "Look, I don't know what today will bring, so I can't take you. But I promise to come back, okay?"

At least she'd put in another call to Jennifer a few minutes ago, after the incident at breakfast, and explained everything that had happened last night and today.

On voice mail.

If she was in serious trouble, well, then, Tracy certainly couldn't count on any immediate help from the marshals. But she reminded herself that she'd been the one to venture out on her own. And she had the support of this whole amazing town behind her.

Tracy led Solomon out of the room and down the stairs, where she told him to be good. In the foyer, Tracy caught David leaning against the wall. Though he was waiting for Tracy, he was watching Jewel and Chief Winters deep in conversation. Tracy smiled to herself. Was there something going on between those two? Jewel deserved a good man, if she wanted one.

David turned his attention to Tracy, his eyes lighting up. "You ready?"

"As I'll ever be."

Once they sat inside the truck, David started it up but he didn't go anywhere. He turned to face Tracy. "Are you okay?"

She blew out a breath. "I'm still frazzled. To think I was that close to the killer. The man who hurt Jay and killed Veronica, who set your truck on fire last night and tried to kill you."

"But to pour coffee on him like that, Tracy…"

"Ah, so Jewel told you about that." Her cheeks warmed. That had been a bold move on her part.

"I don't think you should have done it. You could have gotten yourself killed. Jewel, too, and her guests."

"I slept in the same house with him last night, David.

He made it through our guard. We didn't even think to pay such close attention to the new guest. And then he stared at me through breakfast, like it was all some sick game to him. He was here to toy with me. Hurt people as a way to torture me. I didn't think I was pushing it to find out the truth." She put the window down and sucked in fresh air. "Can we just go now?"

"I don't know if you feel up to this, but I thought we'd go see Jay today."

"In Juneau?"

"Sure. Why not? We'll be far away from here."

"You mean where I should have been days ago. Far away."

"No, that's not what I mean. We want you to stay, Tracy. The town, we stand behind you."

"Can you really speak for the town?" *And what about you? Do you stand behind me?* But she knew the answer.

"Yes, I think I can. People have gone out of their way to tell me."

"And why not me?"

"You're isolated up here. People have more access to me."

She had to admit, she felt more welcome here than she'd ever felt in her hometown in Missouri. She wasn't sure the town where she grew up would be this supportive. But that was all the more reason to feel guilt over putting all these people in danger.

Should she leave again? "I called her, David."

"Marshal Hanes?"

"Yes."

David blew out a breath. "What are you going to do?"

"I got voice mail. Told her there was a manhunt for the killer. He could be caught today."

"But?"

She smiled to herself. He somehow always knew there was more to her story. "This guy is just one of thousands of gang members Santino can order around from prison. If my location isn't secret anymore, then more of them could come. I'll see how today goes and then decide."

"Tracy, what's really keeping you here? I…want the best for you. I don't even know what that is."

Tracy was surprised David had asked. She wasn't sure what to say. Any answer she would give him would be the wrong one. She couldn't give him false hope by telling him he was one of the reasons she wanted to stay, and yet, leaving him out of the equation would also hurt him. She could sense that much. They'd agreed a relationship couldn't go anywhere, and here she was, sitting in his vehicle again. Oh, wait. This wasn't his vehicle, considering what had happened to David's truck last night. If she remembered correctly, this truck looked like his brother Cade's.

The images from last night flared in her thoughts once again and her heart squeezed. Her fault. He'd almost lost his life and he *had* lost his truck. He loved that truck, too. She could tell. So many small things she already knew about him. And liked.

"A lot…just a lot is keeping me here, okay? You already know I'm tired of running. Let's go see Jay. We can talk more on the way."

David steered out the drive, slowly maneuvering around the potholes. Jewel had a beautiful and well-tended bed-and-breakfast but the drive begged for attention. Once they met the real road, David turned to head back to town. He got on his cell and phoned Billy to see if he could meet them at the floatplane dock for a quick trip to Juneau.

Tracy looked out the window and smiled to herself. Must be nice to have such easy access to travel in Southeast Alaska, almost as though David had his own bush pilot on call.

When they drove by the spot where David's truck had burned, the wreckage had been towed off. He kept his gaze straight ahead and didn't look. Probably didn't welcome the reminder, and wanted to think about something else. Tracy noticed he frowned now and then, as though in pain, and she remembered he must be suffering from a headache from being knocked unconscious.

Something in the woods caught her attention. She sat up, wondering if David had seen it, too.

She glanced his way. He was still on the phone, but he appeared to have lost interest in the conversation.

Someone ran out into the center of the road to stand directly in their path.

It was the man who'd called himself Clarence Mercado.

He aimed a weapon at them.

FIFTEEN

A man stood in the road, aiming his weapon at the windshield.

At Tracy.

Police spilled from the forest shouting, pointing guns at the man. It all happened before David could blink.

"Get down!" David called out. He reached over and pressed Tracy's head down toward her knees, shielding her as he swerved. He wanted to veer to the right, putting his side of the vehicle in harm's way, but Mountain Cove police were in the path, forcing him to swerve left.

Not good.

Gunfire erupted. A bullet shattered the window on the passenger's side. Another bullet ripped through the door.

Tracy screamed.

A tree loomed in David's vision. He swerved and slowed, but Cade's top-heavy vehicle rolled to the side and then over. The airbags exploded.

Seconds ticked by before David shook off his daze, his mind racing to catch up with what had happened.

"Tracy!" He pushed the layers of nylon away, unbuckled his seat belt and reached for her.

Hanging upside down, secured in her position by her seat belt, she didn't move.

"Tracy, wake up." *Lord, please let her be okay.*

He pushed more of the deflated airbag out of the way and angled her face toward him. He felt her pulse. Strong.

Chief Winters pulled open the passenger's-side door. "An ambulance is on the way."

"Tracy," David said. "Come on—wake up."

When he pulled his hand back, it was covered in blood.

Panic sent his heart tripping. He didn't want to move her, but it was difficult to examine her where she was pinned to the seat, held there by the taut seat belt.

God, show me where she's injured. His heart and mind scrambled for traction—she'd been hurt on his watch. Then he found the gunshot wound on her arm, and without moving her too much, he examined it more closely. Looked as though she'd been grazed was all. He pulled off his shirt to stanch the flow of blood.

Had she hit her head when the vehicle rolled or was there another injury? His hands shook, even as he kept his shirt pressed in place and prayed softly. Finally, Tracy's eyelashes fluttered.

She sighed and then groaned. Opening her eyes, she blinked, frowning. Her position was awkward to say the least.

"What…? Where am I?" Her blue irises focused on David. "What happened?"

"The killer tried…" He couldn't say the word. "Almost succeeded."

She closed her eyes. "What happened to him?"

"He's dead." Winters spoke from outside the truck. "Couldn't be helped."

Tracy breathed a sigh of relief. "Any chance I can get out of the truck? The blood is rushing to my head."

"We're waiting on the ambulance and the EMTs before we move you," David said.

She squinted at him. "Aren't you a paramedic?"

How did he tell her his heart rate soared, making his chest hurt? How could he tell her didn't trust himself? Why did he keep trying?

And failing.

Unexpectedly she reached up and put her hand against his cheek.

"David? Are you all right?" She searched his gaze with more intensity than David could stand.

He sucked in a breath. "I thought I'd lost you."

"But you didn't. I'm right here. Are you going to help me out, or what?"

He grinned. "Maybe I can manage that after all."

Sirens blared in the distance. Were others injured, as well? David had failed to ask about them; his focus was on Tracy. "I'm going to release the seat belt. Brace yourself."

But he had every intention of catching her when he released her.

The seat belt didn't want to budge. David whipped out his pocketknife and cut her out. Then she fell against him.

His heart warmed. Releasing a grateful, heartfelt sigh of relief, he was glad she couldn't see his face, and he didn't resist pressing into her neck, breathing her in. If she noticed, she didn't say anything, didn't resist.

"It wasn't your fault." She held on to him as though

she could feel his pain, but she didn't know about the trauma from his past.

"You're hurt. I should have done something differently."

"Shh," she said. "It's over now. If Clarence—or whoever he was—is dead now, then it's over."

She'd stiffened, ever so slightly, when she'd said the words. He should have been the one comforting her. Some hero, some protector, he was.

But was it really over? He wanted to believe that, but he couldn't quite trust in it yet. Even if it wasn't, at least they had a reprieve.

He assisted Tracy out of Cade's damaged truck.

The EMTs took her to check her over, but David stayed nearby. Winters huddled with the police officers as the killer was put into a body bag. Who was this guy, really? Was he working for Santino, as Tracy had said? Why hadn't he tried to kill her last night if he stayed in the B and B? Or had the incident at breakfast forced his hand today, making him move up his timeline? They might never get those answers, now that he was dead.

David shook his head at the sight of Cade's truck.

"That makes two this week." Cade stood next to him, surprising him with his appearance. News traveled fast.

David blew out a breath. "I'm sorry, bro."

Cade trudged closer and looked at the damage. "I'm just glad you're okay, for the second time in twenty-four hours. But you've had—what?—two concussions in a few days. I'm concerned about you."

"Don't be. I'm hardheaded." The symptoms had faded. The concussions were mild, thankfully. Besides, he couldn't rest until this was over.

More vehicles pulled up, crunching gravel. Footfalls resounded. Adam, Isaiah, Heidi and Cade's wife, Leah, joined them.

"Where's little Scott?" David asked. A crime scene wasn't the place for a child, but it wasn't as if they could leave a two-month-old baby alone.

"Grandma gave us a break for a couple of hours," Leah said. "We were heading off to lunch when we heard."

"And I just destroyed your time alone." David sent Cade an apologetic look.

Leah blew out a breath and grabbed her husband's hand. "It's okay, David. We're just glad this wasn't much worse."

"Who's in the body bag?" Heidi asked, her tone grim.

"The killer, and he almost killed Tracy this time." David glanced back to make sure she was being examined. He caught her gaze as they shoved the gurney all the way in. "I have to go."

He left his family behind and caught up with the EMT. "Whoa, there. What's happening? Is she going to be all right?"

"Sure. Just taking her to the hospital to treat that gunshot wound. Get an X-ray or two. You might think of doing the same thing. You look a little banged up yourself."

He was fine. "Can I ride with you?"

The EMT quirked a grin. "If you don't think you're needed here, then no problem."

After a quick glance in Chief Winters's direction, David confirmed the man was busy. He'd been there and had seen things unfold for himself, as had his officers, and didn't necessarily need a statement from David or Tracy. He could always track them down if he did. David gave the EMT a nod to thank him for letting him ride to the hospital with Tracy. It paid to have friends in town. He climbed up and into the back of the ambulance. Tracy's eyes widened.

"Mind if I come along?" He found a place to sit before she could reply.

"Of course not." She tried to smile, but he could see she was in pain from her gunshot wound, and likely the shock to her body was catching up to her.

He ignored his own aches and pains. They weren't anything serious.

Thank You, Lord, that it wasn't much worse.

He tried to still the churning in his gut, and he grinned, hoping to hide his grim mood. He wished he could believe Tracy when she'd said that this was all over, but he knew she'd said that for his benefit. She'd already told him it would never end.

Before the EMT climbed inside, David leaned close, ran his thumb down her cheek. "I'm sorry this happened."

She smiled, softly. "I'm glad it wasn't worse and that you weren't badly injured. I couldn't live with myself if even one more person got hurt because of me."

If she only knew how he related to that sentiment.

"I know what I said earlier." She averted her eyes. "But we can't be sure this is over."

Then her gaze found him again.

He took her hand. "I know."

He wanted to tell her he would see this through with her, but doubt coursed through him. Was he the best man for the job?

"If one more thing happens, then I'm leaving."

His breath hitched. "You mean…"

She nodded. "WITSEC. I can't watch anyone else get hurt. I have to leave Mountain Cove forever. My family. And I have to leave…"

When she didn't voice the rest, he thought he read it in her eyes.

You.

While she programmed her new cell phone, Tracy stared out the window of her room at the bed-and-breakfast main house, looking at what little she could see of the cottage through the trees. She'd already texted her mother with the new number. She had no idea how Santino had found her in Mountain Cove to begin with, so getting a new phone and number was for the best. Still, she hadn't gotten a new address.

As for her mother, Tracy would call her later, but she didn't want to get into a long conversation just now when she was expecting David any minute.

Solomon rested his chin on the windowsill and whined.

She ran her hand over his head and behind the thick fur of his ear. "I know, boy, I know."

He'd had much more freedom to roam when they'd lived in the cottage. Should she move back in, give Jewel a chance to rent this room out? Except Tracy didn't know if it was a good idea. She didn't know if she was safe or not. Or ever would be.

Chief Winters was still conducting the investigation. He seemed to believe that Mercado had come to town to taunt Tracy by harming others, repeating what she and Derrick had gone through before. Then, when his cover was blown and he'd run out of options with the police closing in on him, he'd attempted to finish the job. That was their theory, anyway.

Tracy wished they could have faked her death, somehow, so that no one else would be dispensed to come and get her now that Santino knew where she was. Chief Winters was working with other law-enforcement entities to keep Santino's men from returning, but she wasn't sure how he could be so confident that it wouldn't happen again.

It made her head ache even more to think about a life spent living in fear, looking over her shoulder. And her arm still ached where she'd been shot. The doctor said it would take a few weeks to heal completely. She'd been fortunate the bullet had only grazed her.

Solomon barked at the door. Tracy smiled and opened it just as David was about to knock. "Jewel sent me on up," he said. "I hope you don't mind."

"Not at all."

"Are you ready?"

"Sure." They'd never made it to see Jay and he was scheduled to be released from the hospital next week, surprising them all. But he'd had no back, head or internal injuries. Still, the road to recovering with so many broken bones would take weeks. Tracy was certain he would be glad to recover at home with his family.

Family… Tracy sighed, missing her own family.

Solomon whined again. "You can't come. I'm sorry." To David, she said, "I took Solomon for a walk. He hates being cooped up in the room."

"So let him out. Jewel doesn't care."

"I know, but he knocked a vase over. One of the guests threw a ball and he caught it. They should have been outside. So, I don't want him bothering anyone."

"Let's take him and drop him off at my grandmother's house. She'd welcome the company, and he'd have a little room to roam."

"Oh, no. I couldn't trouble her."

"No trouble at all, Tracy. And in fact, I've been thinking about something."

"Yeah?"

"Wasn't sure when to bring it up, but now is as good a time as any."

Tracy eased into the chair at the desk, both smiling and a little wary.

"I don't think you should stay here anymore. At least, until we're sure this is over."

"I've been thinking the same thing." But she wasn't sure she was ready to stay in the cottage. Not yet.

"No, I don't think you have been."

She cocked her head, unsure what he meant or if she wanted to know. "I've already told you if anything else happened that I'm going into WITSEC."

Frowning, he nodded and moved to stare out the window. His reaction wasn't any surprise. He'd told her on more than one occasion he didn't want her to leave, but he had to be feeling the burden of having her around, too, the same as Chief Winters and the rest of the town.

"When my mother died, over two decades ago, Grandma Katy moved in to care for us and she never left. We all think of it as her house, and we all used to live there. Cade got married and moved out, and the same with Heidi when she married Isaiah a few months ago."

A deep, painful sigh eased from David. Tracy wanted to know what brought on the palpable pain emanating from him. He hadn't mentioned when he'd moved out, but it had probably been after his own marriage. Was he thinking about his wife? Tracy had learned that she'd died, but she didn't know the details.

She understood that kind of pain. She'd felt it after losing Derrick. They hadn't made it to the altar yet, but she had pictured herself with Derrick forever. She'd thought that they were getting close, that he might propose... And then he'd gotten involved in his research to write a dangerous investigative article and Santino had taken him from her.

"David?" She knew his thoughts were far away, and snagged his attention back. "What are you suggesting?"

"That you could stay with her in the house. She's all alone. Or even live in the apartment above the garage— that's where Cade used to live. You wouldn't have to go back to the cottage, it's too isolated, and Jewel wouldn't have to worry about her guests being in danger."

"But what about your grandmother?"

"She'd be fine—all her neighbors look out for her. You'd be closer to town and in a neighborhood. We all live close. It's safer than out here...and it's just in case."

David already knew she planned to leave if she had even a hint that someone else would come for her. Mountain Cove had already paid too high a price as it was, and yet it was for that very reason that she couldn't simply run after someone had lost their life on her account. But how could she stay if it cost them even more?

Her cell rang. She eyed the caller ID. Her mother. Tracy sighed. "How much time do we have before we have to leave?" she asked David.

He glanced at his watch. "Five minutes if we want to make it in time. Billy doesn't like to wait."

Tracy answered. "Mom, hi. I—"

"Tracy, it's your father."

Her mother's voice was shaky, tearful.

Tracy's knees shook. "What's happened?"

Her mother started bawling, trying to speak through the tears. Tracy couldn't understand the words. She felt David's arms around her, supporting her.

"Tracy, this is Carol." Tracy's sister sighed. "We've been trying to reach you. It's Dad. He was beaten and is in the hospital."

"Beaten? What do you mean? How bad is it?"

"I don't want to talk on the phone, but you're so far away. It was…bad. Can you come?"

"Is he going to…?"

"Live. He's going to live, but he's asking for you."

Oh, how she'd missed her family. If she'd gone into WITSEC, she wouldn't have the opportunity to see them ever again, even if someone took ill or was near death. But then again…maybe if she'd left for good this wouldn't have happened. Was the attack against her father from Santino, too?

"Why? Why would someone do that?"

God, please let it be for some reason other than the obvious.

"The police don't know. It appears to be a random beating."

"I'm coming. Text me the details."

She ended the call, hurt and anger boiling inside.

"What is it? Tracy, tell me what's going on." David's voice barely registered, but she was grateful for his presence.

"It's my dad. Someone beat him—he's in the hospital. I have to go." The police might have thought it was random, but Tracy knew this nightmare would never end for her unless she could somehow wake up. "Santino has targeted my family now, too."

And waking from this nightmare meant someone had to die.

Tracy or Santino had to die.

SIXTEEN

David righted his seatback as the 747 prepared for landing in St. Louis, Missouri. Tracy's seat next to him was empty—she'd gone to the restroom. He stared out the window, watching as they approached the city. The flight seemed to have taken much too long to get there.

He'd been surprised that Tracy hadn't balked when he'd insisted on coming with her. But she'd had no one else and was too shaken up to travel alone. David imagined she'd agreed because she'd been so distraught upon hearing about her father and hadn't had much fight left for anything else. Besides, she'd known he wouldn't take no for an answer.

All it had taken was grabbing a few essentials. Billy had already been waiting to fly them to Juneau, where they'd bought tickets to travel the rest of the way.

He scratched his rough chin, thinking he might have forgotten his razor. He really didn't know what he was doing in all this. The moment he'd learned she was in danger, he'd assigned himself as her personal protector. A woman he'd wanted to avoid. A woman who seemed determined to push him away.

David wondered who would be his protector when it came to his heart, because he wasn't doing a good job.

Seeing her anguish at the news of her father had twisted his gut into a knot. He was into her in a way he'd never intended. But it wasn't as if he could bail on her now. He'd see this through and keep her safe.

The plane shifted, angling to the right. Where was Tracy, anyway?

He frowned, wishing she would come back to her seat. He rubbed his forehead, feeling the exhaustion of the past few days pressing down on him.

She was still in danger. What he didn't know was how to keep her safe, how to stop the man running things from prison. Why didn't the authorities have more power to stop this? One of the problems was getting them to believe it was all connected in the first place. Law enforcement, along with any government entity, seemed to move with the speed of a raft across the Pacific.

She'd told him that if something else happened—someone else was hurt—she would leave Mountain Cove for good and go into WITSEC. He didn't know if this event counted because it hadn't even happened in Mountain Cove.

God, please let it not count.

But what was he thinking? He was being selfish.

Tracy returned to her seat and buckled in. When her gaze bounced off David and then went to the window, he saw the torment in her eyes. Reaching for her hand, he held it and squeezed. There weren't any words for this situation, and holding her hand was all he could think to do. She squeezed back and seemed to take strength from him.

With his other hand, he gripped the hand rest as the plane came in for the landing.

"David," she said.

"Yeah?"

"Thank you."

He turned his face to her. In her eyes, he saw her gratitude, and it nearly undid him. When this was all over, he didn't have a clue how he would extricate his heart, but he knew it would be painful. Maybe even for her, too.

"You're welcome."

After they landed and disembarked, Tracy's sister, Carol, met them outside the terminal. Carol was a tall, slender woman with black hair who didn't look as if she could be related to Tracy.

Tracy introduced David. "He's…a friend and, well…"

"I didn't want her to travel alone. I just came along to help," he added. But he could tell by the look in Carol's eyes she thought something was going on between them. Regardless, she didn't say anything as she drove them directly to the hospital.

David and Tracy followed Carol down the sterile hallways and up the elevator. Once they approached the door to Tracy's father's room, David hesitated. This was a family affair.

He decided he wouldn't join her in the room and she didn't even look back as she entered. Her focus was on her father, as it should be. He prayed the man would recover quickly. Though he should wait to hear more news about what had happened, he chose to head to the waiting room area and make the calls he hadn't had a chance to make.

He called Cade first. He told him everything, suggesting he keep an eye out and check on Jewel and on Tracy's dog.

Then he called Winters. "Warren, I don't have time for you to call me every day. We're wrapping up this investigation, anyway."

"I'm in Missouri with Tracy. This isn't over yet."

"What happened?"

"Her father was brutally beaten within an inch of his life."

"I'll contact the investigating officer and find out what they know, but obviously that's out of my jurisdiction."

"Tracy thinks it's related. That her family has been targeted."

"Tracy should go into WITSEC, if it's not too late."

David blew out a breath. Not what he wanted to hear.

"Anyone with eyes can see you have a thing for her, but if you want what's best for her, you'll talk her into it. It's the only way for her to be safe."

"But you assured her that the Mountain Cove police would protect her."

"And she's not in Mountain Cove anymore, is she? For that matter, neither are you."

David was surprised to note that his hand shook. He couldn't believe what Winters was telling him. Maybe David had known this was the only way all along, but his mind hadn't wanted to go there. He glanced across the waiting room and saw Tracy searching for him. Before he could react, her gaze found him and she closed the distance.

For a third time, Tracy pressed her face into his shoulder and sobbed.

* * *

Tracy sat in the chair next to her father's bed.

When she'd first seen him earlier in the week, he'd reminded her of how Jay had looked in the hospital. So many bandages she could hardly recognize him. One side of her father's face remained bandage-free and was black-and-blue.

"Oh, Dad," she whispered, tears in her throat.

It had been all she could do to hold it together at the sight of him, though Carol had warned her about the severity of the injuries. Fortunately, her own gunshot wound was safely bandaged and easily hidden beneath her clothing, so no one asked her any questions.

But nobody could have prepared her to see her father this way. Someone in the family remained by his side at all times in case he needed anything, despite the nursing staff. She'd given her mother and sister a break to go home and shower and eat, and then they'd be back. David was staying with Carol and Tim, in their extra room, and Carol would bring him to the hospital later this morning.

Tracy still couldn't believe he'd come with her. He'd promised to stick with her until this was over and, apparently, he was a man of his word. She wasn't sure how she felt about that. One thing she did know: she felt safe and protected with him near her.

"Tracy." Her father's voice was weak. He held out his hand.

Tracy reached for it. There was none of the usual strength in his grip. "Dad, I'm so sorry."

"Not your fault."

She wasn't so sure. She didn't want to argue with him, and maybe he already knew. "Who did this, Dad?"

"Already told the police. Don't know."

"Did you see a tattoo?"

"Happened too fast."

She squeezed his hand again. She wouldn't ask him more questions. She already knew—this was part of Santino's retaliation. When she was in protection while waiting for the trial, she'd agreed to be a witness, regardless, but she'd extracted a promise that she could go into WITSEC at any time after the trial should it become clear that Santino would try to harm her or her family. Her father, however, had never agreed. Would he now?

"Dad, there's something we need to talk about."

"I can guess what that is." He coughed.

Oh, God, help me to convince him.

"Santino sent someone to Mountain Cove to try to kill me."

Her father squeezed her hand. "Why didn't you tell me?"

"I know I should have. Then maybe you could have avoided this. Been more alert. But the man was killed. And now this. Dad…"

"I won't live in fear. I won't lose everything I've worked for."

"What about your life?" David's voice surprised her.

He came all the way in the room. In his gaze, she saw his apology for interrupting.

"Dad, this is my friend from Mountain Cove. David Warren."

Her father's one-eyed bloodshot gaze looked at David. Sized him up. "What are you to my daughter?"

"Dad!" Tracy stood, feeling the heat creep up her neck. "He's my friend, that's all. He's a fireman and search-and-rescue volunteer in Mountain Cove. A real hero." He'd come along to protect her and didn't deserve to be grilled by her father. But she'd said more than she should, making it sound as if they were more than friends, her words defensive, protesting too much.

The way David looked at her, with appreciation and something much more, as though he could reach across the room and wrap her in his arms with his gaze alone, sent warmth and longing through her. What they had between them was much more than friendship, but she had to shut those feelings down. The ways things looked, she would always live in fear of her life. And caring about him was a big mistake. She couldn't go through losing someone again.

"Back to what David said, Dad. Your business isn't worth your life." Or her mother's. Or her own. Didn't he understand that she wouldn't change her identity and life without him? He was risking all their lives.

The nurse came in to check his vitals and Tracy took the opportunity to leave the room with David. Out in the hall she said, "Where's Carol? Didn't she bring you?"

"No. I rented a car. Didn't want to be in the way, and I wanted to be free to come up here when I needed to."

Tracy shook her head. "I'm sorry about all this. You don't have to stay, you know. You have a job to do in Mountain Cove."

"This is more important. I want you to be safe." He enclosed her hand in his. "What are you going to do?"

"I don't know."

His gaze emanated more concern for her than she deserved. More than she could handle. That first day when she'd seen her father, she'd kept it together until she'd left his room. All she could think about was finding David and losing herself in his protective arms. And then she'd sobbed into his shirt. Again. She wanted to be in his arms right now, too. But she had to maintain her composure, and she was getting too attached to this guy. Something she couldn't allow.

"All I know is that I want this nightmare to be over."

David took her in his arms then and weaved his fingers into her hair. With his arms wrapped around her, she felt as though she was cocooned in protection. That he cared deeply for her was evident. Even though she'd warned him they should keep their distance, he was here, helping her through this. And she hadn't resisted.

Somehow she had to regain clarity. Think things through. Figure out what to do about her family to keep them safe. Figure out how to protect her heart.

She pulled away. "I need to splash water on my face, freshen up. Would you mind hanging out here until I get back or Carol or Mom gets here?"

"Of course not." Studying her, he frowned. "You think someone might try to harm him while he's in the hospital?"

She stared at the floor. "I hope not. But try convincing the police to put someone at his door when they think it was a random act of violence."

The investigative wheels moved much too slowly to make a difference for Tracy and her family, and anyone else who dared to get too close, such as David.

Tracy watched him go back into her father's room and she went to the restroom, washed her hands and brushed her hair. She looked a mess and that embarrassed her, though she shouldn't care what David thought of her. Closing her eyes, she took a few calming breaths and headed back to the hospital room. Tracy peeked in on her father and David, deep in a discussion about the oil business, and decided to head to the first floor to grab coffee for her and David. In the elevator she was alone until the second floor, when a woman stepped on, dressed in long-sleeved scrubs. Behind the woman's ear was a tattoo. Numbers. What did they mean?

Heart pounding, Tracy tried to slow her breathing. The tattoo could mean nothing. Or everything. She wished Derrick had never gone so deep in his research. Wished he'd backed away from his article. Tracy wished she knew nothing at all about gang tattoos. That way she wouldn't be wondering if those numbers behind the woman's ear had anything to do with the number of people she'd harmed.

Glancing down, Tracy stared at the floor, allowing her gaze to flick to the woman's wrist. She caught a glimpse of *the* tattoo.

Tracy couldn't breathe.

SEVENTEEN

Carol and Gina, Tracy's mom, entered the room. Tracy's father was sleeping. David had grown impatient for Tracy to return, but she'd appeared to need a break and he'd given her that. Surely she was safe in a hospital. But she hadn't answered her phone. He knew she'd be upset if he left her father for even one second, so he was glad to see her mother and sister.

"Where's Tracy?" Gina asked.

"She went to freshen up." David stood. "I'll find her."

He didn't see her in the waiting room or down the hallway, so he knocked on the door of the women's restroom. Finally another woman approached the entrance and frowned at him.

"Could you check for me? Ask if Tracy is inside."

Her frown softened. "Sure, I'll look."

A few seconds later she returned. "Sir, there's no one in the restroom."

He hadn't thought she'd stay in there so long. David hurried to the elevator. Maybe she'd gone down to grab snacks or coffee. But he would think she would answer the phone. The hospital elevators took entirely too long.

He made the first-floor main lobby and hurried to the

small shop where they'd spotted the snacks and coffee. No Tracy. Unsure if this was an actual emergency, he opted for calling the police detective who'd left his card on the side table next to Tracy's father's bed in case the man thought of something more. David had snagged the card on his way out of the room in case he needed it. He wasn't all that sure that the police were the right entities to handle this. Organized crime, including gangs, warranted the attention of the Department of Justice or the FBI at the very least. But the police were always the first to handle things until they escalated.

So what about now? What about the attempts on her life? Winters was right. She needed to run and hide.

Phone to his ear, he stood in the lobby, watching for her and praying.

The elevator door swooshed open.

A woman stepped out—hospital staff, by her dress—but no Tracy.

David got the detective's voice mail and ended the call. He wasn't sure what he would say. Not yet. He tried her cell again and got no response. All he could think was that her phone had better be dead. She might be back in her father's room by now. Unwilling to wait on the slow-moving elevators, David took the stairwell this time and on the second floor stood Tracy, pale-faced and huddled in the corner.

David grabbed her shoulders. "Tracy, what's wrong?"

"They're here."

"Who? Who's here?" But he already knew the answer.

"Members of Santino's gang. There was someone dressed in scrubs, either working at the hospital or pretending to work. She had the tattoo." Tracy appeared dazed and shocked, which concerned David more than anything at the moment. "She got on the elevator with me. I don't know if she wanted to harm me because a security officer got on the elevator at the next floor. I got off just as he got on."

"And why are you in the stairwell?"

Her gaze locked with his and a small smile seemed to shake off the dazed look. "I could ask you the same thing."

"The elevators are too slow."

"You don't have to tell me. Those were the longest three minutes of my life. When I got off the elevator I just wanted to hide, so I slipped into the stairwell."

"I was worried about you when you didn't come back or answer your phone. I had to find you." He hugged her to him. She could have been killed on that elevator, right here in the hospital. "We need to call the detective, tell him everything. Your dad needs protection."

"I tried to call but the cell won't work in the stairwell," she said.

That explained why he hadn't been able to get through to her. He tightened his hold on her, fearing he could lose her forever. He couldn't go through that again. He planted a kiss on the top of her head, hoping she didn't mind, but it wasn't exactly a *real* kiss, as they'd shared before. The kind that he'd promised never to give her again.

Even through this dangerous scenario, David hadn't stopped thinking about the kiss they'd shared. He was torturing himself on that one. He couldn't let himself love her.

"David," she whispered.

"Yes."

"You can let me go now. We need to check on Dad. Call the police."

Slowly he released her and looked down into her eyes. "Don't go anywhere else alone—that is, until you're safe and sound in WITSEC and have a whole new life."

At the words, a knot lodged in his throat.

She shook her head. "Didn't you hear my father? He's not going, which means I'm not going."

"But this is insane. It will never stop. You said if anything else happened you would leave Mountain Cove and start a new life as a new person."

"I meant if anything happened in Mountain Cove." She grabbed her hair. "I'm so confused, I don't know what to do. But I'm going back to Mountain Cove. Maybe this happened to my father because Mercado was killed instead of me, and this was a warning. If possible, we need to draw them away from my family."

Protect her family by putting *herself* right back in the line of danger? Yeah. As if that made a whole lot of sense. Couldn't someone do something to stop this kind of criminal activity? When David exited the stairwell with Tracy, his cell phone rang. Detective Palmer. David answered the call and explained everything as he and Tracy made their way to her father's room. At the door to the room, David ended his conversation with the detective.

"What did he say?" she asked.

"He's coming to the hospital to question you. It sounds like he's taking this more seriously now. Should you let Marshal Hanes know about these new developments?"

"Why? It won't change a thing. My father refuses to

leave his life and, by default, I refuse to leave my life in Mountain Cove."

Her words terrified David. Winters was right. He had to convince her to go into WITSEC. "Are you sure that's a good idea?"

"I'm not helping my family by staying here. And this time I want to face the threat head-on."

They stood at the door of David's grandmother's home and knocked.

As soon as she'd made sure her father was on the road to recovery, she'd returned to Mountain Cove—in part, she hoped to draw attention back to her and away from her family. In addition, the detective had discovered solid leads regarding who had assaulted her father and assured her arrests would be made. In the meantime, he'd stationed police to guard her father's room.

Her mother had hired a firm to beef up security around the house. Tracy should be relieved, but she couldn't help but wonder how long they would have to live like this.

David smiled. "I could just walk in. She's family, after all. I used to live here."

He reached for the knob just as the door opened. An older woman's face brightened with a huge smile. "Oh, David. So wonderful to see you."

The woman hugged David to her as she pulled them both inside the house. Then she turned her attention on Tracy. "And this is the woman you were telling me about?"

David looked at Tracy with admiration in his eyes. "This is my friend Tracy Murray. And this is Grandma Katy," David said to Tracy.

Tracy thrust her hand forward. "I'm pleased to meet you."

"Oh, dear, we hug around here." The woman tugged her into an embrace. "And you can call me Katy."

The warm and friendly woman released Tracy. A lump grew in Tracy's throat. "Katy, then."

Katy continued her conversation with David as she led them into an open living room connected to the kitchen. Inside the cozy home, Tracy noticed the same cross-stitched scriptures on the walls that Jewel had in the cottage and in her house. Tracy couldn't help but feel slightly awkward. After all, not even a month ago she'd avoided David Warren, thought he was cold and aloof, and now here she was, already meeting his grandmother. She chided herself—it wasn't *that* kind of meeting, as though he'd taken her home to meet his parents or something. But it was strange how circumstances had thrown them together since that first day on the trail.

Sure, they'd been initially forced together that day, but David had made the decision to stick with her since then, and though she'd tried to keep her heart out of it, she'd welcomed his help in all this. In fact, she wasn't sure what she would have done without his encouragement and support. His unwavering protective bearing. Besides, Tracy had kept herself so separate from everyone in Mountain Cove—except for Jewel—that she hadn't made any real friends.

Who was she kidding? She'd needed David these past few weeks. Needed him in a desperate way.

Katy stood in the kitchen making coffee. "David says you're interested in staying at the house. Renting a room. Only I won't accept that. You can stay with me for as long as you need without worrying about payment."

Tracy glanced at him, unsure what he'd told his grandmother. She was beginning to doubt this idea. How could she put this woman in danger like this? Anyone she got close to would be at risk. "Oh, no, I couldn't do that. I was considering renting the garage apartment."

And she was close to changing her mind on the whole arrangement. How had she let him talk her into this? It might be closer to town and in a neighborhood that felt more secure than being out in the woods in Jewel's cabin, but she'd been in a neighborhood when Santino had destroyed her life the first time.

She took a step back.

David blocked her way as if he'd read her mind.

"Grandma understands everything, Tracy. Don't worry." David winked at his grandmother. "In fact, she's been through this before."

"Besides," Katy said, "David is going to stay in the garage apartment. So you see? You have to stay in the house. It's a big lonely house with all the kids gone. I'd enjoy the company."

Tracy wasn't sure how good of company she would be. She felt a little cornered.

"You're staying in the apartment?"

"I am." His forest-eyed gaze pinned her, sending her heart tumbling.

"And Solomon's free to roam the house and the yard." Katy watched Tracy, waiting for her reaction. It was as if the woman was trying to persuade Tracy, too. How could anyone welcome someone in her situation into their home this way?

And how could Tracy say no to these two?

"My grandmother is the best cook, so at least eat dinner with us and then you can decide."

Oh, so he *had* read her mind.

"Make yourself comfortable, dear. Let David bring in your things." Katy grabbed her hand and dragged her forward, tossing a wink at David.

Tracy liked David's grandmother a lot.

Later that evening she settled into a bedroom upstairs, Solomon at her side. David and Katy and her amazing home-style cooking had worked against her, convincing her to stay when alarms had gone off in her head. But if not here, where would she stay? Anywhere else and she would be all alone and an easier target.

She didn't know how, but this family and this town made her feel more protected than she'd felt since this ordeal had first begun—when Derrick had started researching his story. Chief Winters had even stopped by the house to speak with her and reassure her they would keep an eye out with all vigilance.

But they couldn't go on like this forever. Though Tracy wanted this to end, she couldn't foresee any ending that wouldn't cost more lives.

Tracy woke at dawn when her SAR pager went off. She dug around in her backpack, realizing she'd almost forgotten about the thing with everything that had happened.

She read the callout information. They needed Solomon for a wilderness search. A little girl was missing. Tracy couldn't abide that, couldn't sit around and do nothing. She'd moved to Mountain Cove to be free and she intended to live her life. Besides, she'd be with

others on the search, and needed to get her mind off
herself and onto others.

Solomon looked up at her, wagging his tail. He'd recognized the sound and knew what it meant. Wondering
if David had also received it, she peeked out the window. His truck was gone. That was right; he was at the
fire station for his shift. He'd taken off far too much
time on her account already, she was sure.

Tracy geared up and headed down the stairs. Katy
was already up and drinking coffee, a deep frown
etched in her face. What could that be about? Her eyes
grew wide when she saw Tracy.

"Good morning, Tracy. You're up early for work."

"Not exactly. I don't start back helping Jewel until
next week." Tracy shrugged as she took the mug Katy
poured her, feeling guilty and yet so grateful to Jewel
for her understanding. Who could ask for a better em-
ployer? "I need to go now, though, because I received
a callout. They need a SAR dog to find a little girl. She
went missing this morning."

Katy nodded, her frown deepening. "There was a
fire in town last night. I've been praying for David and
the other firefighters, and for Adam. It was his business that burned."

Tracy stiffened, fear curdling in her stomach. She'd
slept so hard she hadn't heard the sirens. And poor
Adam. Had it been another attack related to Santino?
A warning that hit closer to the Warren home, targeting
David's family this time? Tracy prayed it wasn't related.
Everything couldn't be because of her situation, could
it? *God, please, no...* She composed herself. "Anyone
hurt? Have you heard from David?"

"He said he would text when he could. I would have

gone up there, but David wouldn't have it, and I didn't want to leave you here alone. But I believe that God holds my grandchildren in the palm of His hand. Who am I to worry? But instead I pray. Can I pray for you?"

Seeing the strength of those words in Katy's eyes, Tracy wished she had that same kind of faith. "Sure, you can pray. I'll pray, too. I'm so sorry for Adam."

She hung her head, not knowing how to express everything she felt. Then, finally, she said, "Thank you, again, for letting me stay. I should get going."

She wanted to see David and Adam, but knew she would only distract them. Besides, she and Solomon had a job to do. Something to help others.

To Solomon she said, "Come on, boy. We have work to do today. We have to help find a little girl who is lost."

EIGHTEEN

Tracy and Solomon were one of three dog teams deployed to different areas near where the family had camped. She wore a bright orange jacket, as did Solomon, so they could be easily spotted. Dog teams were the most effective first response in searching for a missing person, especially in this wilderness. Especially since it had started raining early this morning.

Solomon was a good air-scent dog, and the weather wouldn't keep him from locating someone, because the little girl would continue to emit a scent, and Solomon would find it. But that was the problem—he wasn't a tracking dog and couldn't tell people's scents apart. When he followed what he could tell was a human scent, it could be anyone. That was why they were on their own now, so Solomon would pick up only the little girl's scent. Her name was Emily and she was only ten years old.

Her parents had discovered her missing this morning. It was likely that she had left the tent sometime during the night while her parents were sleeping and somehow gotten lost. Tracy prayed for Emily and knew Katy and others would be praying, as well. For some reason, she felt as though Katy's prayers would surely be answered. The faith in that woman was palpable.

Following Solomon as he searched the wooded area, Tracy recalled when she and David had been searching for him in the woods, only to find him in the mining shaft. At least the undergrowth was thinned out here and easier to walk through. Easier to see. Maybe Emily had gone this way, since she wouldn't have had to work her way through the thick undergrowth and greenery. The thoughts sent her mind to David again.

She hoped David and the other firemen had extinguished the fire by now, but of course, the rain would help. She couldn't shake the feeling the fire was related to Santino, as well. She prayed it wasn't. Plenty went wrong in life that had nothing at all to do with Tracy and the man intent on retaliation.

But Tracy focused on the situation, shoving her own predicament out of her mind. At least for now. It felt good to think about someone else for a change.

After an hour searching, Tracy was surprised they hadn't found Emily yet. How could the girl have wandered so far? Tracy called Solomon back to give him water and take a break.

Her radio squawked. Tracy answered.

"Emily is alive and well!"

"Oh, thank the Lord." Tracy sighed in relief. She leaned against a tree and took a swig of water. "You hear that, Solomon? We can head back now."

The rain had eased up to a trickle.

A sound startled her. A spattering of leaves. A *thunk* of something hitting a tree behind her head. Tracy froze, her mind slowly comprehending…

A bullet.

Then another bullet whizzed by her and hit the tree a few feet away.

She ducked for cover behind the tree, holding Solomon to her. She wasn't sure if Solomon would be safer on his own, since Tracy was the obvious target, but she wasn't about to risk him out in the open when there were bullets flying. She wished they'd been in a thicker part of the woods and then she'd be harder to spot.

Tracy got on her radio. "Get everyone out. There's a shooter up here. He's taking shots at me!" She relayed her location.

"Are you all right?" Cade's voice came over the radio.

"Just…make sure everyone gets away." She choked back sobs and fear. She couldn't believe she'd actually put everyone in danger on a search and rescue. But for the life of her, she hadn't imagined this outcome.

"Get down and stay hidden."

She was glad the sniper wasn't a good shot or she would already be dead. But maybe that was the point— to drag it out so as to torture her before he killed her. She pressed her face into her hands.

"Oh, God, please, help me! Please keep others safe. I need this to end."

The tree next to her took a beating. She needed to get out of her bright-colored jacket, but instead she was forced to slink even lower onto the ground, into the spruce needles and ferns, pressing Solomon down beside her. He whined and barked, understanding she was in distress.

"Shh." She comforted him. He couldn't understand their dangerous situation.

But she'd protect him. He'd been the one to save her that awful night, but now she faced a new threat by the same man. This was it, then. If she survived this, she would get a new identity and leave her family behind. Maybe they could fake her funeral so all attempts at retaliation would stop. She wasn't indecisive anymore. This had to stop.

She'd thought that either she or Santino had to die, and now she knew. That was the only way. She had to die.

But not today!

Another bullet whizzed by, taunting her. Tracy removed her jacket and Solomon's, then crawled away from them while she tried to maintain the protection of the trees.

Sweat slid down her temples and back. At any moment a bullet could blast through her skull. Though a fierce will to survive rose up in her, tears slid down her cheeks. Almost nothing she'd experienced so far could compare to the terror she felt right now. Each incident seemed to increasingly terrify her until she knew she couldn't take any more.

Flat on the ground, she crawled, the foliage scratching her. Insects scuttled over her and mosquitoes buzzed in her ear. She remained still as best she could and listened, waiting for the next shot. Solomon grew antsy, but she pressed him next to her.

"There now, you're a good dog," she said, twisting her fingers through his fur to calm him.

Another bullet slammed a tree much too close. So taking off her jacket hadn't thrown the shooter off. She was a dead woman if help didn't come soon. They knew she was in trouble, but how could they get to her in time? How could the police find her exact location without endangering themselves?

Any rescue would mean taking out the sniper first.

Solomon growled and bolted from her grasp.

"Solomon! No!"

Next she heard him yelp. Her pulse jumped as she peered through the foliage. Whimpering, Solomon lay still.

Gasping for breath, David ran through the woods. Pushing off trunks. Jumping a brook. The movements reminded him of the day they'd found Jay. Solomon had sounded off and David had known something was wrong. He'd run through the woods, looking for Tracy. He hadn't known then what he knew now.

Someone wanted her dead.

He wanted to call her name. Shout out for her. But a sniper was shooting at Tracy, and he couldn't call attention to either of them. If she had remained at the coordinates she'd given Cade, he knew exactly where she was.

Rotor blades thumped in the distance. Winters had already called the Alaska State Troopers to help. Mountain Cove police were preparing to move in to catch the sniper. But none of them were moving fast enough, as far as David was concerned.

He heard the sound of the suppressed rifle and the ping against trees. How much ammo had this guy brought with him? And how many shots would he take before he hit Tracy? He either wasn't much of a sniper or was toying with her. Or maybe the thick forest had protected her. The forest and God. But David was getting close to her. He pressed his back against a trunk.

"Tracy, can you hear me?" He kept his voice low so it wouldn't carry too far.

Let her be okay, God.

He banked on the fact that the sniper continued shooting meant she was still alive.

"Tracy, are you there?" *Please, be there.*

A bullet hit the tree near David's head. Compared to everything that had happened so far, a sniper in the woods brought everything to a whole new level. City gangs tended to prefer their hits up close and personal— their ranks wouldn't include a trained sniper. Was this a soldier who'd become corrupted, hired by the gang, or a gang member who'd gotten his training somewhere? David slipped behind another tree trunk, moving closer to the sniper's target area, and slid to the ground. He didn't know what he would do if something happened to Tracy.

Then he heard it.

Quiet sobbing.

David peered around the tree, close to the ground, hoping the troopers in the helicopter would get the sniper or at least distract him. Crawling forward, he peered through the foliage and thought he saw her just through the thicket.

"Tracy." Louder this time.

"David?" Her voice was choked with tears.

But hearing her ignited hope in him. "I'm here. Stay there—I'm coming to you."

"No! I don't want you to get killed!"

David ignored her and crawled forward until he found her leaning over Solomon. The dog had been shot. Grief squeezed his gut. He closed the distance and pulled Tracy to him. Trembling, she sobbed in his shoulder.

"It isn't safe for us to stay. I have to get you out of here."

"I won't leave Solomon. He's still alive."

"The police and troopers are closing in on the sniper. Maybe that will give us the chance we need."

She vigorously shook her head. "He could have killed me already. He's just playing with me. Torturing me before the end. That's why he shot Solomon. We can't wait here for him to die. I would have carried him out myself if I could have."

In the distance they heard a voice blasting over a megaphone, telling the gunman to give it up.

More gunfire ensued. An exchange between the police and the sniper?

If they'd engaged him, David could carry Solomon out now. The dog wouldn't make it if he didn't get medical attention soon.

He peered through the tree crowns and in the distance saw the men lowering from the helicopter into the woods. Had they caught the sniper?

David got on Tracy's radio to the ICC. "What's the news?"

"They got him," the dispatcher at the Incident Command Center reported.

"We're coming in," he said. "I'm carrying Solomon. He's been shot."

Carefully he lifted Solomon. "Let's keep to the trees as much as possible. In case he wasn't alone."

He hoped he wasn't making a mistake, but they couldn't stay here and watch Solomon die.

Together they trekked through the woods, David hurrying as fast as he could, careful not to hurt Solomon more and conscious that every second counted in getting the dog the help he needed. Still, David couldn't help but be glad it wasn't an injured Tracy that he carried now.

After a couple of miles, sweat was like a second skin on him, even though he was in Alaska. Behind him, Tracy stumbled.

He paused and turned, prepared to help her up. "Are you okay?"

Her expression more distraught than he'd ever seen, she nodded. "I'm okay. Keep going. Get Solomon help. I'll catch up if I have to."

He wouldn't argue with her, but if she slipped too far behind, David would slow and wait. She might disagree with him, but her safety was still his priority.

"Just hold on, Solomon." He knew the dog meant everything to her, especially since he had saved her life.

David had yet to hear the full story even though they'd spent ample time together traveling to and from Missouri. He understood her reticence well enough— she didn't want to talk about that night. It was something she wanted to forget even while she went through retaliation for being the witness to put Santino in prison.

Winters appeared in his vision in the distance and jogged toward him. He reached for the dog. "Let me help."

"I've got him," David said. "Call the vet—Harrison—for me. I'm heading to his office now."

"Already done," Winters said.

Tracy followed David to the new truck he'd bought in Juneau and parked at the trailhead. She opened the door and got in, and David placed Solomon in her lap. The grief constricting his chest matched the fear and sorrow written across her face. Her gaze locked with his.

Would they lose Solomon?

Not on his watch. Not if he could help it.

He ran around to the driver's side and threw out questions to Winters. "Is he still alive? Can you question him? Put an end to this?"

A dark shadow fell across the police chief's face. "No. Take care of the dog and Tracy. I'll check in with you later. Maybe I'll know more by then. But we need to talk soon."

David burned rubber, headed toward town. He'd gone nuts when he'd come back from putting out the fire that took down Adam's bike shop. That had been bad enough, but then he'd learned that Tracy had been targeted by a sniper while she was out on a search. He hadn't had a moment to think through any of that, but now all his frustration came rushing in. What had she been thinking? What had *anyone* been thinking to let her go out on her own like that?

God help him, he couldn't live without her, and yet, apparently, he couldn't live with her, either, because she wouldn't be allowed to live. Not this way. But he would bring none of that up now. It wasn't the time.

He risked a glance in her direction, reining in his emotions and anything he might say. Tears brimmed in her eyes. The way she looked at him, he could swear he saw feelings for him in her eyes. And though he'd denied it for so long, if he let himself be honest, he loved her, too. But as God would have it, he would lose a woman he loved—again.

NINETEEN

Tracy cradled Solomon, fearing his life was seeping out of him with every passing minute. She held tight as David raced down the road, passing cars, even receiving a few honks, and steered into the small parking space at the veterinarian's office. Chief Winters was supposed to tell the vet to expect them, and she hoped he was available to deal with this emergency right away.

And it was an emergency. She couldn't lose Solomon.

David opened her door and reached for her dog. He carried Solomon to the door, David's long legs making strides she couldn't keep up with. Someone was there waiting and opened the door for him.

Once they were inside, the tall, lanky vet opened the door to his operating room. Relief swelled in Tracy—he'd been ready and waiting to save her search-and-rescue dog. Solomon had saved lives. He deserved this. David laid the dog on the table and nodded at the vet, his expression conveying he trusted the man to save Solomon.

His efforts and concern for her dog broke through her grief. David ushered her out of the room and closed the door behind him. "Let him do his job and we'll do ours."

Tears swelled but they didn't fall. Not yet. She didn't think she could cry any more and didn't want to. "What's our job, David?"

"Pray. We're going to sit here and pray."

The past few hours crashed in on her and sent her into a daze. She took the seat next to David and let him hold her hand. He started praying, but her mind kept drifting to images of David trekking through the woods, holding Solomon. The dog had saved her from the flames. But fire had taken Derrick's life for the investigative reporting he was doing on Santino's gang. Three long years later and she was still in this nightmare, orchestrated by the same man.

David squeezed her hand and continued his soft prayer, then slipped into a silence of his own. She'd never forget the way he'd carried Solomon through the woods, undaunted against all obstacles, as though his own life depended on it. The title "hero" didn't begin to describe this man sitting next to her. Or what he meant to her.

Tracy finally realized there were others sitting in the waiting room with their pets. And they were wide-eyed as they looked at David and Tracy.

David squeezed her hand. "He's going to be okay, Tracy. You have to believe that."

"Can we go outside for some fresh air?"

"Sure." He got up and led her out the door.

They walked around to the side of the building facing the woods.

David lifted her chin, forcing her to look at him. A tangle of emotions emanated from his gaze. "Are you hurt? In all the rush to save Solomon, I failed to ask you."

"I'm fine. Not even a bullet graze this time. Which

is why I don't get any of this. Does Santino want to kill me or not? Or is he laughing from his prison cell while he attacks everyone around me? I think…I think he enjoys letting me know that he can get to me if he wants to. And once I'm dead, the fun will be over for him. What I never understood is how he found me."

"Come here." David pulled her into his arms. "Winters said he would call me with more information. But the shooter is dead, at least. It's over."

Tracy clung to David. She soaked up his reassurances and strength, wanting to believe those words with everything in her. For today, they were enough to get her through. She'd wait until Solomon was strong enough and then she must make the ultimate sacrifice. She never dreamed she'd be in this position, but she would have to leave this man.

A man she loved.

A man she couldn't love—it would cost him his life.

"David? Tracy?" The veterinarian's assistant stood a few feet away.

David released Tracy.

"Yes?" they said together.

"Solomon is out of surgery. We removed the bullet and he's going to be fine. We need to keep him a few days."

"Yes, whatever he needs, do it." The tears chose that moment to spill. Tracy wiped at them furiously. "Can I see him?"

Tracy and David followed the petite blonde into the room where they kept Solomon. Tracy pressed her hand on his head and wound her fingers through his fur. Asleep, he couldn't respond.

"That was much too close," she said.

She glanced up at the vet, respecting his time and that he had other patients to attend to. "Will he be able to return to work as a search-and-rescue dog?"

The man frowned, uncertainty carved in his features. "It's too early to say. We removed the bullet, but the penetrating trauma collapsed his lung. We had to insert a chest tube until his lung heals."

"And how long will that be?"

"Days before we remove the tube. Weeks before he's completely healed. As far as him returning as a work dog, only time will tell. If you'll excuse me, I need to get to my other patients."

"Of course." Tracy forced a smile and thrust out her hand to shake his. "Thank you for saving him."

"Always my pleasure." He exited the room.

When he was gone, Tracy's knees grew weak. She pressed her face into her hands. "How can I ever love anyone, if my family, friends, someone I meet at the grocery store, if even my dog isn't safe?"

David's cell buzzed in his pocket.

Wanting to comfort Tracy, he ignored the call and tugged her to him. He was still running on the adrenaline that had carried him through the woods to find her and then had sustained him as he'd brought Solomon back and rushed him to the veterinarian. But he inhaled a deep breath, bracing for the expected crash.

He held on to her, knowing she would leave Mountain Cove as soon as Solomon recovered enough to travel. She could never leave her dog behind. But she would leave David and her family behind. And he'd never see her again. There was no way she could stay.

She'd tried to make it work. They both had. But they were no match for Santino and his resources.

His cell buzzed again. Must be something important.

Tracy pulled from his arms. She wiped at her eyes and looked at him. "We need to get out of here, and you need to answer your phone."

David followed her out as he tugged the phone from his pocket. Chief Winters.

David answered the call.

"Where are you?" Winters asked.

"At the vet's office. Solomon will live. But he'll be here for a few days and won't fully recover for a few weeks."

"Good. Now, listen. Get her out of there."

"What?" David kept his voice low as they walked through the lobby. He opened the door for Tracy and they stepped outside.

"Take Tracy and leave Mountain Cove. Don't stop to get anything." His tone was urgent.

David eyed Tracy, who watched him intently. "Hold on," he said into the phone. He unlocked his truck and opened the door for Tracy. Still watching him, she climbed inside.

Once he'd closed the door, he continued his conversation with Winters as he walked around to the driver's side. "What's going on, Winters? Tracy is going into WITSEC after this. She'll be leaving Mountain Cove as soon as Solomon heals."

"I'm not sure that's good enough at this point. Or fast enough. I have my suspicions. I'm following a lead, and I don't want to say anything until I know more, but drive to the floatplane dock and catch the next flight out. Take a boat. I don't care. Just get her out."

David stood by his door, but didn't open it. Tracy eyed him from inside the truck. The police chief was telling him that Mountain Cove police couldn't protect her. "Where am I supposed to take her?"

"I don't care. But don't tell anyone your plans." Voices resounded in the background. "Listen, I don't have time to say more, but I'll be in touch as soon as I can." Winters ended the call.

David stared at his phone. What was going on? And what was he supposed to tell Tracy? She wouldn't want to leave without Solomon. He climbed into the truck and avoided her gaze.

"What was that about?"

"I don't know. I'm still trying to figure it out." He ran both hands through his hair. Puffed his cheeks and blew out a breath. He needed a plan and fast.

Tracy sighed and stared out the window. Her thoughts were clearly on Solomon's injuries and what she'd just endured. "You know what this means, don't you?"

"Tell me." David started his truck and steered from the parking lot. He suspected he knew what she was going to say, but what Winters had said to him, which wasn't much, changed everything. Deep down he'd mentally prepared for the moment when she would say goodbye to him forever. And maybe that moment would come. But not yet.

"Nothing you don't already know. This is it, David. I can't take this anymore. They hurt my father and now Solomon. I have to go. Maybe the marshals can just fake my death. Have a funeral and this can all be over for everyone I love. This won't end until Santino thinks I'm dead. I have to wait for Solomon to get strong, though. I knew this would happen, I just…I just hoped it wouldn't come to this."

She was right. He already knew, but he'd hoped as she had. And there was more going on than either of them knew about. David steered toward downtown.

"I know they were supposed to move Santino into isolation," he said. He needed time to figure out how to tell her his plans. "Or away from the prison gangs. They were looking at options to keep him from directing his retaliation. But clearly that isn't working."

"It's just a matter of time before someone else gets hurt." The intensity in her gaze let him know the words had double meaning. She was worried about *him* getting hurt.

Didn't she know it was too late? Her leaving him would leave a long, painful gash in his heart. Yeah, the one he'd protected so well. Though he'd known all along, that hadn't prevented him from taking this fall. But he was going with her now, taking her out of Mountain Cove. How would she feel about that? And what if…what if he went into WITSEC with her? Was that even an option? He hadn't seriously considered that before. He had family here that counted on him. He understood Tracy's turmoil and why she had refused to consider leaving her family before now.

He'd spent almost a decade trying to figure out why God would let Natalie die in that fire. Though he might not ever get the answer to that question, he had a feeling that God was giving him a second chance at love but David had to choose to take it.

He turned off Main Street and headed to the float-plane dock, hoping he could get a ride on something to somewhere. Hoping he could convince Tracy to come with him. That would be the hardest part. He'd call one of his brothers and get them to move his truck. Didn't need anyone figuring out they'd gone too soon.

He turned into the parking lot near the seaplane dock and parked. As if only now realizing where they were, Tracy sat taller. Took in a breath.

"What are we doing here? I thought we were heading…home." She frowned.

Was that her choice of words? Calling his grandmother's house "home"? He liked that. But they might never see this place again.

And, yeah, he was in it for the long haul if she'd let him. That reality slapped him dizzy.

David turned to face her and leaned closer. "That was Chief Winters on the phone a few minutes ago. He said you need to leave now. Don't pass go. Don't collect two hundred dollars."

Her eyes widened. "But I can't leave. What about Solomon?"

"Solomon will be fine. My family will care for him until we get back."

"We?"

"Yes. I'm going with you. We're leaving now."

She frantically shook her head. "I don't understand. What's going on?"

David climbed out of the truck and opened her door, assisting her. She appeared stunned. Why hadn't she been prepared to be instantly whisked away? Wasn't that how the marshals protected witnesses? Maybe she'd gotten accustomed to the pace she'd had in Mountain Cove. Regardless, things had escalated.

"I have no idea, but he said he would call me. It sounded like he'd come across some information he needed to check into. But I've never heard him sound so urgent. I trust him."

"I need to call Jennifer and have her take care of things from her end."

David spotted Billy. "And you'll get your chance. Winters didn't think we had time for that just now. Priority one needs to be getting away from here."

"Where are we going?"

"Just trust me, will you?" He was making this up as he went. But David had already thought of friends he knew in the Seward area. He'd spent a lot of time on the Kenai Peninsula fighting fires. From there, they could take the Alaska Railroad or drive into Anchorage. There were a lot more options. More places to hide in Interior Alaska. More ways to get in and out.

Let Santino find her there.

He'd have to go through David if he did.

TWENTY

Tracy was on the ride of her life.

Or at least it felt that way as she disembarked from the plane at Seward with only the clothes on her back. And no Solomon. David came up behind her, wrapped his arm around her waist and ushered her forward.

She'd left her bright orange jacket in the forest, and now she shivered. It was colder here.

She'd never felt so lost in her life. "So it's come to this. I'm literally looking over my shoulder to watch for someone trying to kill me as I run and hide."

Disquiet surfaced in his gaze. And this man—she swallowed the lump in her throat—this man had chosen to go with her. But she couldn't let him do that. At least not all the way. She couldn't allow him to disappear with her for good. That was asking too much. Yet at this moment, she had no choice but to stay close to him. He was the one who knew where they were going for now.

"What next?" she asked.

"I contact my friends. See if there's someplace we can stay tonight while we figure things out. At least we're out of Mountain Cove. At least you're safe. No one knows I have friends here. No one will think to look for you here."

As if that had mattered before.

"And I need to get us transportation."

He riffled through a thick wad of bills he'd pulled from his pocket. Nausea roiled in her gut. Did he normally keep such a large amount of cash on him?

"David, I can't let you pay for all this." Then again, she was close to running out of money. She couldn't sustain this kind of life—staying on the move to stay alive—for very long. Not without turning to her family for money they couldn't easily spare, on top of the medical bills and the cost of beefing up their home security.

Oh, Lord, when will this ever end?

He eyed her then pulled out some twenties. "This is a matter of life and death, Tracy. Let's find a place to stay. I'll call Chief Winters to find out more about what is going on. But the important thing is your safety."

Tracy nodded and let David take the lead. He knew what he was doing in this part of the world. Tracy didn't have a clue where they were other than a name on a map.

An hour and a half later she was sitting in the kitchen of a cozy log cabin just outside of the small town, getting acquainted with David's friends—an older couple named John and Kari Nash, who eagerly welcomed them into their home.

Of course they could stay for as long as they needed.

Of course they had plenty of space and Tracy would have her separate room. The couple was old-fashioned that way. Besides, Tracy and David weren't a couple.

Were they?

David settled into an easy conversation with them

about the local wildfire threat. She'd known he was a
firefighter in Mountain Cove, but was stunned to hear
of his extensive experience fighting wildland fires all
over the region. Stunned to realize how much time she'd
spent with the man lately and how little she really knew
him. But that was just as well. Her life was not her own,
she finally realized.

Her head was spinning with all that had happened
within a few hours. She'd been all set to tell David goodbye, to say goodbye to everyone including her family,
but today she'd said that word to no one. And she'd
left Solomon behind, something she would never have
willingly done.

John took David outside to show him something and
left Tracy alone with Kari. The woman showed her the
cozy room upstairs decorated in the same country style
as Jewel's cottage, which made her feel more at home.
As though she could breathe for the first time in weeks.
Kari found Tracy some extra clothing, including a coat.
Tracy hadn't exactly come prepared. After she took
a long, hot bath and changed into comfortable, warm
sweats, she sneaked downstairs to see if she could catch
David. She needed to know what was going on and
hoped he'd talked to Chief Winters again by now. But
he wasn't there. The lights were out in the house except
for the fire in the fireplace. Daylight waned outside, but
it would be hours before dark.

Tracy crept back to her room and called Jennifer
to let her know she needed a new life and fast. The
thing was, she'd have to leave Solomon until someone
could bring him to her. As usual, she left a voice mail.
Through the window she spotted David and John ex-

iting the barn and assumed they were heading back to the house, until John got in his vehicle and drove off.

Tracy went downstairs to wait for David. When he didn't immediately come inside, she moved to the sofa near the fire, glad for the warmth.

When David finally came inside he made for the stairs and then paused when he spotted her. "I didn't see you."

"I've been waiting for you."

He moved to the sofa and sat next to her, but not too close. "Sorry. Had some catching up to do with John. And I had to call Chief Winters."

"And?"

"I didn't get through, but left a message. He'll call me back. Don't worry."

"And then what, David?"

He leaned back on the sofa and reached over. Twisted her hair around his finger. "We do whatever we have to do to keep you safe."

"I appreciate all you've done for me. But I can't let you go any further."

Sitting here next to him in the soft firelight, she saw in his eyes the hurt she'd wanted to avoid, the same hurt she felt inside. But they were both adults, both knew they shouldn't get involved. She realized she wanted much more with him, but life had been so unfair.

Tracy couldn't help herself. She tilted forward and gently pressed her lips against his. "You said you'd never kiss me again, I know. But I'm kissing you now."

She slipped her hands around his neck and pulled him closer. David responded as she knew he would and enclosed her in his arms, deepening his kiss. Their kiss was filled with regret and longing and a forbidden love that neither could afford. Deep down, she knew this fireman hero in a way she'd never known Derrick, a man she'd once hoped to marry.

And here she was, letting Santino destroy her life again. But he'd taken so much more than her existence—he'd killed people, hurt them in devastating ways, all because of his need for retaliation against her testimony that had put him away. The pain and memories jarred into her emotions.

David gently eased from her lips. "What's wrong?" His voice was husky, filled with the passion of the moment.

She leaned her forehead against him. "It's not you, David. It's that in the end I'm letting Santino destroy my life. I'm going to run and hide. I'm going to disappear."

He tipped her chin up so she'd look at him. "You never told me what happened."

He definitely deserved to hear the story before she left.

David wrapped his arms around her as they both stared into the fire and she spilled everything she'd kept pent up inside. She'd wanted to forget that night, but apparently she couldn't leave her past behind her.

"I loved a man I worked with at the newspaper. We had talked of marriage, and I'd hoped he would pop the question soon. But he'd wanted to finish the dangerous project he was working on first.

"Derrick was an investigative reporter digging into Santino's gang and their crimes, including the recent arsons that had set the city on fire. The people that died. None of it typical of gangs, and Santino wasn't even a suspect until Derrick dug deeper. He'd received death threats, and then when I started getting them, Derrick was prepared to back out. But I convinced him to keep going. I believe in doing the right thing and not letting criminals win the day. Me… I'm the reason."

Tracy burst into tears and kept crying until they were spent. David sat next to her. He didn't say a word, just waited patiently for her to finish. He understood what she needed—not judgment or platitudes, but for him to simply listen.

"Solomon jumped on the bed, barking at me—that's what woke me. Flames engulfed my house. I was tied up in my bed. Apparently, I'd been drugged. Solomon had been locked away, but he'd clawed his way free. I barely got the two of us out before succumbing to the smoke and flames. But before I passed out, I saw Santino himself and a few others, dousing the house next door with accelerant. He was definitely a pyromaniac. But Derrick? He hadn't been so fortunate. He didn't have Solomon to pull him from a drugged stupor. His house—on the other side of town—burned down with him inside…like the other victims."

David held and comforted her, and Tracy allowed herself to fully release her anguish for the first time since this had all begun. There'd been no one who could comfort her before, not even her family. But this man next to her had already been through much of this with her in recent days, and he understood her as no one else could.

She wiped her eyes. "How many times have I cried on your shoulder?"

"I don't know. A couple hundred?"

She gently rapped him. "I hope you understand now. I want to care about you, but I can't afford to. I can't stand by any longer while people, even animals, I care about get hurt. I wanted to stand strong like my father, but I'm not doing him any favors by hanging on to this life in Mountain Cove. A life I've grown to love. People…" She leaned her forehead against his chin. "People I've grown to love."

She wouldn't say the actual words directed to him. Saying it would mean letting it happen, and she couldn't do that to either of them—not when she was leaving. "I've given myself tonight to say goodbye. I'm leaving as soon as the marshal can get here."

Surprise rocked through David.

He shoved up from the couch. "You called her?"

She nodded. "I didn't reach her. I never do. But I left her all the pertinent information."

David scraped his hands through his hair and paced in front of the fire. Winters had said not to tell *anyone*. Could he have meant Marshal Hanes, too?

"Why didn't you wait until I talked to Winters?"

"What's the point, David? We know I have to leave."

David sat on the edge of the sofa, next to her again. "The thing is…" This wasn't exactly how he'd planned to broach the subject. It wasn't romantic. And the timing was just all wrong.

Goodbye…

He couldn't let her say that word to him. Yet if he deserved a second chance, how did he convince her to let him disappear with her, too? But his family here needed him, as well. David was more torn than ever.

"Tracy," he whispered. Overcome with what he felt for her, he kissed her again, pushing that one word— *goodbye*—out of his mind. Yet it hovered at the edge, nonetheless.

In her kisses he understood what she would not say to him. Understood what he couldn't say to her. He wished this evening wouldn't end, that tomorrow would never come. At the same time, he knew he couldn't hide anything from her anymore.

Before he lost complete control he pulled back and then kissed her on the forehead. He needed to tell her everything.

"My wife died in a fire, Tracy. So I understand how you feel. You blame yourself, when you couldn't have done anything to stop it. But in my case, I'm a fireman. There's no reason that my wife should have died in our house. It shouldn't have burned down. I shouldn't have left her. I promised her I'd be back.

"But back then I traveled all over Alaska or the Pacific Northwest, wherever wildland firefighters were needed. I was gone for long stretches at a time. She begged me to stay, but I was too pigheaded to listen. I did what I wanted to do. Every time I left, she was afraid I wouldn't come back. I was off saving someone else and while the most important person in my life needed me at home. The night the fire burned down our house, I'd come here, to the Kenai Peninsula to fight a wildfire."

David squeezed his eyes shut. He couldn't bear to think that she had suffered or called for him, but the way he understood it, she'd died in her sleep from smoke inhalation. "I didn't know it, but she had a prescription for sleeping pills. She couldn't sleep for worry when I was gone and that's why she hadn't responded to the smoke alarm in the house. So at the end of the day, I'm to blame for her death."

"You can't blame yourself for that. That was her decision."

"How can I not? Everyone has regrets in life and that's mine. I wish I could go back and change what happened. Second chances don't always come in this life. I didn't feel I deserved a second chance, but God gave me the start of one with you anyway. And even if it all ends tonight, I'll always be grateful for that— grateful that through this hard time, I got to be the one who was there for you, who helped you through it all."

With his words he kissed Tracy again. Eventually, Tracy ended their kiss. Her frown deepening, he saw jumbled emotions spill from her eyes. She scraped her hands through her luscious red hair and David was glad he'd at least had the privilege to run his fingers through it, and to kiss her, though he wasn't sure that had been fair to either of their hearts.

"If there was a way for me to stay, I would. You know that."

"I do." And then what? It wouldn't be safe for her. And he couldn't ask her to put herself at risk for his sake. "I think I've known from the beginning, when you first told me the truth, it would end this way."

Unless Santino died. Or Tracy did.

TWENTY-ONE

Tracy pressed her back against the bedroom door. David had left. Walked out of the house when they'd heard John's vehicle return. Somehow she'd thought their conversation would go much differently. It hadn't gone the way she'd wanted but her life wasn't going the way she wanted.

David Warren.

Just a few short weeks ago that name had conjured much different thoughts of the man.

But now? She'd loved his tender kisses and everything about him. And nothing could ever come of it.

She made a phone call to Jennifer again, this time finally getting the marshal instead of voice mail. Carlos Santino was being moved, Jennifer assured Tracy, and she should be relatively safe. But there was no assurance there would not be future incidents. The only guarantee would come when Tracy Murray disappeared and became someone else in a new life and a new place. Tracy was instructed to stay where she was until the marshals came for her.

This time, Tracy would take the deal.

She bit back tears and managed to work her way

through the rest of the conversation. Time was running out. Tracy Murray would have to die.

This was the first night she'd spent alone since she'd first gotten the puppy she'd named Solomon, after King Solomon. The way his golden fur had crowned his head, she'd thought the name fitting. And since that night he'd saved her, she could sleep easier knowing he was with her. But tonight, she felt numb all over and didn't think she could sleep for thinking about her nebulous future that would include none of the people she loved. At least Solomon would go with her.

Her heart twisted and nausea roiled in her stomach at the thought of leaving everyone behind. According to Jennifer, she would at least have the opportunity to say one last goodbye.

She stared at the ceiling for hours until she fell into a fitful sleep.

Coughing...

Tracy woke to incessant coughing. Smoke alarms screamed. Where was she? Where was Solomon? Why wasn't he barking, waking her up as the room filled with smoke and the smell of fire?

No. This was definitely not a dream. And she didn't think her faked death would come like this.

She made for the door as smoke and heat wrapped around her, sending her into a panic.

Oh, God, no. Not again!

Her eyes burned; she couldn't see. She squeezed them shut, mind racing with thoughts of how to get out of here, get free of the flames. Strong arms wrapped around her and she knew right away that they weren't David's. There was cruelty and hatred in the tight, bruising grip.

She opened her eyes and Santino stared at her, an evil grin on his tattoo-riddled face.

Tracy tried to scream but he covered her mouth with tape. She couldn't cough, couldn't breathe. Darkness edged her vision. With what little strength she had left, she fought for freedom but his grip only tightened. He whisked her down a ladder at the back of the house and then, at the bottom, threw her over his shoulder in a fireman's carry.

Then everything went black.

Tracy woke coughing again. The tape had been removed from her mouth so she could breathe in the fresh air; only the scent of smoke still hung in the air, in her nostrils. She was bound to a tree, the setup sending her back to that night in her house. Solomon had saved her.

He hadn't been there to save her tonight, and in an odd twist, Santino had been the one to carry her out of the house. Why had he done that? Where was David? "Where am I?"

Santino might have carried her out of the house, but he'd started the fire. There could be no doubt there. And he hadn't saved her. He was the one bent on killing her. But what of the others in the house?

God, please keep David and his friends safe.

Footfalls crunched on spruce needles behind her. She stiffened. Santino walked around to stand in front of her, that sinister grin leering at her. "This time your dog won't save you. But I'm hoping your new boyfriend will come for you. That is, if he survives the fire."

"No! You're crazy, the worst kind of evil. David!" She tried to break free as she called his name.

God, please let him live.

She wanted to pray that David would find and save

her, but she couldn't pray that. She couldn't be that selfish. It was enough for David to survive. She didn't want him to risk his life for her. She couldn't be the reason he died.

"What are you going to do to me?"

Santino gestured to the lights coming off Seward in the distance. "Let's see what happens when the forest that surrounds the town where you thought you could hide this time goes up in flames. Your boyfriend thought he was so smart, taking you away, but it didn't work. You can never escape." He stuck his face in hers. "I'm going to enjoy watching the look on your face when I set your world on fire."

Santino walked away from her until she could see only his silhouette. What was he doing? Looked as though, sounded as though he was pouring something from a canister.

Accelerant.

She closed her eyes. This was what she'd seen that night. This was her nightmare all over again.

God, how could this happen? How can You let this happen?

But she understood too well that giving people free will meant allowing evil in the world. That was what the criminal-justice system was for. How had Santino escaped? How had he found her so quickly? The obvious answer snaked around her neck and choked her. She jerked against the rope as though she could free herself. No, no, no, no. She didn't want to die this way.

To die the way Derrick had.

Even in the darkness, she thought she could see Santino's evil grin as he dropped a match. Flames erupted behind him. He strode toward her, a wall of fire quickly spreading behind him, cutting her off from the town and any possible rescue.

"See you on the other side of this life," he said as he walked past her.

If only Tracy had gone into WITSEC from the beginning, then none of this would be happening. David would be safe at home. John and Kari's home wouldn't be burning, and the forest wouldn't be ablaze.

How could she have made such a colossal mistake? Cost more lives?

Tracy prayed for her life and for the lives of others. The fire spread out hard and fast against the dry foliage of summer. Flames inched toward her, as well. Thankfully the wind was blowing away from her. Maybe Santino had planned it that way so she could suffer longer. She didn't know. But the wind could shift at any moment and then she would be consumed.

Now she understood why she hadn't been killed before now. He'd wanted to kill her himself. He'd wanted the chance to set her on fire.

The bright orange and yellow flames licked the sky, illuminating the area near Tracy. Behind the blaze, the sky was black with smoke in the thick of night. Surely firefighters would see and respond. If they weren't already busy putting out the fire at the house.

Squeezing her eyes shut, Tracy hung her head, the last of her prayers slipping from her heart. Nobody could save her this time.

Adrenaline coursing through his veins, David raced toward the wall of fire, his lungs burning from smoke and exertion.

He'd seen a man carry Tracy away from the house

and into the woods, but he'd been trapped and couldn't get out in time to stop him. John had been the one to free David. He and Kari were safely out of the house.

He'd told John. He'd told him everything about the danger he and his wife would be facing if they allowed him and Tracy to stay with them, but the man had still wanted them to stay.

Fire trucks were on their way. The firefighters would save as much of the house as they could. He didn't have time to explain to anyone that he had to get to Tracy before someone killed her.

And when he'd looked into the darkness of a short Alaskan night, he'd seen the very instant the ground had been torched. Tracy had to be there. She had to be on the other side of the growing wall of fire. And David had to save her—he *had* to succeed in saving the woman he loved this time. He couldn't live with any other outcome.

But to see those flames licking this part of the world again—he'd been here nearly ten years before and the memory crushed the breath from him.

He raced toward the fire and fought his way through the thick, dry underbrush, racing the flames that blazed up the trees and into the crowns. He had to beat the fire, get to the other side before it spread and blocked his path to Tracy. Firefighters had to have seen the fire by now, but he wasn't sure they had the resources to battle it without calling in help. He'd been part of that help years ago. This wildland fire could blaze out of control before the required resources could be brought in.

What he wouldn't give to be wearing his firefighting gear at this moment.

God, please let me find her. She has to be here.

This was Santino's plan.

"Tracy! Where are you?"

"Here, I'm over here." Tracy's voice barely rose above the crackling roar of a growing wildfire.

David couldn't believe he'd heard her. The flames illuminated the woods, and in the distance, he spotted her tied to a tree. Anger burned in his gut. But he'd found her in time—hope burst through, infusing him with energy. He would beat the flames and save her.

The fire was growing dangerously close and heat licked his limbs. When he made it to Tracy, he slid to his knees, took out his pocketknife and cut the rope. He couldn't catch his breath enough to talk, but he doubted she could talk, either, if not from the stifling heat and choking smoke then from the shock evident on her face. Reflecting in her grateful eyes.

"It's Carlos Santino. He escaped. He's here." Her eyes grew wide. "David, behind you! It's Santino!"

David jerked around and jumped to his feet, prepared to fight.

A sneering man with a face covered in tattoos laughed in reply. "You came for her, like I knew you would."

Why did the man care if David had come for her? But David didn't need to know the answer to that.

"Tracy, get out of here." Anger boiling over, he lunged at the man.

They fought, and as the blows came, David knew he was no match for the man in terms of muscle and sheer strength. A man who'd been training for this moment in prison. But David had something Santino didn't have— the gut-wrenching determination to free the women he loved once and for all.

David had him in a headlock, but Santino escaped his grip and David saw the fear in his eyes—a haunting look David would never forget.

To his surprise, Santino turned and fled, running toward the flames. With Tracy's cries in his ears, he ran after him. He couldn't let him get away. Tracy would never be free if Santino escaped.

Unfortunately, even when he went back to prison, Tracy would never be free of Santino's grasp.

Tracy screamed, calling after David.

She couldn't believe it. Had she just seen David and Santino disappear through the fire? There must be someplace to run between the flames. Surely he'd found a way through to the other side… But Tracy was alone. How did she escape? The heat felt as if it would melt her even standing a few hundred yards away.

David had told her to run and get to safety, but safety was something she had felt only when she was at David's side. She couldn't run away and leave him behind. She bent over as racking coughs took control of her body.

Someone approached from behind. Tracy turned. Fearing it was Santino. Hoping it was David. But, no, it was a firefighter in full gear. He reached for Tracy, but she pulled away.

"David went that way. You have to save him."

The firefighter looked in the distance and shook his head, as if there was no hope of David surviving. He reached for Tracy again. She didn't want to go, but he tugged her with him, intent on getting her to safety.

"No!" Tracy yelled, reaching in the direction she'd seen David and Santino go.

But it was no use. The fireman carried her to safety.

* * *

At the Incident Command Center, Tracy stood in the parking lot, emergency vehicle lights blinking all around her. She tugged a blanket someone had thrown over her shoulders closer and stared at the fire blazing in the distance. It was consuming the side of the mountain and heading for the town, which could be yet another casualty of Santino's retaliation against Tracy.

The firefighters were creating a firebreak to save the town.

A backfire.

A fireman had saved her life, carried her to safety down a path she could never have found on her own to escape the flames. But David hadn't emerged, and she feared he'd perished in the flames trying to keep Santino away from her. And that was why she hadn't wanted to love. She couldn't stand to go through it all over again.

And yet here she was, reliving the nightmare.

How could Tracy live with this? Even if free will was to blame for Santino's actions, rather than God, how could she hold on to faith in a life where everything she loved was taken away from her?

Admittedly, she'd lost touch with God. Stopped praying as much as she should, when her reaction should have been the exact opposite. Seeing David's faith, and hearing the way he prayed, and his grandmother, too, had taught her that much. Reignited her own faith. But now it was faltering again.

She pulled the blanket around her tighter. When the smoke settled, literally, maybe things would look differently. And she knew in the end, God took bad things and turned them to good.

Tracy was still waiting to see good come of this.

That scripture from Isaiah 61 came to mind. Maybe because she'd recently seen it in a framed cross-stitch at Katy's house.

The Spirit of the Sovereign Lord is on me, because the Lord has anointed me to proclaim good news to the poor. He has sent me to bind up the broken-hearted, to proclaim freedom for the captives and release from darkness for the prisoners, to proclaim the year of the Lord's favor and the day of vengeance of our God, to comfort all who mourn, and provide for those who grieve in Zion—to bestow on them a crown of beauty instead of ashes, the oil of joy instead of mourning, and a garment of praise instead of a spirit of despair. They will be called oaks of righteousness, a planting of the Lord for the display of his splendor.

Tearing her gaze from the scene that had exploded and expanded in front of her over the past couple of hours, Tracy hung her head.

Beauty for ashes. That was what she needed. What they all needed out of this.

Lord, we definitely need the ruined cities—or in this case, forest—repaired. We need those who have suffered because of Santino to be comforted.

When the gray of twilight tinted the skies in the wee hours of an early Alaska morning, the flames still were only partially contained. Tracy watched a figure emerge from the smoke in the distance. She expected a fireman, but the man wasn't wearing any gear. She feared Santino had come for her.

But no. She knew that cadence. That set of his shoulders.

Her pulse ratcheted up and she dropped the blanket, rushing forward. A man pulled her back— Adam, the Warren brother who'd lost his business to fire just yesterday and had arrived on the scene not long ago, along with the other Warren siblings and Isaiah. Leah had stayed behind with her new baby.

Right now she didn't want their interference. "But... it's David."

"You know, I think you're right." Adam let her go.

Tracy hurried across the ground, closing the distance. As she grew near, she saw David's stern features soften into a smile when he saw her. Tracy jumped into his arms. Covered in soot, he smelled of smoke and earth. He buried his face in her neck and shuddered.

She hadn't wanted to love again with good reason. But David's courage and bravery, his arms around her, brought her to her senses.

She *could* love again.

She *must* love again. Her heart would give her no other choice.

David finally released her, though she could have remained in his arms forever.

"I did it, Tracy. I saved the woman I love this time."

The look in his eyes, his words, made her heart flip-flop. "Love?"

"Yes, love."

Someone cleared a throat.

Tracy didn't want the interruption.

"Tracy. David." Chief Winters stood there, two US

marshals next to him. "As soon as I learned where you were, and what had happened, we headed this way. Made it just in time, I see."

He introduced the marshals.

"Where's Jennifer...er...Marshal Hanes?" But Tracy feared she already knew.

"I was afraid we were too late," Chief Winters said. "I only just learned that Santino escaped tonight. Marshal Hanes was compromised, her family threatened, traumatized in such a way that she gave your location away. I'm sorry it took me so long to figure things out. But I had to know how you were discovered in Mountain Cove to begin with."

One of the marshals stepped forward. "I'm sorry, ma'am. But we'll handle things from here."

Reality forced its way into the moment. Tracy moved to step from David's arms. "I'm sorry, David. But you can't love me. I have to leave now. We talked about this. It's the only way. I wish I had done this before I brought such havoc on everyone."

But David wouldn't let her go. "You don't have to go anywhere. Santino is dead."

Dizziness swept over her. She couldn't find words.

"How do you know?" Chief Winters asked.

"He tried to kill Tracy tonight, but I wouldn't let him. I chased him and we ended up nearly surrounded by a wall of fire. I escaped before it was too late." Weariness crept over his haggard features. "God help me, I tried to save him. Tried to pull him from the flames he'd stepped into. No matter what he'd done, I couldn't watch him die. But he...wouldn't let me help him. He thought he could save himself."

David hung his head. Tracy never wanted to see that

look on his face again. He was a fireman and a hero. He never wanted to lose anyone—even someone who had committed heinous crimes. In the end, by fighting Santino, he'd saved Tracy.

Set her free.

"You saved me, David. You risked your life for me and saved me in the most important way."

"And I'd do it a hundred times over to keep you safe." David pressed his forehead against hers, oblivious to the US marshals and officials standing around them. "I only wish I hadn't avoided you for so long. I love you."

"I love you, too, David."

"Santino might be dead, Tracy," the marshal said, "but that doesn't negate efforts by his people. The door is still open for you to enter WITSEC, and I'm here to take you away to your new life."

How could she leave David? But then…how could she stay?

"Maybe a married name would help keep you under the radar," David said.

Tracy gasped.

"Will you marry me, Tracy?"

"Are you sure?" She wanted to make sure his proposal wasn't some sort of heroic act. "There's no need for you to go that far to save me."

He chuckled. "Then go that far to save me, Tracy, and marry me. I don't want to live without you."

"Yes. Oh, yes, David."

She had her beauty for ashes.

* * * * *

Margaret Daley, an award-winning author of ninety books (five million sold worldwide), has been married for over forty years and is a firm believer in romance and love. When she isn't traveling, she's writing love stories, often with a suspense thread, and corralling her three cats, who think they rule her household. To find out more about Margaret, visit her website at margaretdaley.com.

Books by Margaret Daley

Love Inspired Suspense

Lone Star Justice

High-Risk Reunion
Lone Star Christmas Rescue
Texas Ranger Showdown
Texas Baby Pursuit

Alaskan Search and Rescue

The Yuletide Rescue
To Save Her Child
The Protector's Mission
Standoff at Christmas

Visit the Author Profile page
at Harlequin.com for more titles.

TO SAVE HER CHILD

Margaret Daley

If God is for us, who can be against us?
—*Romans* 8:31

To all my readers—thank you for choosing my book.

ONE

Ella Jackson looked longingly at the black leather couch against the far wall in her office. If only she could close her eyes for an hour—even half an hour—she would be ready to tackle the rest of the data entry for the upcoming Northern Frontier Search and Rescue training weekend.

She trudged to her desk, staring at the stack of papers she needed to work her way through before picking up her eight-year-old son from day camp, then heading home. She should have been finished by now, but in the middle of the night a search and rescue call had gone out for an elderly gentleman. She had manned the command center for his search, which had ended with the man being found, but her exhaustion from lack of sleep was finally catching up with her.

When she saw her son, Robbie, he would no doubt have a ton of questions about the emergency that had sent him to her neighbor's. This wasn't the first time she'd disturbed her son's sleep in the middle of the night because of a search and rescue, and Robbie was a trooper. Once he'd come with her to the command center when she couldn't find a babysitter. He'd begged to go with her ever since then, but it was impossible to watch over him and fulfill her duties. She'd promised him when he was older, he could.

The sight of the training folder on the desktop screen taunted her to get to work. David Stone, who ran the organization, would return soon and need the list, since the instructional exercises would take place in two days. So much to get done before Saturday. As she sat in her desk chair, she rubbed her blurry eyes, then clicked on the folder. The schedule and list popped up, the cursor blinking hypnotically. When her head started dropping forward, she jerked it up. Not even two pots of coffee were helping her to stay alert.

The door into the hangar opened, and her boss entered. He'd conducted the aerial search for Mr. Otterman, who had finally been found wandering in the middle of a shallow stream two miles from his nursing home.

Her gaze connected with David's. "Mr. Otterman checked out fine, according to your wife, and he's safely back at Aurora Nursing Home."

"Thankfully Josiah and Alex got to him before he made it to the river the stream fed into." He looked as tired as she felt. "Josiah is right behind me. Send him into my office when he comes in."

For a few seconds, Ella was sidetracked by the mention of Josiah. There was something about the man that intrigued her. His short black hair, the bluest eyes she'd ever seen and a slender, athletic build set her heart racing. Although he was handsome, she'd learned to be leery of men with those kinds of looks. No, it was his presence at a search and rescue that drew her to him. Commanding, captivating—and a loner. She knew one when she met one because she was much more comfortable alone, especially after her marriage to an abusive man. For a second, thoughts of her ex-husband threatened to take hold. She wouldn't go there. He'd done enough to her in the past. She wouldn't allow him—even in memories—into her present life.

"Ella, are you all right?"

David pulled her away from her thoughts. "I'm okay. Bree wanted me to tell you to go home and get some sleep since you never went to bed last night."

"My wife worries too much. Josiah and I need to work out some details about the training this weekend." David studied her. "But *you* should definitely go home. You were here before I was this morning."

"But these lists—"

The jarring ring of the phone cut off the rest of Ella's sentence. She snatched it up and said, "Northern Frontier Search and Rescue. How may I help you?"

"Mrs. Jackson?" a female voice asked.

It sounded like one of the counselors at the day camp Robbie went to during the summer. "Yes. Is this Stacy?"

"Yes. I'm so sorry to call you, but your son and two other boys are missing. We've looked everywhere around here and can't find them. We'll continue—"

"What happened?" Stunned, Ella gripped the phone tighter. Surely she'd misheard.

"We don't know. Robbie, Travis and Michael were playing together during free time between activities, but when the counselor rounded up everyone for the Alaskan bear presentation, they were gone."

"I'll be right there with some help to search for them." She didn't know how she managed to speak a coherent sentence, her mouth was as dry as the desert.

Phone still in her trembling hand, Ella rose, glancing around for her purse. Where did she put it?

"I'd hoped you would say that. It's not like them to run off."

"I'll be there as soon as possible." She nearly dropped the phone as she looked around trying to find her leather bag. Beads of perspiration broke out on her forehead. Usually it was on the floor under the desk near her feet.

Where is it? I need my keys. The camp wouldn't call me unless...

Her heartbeat raced. Tears pooled in her eyes. She put the phone in its cradle, and then rummaged through her desk drawers.

David clasped her arms and forced her to stop her search. "What's wrong?"

"It's Robbie. He's missing from Camp Yukon with two other boys."

David released his grasp and reached toward the filing cabinet. "Here's your purse." He put it in her hand.

She hugged her handbag against her chest, then started for the door.

"Wait, Ella. Let me make some calls. We'll get volunteers out to the campsite. Josiah is still out in the hangar with his dog, Buddy. Catch him before his sister leaves. She was heading out to her car when I came in. Have one of them drive you. You shouldn't go by yourself, and it might take me some time to get the search organized and notify the authorities in case the camp hasn't."

As though on autopilot, Ella changed directions and headed to the hangar, scanning the cavernous area for Josiah Witherspoon and his search and rescue German shepherd. They had just been successful in finding Mr. Otterman. But then she thought back to the ones they hadn't found in time. *Not my son. Please, God. Not my son.*

Ella spied Josiah coming into the open hangar from outside, Buddy, a black-and-brown German shepherd on a leash next to him. He walked toward her, his long strides quickly cutting the distance between them.

"What's wrong, Ella?" His tanned forehead scrunched and his dark blue eyes filled with concern. "Another job?"

Words stuck in her throat. She nodded, fighting the tears welling in her. "My son is missing," she finally squeaked out.

"Where? When?" he asked, suddenly all business.

"About an hour ago at Camp Yukon, which is held at Kincaid Park near the outdoor center. They did a preliminary search but couldn't find him or the two boys with him. David said—" She swallowed several times. "I hope you can help look for them."

Josiah was already retrieving his cell phone from his belt clip. "I'll let Alex know to go there. She just left with her dog, Sadie." He connected with his twin sister and gave her the information. "I'll be right behind you. I'm bringing Ella," he told her. Then he hung up.

"You don't have to. I can…" She gripped her purse's straps tighter, the leather digging into her palms. Robbie was all she had. *I can't lose him, Lord.* "Thanks. It's probably wiser if I don't drive."

"Let's go. My truck is outside." Josiah fell into step next to her.

Ella slid a glance toward him, and the sight of Josiah, a former US Marine, calmed her nerves. She knew how good he and his sister were with their dogs at finding people. Robbie would be all right. She had to believe that. The alternative was unthinkable. She shuddered.

On the passenger side he opened the back door for Buddy, then quickly moved to the front door for Ella. "I'll find Robbie. I promise."

The confidence in his voice further eased her anxiety and momentarily held the cold at bay. Ella climbed into the F-150 extended cab with Josiah's hand on her elbow, as if he was letting her know he would be here for her. She appreciated it, but at the moment she felt as though she was barely holding herself together. She couldn't fall apart because Robbie would need her when they found him. He was probably more frightened than she was. Once, when he was five, they had been separated in a department store, and when she'd found him a minute later, he had been sitting on the floor, crying.

As Josiah started the engine, Ella hugged her arms to her and ran her hands up and down them. But the chill had returned and burrowed its way into the marrow of her bones, even though the temperature was sixty-five degrees and the sun streamed through the truck's windshield, heating up the interior.

Josiah glanced at her. "David will get enough people to scour the whole park."

"But so many just came off working Mr. Otterman's disappearance."

"That won't stop us. There are three lost boys. Do you have anything with Robbie's scent on it?"

"I do. In my car."

He backed up to her ten-year-old black Jeep Wrangler. "Where?"

"Front seat. A jacket he didn't take with him to the babysitter last night." Ella grasped the handle. The weatherman had mentioned the temperatures over-night would dip down into the forties, and all Robbie was wearing was a thin shirt.

"I'll get it." Josiah jumped out of the truck before Ella had a chance to even open her door.

She watched him move to her car. She'd only known Josiah and his sister for six months, since they'd begun volunteering for Northern Frontier Search and Rescue, but they'd quickly become invaluable to the organiza-tion. Alex had lived here for years, whereas Josiah had only recently left the Marines. They were co-owners of Outdoor Alaska, a company that outfitted search and rescue teams and wilderness enthusiasts.

Although he was a large man, she'd seen Josiah move with an agility that surprised her. He returned with Rob-bie's brown jacket in his grasp.

He gave it to Ella. "This will help Buddy find your son."

The bright light of a few minutes ago began to fade. Ella leaned forward, staring out the windshield at the sky. Dark clouds drifted over the sun. "Looks like we'll have a storm late this afternoon."

When Josiah flowed into the traffic on Minnesota Drive, an expressway that bisected Anchorage, his strong jawline twitched. "We can still search in the rain, but let's hope we find them beforehand or that the weatherman is wrong."

Ella leaned her head against the headrest and closed her eyes. She had to remain calm and in control. That was one of the things she'd always been able to do in the middle of a search and rescue, but this time it was her son. Now she knew firsthand what the families of the missing people went through. The thundering beat of her heart clamored against her chest, and the rate of her breathing increased. Sweat beaded on her forehead, and she scrubbed her hand across her face.

"Ella, I won't leave the park until we find the boys."

"There are a lot of trees and animals in the park. What if he runs into a bear or even a moose? They could…" She refused to think of what could happen. *Remain calm.* But no matter how much she repeated that to herself, she couldn't.

"How old is your son?"

"Eight."

"Has he had any survival training in the outdoors?"

"A little. One of the reasons I signed him up for the day camp was to start some of that. We've made a few excursions but haven't camped overnight anywhere." Robbie was timid and afraid of everything. If she'd left her ex-husband sooner, her son might not be so scared of loud noises, or the dark. At least Robbie wasn't alone and it was still light outside.

"We'll be there soon."

In the distance Ella glimpsed Ted Stevens Anchorage International Airport, which was north of the park. Maybe the counselors had found Robbie by now. Then she realized that they would have called her if they had. She checked her cell phone to make sure the ringer's volume was up.

Josiah exited the highway, and at an intersection he slanted a look toward her that made Ella feel as though he were sending her some of his strength and calmness. "Thank you for bringing me."

"Remember how successful we were at locating Mr. Otterman? The park is big, but it is surrounded on two sides with water and one with the airport. The area is contained."

"But it's fourteen hundred acres. That's a huge area to cover."

"Can he swim?"

Ella swiped a few stray stands of her blond hair back from her face. "Yes, but why do you ask?"

"I'm just trying to get a sense of what Robbie knows how to do since the park has water and Cook Inlet butts up against it."

"He loves to fish, so I made sure he learned to swim at an early age."

"I love to fish. Nothing beats a fresh-caught salmon."

Ella rubbed her thumb into her palm over and over. "That's how the bears feel, too. What if he runs into one and forgets everything he's been taught?" Her heartbeat raced even more at the thought.

Josiah turned onto Raspberry Road. "If he doesn't run from one and makes noise as he walks, he should be okay. Neither one wants to be surprised. I'm sure the first day the counselors went over how to behave in the wilderness."

"Yes, but…"

Josiah slowed and threw her a look full of understanding. "You've dealt with family members when someone is lost, like Mr. Otterman's son and daughter-in-law earlier today. I've seen you. You always seem to be able to reassure them. Think about the words you tell them and repeat them to yourself."

"I pray with them. I tell them about the people who are looking for their loved one. How good they are at what they do."

"Exactly." Josiah tossed his head toward the backseat

of the cab. "Buddy is good at locating people. I know how to track people through a forest. Tell you what—I'll start the prayer. You can add whatever you want."

As Josiah began his prayer for Robbie, something shifted inside Ella. The tight knot in her stomach began to unravel.

"Lord, I know Your power and love. Anything is possible through You. Please help Buddy and me find Robbie and the other two boys safe and unharmed." Josiah's truck entered the park, and he glanced at her.

"And please bless the ones searching for my son and his friends. Comfort the families and friends who are waiting. Amen," Ella finished, seeing Josiah in a new light today. They'd talked casually the past few months, but there was always a barrier there, a look of pain in his blue eyes. She knew that expression because she fought to keep hers hidden since she dealt with so many people who needed someone to listen to them when they were hurting. She could help them, but she wasn't sure anyone could help her.

In the woods, Josiah gave Buddy as much leash as possible and let him dictate where they went. Having insisted she couldn't stay at the command post, Ella trailed behind him as they searched farther away from the base at the day camp. His sister and her dog, Sadie, were following Travis's scent, while another search and rescue worker, Jesse Hunt, had the third boy's backpack, and his dog was tracking that child.

Josiah glanced over at Alex to his right and Jesse to his left, both within ten feet of him. Suddenly the dogs veered away from each other. Buddy went straight while the others made an almost ninety-degree turn.

"They separated?" Ella asked, coming up to his side.

"I believe so." Tearing his gaze away from her fearful eyes, Josiah examined the soft ground. "Someone else has been here recently." He pointed to the ground. "That's Robbie's shoe print and that's someone with a size twelve or thirteen boot."

"A man? Someone else searching for the kids?"

His gut clenched. "Maybe one of the counselors came this way." Or maybe it was someone else who had nothing to do with the day camp. He wouldn't voice that to Ella. She didn't need to worry any more than she already was.

Josiah continued following Buddy, scanning the ground for any signs that would help him find Robbie. He didn't know how Ella could deal with the people who waited to see if their family member or friend was found. While bringing her to Kincaid Park, he'd felt unsure of what to say to help her. He was used to being alone. He was better off working alone with Buddy. He'd learned that the hard way.

Buddy stopped at the base of a spruce tree, sniffing the trunk, then taking off to the left. Josiah inspected the lower branches and found a few of the smaller ones were broken off—recently.

"I believe he climbed this tree." Josiah pointed at the damaged limbs, then headed the direction Buddy went.

"If only he'd stayed here. It's been hours since he disappeared. It's starting to get colder, and he has no jacket on." Falling into step next to Josiah, Ella scanned the dense woods surrounding them.

The quaver in her voice penetrated the hard shell he'd placed his emotions in to put his life back together after being a prisoner of war in the Middle East. "He's walked and even run a long way from where he was last seen. He'll get tired and probably find a place to rest."

Ella's wide brown eyes were riveted to his. "What made them separate? I saw the lengthening of the spaces between the footprints. He was running then, wasn't he?"

Her gaze drew him in, so much pain reflected in it. He gritted his teeth, not wanting to answer her question, not wanting to add to her distress.

"You don't have to say anything. I can see it on your face. Something or someone scared him. The person whose boot prints we found with his. I saw them under the tree, too. He's being stalked." Ella came to stop.

"It could be someone searching for the kids. Don't jump to any conclusions. Speculation can drive you crazy."

"Just the facts, then. We're on point on this search. The rest are spread out and going much slower behind us." Her teeth dug into her lower lip.

Before he realized what he was doing, he touched her shoulder, feeling the tension beneath his fingers. "Let's go. We don't need to stand around speculating." He squeezed her gently before he turned toward Buddy, who was sniffing the ground five yards away.

His dog barked and charged forward, straining against the leash. Five minutes later, Buddy weaved through some trees, yelping several times. Josiah kept pace with his dog, his body screaming in protest at the long hours he'd been awake without much rest. His German shepherd circled a patch of ground.

Josiah came to a halt at the spot with Ella next to

him. She stared at the ground, her face pale. Bear prints. Fresh ones.

"A bear is nearby, possibly after Robbie," Ella whispered in a squeaky voice, her eyes huge.

TWO

Ella sucked in a deep breath that she held until pain shot through her chest. Finally she exhaled, then managed to ask, "Is the bear following him?"

"No, but it looks as though Robbie stopped, turned around, then began running this way." Josiah pointed to the right. "The bear is going straight."

"Oh, good." Relief sagged her shoulders until she realized the bear might not be the only one.

After taking his dog off the leash, Josiah signaled to Buddy to continue tracking Robbie. As Josiah followed behind the German shepherd, he said over his shoulder, "I think Robbie is slowing down. His strides are closer together."

Her cell phone rang, and Ella quickly answered it. It was David. "Has anyone been found?"

"Yes, Travis."

Ella said a quick prayer of thanks.

David continued. "Alex located him not far from Little Campbell Lake. She's bringing him in."

"Did he tell Alex anything? What happened? Why did they part?"

"They thought if they split up, one of them could get help."

"How did they get lost?"

"They snuck away from Camp Yukon and were playing in the woods. All I know was a man spooked them."

A man? Were those boot prints they saw *that* man's? If so, the man had not only spooked them but followed them—followed Robbie. What if it was her ex-husband? Could Keith have found them? He'd never cared about his son, but he might kidnap him to get back at her. Her chest suddenly felt constricted. Each breath of air she inhaled burned her throat and lungs.

No. Keith couldn't have found them. *Please, God, it can't be him.* Memories inundated Ella as she fought for a decent breath.

"Ella?" David's concerned voice wrenched her back to the present. "Ella, are you all right?"

No. "We're following Robbie's tracks. We should find him soon." If she said it often enough, it might come true.

"I'll find out more when Travis gets here. I'll call you when I hear something else."

When Ella hung up, she realized she'd slowed her gait to a crawl as she'd talked with David. The space between her and Josiah had doubled. She hurried her pace to catch up with him.

"That was David. Your sister found Travis. That's encouraging." But Robbie and his friend Michael could still be in danger. And there was still a possibility that her ex, Keith, could be the man who had spooked the kids.

"Any info on what happened?" Josiah kept trailing Buddy.

"They were playing in the woods when a man scared them. That's all I know."

Josiah paused and twisted around, his tan face carved in a frown. "I don't see any evidence now that anyone is following Robbie."

"But what about the man? The boot prints we found? He could—"

Suddenly a series of barks echoed through the trees.

"Come on. Buddy has something."

Ella ran beside Josiah, who slowed down to allow her to keep up. Buddy sat at the base of a tree, barking occasionally, looking up, then at them.

"Robbie's up in the tree," Josiah said, slightly ahead of her now.

She examined the green foliage and saw Robbie clinging to a branch. He was safe. *Thank You, Lord. Thank You.*

But what about the man? The threat was still out there. The threat that could be Keith.

As she neared, she noticed her son's wide brown eyes glued to Buddy. The fear on his face pierced through her. He might not recognize the German shepherd. "We're here, Robbie," she shouted. "Buddy is a search and rescue dog. He belongs to Josiah Witherspoon. You remember Mr. Witherspoon?"

Robbie barely moved his head in a nod, but he did look toward her. "Mom, I'm stuck."

Standing under the cottonwood, Ella craned her neck and looked up at him. She wasn't even sure how he'd managed to climb so high. He must be thirty feet off the ground. "Don't do anything yet. You'll be all right. Josiah and I will talk about the best way to get you down safely. Okay?" Her heart clenched at the sight of tears in her son's eyes. His grip around the branch seemed to tighten. He was so scared. All she wanted to do was hold her child and tell him she wouldn't let anything hurt him.

Josiah moved closer. "I can get him down. I have a longer reach than you."

"You don't think he can back down, keeping his arms around the limb?"

"Sometimes people freeze once they get into a tree and see how high they are. I have a feeling he was scared when he climbed up, then realized where he was. I did that once when I was a boy, not much younger than Robbie."

"But should I—"

"You should be a mom and keep him calm."

She nodded, relieved Josiah was here because she was afraid of heights. She would have climbed the tree if she had to, but then there might have been two people stuck up there. "Thanks."

Josiah hoisted himself up onto the lowest branch that would hold his weight, then smiled at her. "I once had a tree where I loved to hide from the world, or rather, Alex when she bugged me. She never knew where I went. I used to watch her try to find me from my perch at the top."

For the first time in hours, Ella chuckled. "I won't tell her, in case you ever want to hide from her again."

He began scaling the branches. "Much appreciated."

"I won't, either," Robbie said in a squeaky voice.

"Thanks, partner," Josiah said to her son, halfway up the main trunk of the cottonwood. "Ella, call David and tell him we found Robbie."

Robbie stared down at the German shepherd. "What's his name?"

While her son talked with Josiah about his dog, Ella gave David a call. "He's in a tree, but Josiah is helping him down. We'll return to base soon." She lowered her voice while she continued. "Has Michael been found yet?"

"No, but I'll pull everyone off the other areas to concentrate on the trail Jesse is following."

"Are the police there?"

"Yes, Thomas Caldwell is here. He's talking with Travis and getting a description of the man."

Thomas was a friend of David's and Josiah's as well as a detective on the Anchorage police force. "Good. We'll be there soon."

When Ella disconnected the call, she watched Josiah shimmy toward Robbie as far as it was safe for him to go on the branch. He was probably one hundred and eighty pounds while her son was forty. Josiah paused about seven feet from Robbie.

"I can't come out any farther, Robbie, but I'm here to grab you as you slide backward toward me. Hug the limb and use one hand to move back to me." Josiah's voice was even and calm, as though they were discussing the weather.

"I can't. I'm...I'm scared. What if I fall?" Robbie peered at the ground and shook his head.

"Don't look down. Do you see that squirrel on the branch near you? He's watching you. Keep an eye on him."

"He's probably wondering what we're doing up here." Robbie stared at the animal, its tail twitching back and forth.

Her son scooted a few inches down the limb, which was at a slight incline from the trunk. When the squirrel scurried away, Robbie squeezed his eyes shut and continued to move at a snail's pace. Finally, when he was within a foot of Josiah, her son raised his head and glanced back at Josiah. His gaze drifted downward, and he wobbled on the branch, sliding to the side.

Ella gasped.

Josiah moved fast, latching on to Robbie's ankle. "I've got you. You're okay."

But her son flailed again. "I'm gonna…"

He fell off the limb, screaming. Then suddenly he was hanging upside down, dangling from the end of Josiah's grip. Robbie's fingertips grazed a smaller branch under him, but it wouldn't hold his weight. Ella's legs went weak, but she remained upright.

"Okay, Robbie?" Josiah adjusted his weight to keep balanced.

"Yes," her son barely said.

"You're safe. Nothing is going to happen to you. Hold still. Can you do that?"

"Yes," Robbie said in a little stronger voice.

"I'm lifting you up to me, then we'll climb down together."

Josiah's gaze connected to Ella's, and she had no doubt her son would be safely on the ground in a few minutes. She sank against the tree trunk, its rough bark scraping her arm. She hardly noticed it, though, as Josiah grabbed her son with both hands and brought Robbie to him, the muscles in his arms bunching with the strain.

When Robbie was in the crook of the tree between

the trunk and limb, he hugged Josiah. Surprise flitted across the man's face.

He patted her son on the back several times. "Let's get down from here. I don't know about you, but I'm starving for a hamburger and fries."

"Yeah!" Robbie's face brightened with a big grin.

With Josiah's help, her son finally made it to the ground. Robbie threw his arms around Ella, who never wanted to let him go. She kissed the top of his head as he finally wiggled free.

"Can we go eat a burger with Mr. Witherspoon? Can we?"

The eagerness in his voice made it hard to say no, but it wasn't fair to keep Josiah any longer than necessary. "I'm sure he's—"

"I think that's a great idea, Robbie. There's a place not too far from here that's a favorite of mine. After we eat, then I can take you two to the hangar so your mom can pick up her car."

Robbie looked at Buddy. "What about him?"

"He'll be fine while we're inside. I imagine he's pretty tired. He's been working a lot today."

So have you, Ella thought, glimpsing in Josiah the same weariness she felt, but he must have sensed how important doing something normal and nonthreatening was for her son. Usually when Josiah came to a SAR operation, he did his job and went home. He was all business. But not now. The smile he sent her son made her want to join in.

"Can I pet Buddy?" her son asked.

"Sure. He loves the attention." Josiah squatted next to Robbie after he moved to the German shepherd.

"I wish I had a dog like this. No one would bother me."

Josiah peered up at Ella. "You don't need to worry about that man now."

"You know about the man?" Robbie's forehead scrunched.

"Yes." Ella clasped Robbie's shoulder. "Honey, when we get back to camp, you can tell the police what the man looked like. They'll find him."

Robbie ran his hand down Buddy's back, stroking the dog over and over while Josiah stood next to her son. "How's Travis and Michael?"

"Travis is at the command center. They're still looking for Michael. He may even be with Travis by the time we arrive at camp." At least she hoped that was the case. The idea that Michael might still be lost while the man hadn't been found gave her shivers. She rubbed her hands up and down her arms.

The realization it could still be her ex-husband mocked her. Until she found out for certain, she needed to start making plans to leave Anchorage. She'd disappeared once before. She could again. But the thought of leaving the life she had carved out for her and her son in Alaska swelled her throat with emotions she tried not to feel. She loved Anchorage and the people she'd become friends with. She didn't want to leave.

"Let's go. I imagine you've got a camp full of people anxiously waiting to see you." Josiah rose and said to Robbie, "You want to hold Buddy's leash and lead the way?"

Her son's smile grew even more. "Yeah."

Ella fell into step with Josiah while her son took off

with Buddy. "Maybe I should think about getting a pet for Robbie."

"I can help you with that. Buddy became a daddy eight weeks ago. My friend will be selling most of the puppies soon, but I can have the pick of the litter free. I hadn't intended to get another dog, so if Robbie wants one, he can have my free one."

"A mix breed or a German shepherd?"

"A purebred German shepherd. This guy trains dogs for search and rescue. He'll keep two pups to train, then sell them later."

Her pride nudged forward. Ever since escaping her abusive marriage in Georgia and relocating to Anchorage, she hadn't depended on others to help her. It had taken all her courage to seek aid through the New Life Organization and break free of Keith. She was thankful to the Lord that she and Robbie had been able to make it on their own without constantly glancing over their shoulders, looking for Keith, who should have been in prison for years. For four years, she'd been able to live without being scared for her life and now... "I can't accept one. You should take the puppy and sell it."

"I don't need the money. Outdoor Alaska is a successful business. I'd much rather see a child happy with a new pet. I always had one while growing up, and they were important to me."

What if it really was Keith in the woods? A dog would only complicate their lives if they had to move. "I appreciate the offer."

He tilted his head, his gaze slanting down at her. "But?"

Her gaze drifted to Robbie with Buddy. "A German

shepherd is a big dog. He'll need to be trained. Any suggestions?"

"I can help when the puppy's old enough."

Again the words *I can't accept* perched on the tip of her tongue, but one look at her son petting Buddy shut that impulse down. Her son was frightened more than most children because of the memories of his abusive father and his temper, all directed at her. Although he'd only been four when she'd finally successfully escaped Keith, a raised voice still shook Robbie, and any man with curly blond hair like his father's scared him to the point that he tried to hide if he could.

She didn't realize she'd stopped walking until Josiah's worried voice said, "Are you all right?"

She blinked, noting her son had paused by a big tree and waited for them to catch up. "Thanks for the offer to help train the dog when we get it." She hoped by the time the puppy was old enough to be separated from its mother, she'd know for sure who the man in the woods was.

The corners of his eyes crinkled as he grinned. "Good. My sister has been teasing me lately. Accusing me of being a hermit when I'm not working."

"When did you leave the Marines?"

"Eighteen months ago. Alex and I grew up in Anchorage. We both left, but she came back when our parents died in a small plane crash and took over the running of the family business, Outdoor Alaska."

"Your store has really grown since I first arrived."

"That's all my sister. She's driven."

"And you aren't?" She started walking again, the darkness of the woods throwing Josiah's face in shadows.

"*Driven?* I'm not sure I would use that word to describe me."

"What word *would* you use to describe yourself, then?"

"I'm just not as driven or singularly focused as I once was. Except when searching for a lost person—when someone else's life is in the balance."

What was he not telling her? Studying his closed expression, she knew there was so much more he kept to himself—like she did. She couldn't share her past with anyone. That would put her and her son in danger. What happened today had ended well for Robbie, but if Keith ever found them, she knew it wouldn't. The thought sent a shudder down her spine.

When they arrived at the camp, Robbie saw Travis and ran toward him with Buddy trotting alongside.

Ella scanned the area and glimpsed Detective Thomas Caldwell talking with David. "I hope Michael was found," she said to Josiah.

"I'll get Robbie and Buddy and be right there," Josiah said, and then headed toward the two boys, who stood near a couple of camp counselors and Travis's parents.

Both Thomas and David were frowning. That didn't bode well for Michael. Ella's chest constricted at the thought of the boy still out there. Not far from David stood his wife with Michael's mother. Tears ran down the young woman's face while Bree consoled her.

When Ella joined David and Thomas, she asked in a low voice, "Has Michael been found yet?"

David's mouth lifted in a grin. "Yes, just two minutes ago. He hurt himself. Jesse thinks it's a sprained ankle. He's bringing him in."

"Thank God he's safe. Good thing Bree is here. She

can check him on-site." Ella spied her son and Josiah making their way toward her.

David peered at his wife with love deep in his eyes.

David had been fortunate last winter to rescue Bree, a doctor who flew to remote villages, from a downed bush plane in the wilderness. That had been the beginning of a beautiful relationship, which had just culminated in their wedding on Valentine's Day. Sometimes Ella wished she had a special man in her life again, but her marriage to Keith had soured her on marriage. But David deserved some happiness.

How about you? a little voice in her head said.

She was happy. She had her son, friends, a good church and a fulfilling job. She didn't need a man to be happy. And yet, when she saw other married couples who obviously loved each other, a twinge stabbed her with the idea of what could have been if she hadn't married Keith.

"Travis's dad told me Michael has been found," Josiah said.

"Yeah, Mom. Can we wait until he arrives before going to dinner?"

Ella slid a look to Josiah, and he answered her son, "Yes, of course."

"Good. Travis is staying, too. I'm gonna sit with him until Michael shows up."

"Ella, I'd like to ask Robbie a few questions," Thomas said.

"Yes, of course."

Thomas smiled at her son. "It's nice to see you again. That picnic David threw on the Fourth of July was great. We'll need to work on him to have one for Labor Day, especially if his father is going to be the chef."

"Yeah. My favorite part was the fireworks." Still clutching Buddy's leash, Robbie stroked the German shepherd as he craned his neck to peer up at Thomas.

"Travis told me what happened, but I'd love to hear it from you, too."

The grin on her son's face vanished. "We were over there." Robbie gestured toward the line of trees near the camp base. "We heard an owl but couldn't see it so we thought we would try to find it." He swung his attention to Ella. "I know we shouldn't have gone away from the camp, but I love birds. I saw a bald eagle earlier today."

"We'll talk about that later. Right now, just tell the detective what you remember."

Pausing for a moment, Robbie tilted his head. "Mom, I think I need to learn how to track. That way I would have known how to get back to camp. We walked for a while, listening to the owl hoot." He closed his eyes for a few seconds, balling his hands. "When I saw a man with a mean face standing by a tree staring at us, I looked around. None of us could really tell which way we'd come from. We were talking and not paying attention. I was gonna inspect the ground for footprints, but the man started heading for us. We ran. Me and Michael followed Travis, thinking he must know the way. He didn't."

"I understand you all split up. Why?" Thomas asked.

"Because the man was still behind us. I've seen it on a TV show. People split up when they are being chased. That way one of us could run back and get help."

"What happened when you did that?" Thomas asked.

"At first, he went after me, but then suddenly he turned and started in the direction Michael went. I decided to climb a tree, but the first one wasn't good. The second one was better." He dropped his head. "Except I couldn't get down. Then Josiah saved me." Robbie's gaze fixed on Josiah.

"What did the man look like?" Thomas wrote on his pad.

"A grizzly bear."

"Robbie, no kidding around. This is serious," Ella scolded him.

"Mom, I know. He was *huge*—" Robbie's arms spread out to indicate not only tall but wide "—and had so much dark brown hair all over him. When I was running and looked back, that was what he reminded me of." Her son trembled. "I don't ever want to see him again. I promise, Mom, I won't ever go off like that."

Relieved that the description didn't fit her ex-husband at all, especially all that dark hair, she released a slow breath. "I'm glad you learned a good lesson." Ella patted his shoulder, realizing the fear Robbie had experienced would be more effective than if she grounded him for a week.

"Anything else about the man that might help me find him?" Thomas scribbled a few more notes on his pad.

Robbie stared at the ground, then slowly shook his head. "Nope. I was running most of the time. I didn't want him to catch me."

"Thanks, Robbie, for helping me. You can go sit with Travis if you want now." While her son handed Buddy's leash to Josiah then left, Thomas gave Ella his card. "Call me if he remembers anything else. I've got police combing the woods right now. Hopefully we'll find the man. We'll work on a composite sketch after I talk with Michael. I'd like to show the boys the picture our artist comes up with and see what they think. Okay?"

"Yes. I want him found. I don't like the idea someone is out there chasing children."

"Neither do I. My partner is checking the database of criminals who target children in Anchorage to see if one matches the description."

The realization of how close Robbie had come to being taken by a stranger finally took hold of Ella. The campsite spun before her eyes while her legs gave way.

THREE

As Ella began to sink to the ground, Josiah grabbed her and held her up. "When was the last time you ate something?" He looked into her eyes, making sure she hadn't fainted.

"I don't remember," she answered with a shaky laugh. "I was so worried about Robbie, I wasn't thinking about eating."

"Let's go sit on the bench over there." Josiah's arm held her protectively against his side, and he moved toward the wooden seat off to the side.

"Thanks." Ella closed her eyes and breathed deeply.

When David approached, he said, "I'll get something to hold you over until you can eat a real meal." He left for a moment and was back with a granola bar and a bottle of water. "Sorry it's not more, but this should tide you over for the time being."

She took a bite of the granola bar and took a sip of water. "I started thinking about what could have happened if that man had caught Robbie or one of the other boys."

"But he didn't. Keep your focus on that. What-ifs don't matter." The feel of her close to him accelerated his heart rate as if he were running with Buddy. He gently eased her onto the wooden bench, then sat next to her, worried about her pale features.

She dropped her head, her chin nearly touching her chest. Her long blond hair fell forward, hiding her delicate features. What had drawn him to her from the beginning, when he'd met her months ago, were her large brown eyes. One look into them and he'd experienced a kinship with her, as if she'd gone through a nightmare that equaled his. He hoped he was wrong, because being a prisoner of war was intolerable, even for the strongest person.

"Robbie is all I have. I can't let anything happen to him. That man could have hurt him today." Ella finished the granola bar and gulped down some water.

"He could have, but he didn't. The boy is safe. The police will find the man who chased the kids. If he has any kind of record, it'll only be a matter of time before he's found and arrested."

She angled her head to look into his eyes. For a few seconds everything around him faded. His focus homed in on her face. When she smiled, her whole face lit up, and for a moment, he thought he was special to her. Why in the world would he think that? For the past eighteen months, he'd slowly been piecing his life back together, but at the moment he felt as if all he'd been able to do was patch over the wounds.

"Thanks, Josiah. You've gone above and beyond for me. Neither of us got much sleep last night because of Mr. Otterman's search, but I wasn't following a dog on a scent. You were. I hate to impose on you about dinner—"

He covered her hand with his. "I usually have dinner alone after a long day at Outdoor Alaska. Going out with you and your son will be a nice change of pace. Besides, Robbie is expecting me to go. I don't want to let him down. And you are *not* imposing on me."

For the past six months, since returning to Alaska, he'd gone through the same routine every day—wake up, grab breakfast on the run, work long hours at the store, then go home, eat dinner, play with Buddy and then go to bed. Not much else in between. The only time he deviated from the schedule was when he and Buddy helped in a search and rescue. His volunteering had been a lifesaver for him.

Dimples appeared on her cheeks. "All right, then. Dinner it is. And there's more to life than work, you know. I would have thought you would enjoy camping at this time of year."

For a second, all he could do was stare at her smile until he realized she was waiting for him to say something. "I used to camp a lot, but since I left the Marines, I haven't."

"Alaska is a great place to enjoy the outdoors, even in the winter. That's what I love about this state."

"I know what you mean." He wanted to steer the conversation away from him. He glimpsed fellow searcher Jesse coming out of the trees, carrying a boy. Jesse's dog trotted next to him. "There's Jesse and Michael." He pointed in their direction.

Before Ella could say anything, Robbie and Travis raced toward them. "Well, I guess I don't have to tell my son Michael is back."

"We'll give him a few minutes to talk with his friend, then leave. I've worked up quite an appetite."

"It's all that exercising you did today."

"You were right there by my side, looking for Robbie. You must be hungry, too." Josiah rose and offered his hand.

She took it and stood. "Thanks for all your help." When Michael was taken to the first-aid tent, Ella motioned to Robbie to join her.

Her son skidded to a stop. "Let's go. I could eat a bear." Suddenly he swung his head from side to side. "No one has seen a bear, have they?"

"No."

"Good. I really can't eat a bear, but I'm so hungry."

"Then let's go." Josiah indicated where his truck was parked. "Would you like to take Buddy, Robbie?"

"Sure!"

"I need to talk to the camp director first," Ella said, approaching the man.

Josiah watched Ella talk with the guy. From her body language, he could guess what she was saying to the director. It was clear she wasn't happy with what happened today, and Josiah couldn't blame her. She was more restrained than he would have been if Robbie were his son. At one time he'd envisioned having a family, but not after his fiancée, Lori's, betrayal. The thought of her had been what kept him going while he'd been a prisoner of war, but when he'd escaped his three-month captivity, she'd already moved on with her life with another man.

When Ella returned, her expression was blank except for a glint in her brown eyes. "Okay, I'm ready."

"I need to see Thomas for a second." He gave Ella his truck keys. "Go on. I'll be there shortly."

Josiah jogged toward the tent and waited in the entrance while Thomas finished interviewing Michael. He caught the detective's attention, and Thomas walked to him. "I know you're going to let Ella know your progress in finding the man who scared the boys, but I'd appreciate it if you'd call me first."

Thomas's eyebrows shot up. "I didn't realize you two were so close."

"We aren't. Not exactly. But she's a single mother. I don't want her to feel she's all alone in this."

"She isn't. David and Bree asked me to do the same thing." He tried to maintain a tough expression, but his mouth twisted in a slight smile.

Exasperated at Thomas, who he'd known since childhood, Josiah asked, "Does that mean you'll call me first?"

"Yes. Count this as me informing you before Ella. One of my officers at the station just called me. He found a match in the database from the description Travis and Robbie gave me, and I showed Michael the guy's photo. He positively ID'd the guy, so I sent some patrol cars to the last known address of Casey Foster to bring him in for questioning."

"It's probably too much to ask that he'll be home."

"Many criminals do dumb things and get caught." Thomas looked toward Josiah's truck. "I see Ella and Robbie waiting for you."

"Yeah, we're going to grab dinner." Josiah looked up at the clouds as drops of rain began to fall.

"Go on. I'll show Travis the guy's photo. I won't show Robbie until later. I know what a long day you and Ella had, with the earlier search for Mr. Otterman."

"See you later." Josiah turned to leave and nearly collided with his twin sister. They had similar coloring—black hair, blue eyes—but that was as close as they got to being alike. He and Alex were polar opposites in many respects. They were close, though. She was all the family he had left.

"Just got back from helping to search for Michael. I saw Ella and her son in your truck. Is Robbie okay?"

"Shook up but not hurt."

"Travis, too. But I understand Michael sprained his ankle."

"He hurt it while running, I hear."

"At least this one ended well. It's been a good day for us. Will you be home for dinner?"

Alex lived in their large family house with a housekeeper and caretaker while he stayed in a small cabin behind his childhood home. He would sometimes eat dinner with his sister and discuss business. The place was really too big even for the both of them, but they hadn't wanted to sell the house they'd grown up in after their parents died, which was one of the reasons he'd wanted to be involved in search and rescue. It had been the cold, not the plane crash, that had killed them before they could be found. "No, I'm taking Ella and Robbie for a hamburger at Stella's Café."

"I love Stella's. I'd join you, but I'm half-asleep right now."

"See you later, sis." His stomach rumbling, he quickened his pace.

The sight of Ella looking out his windshield—as if she belonged there—spurred his pulse rate. He'd avoided getting too close to others since he'd come home, except for a few he'd known all his life like Thomas, Jesse and his sister. But even with them, he couldn't reveal the horrors he'd endured. His body had healed, but his heart still felt ripped in two. He'd closed part of himself off in order to survive for those three months as a captive.

He climbed into his cab and twisted around to look at Robbie. "You okay back there with Buddy?"

The boy smiled from ear to ear. "Yup."

Josiah started his truck just as the forecasted rain finally started falling. Twenty minutes later, when he pulled into the parking lot of Stella's Café, the small storm was already clearing up. When he switched off his engine, he looked at Ella, her head leaning against the window, her eyes closed. Then he peered in the backseat. Robbie, curled against Buddy, slept, too. He hated to wake them up. But before he could do anything, his dog lifted his head and barked a couple of times.

Ella shot up straight in her seat while Robbie groaned, laid his hand on Buddy and petted him. The sight of both of them shifted something deep inside Josiah.

"That wasn't exactly how I planned to wake you up, but it was effective."

Ella laughed. "That it was."

Robbie stretched and pushed himself up to a sitting position, rubbing his eyes. "We're here?"

"Yes, but if you two want, I can get it to go."

Ella shook her head. "No, burgers are best eaten right away, especially the fries."

Within five minutes, Robbie sat across from Josiah while Ella was in the seat next to him.

Robbie glanced around, his eyes lighting up when he saw a couple of video games lining one wall. "Can I play?"

"Just until our food arrives." Ella dug into her purse and gave her son some quarters.

When he left, Josiah knew this might be the only time Robbie wasn't around to hear the news Thomas had told him about Casey Foster. Dread twisted his gut just thinking Foster had been in the park near the boys. "Thomas has a lead on a man he suspects scared the children."

She clasped her hands tightly together on the table. "Someone with a record?"

"Yes. His name is Casey Foster. The police have been sent to pick him up. Michael identified a photo Thomas showed him."

"Good. I don't want him frightening any other children at the camp."

"Speaking of the camp, how did it go with the director?" The second the question was out of his mouth, he wanted to snatch it back. He didn't usually pry into other people's lives, especially someone who was an acquaintance—well, a little more than an acquaintance, especially after today. Search and rescue operations tended to bring people closer. But when that happened, he felt too vulnerable and often needed to step away.

"I'm pulling Robbie out of the camp. It's no longer a safe environment. Mr. Waters assured me the counselor who failed to watch the boys would be fired, but I can't take that chance again. Of course, I'm going to have to find other arrangements for Robbie until school starts. I'll talk with David tomorrow. I might have to take a few days off while I look."

"That camp has a good reputation."

"I know. I wanted Robbie to learn about Alaska, some survival tips and how to take care of himself. It was a bonus that a couple of his friends were going to the camp, too. I'll call Michael's and Travis's parents to see what they're going to do. Child care is a big issue, especially when I don't have any family here."

"Where are you from?"

Ella averted her gaze for a few seconds before answering, "Back east."

A shutter fell over her expression, and her eyes darkened. He could tell when someone didn't want to continue a thread of conversation, and he was definitely getting vibes on that score. What was she hiding? The question aroused his curiosity, which wasn't a good thing. He needed to step away before she became more than a casual friend, someone he worked with from time to time.

Ella stood. "I see the waitress coming. I'm going to get Robbie."

The older lady placed their burgers and fries on the table as Robbie hurried back to his seat.

"This smells great." The young boy popped a fry into his mouth.

"Where's your mom?"

"She went to the restroom."

As though she needed to step back. *Interesting.* More and more Ella reminded him of himself. He knew why he was reluctant to become emotionally close to a person. What was her reason?

"How long have you had Buddy?" Robbie asked before taking a big bite of his burger.

"Eighteen months, since I left the Marines." Buddy had entered his life as a service dog because he'd been diagnosed with post-traumatic stress disorder. Out of the corner of his eye, Josiah caught sight of Ella returning to the table.

"How long has Buddy been a search and rescue dog?"

"I started training Buddy a year ago." Buddy had helped him so much, Josiah wanted to help others with his German shepherd.

Ella slipped into her chair, her expression closed. "Is the burger good?" she asked her son.

"Great. Mr. Witherspoon did good choosing this place. We need to come back here."

"Call me Josiah. Mr. Witherspoon makes me sound old."

Finally she looked at him. Again he couldn't tell what she was thinking.

"Is that okay with you?" Josiah drenched his fries with ketchup.

She nodded, then began eating. If it hadn't been for Robbie, the tension at the table could have been cut with a hunting knife. More questions filled Josiah's mind. Did this have to do with the reason she was a single parent? A bad marriage? Did her husband die?

Stop! Don't go there.

"Who was the first person you rescued?" Robbie asked, pulling Josiah away from his thoughts about Ella.

"It was a couple who got lost in Denali National Park." Josiah went on to tell the boy about how Buddy had located them.

By the time the meal was over, Ella's stiff posture had finally relaxed. "I know David appreciates all the time you and your sister give to the organization."

"Alex and I have some freedom in our work because we own the business. We can often leave at a moment's notice. I know others like Jesse can't because he works as a K-9 officer for the Anchorage Police."

His plate empty, Robbie sat back, yawning.

Ella chuckled. "I think that's our cue to go home. It has been a *long* day."

Josiah laid money on the bill the waitress had left and rose. "Let's go. I need to see if David is at the office. We still need to discuss Saturday's training."

"I forgot all about that." Ella made her way to the exit. "Robbie, I guess you'll be going to work with me tomorrow."

Robbie perked up. "I will? Neat."

"I think you'll find the everyday operations of the Northern Frontier Search and Rescue are boring," Ella said when they were back in the truck.

Robbie sat next to Buddy. The dog opened his eyes to note who was in the cab, then went back to sleep. "Buddy has the right idea." He yawned again.

Ella looked sideways at Josiah. "He'll probably fall asleep on the way home. I would, too, but since I'm driving, I can't."

"I can take you two home and even pick you up and take you to work tomorrow, if you'd like. I wouldn't want you to fall asleep at the wheel."

"No, I'm fine. I'm tired but not that sleepy."

At Northern Frontier's hangar, where the organization's office was located, Josiah parked next to Ella's Jeep at the side of the building. While she and Robbie climbed into her car, he headed into the open hangar since he saw David's SUV inside it.

David emerged from the office and halted when he spied Josiah. "Thanks for the help today."

"I'm glad both situations ended well. I just brought Ella back to pick up her car. She's taking Robbie home right now."

"After you all left the park, Thomas received a report that another boy went missing nearby in a residential area."

"Taken by this Casey Foster?" Anger festered in Josiah. What if he hadn't found Robbie?

"Don't know yet. Thomas promised to let me know. It may turn out to be nothing."

"Let's hope. When he calls, make sure he keeps me informed. Is there going to be a search?"

"Maybe. I won't know until Thomas assesses the situation. If there's reason to believe foul play, the police may use their K-9 unit and not need any extra help."

"I know it's hard to think about this on top of all that's happened, but what about the training on Saturday? That's why I came in here, to see when you and I can meet about it."

"I don't know how effective I would be right now. Let's meet tomorrow morning, say eleven?"

"Sounds good." Weariness finally began to set in as Josiah returned to his truck to drive home.

As he left the airport, his cell rang. When he realized it was Thomas, he pulled to the side of the road to take the call. "David told me there's another boy missing."

"No, he was found, but he ran from a man in a vehicle, who was trying to get him into it. The car had been reported stolen earlier—guess where from? An address a few houses down from where Casey Foster lives. I'm at Foster's house right now. He's not here. I have a BOLO out on him and the car. We'll stake this place out and see if he turns up."

"Have you called Ella yet?"

"No, but I feel like she needs to know Foster hasn't been found."

"I'll swing by her place and tell her. I'd hate for her to hear this over the phone."

"Are you sure? This has been an extralong day for you." There was a hint of curiosity in his friend's voice.

Josiah could imagine the grin on Thomas's face. He and Jesse were longtime friends who knew about his ex-fiancée. Thomas had even tried to fix him up on a date when he had returned to Anchorage. Josiah had declined the offer. "Yes. I want to make sure Robbie is okay."

"Sure. See you at Saturday's training."

If not before hung in the air for a few seconds before Josiah said goodbye and disconnected the call.

Fifteen minutes later he arrived at Ella's house and walked up to her porch with Buddy. If Robbie was still awake, he'd want to see his dog. Before he pushed the doorbell, he steeled himself. He hated telling Ella that the police hadn't found Foster yet, but she needed to know.

When she appeared at the front door, he smiled at the sight of her. She was a beautiful woman who cared about people. And he wanted to know who or what had put that sadness in her eyes.

"Josiah? What brings you by?"

"I heard from Thomas."

"Come in." After she closed the door, she swept her arm toward the living room. "I have a feeling I need to sit down to hear what you have to say."

What was he doing here? Why did he feel he needed to be the one to talk to her? Josiah cleared his throat and proceeded to impart the news concerning the attempt on another boy and the disappearance of Foster.

The color drained from Ella's face. "So he's out there looking for his next victim."

"Everyone is searching for him."

"Then I'll pray the police find him soon before another child is terrorized."

"Where's Robbie?" Josiah sat across from Ella with Buddy at his feet.

"He went right to bed. Fell asleep on the ride home from the airport."

"Good. He needs the rest."

Buddy rose and began growling. Josiah bolted to his feet at the same time Ella did.

She opened her mouth to say something, but a scream reverberated from the back of the house. "It's Robbie."

FOUR

Ella froze at the sound of her son's scream. Josiah and Buddy charged toward the living room doorway. Ella raced after them, overtaking them in the hallway.

"This way." Ella told them, hoping it was only a nightmare caused by today's events.

"Mom! Mom!" Robbie yelled, flying out of his bedroom at the end of the hall.

But the fright on his face belied that hope. He pointed a shaking hand toward his doorway, his eyes wide with fear. "He's...outside my...my window." Robbie swung his attention from her to Josiah then Buddy.

As Ella knelt in front of Robbie and clasped his arms, Josiah said, "I'll take a look outside."

"Use the back door in the kitchen." Ella kept her focus on her son while the sound of Josiah's footsteps faded. "Tell me what happened, honey."

"I woke up. Don't know why. When I sat up, I looked out the window." In the entrance to his bedroom, Robbie lifted his arm and pointed at the closed window at the end of his bed. "I saw..." Robbie began to tremble.

Ella hugged her son as though she could protect him from anything. She wished. "What did you see, honey?"

Robbie hiccupped, then said, "A man staring at me."

Chills flashed through Ella, her heartbeat thumping against her chest like a ticking bomb. "Did you know the man?"

"I don't know. Maybe the guy at the park. It all happened so fast. When I yelled, he ran away."

"Josiah and Buddy will check it out. I see them outside right now." She crossed to the window, watching while Buddy sniffed the ground before she closed the blinds. Her son liked to fall asleep in the summer with the blinds open since he was scared of the dark. From now on, he would have to be satisfied with a night-light. "No one can see you now. You're safe."

Standing in the entrance, Robbie clutched the door frame. "I don't feel safe."

"Tell you what. Why don't you camp out in the living room?"

"By myself?"

Ella pulled the navy blue comforter and pillow off his bed. "There's no way I'm gonna let you have all the fun. I'm camping out, too."

"Can we ask Josiah and Buddy to stay?"

Before today, the question would have been totally rejected. But after everything that had happened, the thought of being alone made her afraid.

Under Robbie's window, Buddy caught a scent and tugged on his leash. Josiah followed him around the side of Ella's house and across the front yard into the street. Buddy headed to the left along the curb past three of Ella's neighbors before his dog stopped and sniffed the road. Buddy stared at Josiah and barked.

He petted Buddy. "It looks like the person left in a car. At least we know he's gone."

He prayed that was the case, but as Josiah walked back to Ella's, his concern for her and Robbie grew. What if it was Foster, and he'd snatched the boy? After what happened earlier today, he would have thought the man would lose himself in the wilderness north of Anchorage rather than stick around and go after one of the kids he'd harassed in the park.

He retrieved his cell phone from his pocket and called Thomas. When his friend came on the line, Josiah said, "I came over to Ella's house to let her know about Foster, and while I was here, Robbie saw a man outside his bedroom window looking in. Buddy and I checked it out and Buddy trailed the scent down the street until it vanished between the third and fourth house to the left of Ella's."

"You think it was Foster and he drove away?"

"Maybe it was Foster. I can't be sure. But how would Foster know where Ella lived?"

"Wish I knew. It could have been someone else, but either way, a man was peeking into Robbie's bedroom. Not good." The controlled anger in Thomas's voice conveyed his concern about the situation. "I'll come out and take a look. Not sure there's much the police can do. I've got everyone out looking for Foster. If he's still in Anchorage, hopefully we'll find him soon. We're notifying the public to be on the lookout. Maybe a citizen will see him and report his location."

Josiah climbed the stairs to Ella's porch. "See you in a while." After disconnecting, he knocked on Ella's door.

When she let him in a minute later, her arms were

full of bedding. "We're camping out in the living room and making sure the blinds are pulled tight. I'm hoping it helps take his mind off the man peeking in the window." She lowered her voice and asked, "Did you find anything?"

He nodded. "I called Thomas. He's on the way."

Ella pressed her lips together, walked into the living room and set the covers on the floor. "I was hoping he was wrong."

"Where's Robbie?"

"The bathroom. He'll be here in a minute."

Josiah quickly told Ella what he and Buddy found, the whole time keeping an eye on the hallway. He didn't want to upset Robbie any more than he already was.

She sighed. "I know Thomas will want to talk to Robbie, but can you explain and show Thomas the window? I don't want Robbie traumatized any more than he already is. My son doesn't know who it was for sure. If he remembers something, I'll call Thomas."

"I'll take care of it. There might not be much he can do, but I wanted Thomas to know about it. When he comes, I'll talk with him out on the porch."

"I've decided it's time we get a dog. Is the offer still good for one of Buddy's puppies?"

"Yes, but it'll be a while before the puppy could be a watchdog."

Ella edged closer, glancing back at the hallway. "Just having a dog in the house would make my son feel safer." Her gaze locked with his. "Me, too."

"Then I'll talk to the breeder and see about arranging a time to see the puppies. Robbie can pick out one, and when the breeder thinks he's ready to come home with you, I can start working with you and Robbie. That is, if you want me to."

A smile spread across her face. "I was hoping you'd say that."

His pulse kicked up a notch. "I said I would, and when I make a promise, I keep it." Josiah caught sight of Robbie coming toward them and turned toward the boy. "I hear you and your mom are going to have a campout in the living room. You could even make a fire in the fireplace and roast marshmallows."

Robbie's eyes grew round. "Mom, can we?"

"Only if Josiah goes out and gets the firewood," she said with a chuckle.

"Will you? We could make s'mores. Isn't that right, Mom?"

"I think I have everything we need."

Josiah remembered having s'mores as a child. He once ate so many he got sick, but that didn't stop him from loving them. "Sounds good to me. Just point me in the right direction."

"On the right side of the house by the garage."

Seconds later the doorbell rang.

"Do you want me to get it?" Josiah watched Ella struggle to contain her concern. He tried to imagine what she was going through. To have a child threatened or hurt had to be a parent's worst nightmare.

"Yes. Robbie and I will be checking to make sure we have enough of everything for the s'mores."

"I'll leave Buddy with you two." Josiah passed the leash to the boy. "You're in charge of him."

"Sure thing. I'll take good care of him. I promise." Robbie petted the top of Buddy's head.

The chimes sounded again.

"I'd better get the door." Josiah walked toward the foyer.

"And we gotta get some wire coat hangers," Robbie said as he and Ella headed to the kitchen.

Josiah waited until they disappeared before he opened the front door. He walked out on the porch to talk with Thomas.

Thomas frowned. "I was beginning to wonder if something else had happened."

"Sorry about that. Ella didn't want Robbie to know you were here. She asked me to talk to you and show you where the guy was."

"But I need to talk with Robbie."

"Can you wait until tomorrow? The kid is pretty shook up, and she's trying to divert his attention from the day's incidents." Josiah descended the steps.

Still on the porch, Thomas nodded. "I understand. I'll take some pictures and check for latent prints on the windowsill. Did Robbie tell you anything about the man?"

"No, he didn't. He might remember something later." Josiah rounded the back of the house and stopped near Robbie's bedroom window. "This is one of those times when I'm glad it's light out till ten-thirty at night."

Thomas took photos of the boot prints in the dirt and then dusted for fingerprints on the ledge. "You didn't touch any of this?"

"No. I think the boot print looks similar in size to the one I followed earlier today in the woods."

Thomas turned toward Josiah. "Let's hope one of these prints on the sill is in the system."

"Will you let me know before you call Ella? If it's

Foster, that means the man discovered where Robbie lives and came after him."

Thomas's forehead wrinkled. "You think he targeted Robbie in the woods?"

"Not exactly, but maybe he's fixated on the boys. After all, they got away from him."

"I'll talk with the parents of the two other boys and alert them, especially if one of these prints ends up being Foster's."

Josiah started for the right side of the house. "Good. I'm going to stay the night. I'd never get any sleep if I left them unprotected."

Thomas grinned. "Does Ella know you're staying?"

Josiah shot him an exasperated look as he bent over and lifted several logs. "Not yet. If I have to, I'll guard them from outside."

"This is the first time I've seen you so invested in a search and rescue case."

"Ella is a friend, and she's alone with an eight-year-old. If you were me, you wouldn't walk away, either." Josiah started for the front of the house.

"No, I wouldn't. I'm glad to see your interest. Since you returned home, you haven't gotten involved in much other than work and volunteering for Northern Frontier. Jesse and I have to practically kidnap you to get you to do anything else."

"Most of my spare time has gone to training Buddy."

Thomas stopped at the bottom of the porch. "Your dog is trained better than most. I think you can relax and enjoy yourself from time to time."

Josiah glanced at his childhood friend. "Look who's talking. When was the last time *you* went out on a date?"

"Okay. I know work has demanded more of my time

lately, so maybe when things settle down you, Jess and I can go camping before winter sets in."

"Sounds good. See you." While Thomas headed for his car, Josiah scanned the neighborhood. Everything appeared peaceful, but as he knew firsthand, that could change in an instant.

He entered Ella's house with the logs, locked the front door and made his way to the fireplace. Robbie, Buddy and Ella came into the living room as he stacked the wood for a fire.

"Do you want me to start it now?" When Josiah peered over his shoulder at Ella, he caught her staring at Robbie kneeling next to Buddy and stroking him.

Her gaze shifted toward Josiah, and a blush tinted her cheeks. "I was telling Robbie in the kitchen about getting a puppy soon."

The boy grinned so big, a gap in his upper teeth showed a missing incisor. "Can we go get it tomorrow? I'm ready. See how good I am with Buddy?"

"I'll have to call the breeder and see what day works for him." Josiah finished setting the logs on the grate, started the fire and stood up.

"Robbie, I know you're excited, but I told you it might be a few days. Besides, I'll be tied up tomorrow at work, then Saturday I'll be working at the training session. All day."

"But, Mom, I *need* a dog."

"You don't need a dog. You want one. And I realize that." She faced Josiah. "So we'll be available anytime after Saturday."

"Okay. I'll let you know what I can arrange." The sight of Robbie's shoulder drooping prompted Josiah to add, "I'll be busy with the training session all day Saturday, too."

Robbie opened his mouth to say something, but Ella interrupted. "No arguing."

The boy pouted. "How did you know I was gonna do that?"

She smiled, her brown eyes sparkling. "Let's just say it's a mom thing."

"Did you have all the ingredients for the s'mores?" Josiah asked. "I can fix the hangers if you want."

"Good. I couldn't find my pliers." She gave him the two wire hangers she held. "We have more than enough supplies, except for hangers. It's getting late, Robbie, so I'll let you fix a couple of s'mores but that's all. We have to go to work early tomorrow."

"Can Buddy—" Robbie glanced at Josiah "—and you stay the night? We're camping out in here. It'll be fun." The boy grinned, but the corners of his mouth quivered as though he was forcing the smile. Trying to be brave.

Josiah could remember he'd done the same thing. Putting on a front for everyone around him when things were wrong. "It's your mother's call." He switched his focus to Ella, whose expression was unreadable.

"Robbie, I think we could use something to drink. Get the milk and three glasses, please."

The boy trudged toward the hallway, his shoulders slumped, his head down. At the doorway, he swiveled toward his mother. "Please, Mom. I know you can take care of me, but you're a girl."

Ella gave her son *the look*.

Robbie hurried away.

"What do you want me to do?" Josiah said when the boy disappeared.

"I…" Her chest rose and fell with a deep inhalation and exhalation.

He closed the space between them and almost clasped her upper arms, but stopped himself and left his hands at his sides. "I think I should stay. I'm not comfortable leaving you alone after what happened at the park and then here today. There's safety in numbers." One corner of his mouth tilted, hoping to coax her into a smile.

"Don't feel obligated to stay. I don't want to be…" She swallowed hard.

"What?" This time he did take one of her hands. "If you're going to say a burden, stop right there."

She grinned. "I was going to say a nuisance. Tonight was probably not connected to the park. I know the Millers down the street were robbed last month. Maybe it was someone casing my house."

"That's not a good thing, either. Let me put it this way. I wouldn't sleep at all if you and Robbie were here by yourselves after this scare." He didn't want to tell her he was pretty sure it was Foster outside Robbie's window. The boot print was too similar. "Do me a favor and let me stay. I need some sleep, especially after last night."

She sighed. "Okay."

"Yippee!" came from the direction of the kitchen.

Ella's cheeks flamed. "Quit eavesdropping, Robbie, and bring the drinks." Then to Josiah, she said, "Sorry about that."

She gently tugged her hand from his, and Josiah instantly missed the contact. He was thankful Robbie entered the living room when he did.

While Ella organized the s'mores production, Josiah

watched her work with Robbie. Ella was a wonderful mother. He and Alex had had good parents who expressed their love all the time. Their deaths had been hard on them, but he'd grown up thinking one day he would have his own family and be a dad like his. Now he didn't know if he could.

His captors hadn't taken just three months away from him, but much more. They'd left him with deep emotional scars he wasn't sure would ever totally heal. Since he'd come home, he'd had only one episode of anxiety when he'd heard a car backfire. Maybe he wasn't the best person to guard Ella and Robbie, but there wasn't anyone else right now.

Early the next morning while Robbie and Josiah slept in the living room, Ella sat at the kitchen table, sipping coffee. She'd opened the blackout blinds in the alcove and stared outside into the backyard, which afforded her a view of her neighbors' homes on each side and behind her. If she got a dog, she would need to fence off the area. Maybe she needed to reconsider. She didn't have a lot of money to spend on something like that.

And yet, having an animal in the house appealed to her. A dog like Buddy would make her feel safer—like an alarm system. After the first two years living here in Anchorage, she should have looked into getting a pet. Robbie had wanted one, but she'd still been worried Keith would find them somehow. And having a pet would make fleeing harder.

Yesterday for a short time, that fear had dominated her as she searched for Robbie. She'd actually been thankful it had been Casey Foster. That meant her ex-husband hadn't discovered their whereabouts.

Thank You, Lord. I don't know what I would have done if Keith had been the one in the woods. It was hard enough fleeing him the first time and giving up my friends and family. At least I have You and Robbie.

"You're an early riser," Josiah said from the doorway into the kitchen.

He'd finger combed his hair, and his clothes were rumpled from staying in the sleeping bag that he kept in the storage container in his truck. But the sight of him soothed any anxiety she felt thinking about her ex-husband.

"Want some coffee? I have a full pot." Ella started to rise.

Josiah waved her down. "I can get it. Do you want a refill?"

She looked at her near-empty mug and nodded. After Josiah poured coffee for them both, he returned the pot to the coffeemaker and settled in the chair across from her.

He peered out the window, his hands cradling his mug. "Five in the morning and it looks like eight or nine anywhere else. I'm still getting used to the long days."

"I thought you were from Alaska."

He took a sip of his coffee. "But I was away for years serving in the Marines and got used to more normal days and nights."

"This winter must have been difficult for you, then. I remember that was the harder adjustment for me than the long days."

"The dark doesn't bother me as much as it being light most of the time." Josiah stared at his coffee, and for a long moment silence descended between them.

His thoughtful look made her wonder if he was

thinking about something in his past. She'd known he'd served in the Marines in combat situations, but he'd never discussed that time in his life. Then again, she wasn't a close friend.

"I appreciate your staying over. I don't think Robbie would have gone to sleep if you hadn't been here. In fact, I'm not sure I would have, either. Then I'd probably be fired when David found me slumped over the computer keyboard at work later today sound asleep."

Josiah lifted his head, his gaze connecting with hers. "I don't think you have to worry. You've got David wrapped around your finger."

For a few seconds his eyes reflected sadness before he masked it. Again she felt a bond with Josiah, and she wasn't sure why. "I hope so. I'm bringing Robbie to work with me today." She drank several swallows of her coffee. "David is a great boss. He's part of the reason I love my job."

"How did you come to work for Northern Frontier?"

"I was working as a waitress at a café not far from the airport. The man who began and oversaw the search and rescue organization was a frequent customer. He'd come in sometimes, exhausted and frazzled. We started talking, and one thing lead to another. He decided he needed an office manager to run the day-to-day operations of Northern Frontier because of its continual growth."

"I understand David took over Northern Frontier not long before I started volunteering."

"Yes. I've been with the organization for over three years and it has grown in the number of searches we're involved in, as well as in reputation." She loved talking about her work because she felt she was assisting people who needed it.

"My sister had read about Northern Frontier, and when she decided to help, she gave me the idea to volunteer with Buddy, as well."

"Alex has been great to work with. She can rearrange her job to help whenever we need her. You, too."

Josiah grinned. "It helps that we own the business we both work for."

The warmth in his smile enveloped her like an embrace. "Robbie loves Outdoor Alaska. We went to the store right before camp started to get some items he needed. I had a tough time getting him to leave."

"It's more than a store. It's a destination if you're interested in the outdoors, hiking, camping or sports related to Alaska."

"Then what's that mini basketball court doing there?"

"Basketball is alive and well in Alaska. It's a sport that can be played indoors or outdoors. Also, the small court is a great place for kids to pass their time while parents are shopping."

"Who came up with the idea?"

"Me. I like basketball, and sometimes it's a great way to let off steam."

"Must be working. I've never seen you angry. Even in the middle of a crisis, you're calm." Contrary to her ex-husband, who flew off the handle at the slightest provocation, to the point she'd been afraid to say or do anything around him.

"Everyone has a breaking point."

Yes, she of all people knew that. Her limit had been when Keith pushed her down the stairs. Unfortunately, it had been a year after that before she and Robbie could escape him safely.

"Mom. Mom, where are you?" Robbie yelled from the living room.

"I'm in the kitchen." She rose and started for the hallway when her son and Buddy appeared at the other end. "I was about ready to fix us breakfast. Are you up for some blueberry pancakes?"

Robbie's furrowed forehead smoothed out. "Yes." He looked beyond Ella. "Can you and Buddy stay for breakfast? Mom makes the bestest pancakes in the whole state."

"How can I say no to that? I love pancakes and blueberries." Josiah moved closer to Ella. "Is that okay with you?"

She shivered from his nearness. "It's the least I can do after all you've done for me and Robbie."

"Yes!" Robbie pumped his fist in the air. He turned and headed toward the living room, saying, "That means you get to stay, Buddy."

"Can Robbie go with me to walk Buddy? It'll give me a chance to check out your neighborhood."

"Sure. That'll give me time to cook breakfast."

While her son and Josiah walked the German shepherd, Ella hurried to her bedroom and changed for work, then returned to start the pancakes. Twenty minutes later, the batter ready, more coffee perking and the orange juice prepared, she made her way toward the porch to see how much longer Robbie and Josiah were going to be. Halfway across the foyer the doorbell rang. Glancing at her watch, she saw it was seven in the morning.

A bit early for visitors, Ella thought as she cautiously peered out the peephole and heaved a sigh of relief. Detective Thomas Caldwell. Then she wondered why he was here so early.

When she swung the door open, she glanced around. "Did you see Josiah and Robbie with Buddy?"

"Yeah, they're heading back here. Josiah got a chance to show me where Buddy lost the scent of the intruder. I thought later I'd check with your neighbors to see if anyone saw a strange car parked there."

She glimpsed Josiah with Robbie and the German shepherd walking across the yard toward the house. "Come in. Would you like to join us for breakfast?"

"Sounds good, but before your son returns, I wanted to let you know about the fingerprints on Robbie's windowsill."

FIVE

Thomas looked over his shoulder at Robbie and Josiah coming up the steps. The detective quickly whispered, "One set of prints isn't in the system, but the other is Foster's."

"So he found out where Robbie lives." Ella clutched the door frame in the foyer.

Her stomach roiled at the confirmation Foster had been watching her son sleeping last night. A sudden thought blindsided her. She whirled around and raced toward her son's bedroom. She yanked the blackout blind up, then examined the window lock. She sagged against the ledge, gripping the sill as she tried to relax. She couldn't. It was locked. But what if it hadn't been?

The sound of footsteps behind her caused her to turn around. She hoped it wasn't Robbie. Josiah stopped a few feet behind her.

"Thomas told you about Foster being outside the window?"

She nodded and stared out the window at the spot where Foster had stood. "Why has this happened?" *On top of all that I've dealt with in the past, now Foster is after Robbie.*

"Thomas told me he'd do everything he could to find this man. Until then, I'd like you to come stay at my family's home."

She faced him again. "I can't—"

He touched his hand to her cheek, setting her heartbeat racing. "All I ask is that you think about it. I know Alex would love to have you. And Robbie will have two dogs to fall in love with. It would just be until Foster is caught."

Tears clogged her throat. She took in his kind expression, full of compassion. She couldn't remember anyone looking at her quite like that. She swallowed several times before saying, "I'll think about it. I still need to make arrangements for someone to care for Robbie while I work."

"Have you taken any vacation time lately?"

She shook her head.

"Then do. Spend time with Robbie at my family estate. When my sister and I are at work, both Sadie and Buddy stay there along with a couple that take care of the place. Harry is an ex-Marine, and his wife, who is the housekeeper, was a police officer."

"A Marine and a police officer? That's quite a combination. And they're caretakers now?"

"Yup. They've been working for my family for twenty-three years. Harry was my hero growing up. Still is. When he retired after twenty years in the US Marines, he married the love of his life, Linda, and they moved to Alaska. I learned so much of what I know about life and the wilderness from him. My parents were busy people, and Harry and Linda basically raised Alex and me."

"Now I understand why you became a Marine."

"He instilled in me a sense of duty to my country."

"How long did you serve?"

Josiah turned away from her and started for the hallway. "Ten years. You have a lot to do today. We better get moving."

What is he not telling me? She knew when someone was shutting down a conversation. She hated secrets. Keith had always kept a lot of them. She didn't want to go down that road with Josiah, also.

After dropping Ella, Robbie and Buddy off at the Northern Frontier hangar at the small airport, Josiah went to his cabin on the grounds of the estate, showered and changed, then headed for work.

"How's Ella doing after yesterday?" Alex asked Josiah when he entered her office at Outdoor Alaska, on the second floor of the main location.

"Foster came to her house and was peeping into Robbie's room last night. Buddy and I stayed the night with them."

"The police haven't found him yet?"

Josiah settled in the chair in front of his sister's large oak desk, which was neat and organized as usual. "No. Thomas came out to the house and looked around last night, then came back this morning. He showed Robbie some photos, and the kid picked Foster out of the lineup."

Alex scowled. "Eight-year-olds shouldn't have to be doing that."

"That's why I'm here. Ella hasn't said yes yet, but I've invited her and Robbie to stay at the estate. I thought they could stay in the main house with you. If not—"

She waved her hand. "Of course they can. It'll be nice to have a child around, and Sadie will love it."

"Yeah, Buddy has taken to Robbie. I'm going to let them have the pick of the litter."

"Where's Buddy now? Sadie missed her playmate last night."

"I left him with Robbie at the hangar. He promised to walk Buddy and play with him."

"But mostly you want Buddy protecting the boy?"

Josiah nodded. "It's hard for me to comprehend people going after children. I also saw that in the war zone. Too many kids being hurt or killed."

"I don't understand how such evil can exist in this world. Look what happened to you. You were tortured and held captive for months in the Middle East. How could God let that happen when you were saving a group of children from a burning building?"

His sister's faith had been shaky after their parents' deaths, but his captivity had caused her to question even more what the Lord's intentions were. He hated that, and nothing he said would change her mind. "At least the children were saved."

"And I'm glad for that, but you shouldn't have had to pay for it like you did." She pushed to her feet. "Let's just agree to disagree about God. He's constantly letting me down."

"But I'm alive and helping others with Buddy." He'd struggled while a prisoner, but his fiancée and his faith had pulled him through. It was hard enough losing Lori and rebuilding his life because of his capture. He was not going to turn away from the Lord, too.

"Will you still be able to go to the Fairbanks store

and meet with the employees and city officials about the expansion on Monday?"

"Yes."

"What about Robbie and Ella?"

"I might take them with me. A change of scenery could be good for both of them."

One of Alex's eyebrows rose. "First you loan Buddy to them, and now you're including them in your life. Is there more going on than simply protecting the child?"

He frowned. "If I'm protecting them, then I need them close by."

"You haven't been apart from Buddy since you got him."

"I don't need him like I did when I first came back to the States."

"But what if you have an anxiety attack or nightmares?"

"I haven't had one in months, and besides, I have other techniques to help me." Having PTSD after his release from captivity had nearly destroyed him until Buddy had come into his life and he'd gotten help for his panic and anxiety attacks.

"Still, it's good to see you forming friendships outside your small circle of close friends."

"Quit worrying about me, big sis."

"I'm only five minutes older than you, little brother," Alex said with a laugh.

The intercom buzzed, and Alex pressed it down. "Your ten o'clock appointment is here."

"I'm leaving." Josiah stood. "See you tonight."

"Let Linda and Harry know if Ella and Robbie come to the estate. You know how they are if they don't have any warning."

At the door, Josiah glanced back. "I'm surrounded by organizational freaks. As soon as I know, they'll be informed."

In the reception area, he passed a young gentleman dressed in a three-piece business suit that mocked Josiah's casual clothing of tan slacks and black polo shirt. Later he would load some equipment into his truck to use at tomorrow's training session, but for now he had reports to write on last month's sale numbers.

As he left his sister's office, he again wondered at the differences between Alex and him. She would fit right in with the man who had an appointment, whereas Josiah would be more comfortable in jeans and a T-shirt, but that would shock his sister. If Alex ever saw how messy he was at the cabin, she would be appalled. On second thought, she probably wouldn't be. They knew each other well—in fact, she was the only person who knew how much his captivity had changed him. He hadn't shared that with anyone but Alex and God, and even his sister didn't know all of it.

Ella finished a chart for the training session tomorrow and printed off the copies she would pass out to the participants. Robbie, Buddy and David were out in the hangar setting up some of the areas concerning search and rescue. She checked the wall clock and noted that it was three-thirty. She almost had everything ready to go, then she could go home, get some rest and—

The phone on her desk rang. She snatched up the receiver. "Northern Frontier Search and Rescue. How can I help you?"

A few seconds' silence, then deep breathing filled the earpiece.

She started to repeat herself when the caller hung up. Ella slowly replaced the phone in its cradle. The second call today. She looked at the caller ID and saw the number was blocked. Since the people who contacted her needed help finding someone, even when she was sure it was a prank call, she stayed on the line in case the person was in trouble.

Was that Foster? If so, why was he calling?

"Mom, what's wrong?" Robbie asked when he came into the office.

"Nothing. Counting down the time until Josiah picks us up."

David appeared in the doorway. "He should be here in an hour with the equipment he's loaning us."

Robbie held on to Buddy's leash. "It's time I take him for a walk. I can do it by myself. I'm only gonna be on the grass near the hangar."

Ella shoved back her chair. "No. I'll come with you. David, I finished the last chart. It's still in the printer. When I get back, I'll put the packets together, and then we should be all ready."

"Great. I want to call it an early evening. Let's pray there aren't any search and rescues tonight or tomorrow." David headed for his office.

"I hope there aren't any the whole weekend. I have some sleep to catch up on." *And how am I going to do that unless I accept Josiah's invitation to stay at his family estate?* He would expect an answer when he came to take her and Robbie home. For the past four years she'd depended only on herself to keep her and Robbie safe. She couldn't tell anyone about her ex-husband. The more people who knew her real past, the greater the risk. The New Life Organization had stressed that to her.

"Mom, Buddy is pacing around. He needs to go outside *bad*." Her son waited by the door that led to the airfield.

"Okay, I'm right behind you."

That was all Robbie needed. He shot out of the office and made a beeline for the patch of grass on the left. At a much more sedate rate Ella followed and gave her son freedom to move in a wide arc with Buddy while she lounged against the building, wondering if it was possible to fall asleep standing up.

Robbie let the dog off the leash to get some exercise. He threw a tennis ball across the grassy area at the side of the hangar to the other end. Buddy barked and raced after it.

Behind Robbie there was a road that was only a few yards from the main street. A black truck, going five or ten miles over the posted speed limit, headed out of the airport. Suddenly the driver swerved the pickup onto the grass, going straight for her son.

"Robbie!" Ella screamed, sprinting as fast as she could toward him. "Run."

Eyes big, Robbie pumped his short legs as fast as she'd ever seen him do. Buddy charged toward the truck, barking. Her son flew into her embrace while Buddy raced after the vehicle.

The driver swerved his pickup back toward the road, the rear tires spinning in the dirt and grass. Even when the black truck bounced onto the pavement, Buddy continued to chase it.

Robbie twisted to watch the German shepherd. "Mom, I can't lose him."

"Cover your ears." Then Ella blew an ear-piercing whistle. "Buddy. Come."

The dog slowed and looked back at her.

"Come!" She shouted the command she'd heard Josiah use with his dog.

Buddy trotted toward her and Robbie. When the animal reached them, her son knelt and buried his face in the black fur on the German shepherd's neck.

Robbie peered up at Ella, tears running down his face. The sight of them confirmed that she would be staying with Josiah and his sister. She needed all the help she could get to keep her son safe.

"Let's go inside."

Her son rose, swiping the back of his hand across his cheeks. "Was that the man from the woods?"

"I couldn't tell. The truck's windows were tinted too dark, and there was no license plate."

"Is…is—" he gulped "—it my—" his chest rose and fell rapidly "—my dad?" The color drained from her son's face, and he continued to breathe fast.

Halfway back to the hangar, Ella stopped and squatted in front of Robbie and clasped his arms. "No. The photo you and the other boys identified looks nothing like your father."

"I'm scared."

So am I. "I won't let anything happen to you. I promise. Josiah has asked us to stay with him and his sister at their house. You remember his twin, Alex. Her dog's name is Sadie. So you'll get to play with two dogs. That should be fun."

He nodded.

Ella fought to suppress her tears. If she broke down, it would upset Robbie. He hated seeing her cry. She'd done enough of that while living with her ex-husband. "I told David earlier that I was going to take at least a week off to spend time with you."

"Can we go camping?"

"Maybe."

"If we leave, the bad man can't get me."

She couldn't tell her son that wasn't always the case. If Keith ever found out where they were, he'd come after them, even though he'd lost his paternal rights because of his criminal activities working for a crime syndicate and his violence against her. "I'll talk with Josiah and the Detective Caldwell to see what's best."

The sound of a vehicle approaching drew Ella's attention. Josiah parked at the side of the hangar. When Robbie saw him climb from the Ford F-150, he snapped the leash on Buddy, then hurried toward Josiah. Ella watched her son run to him, pointing to the area where the black truck had driven off the road.

Even from a distance Ella could feel the anger pouring off the man. As he bridged the distance between them, a frown carved deep lines in his face. A storm greeted her in his blue eyes, but she didn't feel any of the fury was directed at her.

"Robbie, will you let David know I'm here with the supplies?" Josiah asked. "Take Buddy with you."

"Sure."

While her son led the German shepherd toward the hangar, Josiah asked, "Was it Foster?"

"I don't know. Maybe. The license plate was missing from the truck."

"Will you stay with Alex and me?"

"Yes."

"Can you leave now?"

"Right after I put the training session packets together. It shouldn't take me long."

"Good. I'll take you home so you can pack what you'll need. I'll have Robbie help David and me unload the truck while you finish up." He started for the hangar.

"Is this all right with Alex?"

"Are you kidding? She's thrilled to have others in that big old house she lives in."

"You don't live there?"

"I'm out back in the caretaker's cabin. Harry and Linda have a suite of rooms in the main house. They're more like family than employees." As David and Robbie emerged from the office door, Josiah caught her arm to pull her around to face him. "I'll call Thomas while you're packing. He'll want to know about this incident."

Ella nodded. She'd give whatever information she could to the police and pray it would help them find whoever was doing this to her and Robbie.

Later that evening, Josiah sat on the deck at the estate, watching Robbie play with both Buddy and Sadie. The sound of the boy's laughter penetrated the hard shell around Josiah's heart, put there to protect him from further pain after Lori's betrayal. He'd always wanted to be a father but had pushed that dream aside. Having a family meant trusting a woman enough to open up to her. He couldn't do that. If he couldn't give his heart to a woman, how in the world could they ever build a lasting relationship?

When Ella's son finally sank to the thick green grass and stretched out spread eagle, he called Sadie and Buddy to him. One dog lay on his right while the other sat on the left. Robbie stroked each one and stared up at the sky. It was good to see the child lose himself in the moment and forget for a while that someone was after him.

The French doors opened behind him, and he spied Ella coming toward him. Beautiful. Kind. But something was wrong. He could see it in her eyes, even before Robbie had been threatened. Had she been betrayed like him? She never talked about Robbie's father.

He turned his attention back to the boy playing between the dogs. He shouldn't care about Ella's past. But he did care. Why did she always look so sad?

"Well, we're all settled in our rooms." Ella sat in the lounge chair next to him.

"Good. I've decided to stay down the hall, and I want Buddy to sleep in Robbie's room, if that's all right with you."

"I couldn't say no. My son would disown me. He's so attached to Buddy. I need to get him his puppy soon or you'll have a problem when all this is over."

"We can go to the breeder on Tuesday. On Monday I'm driving to Fairbanks to talk with the team at Outdoor Alaska. I hope that you and Robbie will come with me. I'll only have to work a few hours, and then we can spend the rest of the time sightseeing or whatever else you'd like to do."

"Sounds wonderful. Robbie wants to go camping while I'm off. I'm not sure we should."

"If Robbie wants to camp out, we could do it here on the estate. We have woods." Josiah pointed toward the grove of trees along the back and side of his property. "It's not big, but it should give Robbie the sense of camping out in the forest."

"Is it safe?"

"It should be. We live in a gated community and even have private security guards patrolling the area. But the best security will be Buddy and Sadie. Nothing gets by them."

"Thanks. I don't want my son obsessed about the man stalking him. Did you notice on the drive here he didn't say a word?"

Josiah slid his hand over hers on the arm of her chair. "Yes. Young people generally never think anything bad will happen to them, and it is very sobering when that illusion is challenged or broken."

Ella rolled her head and shoulders. "And a challenge for parents to balance letting our children feel safe and really being safe. We want to protect them from every harm that comes their way, but we aren't with them 24/7. I know it was wrong for the boys to leave the camp area, but where were the counselors who were supposed to be keeping an eye on them?"

"It has to be doubly hard being a single parent. What happened to Robbie's father?"

She tensed, withdrawing her hand from his.

She began to rise when Josiah said, "I'm sorry. It's none of my business. I just thought his father might be able to help."

A humorless laugh escaped her lips. "His father is no longer in his life. I'm telling you this so you don't ask about him anymore. It's a subject that distresses my son."

And Ella. Why? It was none of his business, and he usually respected a person's privacy, but he had a hard time letting it go.

"I'm sorry. I didn't mean to upset you."

She took a deep breath and tried to relax in the

lounge chair, but her grasp on its arms indicated the tension still gripping her. "My philosophy is to look forward, not back. I can't change the past so I don't dwell there."

Easier said than done, he thought. He tried not to look backward, but what had happened to him was an intrinsic part of the man he was today. Ella's past was part of her present, too. She didn't have to tell him that Robbie's father was the one who'd hurt her so badly. He curled his hands into tight fists until they ached. Slowly he flexed them and practiced the relaxation techniques his counselor had taught him.

The sound of the French doors opening pulled Josiah's attention toward Thomas coming out on the deck. The fierce expression chiseled into his friend's face meant he was the bearer of bad news.

SIX

Ella saw Thomas heading for her. She straightened in her lounger on the deck at the Witherspoon estate. Not good news.

Thomas grabbed a chair and pulled it over to Ella and Josiah, checking to see where Robbie was.

Her son threw a Frisbee that Buddy caught in midair. "Did you all see that?" he yelled over to them.

"Yeah, both of the dogs love to catch Frisbees," Josiah answered while Thomas settled in his seat next to Ella. "So, Thomas, what happened?"

"A child a year older than Robbie, same hair coloring and height, has been taken by a man that fits Foster's description. A black truck like the one you described was identified near the abduction. We have an Amber Alert out on Seth London."

"Where did Foster get the black truck?" Ella asked, remembering that wasn't the description of the vehicle that his neighbor had reported stolen.

"It was reported stolen. He took the license off it, but we're looking at all black trucks, including those with plates, because we have a report of several license plates missing from a parking lot. We're also immediately investigating any car thefts in case he steals another one. Just like the first car, he probably won't keep the black truck long."

Josiah leaned forward, resting his elbows on his thighs. "What else?"

"We dug into Foster's past and found his record. He went crazy when his girlfriend sent her son to live with her grandparents, and he attacked her. The grandparents moved away from Alaska and disappeared. This month was the anniversary of when that happened."

"Was the child his?" Josiah glanced toward Ella.

Seeing the compassion in Josiah's gaze nearly undid her. Josiah was so different from the type of man Keith was, but then, she'd been fooled by her ex-husband, too.

Numb with all that had happened the past couple of days, Ella averted her head. She didn't want to hear about Foster, and yet she needed to know. The man had come after her son several times and might still try again.

"The girlfriend said no. Foster insisted he was the biological father and should have a say in where the boy lived. I'm joining the manhunt, but wanted you to hear what happened from me."

Finally Ella focused on the conversation. "It sounds as if he's gone crazy again."

"Yes. I'm speculating he saw the boys playing in the woods, and it made him snap. Michael, like Seth, looks similar to Robbie."

After the horror of my marriage, Lord, I don't know if I can do this. Ella lowered her head and twisted her hands in her lap.

"Do you need me to help with the hunt?"

The calm strength in Josiah's question reminded Ella

that she wasn't alone this time. She had people who cared about her.

"We don't have an area narrowed down. Once Seth was taken into the truck, there was no scent for the dogs to follow. I'll let David know if we need Northern Frontier's resources. Right now the police are handling it, but David is on alert."

"I didn't receive a call from him. Did he say the training session tomorrow is still on?" Ella looked toward Josiah, his gaze ensnaring her. "Did he call you, Josiah?"

"No, not yet. I would have said something to you." Josiah's expression softened.

"He told me he's canceling it. He wants everyone ready if there's a need for civilians to search for Seth." Thomas stood.

"But he should have let me know," Ella said. "I usually make the calls when something is cancelled."

Thomas clasped Ella's shoulder and squeezed gently. "He knew I was on my way to talk with you. He wanted me to remind you that you're on vacation and he can handle everything for the next week."

Ella pursed her lips. "There are a lot of people to get in touch with."

"Bree is helping him. I want you to keep your son here. If Foster is fixating on kids like Robbie, he may still try to come after him. Michael and his mother have gone to Nome to visit some relatives." Thomas peered at Josiah. "I'll call with any news."

"I take it Alex knows about the most recent developments." Josiah got to his feet and walked to the railing of the deck.

"She wouldn't let me into the house until I told her."

"Yup, that's my sister. She wants to know what's going on before it happens."

When Thomas left, Ella stood beside Josiah at the railing. "I think if Buddy hadn't been with him, Robbie could have been Seth today."

"I hope someone sees Foster or the truck or something to give the police the break they need, but I am not going to let anything happen to Robbie."

Alex came out on the deck. "Dinner is ready. I would suggest you keep the TV and radio off. The story about Seth is all over the news. Tonight, while Buddy is staying with Robbie, I'm going to let Sadie loose downstairs to prowl. Ella, the alarm system here is top-notch. No one is going to get to Robbie with us around."

"Thanks. It's nice to have friends to turn to for help." Both Josiah and Alex had reassured her that she and Robbie weren't alone. She had to keep reminding herself of that. This wasn't the same as four years ago when she'd fled her husband. When she'd arrived in Alaska, she'd had no friends and a four-year-old to raise by herself.

Ella yelled out, "Robbie, it's time to come in."

Her son stopped before throwing the Frisbee and faced her, a dog on each side of him. "Do I hafta come in? We're having fun."

"Tuesday won't come fast enough. He needs a dog of his own," Ella murmured to Josiah and Alex, then shouted, "Yes. Now. Dinner is ready."

"It's still light out."

She shook her head. "It'll still be light at eleven o'clock when you'll be in bed."

Robbie shrugged his shoulders and plodded toward the steps to the deck with both dogs following closely.

When he arrived in front of Ella, his mouth set in a pout, he said, "We were having so much fun."

"I know, and you'll be able to come out here tomorrow with Buddy and Sadie again, if you want."

"What about the training session? You told me we had to go there early."

"We're not going."

"Why not? You're in charge. David told me you were indi—indispensable."

Ella chewed on her lower lip. She shouldn't have said anything. Robbie didn't need to know about the little boy abducted today. He didn't need to worry. She'd do enough for the both of them. Then she remembered her granny telling her that when she began to worry, she should pray. Give it to God. Easier said than done. "I'm on vacation, remember? David wants me to start right away."

Robbie turned to Josiah. "Are you going?"

"Nope. I'm staying here, too."

A serious expression descended on Robbie's face, his forehead crinkling. "It's because of me and what happened yesterday."

Josiah nodded. "You're my priority and Buddy's."

"Yeah, he and Sadie are great. I can't wait to get my own dog."

"Soon." Ella started for the French doors. "I don't know about you two, but I'm starved. I didn't eat much at lunch."

Robbie peered up at Josiah and fell into step next to him. "That's because she ate while working at her desk."

"I've done that a few times and don't even remember what I ate an hour later. When we sit down for a meal, we should focus on the food and savor it." Josiah cocked a grin. "Or at least that's what my sister keeps telling me."

Robbie giggled. "I don't want a sister, but I'd love to have a brother."

Ella's cheeks flushed with heat. That wasn't going to happen, but at one time she'd wanted three or four children.

"My big sis isn't too bad, but I've always wanted a brother, too."

The laughter in Josiah's voice enticed her to glance toward him. His twinkling blue eyes fixed on her, and he winked.

Her face grew even warmer, and she hurried her pace to walk with Alex toward the dining room. She couldn't deny Josiah's good looks and kindness, but then Keith had been handsome and nice in the beginning. How could she ever let down her guard and trust any man?

Driving toward the Carter Kennels outside Fairbanks on Monday, Josiah took a peek at Robbie in the backseat, looking out the window. Ever since he'd told him he had something special planned for him, Robbie had kept his attention glued to the scenery as though that would tell him where he was going.

"When are we gonna be there? We've been driving *forever*." Robbie turned forward. "I wonder if Buddy is doing okay."

"Robbie, you need to be patient." Ella shot her son a look that said *knock it off*. "That's the third time you've asked in the past forty minutes."

Josiah saw the mountain, at the base of which the kennel was located. "We're almost there."

"Where?"

"A surprise. After sitting around all morning at Outdoor Alaska, I thought we should do something I think you'll love."

"I miss Buddy."

"He needed a rest."

"He slept all night in my bed."

Josiah smiled and sliced a glance at Ella who rolled her eyes. "Yeah, but he was on guard duty."

"But he was snoring last night."

"Trust me, Robbie. You'll enjoy this."

When the large Carter Kennels sign came into view, Ella twisted toward her son. "This is a kennel for sled dogs. They train them here. One of the owners takes part in the Iditarod Race every year."

"Did he ever win?" The excitement in Robbie's voice infused the atmosphere in the truck.

Josiah chuckled. "He is a she, and Carrie has come in fifth and third. She told me next year she'll definitely win."

"I'd like to do something like that one day. I followed it this year."

"Yeah, your mom mentioned that to me when I asked her about coming here." Josiah pulled into the driveway. "Carrie has tours of the kennels in the summer, but she'll have time this afternoon to give us a private tour."

"She will? Yippee!" Robbie shot his arm into the air. "Will I be able to pet the dogs?"

"Carrie will have to let you know that. She's a trainer and has some great mushers." Josiah parked in front of a small black building where Carrie ran her business while the dogs stayed in a building off to the right.

As Carrie came outside, Josiah, Ella and Robbie climbed from the truck. Carrie was a fellow dog lover as well as a good customer of Outdoor Alaska. "It's nice to see you again." He shook the forty-year-old woman's hand.

"It's been a while since the Iditarod. You need to come out here more often. Great place to relax." Carrie turned her attention to Ella, then Robbie. A smile blossomed on her face as she greeted the boy. "You must be Robbie. I've been looking forward to meeting you today. Josiah said something about how much you love dogs and that you're a big fan of the Iditarod."

Eyes big, Robbie nodded his head. "Yes, ma'am. I was at the starting line this year rooting everyone on. One day I'd like to be at the finish line in Nome."

"Maybe you can drive a team one day."

Robbie grinned from ear to ear. "I hope so. I'm getting a puppy soon."

"An Alaskan husky?"

"No, a German shepherd from Buddy, Josiah's dog."

"Let's go meet my huskies." Carrie began walking toward the kennel area.

"I hope to train my dog to do search and rescue." Robbie's voice drifted back to Josiah, who was trailing them with Ella next to him.

His chest swelled listening to the boy's words. He could remember when he was Robbie's age and thought anything was possible. He was going to conquer the world and save everyone. Then real life had intruded, and he grasped that he didn't need to do it on a grand scale but one person at a time. That realization had helped him deal with the past.

"I think I'm going to stand back and let my son enjoy the special time with Carrie. This is a dream come true for him."

"Good. Hopefully, after the past few days, this will take his mind off someone being after him."

Ella shook her head. "All because he reminds Foster of his ex-girlfriend's little boy. What is this world coming to?"

"Someone once told me that when I wake up in the morning, I should tell myself, 'This is the first day of the rest of my life.'" It was a piece of advice from the chaplain who'd visited him while he was recovering from his captivity.

"Has it helped?"

"When I remember to do it. Changing a mindset isn't always easy."

She looked off toward Robbie. "I know what you mean. I had someone suggest to me to start listing every day what I'm thankful for. To focus on what I have, not what I don't have."

"Has it helped?"

"When I remember to do it," she said with a laugh.

Robbie came running back to Ella. "Mom, I get to feed the dogs, then Carrie is going to show me how to hook up a sled. She is gonna let me go out on a sled run."

"How?"

"She says in the summer and fall she does A..." He scrunched his forehead and thought for a few seconds. "ATV training with her dogs when there isn't enough snow for a sled." Robbie rushed back to Carrie.

Ella released a long breath. "I have a feeling my son quoted her word for word."

"It's good to see him smiling so much."

Ella shifted toward Josiah. "All because of you. I can't tell you how much I appreciate your help. It hasn't been easy for me to accept help, but when your son's life is in jeopardy, you do what you have to do to keep him safe."

"You're a terrific mother."

She blushed.

"And Robbie knows it."

"There were moments this weekend when he wanted to do something I had to nix that I wasn't so sure."

"He shook off his disappointment and each time came up with something else to do." Josiah watched Robbie finish feeding the dogs, then walk toward a shed where he knew Carrie kept the dog sledding equipment. "I guess we'd better join them."

The faint red patches on her cheeks began to fade as she walked beside Josiah. "Thank you for showing Robbie some of Buddy's training. That took his mind off the fact that the activities at Northern Frontier were canceled on Saturday. When I told him last Friday he was going to attend with me, he was so excited. He didn't understand why it was called off, and I couldn't lie so I didn't tell him much of anything."

"It's hard trying to keep him protected from what's going on—Robbie's smart. I think he knows something is up."

"Yes, I'm afraid you're right. I want my dull life back."

As he strolled across the compound, he took her hand and peered down at her. "Dull is good." He'd learned excitement wasn't all it was cracked up to be. He'd joined an elite team in the Marines because he'd wanted more action. Once, when he'd been injured and had desk duty for a month, he'd become so restless he'd tried to get the doctor to clear him for active duty early.

When he and Ella were a couple of yards away, Robbie held up a harness. "I get to put this on a dog, then help set up the tug line and gang line."

"Great," she said to her son, then leaned closer to Josiah. "I know what he's going to be doing the rest of the summer. Reading everything he can find on sled dogs."

"Don't be surprised if he becomes the youngest competitor in the race."

For a few seconds Ella blinked as though surprised. All traces of enthusiasm left her expression as she swallowed hard.

"Is something wrong?"

She angled away from him. "No, nothing's wrong, so long as my son is safe."

Strange. Something didn't fit. He started to ask her about what she'd said, but quickly decided it wasn't his concern. Obviously she didn't want to share it with him, and that bothered him.

Ella opened the garage door to the kitchen, so Josiah could carry Robbie, who was sound asleep, into the house. Buddy and Sadie greeted them at the door when they entered.

Positioned at the sink, Linda glanced at them.

"Where's Alex?" Josiah asked as he crossed the room.

"In the den. She came home right before dinner. I can fix you some leftovers if you want."

"Thanks. We ate in Fairbanks not that long ago." Josiah headed for the hallway.

Ella followed him. "Will you carry him upstairs and put him on his bed? I doubt he'll wake up before morning. He's worn out from today." Josiah had gone out of his way to make the outing to Fairbanks special for

Robbie. That was another reason she was attracted to Josiah when she shouldn't be. He cared about her son, and Robbie hung on to every word Josiah said. Robbie's father had never spent any time with his son.

After he placed Robbie in his room, he backed away. "I'm going to let Alex know how my visit to the store went today."

"I'll be down in a little bit. I'm tired but not ready for bed." Ella removed Robbie's tennis shoes while Buddy settled on the floor next to the bed.

She put a light sheet over her son, then smoothed some of his hair from his face. When she did that when he was awake, he'd act as though he was too old to have his mother fuss over him. In a couple of months he would be nine.

What if I have to leave Alaska?

Ella crossed to the window to pull the shades halfway down but stopped and looked out onto the backyard toward the stand of birch and spruce trees at the rear of the property. It was eleven o'clock at night, and the sun was finally setting but would rise before five. At least she didn't have to worry about a man peeking in at her son sleeping here. Chills shivered up her spine as she thought back to Thursday night, when Foster had done just that. She tugged the blinds another several inches down.

She dug her cell phone out of her jeans pocket and checked to see if David or Thomas had left her a message. Nothing. Still no sign of Foster. People headed into the wilderness all the time to disappear from civilization. What would she do if the police never found Foster?

She'd left Georgia because of Keith. She didn't want to leave Alaska because of Foster.

Her son mumbled something she couldn't understand and rolled over on the bed.

"Robbie," she whispered, checking to see if he was awake.

When she saw his eyes were closed, she released her pent-up breath and headed into the hallway. Her stomach rumbled. She'd worked up an appetite after walking along Chena River at the Fairbanks Downtown Market after visiting the Carter Kennels. She'd enjoyed the music, sampling some of the food and the atmosphere. For a while, she'd felt free, as though they hadn't a care in the world, and she and Robbie were spending the day with a wonderful man under normal circumstances.

Now she wasn't even sure if that would ever be possible. After Keith had been put into the Witness Security Program because he'd turned state's evidence against the crime syndicate he'd worked for, she had no idea where he was. She didn't know if he was in a prison or out there somewhere with a new identity.

Robbie and I are totally in Your hands, Lord. She repeated the prayer as she descended the stairs to the first floor. She'd done everything she could to vanish. She followed the New Life Organization's instructions—as though she and Robbie were in WitSec like Keith—and so far it had worked for four years.

As she neared the den, she heard Josiah ask, "What did David have to say?"

"He's calling everyone about meeting to help with the search now that the state police have found the black truck. What are you going to do?"

Ella paused before entering to hear what Josiah

would say to Alex without her around. She didn't want to keep him from doing what he should do. Josiah and Buddy were a great SAR team.

"I'm staying here. My first priority is Ella and Robbie."

"I'm going. You know how I feel about any child that's missing."

"You should. I would go, too, but—"

"Good, because I'm going to be involved," Ella said from the den's entrance.

Josiah looked at Ella. "You can't. What about your son?"

"Robbie will also go. He'll help me at the command center. David will be there, so we'll be fine, but they're going to need all the trained dogs with good handlers if they're going to locate Seth." When Josiah frowned and started to say something, she set her hand on her waist. "And honestly, do you see Foster walking into the command center to take Robbie? We know what the man looks like. With the police crawling around the area, he won't."

Josiah exchanged a glance with Alex. "Okay, but only if David agrees."

She put her other hand on her waist and narrowed her eyes on Josiah. "You're hoping he says no, aren't you?"

He grinned. "Of course. That's why bosses get paid big bucks."

"He volunteers his services just like you."

"But he has the fancy title."

Alex laughed and rose from the couch. "I'm going to let Sadie outside to check the grounds, then I'm off to bed. Four o'clock will be here soon enough."

Ella sat where Alex had been. "So tell me, what have the police found?"

"The black truck used to kidnap Seth was found off Eagle River Road half an hour ago. The area around there is wooded and vast. Although it's going to be dark soon, the K-9 unit is searching the immediate area, but as soon as it's light, they want us in place so we can blanket the vicinity."

"Maybe they'll find Foster and Seth beforehand." Ella shifted to face Josiah at the other end of the couch.

"I hope so, but there are a lot of places to hide, and the Eagle River is nearby. He could try using the water to throw the dogs off."

"Even in July the water is ice-cold."

"There's a chance Foster isn't even there or Seth. But it has to be searched."

"And you need to be there. Robbie and I are going, too. This is why I work for Northern Frontier Search and Rescue. I'm good at running the command center and keeping track of where our volunteers are." She scooted closer to Josiah until they were inches apart. "I'm going, and David can't do anything about it once I'm there."

His blue eyes softened. "Fine. Both Alex and I are dedicated to searching for any child missing, no matter when or where."

Ella wanted to melt under his perusal. "I know. I've seen your dedication."

"Once when we were eleven, a friend went missing. The conditions weren't the best. Only about half the searchers needed arrived. By the time he was found, he'd died. I'll never forget that. That's why I got serious about survival in the wilderness and trained Buddy to be a SAR dog."

"I'm so sorry about your friend."

"The worst part was I couldn't do anything to help him."

The more she got to know Josiah, the more she realized how much integrity he had. But she still felt that he kept a part of himself bottled up and hidden from the world.

She laid her hand over his on the couch. "You were only a kid. Robbie keeps wondering why he can't help search."

His gaze locked with hers, and she felt like she was drowning in those blue depths. "I understand why kids don't join search teams. In Alaska, tragedy can happen quickly. But even knowing the reason doesn't mean it didn't affect me."

The urge to cup the rugged line of his jaw inundated her. She grappled for a subject that would keep her from speculating how it would feel to kiss him. "I wonder how capable Foster is in the backcountry." She relaxed against the cushion, slipping her hand from his. Too dangerous.

"Let's hope he makes a mistake and gets caught."

"That's what I'll be praying for while you all are out searching."

He rose, holding his arm out toward her. "We'd better get some rest. We'll have to leave in less than four hours."

When he pulled her to her feet, she came up close against him. He grasped her, their gazes bound as though ropes held them together. He brushed his fingers through her hair, then cupped her face. He bent toward her, then his mouth claimed hers in a kiss. Suddenly, her legs felt like jelly, so she gripped his arms to keep herself upright.

A series of barks broke them apart as Ella looked toward the door.

"That's Buddy," Josiah said, as he charged from the room.

SEVEN

Could someone have gotten into the house?

Josiah raced for the stairs, taking them two at a time with Ella right behind him. He hit the second-floor landing at a dead run. When he reached Robbie's room and started to open the door, the barking ceased. He slammed into the room, his heart galloping as fast as a polar bear after its prey. Nearly colliding with Robbie a few feet inside, Josiah skidded to a halt.

The boy stood in the center of the room, his arms straight at his sides, a blank expression on his face as he stared into space. Buddy nudged his hand. Nothing. Josiah glanced toward the hallway, not sure what to do.

Ella hurried inside, took one look at her son and relaxed the tensed set of her body. "Occasionally in the past, he has sleepwalked. He used to do it more when he was younger. The doctor thought he'd outgrow it as he got older." She kneaded her neck. "It's been six months since he did it, so I thought he finally had. Usually the age range for sleepwalking in children is between four and eight years old, and he'll be nine in September."

"Then I'm glad Buddy was here. If Robbie had left his room, he could have fallen down the stairs."

"He wanders around his bedroom, and I'd often find him asleep on the floor the next morning." Ella guided Robbie back to the bed and tucked him in. "He doesn't realize he's done it, even when he wakes up in a different place."

Josiah stood with Ella by the door to make sure Robbie didn't get up. She curled her hand around his and took deep breaths.

"I think he's fine."

"If not, Buddy will let us know."

In the hallway she faced Josiah. "You and your sister have done so much for Robbie and me. I can't thank you enough."

"You don't have to thank me. I do it because it's the right thing to do. You can trust me. I won't do anything to hurt you or Robbie."

"I know."

He studied her for a moment. "Do you really? I'm not sure you do."

"Why do you say that? I wouldn't be here if I didn't."

"Someone has hurt you, made you wary. I certainly understand that. I just wanted you to know where I stand."

She pursed her lips and stared at his shirtfront. "I won't deny that I've been hurt. I divorced a man who didn't love or care about his son." She took several steps to her bedroom door. "Good night. I'll see you in a few hours."

Josiah watched her disappear inside the room, closing the door quietly while her body language screamed tension. It was obvious the man didn't love or care about Ella, either. Under different circumstances, he would pursue Ella, but he didn't have any business getting involved with a woman. The last one had left her mark on his heart.

By five in the morning the next day, Ella had signed in most of the searchers at Northern Frontier Search and Rescue. She counted only three left in line.

"Mom, why can't I go out with Josiah? I want to learn all I can about having a SAR dog." Robbie whined as he sat next to her at the check-in table for Seth's searchers.

"Because you'll remain glued to my side the whole time." She took the check-in form from another searcher and gave instructions to the next person.

"But I want to help!"

"You are helping. I wouldn't be here if you weren't with me. You'll be able to search when you're older."

Robbie pouted. "I'm always too young. When I get my puppy, I'm gonna start working with him right away. At least I can do that." He slumped against the canvas back of the chair.

"That's a good plan." Ella took the check-in form from the last searcher. It was two minutes until David would brief the search teams on the situation and objectives.

Ella rose and stretched.

Robbie jumped to his feet. "Can I hang out with Josiah until he leaves?"

She nodded, realizing a good part of the day would be boring for her son. Maybe she shouldn't have come, but that would have meant one less team of handlers and dogs. Like Josiah said last night, this was the right thing to do.

She watched her son hurry to the tent and find Josiah standing next to Buddy. A couple of seconds later, he handed her son his dog's leash, and Robbie grinned from ear to ear.

With a deep sigh, she made her way to the tent, wanting to listen to the briefing but still keep an eye on the check-in table. Two searchers had yet to show up—a husband-and-wife team. She hoped nothing had happened to them. They could use everyone to help the state troopers overseeing the search for Seth.

David signaled for quiet. "I've just been updated. We'll be searching this area." He pointed to area south and west of Eagle River Nature Center, where their staging area was. "A trail from the truck Foster used in the abduction of Seth London headed away from the center toward the south. From the tracks the police have found, there's evidence that Foster went into the backcountry with Seth but the boy didn't come out. A vehicle was reported stolen half an hour ago. They believe, based on the footprints, that Foster took the car. There was no evidence the child was with him. Our job is to search that area and pray we find the child alive."

As David continued to fill the searchers in on what they would do, Ella spotted the couple arriving and walked back to the table to check them in.

"We're sorry. We had a flat tire."

"I'm so glad you are here and safe. David is just finishing up with the group now. Talk to him, and he'll give you the spiel and instructions."

They nodded, then rushed to catch the last part of David's briefing. Ella started back toward the tent pitched near the nature center. Her gaze immediately zeroed in on her son, who hadn't left Josiah's side. In the past days, Robbie had followed Josiah around everywhere. They'd bonded almost overnight, and that scared her. What would happen when Foster was found and they went back to their life without Josiah and Buddy? The thought added a chill to the cool morning air. She zipped up her light parka as though that would warm her. She had a feeling that when Josiah went on with his life, he'd leave a hole in both her life and Robbie's.

Memories of their kiss the night before haunted her again. She'd barely slept because he'd filled her thoughts. She would not fall in love with Josiah. She'd fallen in love with Keith, and her life had become a nightmare not long after the wedding. How could she tell Josiah about her ex-husband?

The searchers began grouping with their team leaders. Josiah knelt in front of Robbie and clasped her son's arm. He said something too quietly for her to hear, but whatever Josiah told Robbie, it turned his frown into a grin.

Robbie hugged Josiah, then gave him Buddy's leash. Josiah rose, and they exchanged high fives. Emotions overflowed her throat. She swallowed hard as Josiah looked around, then caught sight of her. He smiled and waved. Her son had missed out on a male role model. Even when Keith had been around, he hadn't really been a part of Robbie's life. How would she ever be able to make it up to her son for her bad judgment concerning her ex-husband?

"I've noticed you're one of the organizers. Could you answer a few questions?" a woman asked from behind Ella.

When Ella pivoted toward her, she realized a cameraman was standing behind the woman, as well as a photographer snapping pictures as the searchers prepared to leave.

"We just arrived and didn't catch the briefing." The young lady she recognized from a local television station held a microphone up for Ella to reply.

She froze. She always worked way behind the scenes of a search, and usually kept track of any media covering the rescue. Being fixated on Josiah's relationship with her son had caused her to let down her guard.

Ella pointed toward the tent. "You'll want to talk with David Stone. He can answer your questions."

"Thank you." The woman and her cameraman headed for the tent.

But the photographer stayed behind and continued taking pictures. This rescue would generate a lot more media coverage than usual because of the nature of the story. She quickly put some of the searchers between her and the reporters, grabbed Robbie, then headed around the nature center.

She wasn't worried about the TV reporter, because the station wouldn't air anything that didn't contribute to the story, but she would have to stay away from the photographers. For all she knew, her husband could be dead. He'd certainly angered a lot of people, but she wasn't going to take a chance.

Hours ago after being airlifted to one of the sites where a set of tracks, which the authorities thought were Foster's and Seth's, had been discovered, Josiah gave Buddy a long leash. Josiah kept his gaze trained on his surroundings for any footprints to compare with what he'd seen at the start. He prayed to the Lord to guide his steps and help him find the child. He knew of the dangers in the wilderness—bears, moose, freezing water, falling on the rough trail.

The other searchers were behind the handlers with their dogs, covering the ground much more slowly, looking for any signs to help them. To Josiah's left, his sister and Sadie were following Eagle River. He hoped the child hadn't fallen into the ice-cold river or the many creeks feeding into it. From what he'd heard in the briefing, Seth didn't swim well.

Buddy reached one creek crossing that branched out over a large area. Josiah and his dog navigated to the other side by using downed logs and stepping-stones.

Buddy was following Seth's scent from an article of clothing while Sadie was following Foster's. So far the two dogs were going the same direction.

Using an SAR satellite phone, Josiah called in to headquarters. "We've come about three miles from the drop-off site. It looks like Foster and Seth crossed a creek here. We'll pick up their scent on the other side."

"The other teams are calling in, too. So far nothing." Ella's voice sounded strained.

"Is everything all right?"

"Yes, just a media circus here. Thankfully David is the spokesperson."

"I'll check in later."

"Be careful. No sightings of Foster or the car he stole at the parking lot in Girdwood, but the police have confirmed from video feeds that Foster took the vehicle. No sign of Seth in the tapes."

He gritted his teeth, hoping the boy was still alive. "How's Robbie?"

"Asleep right now in the tent. Take care and don't worry. David and Bree are keeping a good eye on us."

"Okay. Bye." As he put his phone into his backpack, visions of them kissing last night appeared in his mind. He was starting to care about her more and more with each day they spent together.

Josiah stepped up to the water. The morning had barely started to warm up. "I'll go first," he said to Alex. "Make sure we can get across."

As he hopped from one rock to another, he slipped and his leg went down into the icy water. He sucked in a deep breath and yanked his foot free. Buddy sat on the other side of the stream, waiting only yards away.

When he reached the other side, Josiah waved to Alex. His sister crossed the creek, learning from his misstep to go another route. As she and Sadie joined him, he said to Buddy, "Search." There weren't too many ways to cross the creek, so he hoped they'd pick up the scent quickly.

His German shepherd sniffed the ground until Josiah finally said, "Looks like Buddy hasn't picked up the scent yet. I'm heading this way."

"I'll go the opposite direction," Alex said.

Josiah only went five yards before Buddy picked up the trail. He gave a loud whistle to indicate that Alex should join him. When she did, Sadie also found Foster's scent.

"What made Foster deviate from the trail?" Josiah looked around at the dense underbrush and forest surrounding the area. "Maybe there was someone he wanted to avoid."

"Whatever the reason, this is the way we go. They're still together."

"This doesn't make sense. Why is Foster even bringing Seth here? This isn't isolated."

"This is pure speculation," Alex said, "but he used to think of his girlfriend's son as his own. What if he's trying to do stuff he would have done with a son?"

For the next hour, he and Alex went along the trail part of the way then off it then back on the path. When the vegetation thickened, Josiah suddenly veered away from Alex.

"Seth is going this way." He glanced back at his sister.

She took several more steps before Sadie dived into the thicket, as though Foster was chasing after Seth. Off the trail Alex and Josiah came together about forty yards into the thick woods, following the course of a creek upstream.

Josiah let Buddy off the leash so he could go faster through the brush. A couple of minutes later, his German shepherd barked, followed by Sadie. Although Foster had been sighted in Girdwood, Josiah removed his gun. As a soldier he'd learned it was better to be prepared rather than surprised.

He forged through the vegetation, spotting a small green tent nestled among the trees. Alex and he exchanged looks. He motioned for her to stay in case Foster had somehow returned. Taking off his backpack, Josiah left it next to Alex and crept forward, always keeping his eyes open for a bear.

When he reached the tent, he didn't go in through the front but uprooted one of the stakes on the side and lifted the tarp. Inside, Josiah saw Seth, who was terrified. The boy's mouth had duct tape over it, and his feet and hands were bound, but he was alive.

"I'm here to rescue you, Seth. Your parents have been worried sick." Buddy barked again and Josiah added,

"That's my dog. He found you. I'm going to come in through the opening and untie you. Okay?"

The child's eyes were still round as saucers, but he nodded and struggled to sit up.

Josiah called out to Alex, "I found Seth alive. Call base and let them know."

Later that evening, Ella entered the den, tired but so glad that Seth was back with his parents, dehydrated but unharmed. "Where's Alex?"

"She went to bed. She has to get up early for a meeting at the store." With feet propped up on the coffee table in front of the navy blue leather couch, he nursed a tall glass of iced tea while watching TV. He turned the sound down and patted the cushion next to him. "Sit. Relax. It's been a long day."

"Alex is okay that you aren't going into work tomorrow?" She sat at the opposite end of the sofa from Josiah. Getting any closer was just too dangerous. She still couldn't get their kiss out of her thoughts.

Josiah chuckled. "She's fine. Besides, I have a long list of suppliers I'll be contacting tomorrow. I often work from here. That's the beauty of my job. I don't always have to go into the office."

"I was hoping the police would have found Foster by now."

"He'll be found. His photo has been plastered all over town, as well as the description of the car he's driving. Roadblocks have been set up, and all ways to leave the area are under surveillance. He took a child. A lot of people are eager to bring him in. You and Robbie will be home in no time."

Home. The house she lived in now was the first place she'd called that since she'd left her childhood home and married Keith. Sometimes she prayed that she could go back to Georgia and see her parents, but that wouldn't be smart. "I hope so. I hate being an imposition on you and Alex."

"I've told you a thousand times. You aren't."

She relaxed against the couch and sighed. "I'm bone tired, but I wouldn't have traded seeing Seth reunited with his parents for anything. The other day I had a taste of what it feels like to have your child missing. A parent's worst nightmare."

"If it wasn't for Buddy and Sadie, I'm not sure he would have been found before his dehydration became serious. The Lord was with us today."

"Foster must be crazy. I can't believe he brought Seth all the way out there and then left him. What if a bear had come upon the child?"

"Thankfully one didn't. Thomas thinks that Foster is falling apart, which will probably cause him to make a mistake. After Thomas talked with Seth, he told me that Foster had wanted to share a camping trip with the child. Foster had kept saying how he'd promised him one, and finally they could go. I think Alex had it right that Foster thought of Seth as the son who was taken away from him."

"What if he goes after another child?"

"That's definitely a possibility. That's why the news is making it clear to parents to watch their children, especially young boys." Josiah angled himself on the couch toward Ella. "When Thomas went through Foster's apartment, they found a closet with walls plastered with pictures of his ex-girlfriend's son."

"When did this happen?"

"Right after they identified him, they went through it from top to bottom, trying to find a lead."

She straightened. "That was days ago. Why didn't you tell me this sooner?"

A tic in his jaw jerked. His hand on the couch fisted.

"What are you not telling me?"

Silence.

"I'm not leaving until you tell me. What are you hiding from me?"

"In my defense, I didn't hear this from Thomas until late Sunday night after you had gone to sleep. Thomas called to give me an update on the investigation and told me then about the closet..." He uncurled his hand then balled it again. "He had taken a few photos of Robbie, and they were posted over the other boy."

Ella heard his words, but it took a moment for their meaning to register in her mind. She bolted to her feet and rotated toward him. "You should have woken me up and told me this right away!"

"Sunday was the first time you'd gotten a good night's rest. You had been functioning on minimal sleep for days."

"Then yesterday."

"There was never a right moment. I wasn't going to dampen our outing to Fairbanks, then the truck Foster had stolen was found."

"I can think of a few." Ella began to pace. "How many pictures? Where were they taken?"

"There were four. Taken at the day camp, and his friends were in them, so they could have been shot because of one of them. Remember Michael is similar to Robbie and Seth in size and coloring."

She stopped and faced him, her arms ramrod straight at her sides. "And yet, Foster came to my house and peeped into Robbie's bedroom. I would say that meant he'd singled out Robbie."

"With all that's been going on with Seth, I didn't want to add to your worry."

"I'm a grown woman who's been on her own for years. I can take care of myself." Had she been lured into a false sense of safety when she of all people should realize no one was ever totally safe? She got up and started pacing, wound too tight to sit and relax.

"You don't always have to do everything by yourself." He rose and blocked her path. "I've learned the hard way there are some things I can't control. In fact, a good part of life is out of my control. But I can control how I react, what I think."

She began to go around Josiah, but suddenly the fight drained out of her. "I know, and I'm working on it, but with all that's happened lately, past fears have a hold on me."

He clasped her hand, threading his fingers through hers. "What fears?"

For a moment she contemplated telling him about Keith, but the words clogged her throat and she couldn't. "One I need to put to rest," she finally murmured, lowering her gaze.

He lifted her chin until she looked in his eyes. "We all have fears we need to put to rest. Easy to say. Hard to do."

What are yours? she wondered. She exhaled and stepped back, her hand slipping from his. "I'm trying not to worry all the time. To give those concerns to the Lord and trust more, but it's a constant battle."

"Faith can be." Josiah took his seat on the couch.

Ella remained standing in front of the fireplace. "Please let me know if you hear something else from

Thomas right away. I'm not as fragile as you think I am."

"On the contrary, I think you're a strong woman. You help others. You're raising a wonderful son by yourself. There are many qualities about you that I admire."

The heat of a blush slowly swept over her face. If he only knew about her past. It had taken her years to get away from Keith. She'd kept thinking things would change, and when she realized they wouldn't, she'd discovered how controlling her ex-husband really was.

Needing to turn the conversation away from her, she searched for a topic. When she spied Josiah yawning, she said, "I can't believe you aren't asleep after the day you've had, hiking for miles, carrying Seth to the helicopter pickup site. Why are you still up?"

"I wanted to watch the news. See if anything has happened."

"Doesn't Thomas keep you updated?"

"When he has the time. I didn't know about the pictures right away."

She sat at the other end of the couch. "Probably not a bad idea. I don't know what I'll do if Foster isn't found soon. I can't keep taking time off, and I need my job."

"We'll deal with that when the time comes."

We'll? Like a couple? The idea struck panic in her but also gave her a sense of comfort. For the first time in years she actually didn't feel alone. She'd purposefully held part of herself back from others, and the thought Josiah could break down all her barriers frightened her.

He leaned forward, picked up the remote and turned up the sound. "I figure they'll lead with Seth's story."

But the anchorman cut to a national story first. Ella slid a gaze toward him and found him watching her.

A smile lifted the corners of his mouth. "Maybe we'll see our pictures on the news. Our fifteen seconds of fame."

"Maybe you. I seem to remember a reporter sticking a microphone in your face when you hopped down from that helicopter."

"Earlier today, there was a happy ending to the kidnapping of Seth London. He's been returned home safely to his parents," the anchorman said, the picture on the television switching from him to one of Seth's parents hugging their child.

Then Mr. London made a statement to the press praising the searchers who found Seth.

A video of Josiah as he climbed down from the helicopter came on, followed by him saying, "My dog is the one who found Seth. I was just tagging along."

Ella smiled. "You're about as comfortable as I am in the limelight."

"I'd rather face a grizzly than a reporter."

She laughed, her earlier tension melting away while David came on the screen and told the reporter about his dedicated search and rescue team members. Then a picture of her with Robbie flashed on the TV with a voice saying, "This is one particularly hardworking member, Ella Jackson, with her son, Robbie."

She heard Josiah chuckling. "And there's your fifteen seconds of fame." But it sounded as if he was talking from the end of a long tunnel, his voice echoing off the concrete walls.

Her face—and Robbie's—was on the evening news. For everyone to see. What if the national news picked up the story? And Keith saw it?

EIGHT

Ella's face turned as pale as her white shirt, and her eyes grew as large as saucers.

Josiah moved closer to her on the couch. "Ella? Are you okay?" He didn't understand what was wrong. He laid his hand on her arm and said, "I know you'd rather work behind the scenes, but you are just as important as the people out searching. I'm so glad you got some recognition for your contribution."

She yanked her arm from his grasp. "I didn't know they took that photo of me and Robbie. They shouldn't have."

The frantic ring to her words worried him. Something else was going on here. "Ella, what's really wrong? This is good publicity for Northern Frontier Search and Rescue. I won't be surprised if donations flood the office after this piece."

Her hands began to tremble, and she hugged herself, tucking her fingers under her arms. "This is *not* good." She shot to her feet. "I've got to leave Anchorage. I can't stay. It's not safe."

She ran for the hallway. Josiah hurried after her and caught up with her in the foyer.

He held both her hands in his, and waited until she made eye contact to say, "Foster is *not* going to get to Robbie. You're safe."

"No. You don't understand."

"Make me understand." He wanted to hold her until she calmed down, but she strained away from him.

"I need to go home and pack. Leave. Right now."

"Why, Ella? What are you afraid of? I promise I will never let Foster hurt your son or you."

She shook her head. "It's not just Foster I'm afraid of." Her eyes widened even more. She snapped her mouth closed, swept around and raced up the staircase.

Josiah went after her, taking the steps two at a time. Inside her bedroom, she swung her suitcase up on the bed and hurried toward the closet. He stood in the doorway, watching her, not sure what he should do.

She was worried the piece about Seth's rescue would be on national TV. Why? Her ex-husband? From the one comment she'd made about him, he hadn't been a good father to Robbie. Was there more?

Suddenly Ella came to a halt between the closet and bed, a blouse and sweater in her hand. Her gaze fell on him as the clothes floated to the floor. Tears glistened in her eyes, full of fear.

Whatever it was, she was terrified.

He covered the distance to her and embraced her, tugging her against him as though he could somehow erase the panic by holding her. He would do anything to take away that sense of alarm, but at the moment he felt helpless as he listened to her cry against his shoulder.

He stroked her back, her sobs breaking down the wall he hid behind. He closed his eyes and sent a prayer for help to the Lord.

When her tears stopped, he loosened his hold enough to lean away to look at her. "Ella." He waited until she focused on him. "Tell me what is wrong. If I can help, I will. Please."

Ella blinked and moved back, swiping at her cheeks. "I'm sorry for that."

"Don't be. We all hit a wall at different times in our life." He, more than most, had realized that the hard way.

"That's exactly how I feel. For years I've held my emotions inside, and suddenly they just needed to be released."

He drew her to a love seat nearby, sat and pulled her down next to him. "Maybe it's time you share all these emotions with someone. I get the feeling you haven't."

"Not for four years." She wanted to tell him her story, but she was afraid. And yet, the words *tell him* bounced around her mind. Could she trust him? She was so tired of going it alone.

"You don't have to say anything, but whatever you tell me I'll keep in confidence. I know what it feels like to need to talk, but something holds you back."

She started to ask him about it but realized this wasn't the time. Taking a cleansing breath, she stared at her laced fingers in her lap and murmured, "My ex-husband can't find me. If he does, he'll kill me." Slowly, unsure of his reaction, she peered into his eyes—full of compassion and something else. Anger?

A nerve twitched in his jaw as he covered her clasped hands with his. "Why do you think that?"

"I'm the one who turned him in to the police for his illegal activities. Once he was in jail, I ran from him, taking Robbie with me. Through the New Life Organization, a group that helps abused women leave their husbands, I was able to divorce him and get complete custody of my son. If it hadn't been for them, I don't know what I would have done."

Although Josiah's expression was fierce, his touch against her hands was gentle. "Did he ever hit you or Robbie?"

"Only me, but he'd come close to hitting Robbie toward the end. I'd tried to leave him a couple of times, and he always found me, dragged me back home. I discovered the first time I ran away that his associates were ruthless and would stop at nothing to get what they wanted. That was how Keith was, too."

"Then how were you able to finally get away from him?"

"I arranged through our maid to give the police information I'd discovered about Keith's criminal activities. She was a lifesaver and the reason I'm a Christian. I don't know what I would have done without Rosa. Everyone else who worked for my husband was terrified of him. God sent her to me when I needed her."

"What happened to her?"

Ella could remember so vividly when she'd said goodbye to Rosa. The emotions of that parting inundated her, and the tears welled up in her throat. "I gave her some money, and she went back to her own country. Originally she was going to come with me, but she was homesick. I miss her so much, but for Robbie's sake, I've cut off all ties to my past, including my parents."

"If you turned your ex-husband into the police, why isn't he in prison? Or was he released?"

"He was charged but never went to trial. I found out

that he had turned the state's evidence against the crime organization he was part of."

"Is he in the witness security program now?"

"No one will tell me for sure, but I know he disappeared. I imagine he is, but he has his own problems. The people he worked for won't hesitate to kill him if they find him. I've scoured the internet for any trace of him and never found anything."

"And now you're afraid he might see that photo of you and know where you are?"

She nodded. "I've always been so careful not to have my picture taken. Nowadays one photo can live on the internet forever. TV networks and newspapers all put their photos and videos up on the internet. Now I don't know what to do."

"You think he's still looking for you?"

"I have to think he is. To ignore that possibility could mean tragedy. When Robbie went missing, my first thought was that Keith had found us and he'd kidnapped him. For a few seconds, I was relieved it was Foster. But he's become a problem in his own right." The thumping of her heart made breathing difficult.

"Foster will be found."

"I'm not so sure. He's been eluding the police for a while now. Don't forget, Alaska is a big state."

Josiah frowned. "True, but it seems as though he's losing all sense of reality. He'll make a mistake soon and get caught. I have to believe that."

"Because the alternative is that there might be two people who want to come after Robbie?"

"We have some dedicated people looking for Foster, and now the public is involved."

"I hope we catch him. I love living here, and I don't want to run again. I'm tired of running."

He pulled her toward him, and slipped his arm around her. She nestled against him. "Your ex-husband has his own problems. If he has powerful people coming after him, then I can't see him coming after you. He'll do what he needs to do to protect himself. Drawing attention to himself could alert the criminals he turned against."

"Keith always put himself first, so you're probably right." She laid her head against his shoulder and savored the moment. Right now this was the safest place for her and Robbie. She needed to practice putting herself in the Lord's hands, because the alternative was living a life of fear.

"You'll see. After Foster is captured, everything will return to normal." His hand rubbed up and down her back.

Normal? She wasn't sure she knew what that was. Her life hadn't been normal for years.

"But one thing I promise you. Your past is safe with me. You don't have to do this alone."

She'd always dreamed of someone saying that to her, but Josiah had his own problems that he kept secret. Even though she'd become a very private person out of necessity, she'd never fall in love with someone hiding part of himself. Not after Keith. She couldn't go through that again.

"I think we need to plan something fun to do after Foster is caught. Any suggestions?"

"I think Robbie would like a camping trip."

"What about you?"

"Whatever Robbie wants, I want. But I have to warn

you. I'm a complete novice. I'm not even sure I can put up a tent."

"We can remedy that. I'll make my business calls tomorrow, and then we'll set a tent up in the backyard. You need to know how and so does Robbie, especially if we do go camping."

"That would be great."

"Okay, now, what would you like to do for yourself?"

"Robbie being happy is something for myself."

"What's your heart's desire?"

The fact that Josiah had even bothered to ask her that stunned her. Not once had Keith or anyone else asked her. She couldn't tell him her heart's desire was to be loved unconditionally. "I'd love to go out to dinner at Celeste's. I'd never be able to afford it, though," she said instead.

"Celeste's. Done. I suspect that isn't really what your heart's desire is, but I can understand your reluctance to reveal the truth." He smiled, a gleam in his eyes that made her feel cherished. "I hope one day you'll be able to tell me. It's hard being alone."

The way he said that last sentence held a wealth of loneliness. She wanted to ask him what had happened, but she swallowed the question and pushed to her feet. "Thank you for your help."

A glint of sadness winked at her as he rose, clasped her upper arms and leaned toward her to kiss her forehead. "Good night."

Too good to be true. Remember how Keith had been such a gentleman until you got married? Like Dr. Jekyll and Mr. Hyde.

She squeezed her eyes shut, the click of the door

closing indicating he was gone from the room. But not from her thoughts—or her heart.

Josiah watched Robbie help Ella put up the tent in his backyard. The sight of them working together was beautiful to see. After hearing about Ella's ex-husband, he admired her even more. But he worried that he had too much baggage to be the right man for her. She needed someone who didn't have occasional panic attacks, who didn't wake up soaked in sweat in the middle of the night from a nightmare, who was afraid to ever give his heart to another.

"Mom, you also forgot to tie the poles together at the top. If you don't, it might collapse on you."

After following her son's instruction, Ella moved back from the tent. "Is this what you mean?"

"Yup. Good job." Robbie crawled inside, then poked his head out as Ella made her way to Josiah. "Are we going to your friend's to pick out a puppy?"

"Yes, but he wants to keep the puppies another week before you can take your choice home."

"Aw, I was hoping he could come home with me."

Ella placed her hands on her waist. "Young man, we are not going to get a puppy until we're back in our own home."

For a few seconds Robbie pouted, then his eyes lit up, and he grinned. "But I can choose today, and he won't be sold to someone else?"

"Yes. He'll hold him until you can take him home." Josiah began disassembling the tent.

"Even if it's weeks?"

"Yes. Now help me pack this tent up so we can go."

"I'm going in to get our lunch. We'll have a picnic out here first. I don't know about you two, but I'm starved."

While Ella strolled toward the deck, Josiah glanced over his shoulder at her. He couldn't stop thinking about Ella's past. How could a man treat his wife like that? What kind of man was he? He thought about the bullies he'd encountered in his life, and anger festered in the pit of his stomach—the same kind he'd endured while held captive.

"Josiah?"

He looked at Robbie. "Yes?"

"Can Buddy go with us? He might want to see his puppies."

"Sure."

"Does your friend have Alaskan huskies, too?"

"No. Only a couple of German shepherds right now. Why?"

"I want to be a musher in the Iditarod Race when I'm old enough."

"Maybe next spring we can see the race end in Nome." Josiah finished stuffing the tent into its bag, spying Ella heading toward them, her arms full with the food hamper, jug and blanket. "Go help your mom while I put this away."

Robbie hopped up and raced toward his mother, taking the jug from her.

"Stay, Buddy," Josiah said.

His dog's ears perked forward, and he remained still while Josiah carried the camping equipment to the storage building. Inside he paused, realizing that in a short time he'd grown accustomed to having Ella and Robbie here. He cared about them—more than he should. It would be quiet when they left.

A bark, then another one, echoed through the air. He poked his head out of the shed and saw Sadie trying to get Buddy to play. But his German shepherd stayed where he was told to. Buddy had been so good for him at a rough time in his life. The puppy would be good for Robbie, too.

"Lunch," Ella said as she spread a blanket over the grass.

Josiah's stomach rumbled, and he hurried from the storage shed. Robbie plopped down on the cover, reaching toward Buddy and scratching him behind his ears.

"Play, Buddy." Josiah sat on the blanket next to the basket.

On the other side of the food hamper, Ella removed the roast-beef sandwiches. "You have to tell him to play?"

"After I give him a working command like stay, saying *play* is my way of telling him he has free time now."

This time when Sadie barked, Buddy ran after her.

Robbie rubbed his hands together. "I can't wait until I teach my dog that."

"It takes a long time and a lot of patience to have a working relationship with a dog, especially if you want one that does search and rescue. The more we work together, the more in tune we are."

"I can do that, too."

After Ella blessed the food, Robbie grabbed a sandwich and began eating. Josiah smiled, watching the boy stuff the food into his mouth and wash it down with gulps of lemonade.

Five minutes later, Robbie jumped up. "I'm gonna play with Sadie and Buddy. I haven't thrown the tennis ball for them today."

Josiah stared at the two dogs and Robbie. "Buddy and Sadie aren't going to know what to do once your son leaves here."

"They've been good for him. Helped take his mind off Foster."

"I was talking with Alex this morning before she left for the store. She suggested camping on one of the islands. She's been wanting to try out some new equipment."

"That sounds great. I haven't gone to any of the islands off Alaska."

"I'm going to check around to see what would be fun and adventurous."

Both of her eyebrows hiked up. "Adventurous?"

"Robbie told me he wants to have an adventure. Hunt animals but not shoot them. He said he has a camera. He wants to take pictures."

"Shooting photographs, not bullets, is fine by me."

"I thought it would be a good time to teach him about being in the wilderness and how to act around the various animals."

"I could learn that, too," she said with a chuckle. "I freaked out when I saw the bear prints in the park. You didn't. I've heard animals can smell fear."

"I'm going to make you into an outdoorswoman before this is over with. That's one of the beautiful things about Alaska. We're the last frontier in the United States." Josiah took a sip of his drink. "Have you talked to David today?"

"No. When I left the search for Seth, he told me he didn't want to hear from me until Sunday. This was my time off. He said he wouldn't answer my call."

"That sounds like him. I haven't heard yet when the postponed training session will be held."

"He wanted to wait and see if Foster is caught. I think he's worried the man will try to take another child." Ella busied herself putting the trash and bag of chips back into the food hamper. "Has Thomas called with an update?"

"Right before I came out here to demonstrate the camping equipment. And before you say anything, I was going to tell you when Robbie wasn't around." He continued when Ella looked at him, "He dumped the car he took in Girdwood and has stolen another one."

"Where?"

"South Anchorage. The police are tightening the noose, so to speak. Watching traffic cams, keeping a close eye out for any missing vehicles. I don't think it will be long before he's caught."

Ella scanned the yard, her gaze zeroing in on the woods at the back of his property. She shivered. "What if he's back there watching us right now?"

"Not possible without Buddy and Sadie knowing. They guard this property well."

"I knew I should have gotten a big dog when we first came to Anchorage. Foster would never have gotten into my backyard that night, but back then I didn't even know if I would be staying."

"No one should have to live in fear." He could remember each day he was a prisoner, wondering if it was his last one. After a while, he'd become numb to the fear.

"I've forgotten what it's like not to be afraid, but over the years the more I've learned to turn it over to the Lord, the better I've been able to handle it...except last night."

Josiah covered her hand on the food hamper handle. "With good reason. We all have moments of vulnerability."

"Robbie doesn't know most of what I told you last night. In fact, very few people do."

"He won't learn it from me. It's not my story to tell."

"What is *your* story, Josiah?"

"Boring and dull."

"Josiah, can we go now?" Robbie shouted as he tossed the tennis ball for Sadie.

"He lasted longer than I thought he would." Ella picked up the blanket and folded it.

"Let's go." Josiah carried the food hamper toward the house, thankful for Robbie's timely interruption.

Ella's son said goodbye to Sadie and ran toward the deck with Buddy at his side. "I'll get his leash."

Josiah set the basket on the kitchen counter for Linda and walked into the hallway. "I need to get my keys. Meet you two at the truck."

As he climbed the stairs, he glimpsed Robbie leading Buddy toward the kitchen. In a short time, he'd come to feel as though Ella and Robbie belonged here. He'd miss them when they returned to their own house.

More than he realized.

"Okay, David, I'll put the training session on my calendar for that Saturday." Josiah reclined in his desk chair in his home office. "Do you want me to tell Ella, or are you going to?"

"I've been avoiding talking to her. Every time I do, she asks a ton of questions about what's going on with

Northern Frontier and when she can return to work." A heavy sigh came through the line. "I'll call her. I think I have an idea how she can work from your house and get most of her duties done, if you're okay with it."

"Sure. She's been talking about work more and more the past few days and keeps checking the news to see if Foster has been found. That sighting yesterday got her excited, but so far nothing has come of it. I'll keep you informed with what's happening with Ella." Josiah hated seeing disappointment on her face. She tried to hide it, especially for Robbie, but he always saw a glimpse when she didn't think anyone was looking. This was wearing her down.

He swiveled his chair around to stare out the window. Gray sheets of rain fell from the sky. It was a dreary day. Most of the time, when he wasn't working, he, Robbie and Ella were outside enjoying the outdoors. The last thing he'd taught them about camping was how to make a fire without the benefit of a lighter or matches. Robbie learned right away. Ella was a whole different story. They would starve if they depended on her to make the fire.

Suddenly his cell phone rang. He saw that it was Thomas and quickly picked it up. "I hope this is good news."

"It's about Foster."

NINE

Robbie sat in front of the window in the den with his face flat up against the glass. "Mom, it's been raining *all* day. When is it gonna stop? Buddy is bored and wants me to throw the ball for him." He spun around and grinned. "I've got an idea. What if I throw the ball down the upstairs hall? It's long and—"

Ella held her hand up. "You will *not* do that, and if you do, you'll be grounded. You think this is boring. Wait until you're by yourself the rest of the day."

He faced the window again and resumed his staring contest with the rainy day.

She wasn't going to admit to Robbie that she was bored, too. The bleak grayness reflected her mood. The rain had been falling for the past twenty-four hours. Josiah had been working a lot in his home office, which she couldn't begrudge him because he'd rearranged his life to protect her and Robbie. But she missed doing activities with him, and even talking with him. Once she'd opened up about Keith, a deluge had begun. She finally had someone to confide in. She'd felt as though she'd been released from a prison of silence.

Robbie glanced at Buddy. "I'm bored, too."

Ella pressed her lips together. All his toys and books were at their house. Maybe Josiah could take them home so Robbie could get some. She started to say something to her son when her cell phone rang.

"Hi, David. Josiah told me you had an incident you and some of the others helped with a couple of days ago. How did it turn out?"

"Two people died in a plane crash not far from Fairbanks. Pilot error. I'm calling to find out if you'd like to work from home next week or take another vacation week. I think we can set up a temporary office at Josiah and Alex's house. There are some funding reports that are due soon, but if I need to, I can explain they'll be a little late."

"No. I can get them done. You can forward calls to the main number here. It can work. I just need to ask Josiah if it's all right."

"It is. I called him a few minutes ago."

"Good." Ella looked over at what Robbie was doing. He was still at his post at the window.

"I'll come over tomorrow afternoon with what you'll need," David told her.

When Ella disconnected the call, she walked over to her son and settled her hand on his shoulder. "Hon, I think we need to get a few of your toys and games from our house. The forecast is for rain through tomorrow, if not longer."

Robbie hugged her. "That would be great! Do you think Josiah would be okay with it?"

Just then, Josiah came into the den and Buddy greeted him. "Yes, I am. We should have done that in the beginning. Especially for days like this when I'm stuck working and the weather isn't cooperating."

Her son punched the air. "Yes!"

Josiah smiled at Robbie. "We'll leave in a minute. Linda told me she needed a cookie taster. Do you want the job?"

"What kind?"

"Chocolate chip."

"I can do it," Robbie said as he raced from the room with Buddy on his heels.

Ella drew in a deep breath. "Nothing beats that smell. I may have to apply to be Linda's taster, too."

"Before you do, I have something to tell you about Foster."

"You talked with Thomas?"

He nodded. "Last night Foster was spotted at Big Lake by a man who tried to stop him. Foster knocked the guy out, then tied him up. By the time the man was found and reported it, Foster had been gone for twelve hours. They suspect he's heading into the backcountry."

"So he somehow made his way from Girdwood to Big Lake unseen by the authorities."

"The vehicle he was last reported driving has been found. They aren't sure what he's driving now."

She hadn't prepared herself enough for the fact that Foster might never be caught. She couldn't stay at the estate forever. Maybe she would have to leave Alaska and the friends she'd made, not because of her ex-husband, but because of Foster. She didn't want to feel like a prisoner again and certainly didn't want it for her son.

"From the encounter at Big Lake, the police now know Foster has altered his appearance, and has sent out an updated sketch as well as possible variations."

"What does he look like now?"

"Here." Josiah gave her his cell phone.

"Blond hair cut short, no beard, glasses." She could remember when she'd changed her appearance to get away from Keith. It had worked. She prayed Foster's new look didn't work as well for him.

"Mom, can we go now?" Robbie entered the den with a half-eaten chocolate-chip cookie in his hand.

Josiah turned toward her son. "Yes. I'm finished for the day. You'll have to show me your stuff."

"Can I bring it all?"

"Robbie! We are not packing up your room to bring here. You get to pick five or six things you want."

"Mom, that isn't much. It'll be hard to decide."

"But I'm confident you'll be able to do it."

Robbie pouted. "I'm glad you are. I'm not."

Josiah clasped his shoulder. "I'll help. Let's go. Linda said dinner would be ready in an hour."

"And she let Robbie have some cookies?"

"Only one," Robbie said and popped the last bit into his mouth. "She told me I could have more later." He headed toward the garage off the kitchen. "Can Buddy come, too?"

Ella followed her son with Josiah a few steps behind her. "Buddy has been with you every waking moment today. Let's give him time to rest." There was no way the dog had been getting his usual amount of sleep.

Fifteen minutes later, Josiah pulled into her driveway. She hadn't been home for over a week. "Remember, no more than six items. We aren't moving into the estate, just visiting. And we don't have a lot of time."

"Yeah. Alex has a date." Josiah climbed from his truck.

Curious, Ella hopped from the cab and hurried after

Josiah. "With who? I didn't know she was dating anyone."

Josiah chuckled. "Neither did I. Honestly, I think this is a business date." While Robbie ran ahead to the porch, he leaned close to Ella and whispered, "Trust me. She isn't serious. She prefers being single."

"I certainly understand that." Ella dug into her purse and withdrew her key, then opened the front door.

Josiah clasped her arm, stopping her from going inside, while Robbie darted across the threshold. "Not all men are like your ex-husband. Alex was happily married for five years."

"I'm glad," Ella responded, then she turned and called out to Robbie, "Wait up."

Josiah moved past Ella and Robbie. "Let me do a quick walk-through first."

Her son scuffed his tennis shoes against the floor while Josiah checked the house. When the sound of Josiah's footsteps returning to the foyer indicated he'd finished, Robbie ran toward the hallway, leading to the bedrooms.

"He's done. I need all my time to make some serious decisions about what I'm gonna take." Passing Josiah, Robbie disappeared around the corner.

"If I don't supervise, he'll manage somehow to bring his whole toy chest. His school backpack is hanging on a peg in the garage." She heard a slamming sound coming from Robbie's room. "Will you get it while I corral my son?"

"Yeah, sure."

Something else thumped to the floor. She hurried to his bedroom. When she stepped into the entrance, he was looking through a drawer and suddenly plucked a

set of action figures out of it then tossed them on the
bed.

"That's one." Robbie went to his closet and started
to open it.

"That's seven action figures. That's seven items,
so…" Something was wrong here. The overhead light
was on. She shifted her attention to the window with the
blackout shade pulled down. She hadn't left it that way.
Quickly she pulled it up. Her gaze widened at the sight
of the window ajar a few inches. "Don't open the closet."

Josiah walked through the living room and dining
room into the kitchen. He paused at the sink window
and looked outside. The rain had let up as they drove
here, but now it was starting to come down hard again.
He continued his trek to the garage and stepped down
into it. Ella's black Jeep Wrangler was parked close to
the door, but on the other side was a white Honda.

The hairs on the back of his neck stood up. He pivoted toward the house. Something solid came down on
his head. He crumpled to the concrete floor.

As Robbie flung his closet door open, he swiveled
around. "Why not? Some of my favorite toys are in
there."

Expecting someone to come charging out, Ella frantically searched for something to use as a weapon. When
no one came out, with Robbie's baseball bat in hand,
she whispered, "Get behind me," then inched forward.

Using the wooden stick, she poked behind the clothes
hanging up. "Robbie, did you open your window and
forget to close it?" She came out of the closet.

His wide gaze riveted to her. He shook his head, the color washing from his face.

"Stay behind me. Someone might be in the house."

"But Josiah checked each room."

He wouldn't have seen the open window because the shade was pulled down. Her shaky hand withdrew her cell phone from her pocket. She found Thomas's number and punched it as she crept down the hall to the bathroom. "Thomas, this is Ella. Josiah brought us to our house to get some toys. I think someone has been here. May still be here." Her whispery voice rasped from her throat.

"Where's Josiah?"

"In the garage." Ella checked behind the shower curtain in the bathroom.

"Get him and get out of there. I'm on my way."

As she hung up, a crashing sound came from the garage reverberating through the house. Josiah! If she could get to her purse on the hallway table, she could get her gun.

"Robbie, lock the bathroom door and don't open it unless it's me or Josiah. Okay?"

Fear filled his face. He nodded.

"You'll be all right. The police are on their way."

She waited a couple of heartbeats until her son clicked the lock in place, then she snuck toward the foyer to get her Glock. One of the first things she'd done after she'd left her husband was learn to shoot a gun to protect herself.

A large man, his back to Josiah, headed for the door into the house. Josiah fought to keep conscious. If he didn't, Robbie would be kidnapped. He didn't want him to be taken prisoner. Flashes of his own captivity swamped him for a few seconds. He shut down his emotions and went into combat mode.

He struggled to his feet, steadying himself while looking around for a weapon. There was nothing within reach. With his head pounding, he moved forward as the large man glanced over his shoulder at him.

Foster spun around and came toward him like the grizzly Robbie had called him. Josiah charged the man, ramming his left shoulder into Foster's chest. He slammed back against the wall, the shuddering sound resonating like a shock wave through the garage. The man wound his arm around Josiah and squeezed. His breath leaving his lungs, he kicked Foster, then kneed him as Josiah wrestled to loosen the arms about his torso. Again he struck Foster with the toe of his boot.

The hulking man shoved away from the wall and drove Josiah into Ella's car, swooshing out what little air remained in his lungs. Trapped between the hood and Foster, Josiah pounded his fists into the man's back, gasping for oxygen. Dizziness sapped what strength he had left.

The sounds of fighting coming from the garage sent Ella's heartbeat racing as she neared the open door. With sweaty hands, she held a baseball bat in one hand and her gun in the other. At the threshold she peered around the door frame while preparing to help Josiah. Foster outweighed him by at least fifty pounds from the pictures she'd seen of the man.

Her heartbeat thudded against her rib cage as she spied Foster pinning Josiah against her car. Crushing him.

She had to do something, but she couldn't shoot Foster. She might hit Josiah, too. Fortifying herself with a deep breath, she laid her gun on the counter nearby and gripped the baseball bat with both hands.

The police are on the way. I can do this.

She crept toward the pair and raised the bat.

Foster looked back, his dark eyes boring into her.

He started to turn toward her.

She brought the bat down on his shoulder. The first blow stunned him, but he kept turning. She swung the bat again, connecting with the side of his head. The hulk teetered for a few seconds, then collapsed to the floor.

She hurried to Josiah. Drawing in deep gulps of air, he slid down the side of the car.

He reached toward Foster and felt for a pulse. "He's alive. You need to call the police."

"I already did. How do you feel?"

"I think he cracked a rib. Robbie had it right. He's like a grizzly bear even without all the facial hair he used to have." With each breath, Josiah winced.

Ella gave him the bat. "Hit him if he moves. I left my gun in the kitchen."

She hurried inside, snatched it from the counter and returned to the garage. The sight of the pain on Josiah's face tore at her. "I'm calling an ambulance."

"No. I've had worse injuries. After the police leave, we'll go to the emergency room, but I'm not leaving you and Robbie until Foster is hauled away." Laying the bat on the floor, he held out his hand. "I'll trade you."

"I know how to shoot," she said as she passed him the gun. "But I'm not going to argue with an injured man."

"Where's Robbie?"

"Locked in the bathroom."

The sight of red lights flashing across the walls prompted Ella to push the button to raise the garage door.

"I'll take care of this. Go check on Robbie." Josiah pushed to his feet using the car as support.

Ella spied Thomas walking up the driveway. She hurried into the house to let Robbie know everything was all right and to make sure he didn't see Foster. The man had already traumatized her son enough.

"Robbie, this is Mom. You can come out now."

The lock clicked, and Robbie swung the door wide and rushed into her arms. "I was so scared. I..." Sobs drowned out the rest of his words.

She hugged him to her. When he quieted, she knelt and clasped his arm. "Honey, the police will take Foster away. We're safe. And so is Josiah. We have no reason to be afraid anymore."

Tears ran down his cheeks unchecked. "I didn't know—" he gasped for air "—what was going on."

"Foster attacked Josiah in the garage. He must have been out there waiting. The important part is that he'll be put away for a long time."

"Where Josiah?"

"He's with the police, but you and I are going to sit in the living room and wait until Foster is hauled away. I'm sure the police will want to talk to both of us."

"Foster wasn't in the house?"

"No, the garage." She didn't want him to know that Foster had parked a car in the garage or that in all likelihood he'd been in their house—maybe for hours. She'd have to deal with that, but she didn't want Robbie to.

"But my window was opened?"

She wouldn't lie to her son, but she would try to play

down the fact he was inside at some time. "Yes. He might have gotten in that way or another way. We'll let the police figure that out. Let's concentrate on the fact he has finally been caught and we can return home."

"I don't want to," Robbie cried out and ran into the bathroom, locking the door.

"Honey, open up please." She tried turning the knob, hoping she was wrong about the lock. She wasn't.

"Go away. I'm safe in here."

Looking up and down the hallway produced no great ideas of how to get her son out of the bathroom. There was a part of her that wanted to hide in there with him. "Please, sweetie. You're safe now. Come out."

Out of the corner of her eye, she glimpsed movement and reacted. Hands fisted, she rotated as though she would stop anyone from getting to her son. When she saw it was Josiah and Thomas, she sank against the door. The trembling started in her fingers and quickly spread throughout her body.

Josiah strode to her and started to pull her to him. "Okay?"

Remembering his ribs, she sidled away. "I'm okay. You aren't. I need to get you to the hospital."

"Not until I know Robbie is all right. Let me talk to him while Thomas interviews you."

"Thanks." She moved away while Josiah knocked on the door.

"Robbie, this is Josiah. Can I come in and talk to you?"

Ella walked toward Thomas at the end of the hall, praying that Robbie would let Josiah in.

Silence ruled for a long moment.

"Robbie, I'll only stay as long as you want." Josiah's voice softened, conveying concern.

Her son unlocked the door and slowly opened it. Ella stepped out of view. She'd wanted to be the one who comforted her child, but if she couldn't, then she thanked the Lord Josiah was here to help Robbie deal with everything.

Thomas touched her elbow, drawing her attention to him. "Let's go in the living room. This whole situation has been tough for Robbie, but also for you, Ella."

She hugged her arms to her chest and followed Thomas. When she sank onto the couch, the police detective sat in a chair across from her. In the distance she heard a siren. "Is that an ambulance for Foster?"

"Yes. While I was in the garage, he regained consciousness but was groggy. Don't worry. A team of police officers will be guarding him until we get him to the jail. He won't get away from us. I promise." Controlled anger hardened his voice. "He won't terrorize you or any other families again."

As her adrenaline subsided, a chill gave her goose bumps from the top of her head to her toes. "I knew something was wrong when I saw Robbie's blackout shade down and his window cracked open. Now that I think about it, the bed was rumpled." She shivered, picturing Foster lying on it, waiting for her son. "What if he'd been in the closet rather than the garage? Josiah had a hard time fighting him off. I can't imagine me trying."

"You stopped him, though, with quick and calm thinking. Why don't you tell me everything from when you arrived at the house?"

Ella peered toward the hallway, then started from the

beginning, but the whole time her thoughts dwelled on Robbie and Josiah in the bathroom.

Robbie sat on the edge of the bathtub while Josiah leaned against the counter across from him, wincing when he moved the wrong way and a stab of pain pierced his chest. The boy stared at the tile floor, his hands gripping the tub edge so tightly his fingertips were red.

"I watched the police take Foster away. He can't hurt you, partner."

Ella's son didn't look up or say a word.

Not sure exactly how to comfort the child, Josiah cleared his throat. He'd had little interaction with kids in the past. He plowed his fingers through his hair, trying to think of something to say that would help Robbie.

"You and your mom are safe now."

The boy lifted his head, his eyes shiny with unshed tears.

"I promise."

"He…he was in my…house." Robbie shuddered.

Josiah squatted in front of the child. "He isn't now and won't be in the future. He'll go to prison for a long time."

"He scared Mom."

"I know, but she's all right. You saw her."

"He scared Mom like my…" Robbie's eyes widened, and he clamped his hand over his mouth.

Dad? Given what Ella had told him about her ex-husband, Robbie had probably been schooled not to say a word about his past. "But you two are all right now. That's what is important."

"But I was so scared. I was a crybaby. I need to be big and strong for Mom."

"There's nothing wrong with being afraid. Fear is an emotion we have to help us deal with certain situations. I've known people who were fearless, and they ended up hurting themselves and others. Fear makes us consider all possible answers to a problem, then hopefully we pick the best solution rather than just reacting."

"Have you ever been afraid?"

"Yes. I was today. I didn't want Foster to hurt you or your mom."

Robbie straightened. "He's a bad man."

"He's done some bad things, and he will pay for that. There are consequences to our actions."

"Like when me and my friends left camp when we weren't supposed to?"

Josiah nodded. "Are you ready to go see your mom now? She's worried about you."

"Yes."

Josiah put his hand on the edge of the counter and struggled to his feet. The sharp pain sliced through his chest. He needed to go to the hospital.

But at least he'd reassured Robbie that he was safe.

TEN

"Mom, is Josiah gonna hafta stay in the hospital tonight?" Robbie looked up from the paper he was drawing on in the waiting room of the emergency room.

"I don't know. We should hear something soon." Ella's gaze strayed to the entrance, as it had so often done in the past hour since Josiah had been taken to see a doctor. The minutes since then had passed agonizingly slowly. He was hurt because of her. She knew how painful a broken or even cracked rib could be.

"How come Alex isn't here?"

"Josiah made me promise not to call her, but if he's admitted, I will."

"You can't break a promise to him."

"Okay, you're right. I'll make sure he calls his sister. She needs to know if he's in the hospital."

"And Buddy."

She smiled. "Yeah, Buddy, too."

Robbie went back to making a picture for Josiah while she kept looking toward the doorway. Worry twisted her stomach into knots.

Ten minutes later, Josiah appeared in the doorway,

looking worn out but relieved. One corner of his mouth lifted. "Ready to get out of here?"

Robbie jumped to his feet, grabbed his work of art and rushed to Josiah. "I made you a picture."

While he looked at the drawing, she bridged the distance between them. "He's been working the past half hour on it."

He tousled her son's hair. "You never told me you could draw like this. Buddy is going to love this."

"I was afraid you'd hafta stay here and you wouldn't get to see Buddy."

"Let me see." Ella stepped next to Josiah. "He wouldn't show me while he was working."

Josiah held a picture of him with Buddy sitting beside him.

"I still have to put in a few more trees. It's a drawing of you at Kincaid Park."

"Tell you what. I'll loan it to you to finish, but I want it back when you're through." Josiah's voice grew huskier as he spoke. "No one has ever made me a gift like that." He swallowed hard. "Let's go. I hate hospitals."

"Me, too." Robbie took Josiah's hand. "I had to visit Mom in the hospital once, and it scared me."

On the other side of Josiah, Ella leaned forward. "Robbie, they fixed me up. Just like they did Josiah. You love visiting Bree at the clinic. Hospitals are just bigger clinics."

Outside Ella stopped. "You two stay here. I'll bring your truck around."

"I can walk—"

She narrowed her gaze on him, halting Josiah's words. "Let me take care of you for once. Keys, please." She held out her palm flat.

"Yes, ma'am." He tossed her the keys to the F-150. "Just remember a man and his truck have a special bond."

She laughed as she left Josiah and Robbie at the entrance to the emergency room. With the capture of Foster, she felt a weight lifted from her shoulders. No more hiding. No more watching over her shoulder.

Twenty minutes later, she drove the truck into the garage at Josiah's estate. She glanced over at him, the side of his head resting against the passenger window, his eyelids half-closed. "Home sweet home."

"Buddy's probably worried. I'll let him know you're okay." Robbie climbed from the backseat and headed for the door into the house.

"Josiah, do you need me to help you inside?"

He perked up. "No, I can make it on my own. They gave me something for the pain, and I believe it's starting to take effect."

"Good. You need rest."

"Will you do me a favor?"

"Yes, of course."

"Don't go home until tomorrow. I think it would be a good thing if Robbie had Buddy with him when he goes back home for the first time after Foster was caught."

"Sure. It's late anyway, and per your request I didn't tell Alex about your being hurt. Before we go inside, tell me what the doctor said about your injuries."

"A couple of bruised ribs and a knot on my head. Time will take care of everything. I'll be fine soon."

"Yeah, you're one tough guy. It's okay to admit it hurts."

"Was Keith the reason you were in the hospital?"

"Oh, no, you don't. Today is about you and your injuries. Not mine. I'm not going to talk about my past right now."

"I respect that." Josiah glanced toward the house. "I think your son is waiting for us to come in."

Sitting next to Robbie, Buddy barked.

"I think your dog needs to make sure you're all right." Ella opened the driver's door, hopped down and started to round the hood to help Josiah whether he wanted it or not. She owed him so much.

But he eased out of the cab before she could get to him, a grimace on his face.

"I think I remember someone I know telling me it's okay to accept help." Ella closed the space between them.

"I'm putting up a brave front for Robbie and Buddy."

"Sure." She walked next to Josiah and watched as he put on a brave front—no doubt for Robbie. She'd done that herself in the past.

At the door, Robbie stepped to the side to let them into the house. "Buddy missed me badly. So did Sadie."

"Let's go upstairs. You need to rest," Ella said to Josiah, proceeding through the kitchen toward the foyer. "Now that you're home, can I tell Alex, Linda and Harry what happened to you?"

"Yes, I can't hide much from Alex. The twin thing."

"Is there really something to that?"

"Yup, at least with me and Alex there is."

Robbie and Buddy followed behind them to the second floor.

At his bedroom door, Josiah turned toward them. "I'm okay. I'm going to bed. I don't need a nurse."

Ella frowned. He didn't see his face each time a certain movement caused him pain.

Josiah's eyes softened. "I'll be fine. Promise." He opened his door and started inside.

"Wait," Robbie said. "You need Buddy tonight. I don't. Foster has been caught." Robbie waved his hand toward the room. "Go, Buddy."

When Buddy didn't follow the command, Josiah ruffled Robbie's hair. "Thanks." Then to his German shepherd, he said, "Come."

When the bedroom door shut, Ella placed her hand on her son's shoulder. "That must have been hard for you."

"Yup, but Buddy is his dog." He stood up taller. "I'm fine. Josiah isn't."

"It's past your bedtime. You need to get your sleep, too. Tomorrow we go back home and get our normal lives back."

"But I don't want to leave."

"You'll get your own dog soon and be busy taking care of him."

Robbie's face brightened. "And training him. When can I go get him?"

"Maybe sometime next week. I'll be in to say goodnight in a few moments."

Ella slipped inside her bedroom and sank onto the bed, the day's events flooding her mind finally. She'd managed to hold them at bay while talking to the police and making sure Josiah was all right, but now the implications of what had occurred earlier deluged her. Her body shook. She hugged herself trying to control the tremors rocking her, but it didn't stop them.

Today could have ended so badly.

Thank You, Lord. Without You, I couldn't have done half the things I've had to do these past four years.

* * *

While watching Robbie play with Buddy and Sadie in the backyard, Ella sipped her coffee on Josiah and Alex's deck. Earlier she'd called David and let him know she was returning to work the next day. He'd already heard from Thomas about what had happened at her house. She was glad she didn't have to go into details. She just wanted to put Foster behind her and move on. Today she'd need to find a place for Robbie to stay while she was at the Northern Frontier office.

The sound of footsteps invaded her thoughts.

Alex sat in the chair next to her. "I really need this coffee. Thanks for putting a note on my bedroom door about Josiah. I should wring his neck for keeping the fact he went to the hospital from me."

"I tried to convince him I should call you. But he wanted you to enjoy yourself since there really wasn't anything you could do."

"Sometimes my brother exasperates me."

"Just sometimes?"

Alex laughed. "He keeps hoping I'll meet another man and marry again. That isn't going to happen. I had a beautiful marriage and five glorious years. I don't see anyone taking my husband's place. He may be gone, but he still lives in my heart."

Ella had wanted that so much and had thought Keith was the man for her. Now she felt the same way Alex did about marrying again, but for the opposite reason. "You don't get lonely?"

"No. I have friends and my business. Those keep me busy. I don't have time for a man. How about you?"

"I have all those things and my son. I have a fulfilling life." But as Ella said that, something was different than before. She hadn't gotten to know Josiah until recently. Even if he could make her forget the nightmare of her marriage, she didn't plan to make the same mistake twice. She hoped Josiah and her could be good friends. He was wonderful for Robbie. But anything beyond that wasn't possible.

"I'm going to miss you two after today. I've enjoyed getting to know you. And I know Josiah has. You've made him laugh and smile more than I've seen in a long time."

"Did something happen to him?" Ella stopped herself from asking anything further. If she ever learned about his past, he should be the one to tell her. She knew little about him other than that he grew up in Alaska. There were too many years unaccounted for before and after he was a US Marine.

"He doesn't talk about it."

"I can understand. The past is the past."

"I like you a lot. I hope one day he'll share his past with you."

Her curiosity was aroused. Just because she'd shared her past completely with him didn't mean he had to do so, but she'd hoped he would trust her enough to confide in her.

"I hope you two aren't conspiring." Josiah, dressed in jeans and a long-sleeved T-shirt, joined them and took the seat on the other side of Ella.

"Yes, because you've been a bad brother. Next time you go to the emergency room, you better call me or have someone else let me know. If you don't, you're going to rue the day you made that decision." Her voice was calm and quiet, yet as Alex sipped her coffee, her gaze drilled into Josiah.

"I tried to tell him yesterday." Ella shot him a look of satisfaction.

"I see. You are ganging up on me. I'm injured. I need your sympathy." A twinkle danced in his eyes as he carefully leaned back in the lounger, his legs stretched out in front of him.

Robbie raced toward the deck with the two dogs close by. "You're up. How are you?"

Josiah threw Ella and Alex an irritated glance. "At least Robbie cares. Yes, I'm okay."

"Great. Then you can come show me some more commands. I'm getting my puppy this week."

"That's good. I'll be out there in a sec."

Robbie ran back to the middle of the yard and flung the Frisbee for Buddy while Josiah struggled out of his lounger. He winced.

"It's okay to admit you're in pain." Ella hated seeing him like that.

"Nope. I'm not letting it get the best of me. Life goes on."

Slowly Josiah made his way toward her son.

"That's his motto. Mind over matter."

"Has he been injured a lot?"

Alex's forehead scrunched. "Yes, but he doesn't talk about it."

Ella watched him interact with Robbie. She and Josiah were similar in a lot of ways—even about keeping secrets.

"Are you sure you don't want me to leave Buddy here tonight?" Josiah sat on Ella's couch with his German shepherd at his feet later that evening.

She settled next to Josiah. "Robbie slept without him

last night at your house. He should be okay. We're going after work on Wednesday to get the puppy he picked out."

"Does he have a name for him yet?"

"Sam."

"Where did that name come from?"

"He didn't know. It just popped into his head when he saw him at the breeder's house last week."

"Is everything set for you going back to work tomorrow?"

"Yes. My neighbor will watch him for me. I loved staying at your place and we both know Robbie did, but it feels good to be home and back to my normal life."

"The vacation is over," Josiah said with a chuckle.

"If the past week was a vacation, I never want to go on another one. Loved the company but not the reason for being there."

Josiah sobered. "Yeah, a normal life is good, but I still owe Robbie a camping trip."

"That would be nice. Now, that would be a real vacation without a lunatic coming after us."

"That's what I was thinking. I already have one of the islands picked out."

She clasped his hand and cupped it between hers. "You don't have to. Robbie and I have taken up too much of your time." She needed to put some distance between them before she fell in love with him. *I have to listen to my head, not my heart.*

"First, I want to. Second, I promised Robbie and third, I enjoy camping and sharing the experience with others. I've even persuaded Alex to take some time off from work, which is a feat in itself, to join us."

Ella rubbed her fingers across the back of his hand. "What about your injuries?"

"We'll wait until they're better. Thankfully my threshold for pain is high."

"I'm just glad you were here when Foster decided to hide out in my house." She refused to think what would have happened if he hadn't been there.

"So is Thomas. He called today to tell me we've made his life a little easier with the capture of Foster."

"It's always nice to accommodate the police. Although I can't believe Foster had the nerve to use my home as a hideout."

"He figured you weren't coming back as long as he was loose."

"How do you know that?"

"He told Thomas." Josiah rose slowly and carefully. "I'd better go. You have to get up early. You've been a woman of leisure for the past week, and it may take you a while to get used to your work routine again. Do you have someone to watch Robbie beyond tomorrow?"

"Yes, my neighbor insisted she would since she and her husband are back from their three-week trek through Alaska. Both of my neighbors on each side have been a good support system for me."

"Good." He headed for the front door.

Ella went out on the porch with him as the sun was starting to go down. "Thank you again for your help. With everything."

He turned toward her, a smile dimpling his cheeks. "My pleasure. We'll talk before you go to pick up Sam. I'd like to go with you." He inched closer.

"I'd like that." She tilted up her chin, so close to Josiah she could smell mint on his breath. She lifted her hand and cradled his cheek, wanting him to kiss her and yet hesitating to make the first move.

He bent toward her, his lips softly capturing hers. Then he pulled back. "I'd better leave."

No, don't. But she wouldn't say it out loud because he was right. It was better that he left now. She didn't know what to do about the feelings swirling around in her head concerning Josiah. She needed some space between them until she figured out how to be a friend and nothing more.

"Yes, you're right. Talk to you this week."

She waited on the porch until he drove away, thinking back to all that had occurred recently. Josiah had always been there in the center of the action. In that short time she'd become dependent on him. She'd vowed she would never feel that way about a man again. She wasn't a risk taker, although everything in her shouted that Josiah wasn't a risk.

She shook her head, trying to empty her thoughts of him. But she wasn't successful.

With a deep sigh, she pushed open the front door.

To find her son standing in the foyer looking into the living room, fear on his face.

He whirled around and flew at her. "I thought you'd left me alone or something."

"No, honey. I was saying goodbye to Josiah on the porch. Is something wrong?"

"I can't sleep. I tried really hard, Mom." His eyes filled with tears, and he bit his lower lip.

"That's okay. Sometimes it takes a while to fall asleep."

A tear ran down his face. "I'm scared. What if Foster escapes from jail?"

She smoothed his hair off his forehead. "He won't."

"He was in my bedroom."

"We don't know that for sure." Although she thought he had been, she didn't want to confirm it for Robbie.

"He must have opened my window. I didn't. You didn't."

"Well, he can't now. He has police officers guarding him, and he's behind bars."

"I miss Buddy. He made me feel safe."

"He wasn't with you last night."

"That's because Josiah needed him more, and I felt safe at his house."

"You love this house, and your room."

"I want to move to the other bedroom."

"It's smaller."

"I don't care. That man ruined my room for me."

Sadness enveloped Ella, and she wished she could turn back time. *Lord, please help Robbie. He shouldn't have to feel this fear at his age.*

"Will you sit with me while I fall asleep?"

"Of course."

He hugged her. "You're the best."

A few minutes later, Ella sat against the headboard in Robbie's room with her son cuddled up against her. For the first half hour, his eyes kept popping open to check she was still there. Then the next thirty minutes, they stayed closed, but her son twisted and turned. By the second hour, he finally calmed, and soon he fell asleep.

But Ella was wide-awake with no hope of going to bed anytime soon. Darkness shrouded her, and if it wouldn't have awakened her son, she would have turned on a light. She didn't want to take that chance. Like her son, she'd slept well at Josiah's. Now every sound outside spiked her heartbeat. Even staring at the window, she imagined Foster crawling through it and snatching Robbie from her arms.

With thoughts of Keith, it had taken her over a year in Anchorage before she'd gotten a good night's sleep. She was determined Foster wouldn't invade her peace— her son's. She searched her mind for something to think about that brought a feeling of safety, calm.

Josiah.

No doubt about it. She'd never met someone quite like him. She could talk to him about things she didn't with others. That still amazed her.

But a big part of his life was a mystery to her. He held a large part of himself back. She could never allow her heart to become involved. Could she?

Josiah sat at his desk in his home office. "I'll bring Buddy over this evening. He can stay the next two nights until you take Sam home. Do you think that will help Robbie sleep?"

"Thank you, Josiah. Are you sure?"

Hearing the relief in Ella's voice confirmed his decision, even though he'd awakened last night in a cold sweat. "Yes. It's only for a couple of nights. I'll be fine. Remember, you two had Buddy before." If he wasn't, he'd deal with it. He didn't want Robbie becoming so scared he couldn't sleep.

"You're a lifesaver, and I know Robbie will be thrilled. At least let me treat you to a dinner. I hope you'll be able to stay when you drop Buddy off."

"I'll make time in my busy schedule," Josiah said with a chuckle. "Since the doctor told me to rest and take it easy for two or three days, I've been working from home."

"Good thing you have an understanding boss. See you later."

After he hung up, Josiah leaned back in his chair and stared out the window at his backyard. Serene. Peaceful. And yet inside, he couldn't shake the memories of Foster's heavy weight pressing down on him, squeezing all the air from his lungs. The sensation of not being able to breathe had thrown him back to his time as a POW. The past two nights, his nightmares had returned, and Buddy had been there to wake him from the horrors he relived.

A tightness in his chest that had nothing to do with his bruised ribs spread. Before he could call Buddy, his German shepherd was in front of him, nudging his hand. Taking breaths as deep as was possible, he stroked his dog, thinking of his present life. Ella. Robbie. Slowly his panic subsided.

But would it tonight, without Buddy?

ELEVEN

Thursday evening, Ella inhaled a deep breath of the outdoorsy scent of the Russian Jack Springs Park. "It was a good idea to walk Buddy and Sam together. Sam is already responding to Buddy, and he's a great role model for our puppy."

"How was your first night with Sam?" Josiah walked beside her on the trail while Robbie held both leashes.

"Robbie insisted on Sam sleeping in his bed, and somehow there wasn't one accident—at least last night."

"So Robbie slept all right without Buddy?"

"Yes and thanks for the use of Buddy for a couple of nights." She slanted her head and assessed Josiah. He didn't look as tired today. Yesterday she'd wondered if he'd been getting the rest the doctor recommended. "How have you been sleeping with the bruised ribs?"

"When the doc told me to sleep on the side that's bruised, I thought he was crazy. But believe it or not, it actually is much better."

He didn't exactly answer her question, so she said, "I'm glad you're getting the rest he said would help you get better, because my son has already started bugging me about the camping trip."

"I'm adjusting, and over-the-counter pain meds are all I have to take now. I think we could look at the first weekend in August. That's only a couple of weeks away. I know how it is when you're a child and want to do something badly, but Sam should take his focus away. I'll come over after work and help him with the puppy."

"That'll be great. I appreciate it, and so does Robbie. You and Buddy are all he talks about." But what would happen to Josiah and Robbie's relationship if another woman entered his life? He deserved to be married and be a father. He was fantastic with her son.

"Is he going to be at the training session this weekend or staying with your neighbor?"

"He wants to be at the session, but this Saturday is all business for Northern Frontier. Now that it's safe, I need to focus on my job or David might fire me."

Josiah tossed his head back and laughed. "Are you kidding? He knows a great office manager when he sees one. You should hear him rave about you."

A blush heated her cheeks. "Enough, or I might get a big head and grow right out of my ball cap."

Josiah stopped on the path while Robbie let the dogs sniff a tree off the trail. "That's just it. You don't realize how good you are. Efficient. Caring. More organized than most people. Great with people. You remind me a lot of my sister."

She was growing uncomfortable with all his compliments and needed to change the subject fast. "Is she able to come camping with us?"

"Yes, I'm sure."

"Good, because I like her a lot, and it'll give us more time to get to know each other."

"She's looking forward to it. Our love of camping

as children is the reason we didn't sell Outdoor Alaska when our parents died. So it'll be good to get back to our roots. This camping trip will help us to see what new products work or don't."

"So this is a business trip?" The corners of her mouth twitched with the grin she was trying to contain.

"Not really. Not even for Alex. As much as she's a workaholic, she still sees the value in taking some time off."

"But you're not a workaholic?"

"Not like Alex. She's a diehard."

"I'm glad you aren't. There's more to life than just work."

"Believe me. I discovered that the hard…" His voice faded into silence. "We better catch up with Robbie. Sometimes it's hard to control two dogs at the same time."

Frustrated, she chewed on her bottom lip. She wanted to shout at Josiah, *Let me in!* Finally she stopped and blocked him on the path. "Why didn't you finish what you were saying?"

"Because I don't share my life with anyone. Some things are best left in the past." He skirted around her and increased his pace to catch up with Robbie.

At that moment, she realized he'd never really share his life with her. If it weren't for Robbie, she would put some distance between her and Josiah right away before she became even more invested in him. But it would break her son's heart. He'd never had a good male role model, and Josiah was quickly taking that position in Robbie's life.

That realization made her decide that after the camping trip she would have to find other role models for her son. Maybe through the Big Brothers program. She was afraid when Josiah moved on in his life, it would devastate Robbie.

"Mom, what's keeping you? I want to play on the playground before we leave."

There was no easy solution to her dilemma concerning Josiah and Robbie. She exhaled slowly. "I'm coming."

Ella came into the kitchen from her backyard and noticed Robbie hanging the phone up. "Who was that?"

He shrugged. "Wrong number, I guess."

"Josiah will be here soon. After Sam's training, we're going to Outdoor Alaska to get the camping equipment we need, so remember not to get dirty."

"Hurray! We leave in two days, and I need to practice putting up our tent."

"Only when I'm watching." She couldn't afford to buy a second tent if he ruined the first one.

"Sure, Mom. I wish you'd quit babying me. I know what I'm doing. Josiah taught me, remember?"

"True, but that was a couple of weeks ago." She'd tried to stay away from Josiah as much as possible when he came to help Robbie, but it wasn't easy when she saw him being more of a father than Keith had ever been.

"Mom, why can't Sam go with us?"

"We aren't taking the dogs. Linda and Harry will watch Sam. He'll have fun with Buddy and Sadie. I don't want to have to worry about your puppy when what we're doing is new to us."

"We're gonna be on an island. Sam couldn't go too far without meeting the Gulf of Alaska."

"What if we run into a bear? Do you want to worry about Sam doing something to get himself hurt?"

"Bears? I hadn't thought of that. Are there going to be many?"

"It's Alaska. The possibility of a bear encounter is part of living here. Remember that time the moose came down into our yard during the winter and ate our bushes? We live in a big city. That didn't stop the moose."

Robbie giggled. "I doubt much could stop a moose or a bear."

"It would take a lot. That's why you never confront one."

The doorbell chimes resonated through the house.

"That's Josiah. I'll get it," Robbie said as he rushed from the kitchen.

"Check before you open the door," she called after her son, but she doubted he heard her because two seconds later he admitted Josiah into the house, then began telling him about his day.

Ella smiled. Poor Josiah. Sometimes he couldn't get two words in.

When Josiah entered the kitchen with Robbie, he smiled at her, which sent goose bumps up and down her arms. "How was your day?"

"Fine. Just wrapping up the information about the search and rescue of a tourist in Katmai National Park."

"From what I heard, you all did good yesterday."

Robbie looked at Josiah. "Why didn't you go with Buddy?"

"The area where the tourist disappeared has a lot of bears. In the summer they are all over Brooks Camp and the surrounding area. Dogs and bears don't mix, and they prefer that K-9s not be used in the search, at least initially. The personnel working SAR missions will vary depending on where the person went missing and who the person is."

"Sam and I are ready." Robbie started for the kitchen door.

"Good. I'll be out back in a second." When her son left, Josiah moved to her. "Are we still on for the camping trip this weekend? I know Northern Frontier has been extra busy lately."

"That's normal for a summer with so many tourists around. Robbie is counting down the hours until we leave. David has insisted I go and not to worry about Northern Frontier. There are a lot of people who can step in temporarily. Do you still want to go?" Most of the searches were outside of Anchorage, and when that happened, she manned the phones at the office, coordinating and supporting David and the searchers. With her gone a lot because of her job, she hadn't seen Josiah as much as Robbie had. Josiah had ended up helping Robbie with the puppy at her neighbor's a few times.

Josiah stared out the window at her son playing with Sam. "Most definitely. Robbie is like a sponge. So eager to learn everything. His enthusiasm is contagious. It's good to be around him."

"Then it's still a go. Friday we leave."

Josiah went out to the backyard to start the puppy training. She stood at the sink and watched him and Robbie training Sam to obey simple commands. Her heart swelled at the sight. Robbie should have a father who cared about him.

Toward the end of the lesson, Ella went outside to

remind them they still needed to go shopping at Outdoor Alaska.

As Josiah wrapped things up, he caught sight of Ella on the patio and waved. He'd tried to stay away from her after Foster's capture, but he kept being drawn back to her. And Robbie. The boy reminded him of how he'd been growing up. Eager to learn. Curious about everything. Robbie loved Alaska as much as he did. It was one big outdoor park with so much to offer.

"Are you guys ready to leave?" Ella asked as she crossed the yard to them.

"Yes. I can't wait to get my own tent." Robbie grinned from ear to ear, excitement bubbling out of him.

Josiah needed that. To find the joy in life that had been beaten out of him. To truly reconnect with God. "Let's take my truck. Your gear will easily fit in the back."

Rush-hour traffic had subsided, and he drove to the main store in less than fifteen minutes. The moment he entered, an employee approached to help them.

Josiah waved the man away. "Thanks, but I'll take care of this. I know where everything is." He'd been spending more time in the corporate offices and had lost touch with some of the day-to-day activities of the stores. Maybe he needed to become more involved.

"First we need to pick out a tent."

Robbie immediately went to an orange, brown and white dome tent. "I like this one."

Josiah smiled. "That's a good choice. Big enough for up to four people but not too big."

Ella's son beamed. "What's next?"

An hour later, Josiah pushed a cart toward the front

while Ella had a second one. He got in line behind a woman with two kids. A large man, similar in build to Foster, came up behind Ella.

With Robbie next to him, Josiah put his hand on his shoulder. The boy had said little about Foster since the day they'd talked in the bathroom, but from the nightmares he'd had at first, Robbie still needed to talk about it. He, of all people, knew that took time. He wanted to be there for the boy when he did.

When Robbie glanced back at Ella, he stiffened.

Josiah squeezed his shoulder gently. "All right?"

"For a second I thought that man was Foster. He isn't." The child took a deep breath. "I'm okay."

"If you ever need to talk, I'm here."

Robbie slanted a look up at Josiah. "Thanks."

"Remember the other day I gave you my cell phone number in case something happens to Sam or you're having a problem with him? Well, you can use it for yourself, too."

The bright light returned to the boy's eyes. He thrust out his chest and moved up to the clerk to check out.

After the woman rang up the merchandise, he started to pay for the purchases, but Ella quickly moved forward and handed the woman her credit card.

"I wanted to do this for you and Robbie."

"No way. I appreciate the thought, but I'm taking care of it."

"At least let me use my employee discount."

She peered at him for a few seconds, and he wasn't sure if she would even accept that, but then she nodded. He gave the clerk his employee discount information.

When the woman realized who he was, she blushed.

"I didn't realize you were Josiah Witherspoon. So sorry, sir." She hurried to finish the transaction.

As they were leaving, Josiah paused and looked at her nametag. "Pam, thank you for doing such a good job."

As he left the store, pushing one of the carts full of items, he said to Ella, "I need to become more involved with my employees. Make sure they feel important. We're growing, and I don't know the new people working for me like I should."

"How many are there?"

"Three hundred and two."

"That's a lot of faces."

"I know their names on paper, but I've only dealt with the employee representatives."

Ella started unloading her cart and putting the supplies in the back of the truck. "You could always do what David does and have a big shindig once a year."

"Yeah, I love that picnic. The softball game is so much fun." Robbie tossed the ground cloth into the pickup's bed.

"It's a good suggestion, and one of the many parks in Anchorage would be a great place to host it."

The idea of having an annual celebration at the end of the summer season felt right. Since returning to Alaska, he'd held himself back from connecting with others, only stepping out of his comfort zone to help with Northern Frontier Search and Rescue, and even then, he often searched with just Buddy.

It was time to reconnect with the world again.

Ella stared out the window of David's plane at the forest-covered island with mountains jutting up in the middle of it. It was green everywhere she looked. Beautiful. Although she hadn't camped since she was a child, she was getting excited about it.

"We're gonna stay here?" Robbie asked Josiah, her son's eyes big as he took in the eastern shore. "Do people live here?"

"Some. Not many. Hunters and visitors come in the summer, though, so we may run into a few people. But essentially, we're bringing in what we need and will take it back out, even our trash."

David landed on the water of the gulf and steered the floatplane to shore. "I'm going to be back here on Sunday evening to take you all home. Six o'clock. Have fun."

"Yippee, we've got two and a half days of camping." Robbie pumped his fist into the air while Alex exited the seaplane, then Josiah.

Her son hopped down, splashing in the few inches of water David landed in. Robbie hurried toward Josiah.

"Are you ready for this?" David asked with a laugh.

"I'm relying on the others to know what to do. Robbie needs this time away, and I'm glad we know people who have camped a lot. See you on Sunday evening, and thanks for dropping us off." Ella climbed out of the airplane as Josiah came back, minus his gear, to get the rest from the back of the plane.

Josiah placed his arms under her and carried her toward shore. "No sense in your boots getting wet. There'll be enough times when we cross a stream."

"Is that why you told me to bring more than three pairs of socks?"

"Smart woman." He set her on the small beach, then returned to the plane to grab the inflatable boat packed in a duffel bag. When Josiah had retrieved all their provisions, he waved to David. "Last chance to go back to civilization." Josiah planted himself next to her and watched as their friend took off.

"Is that what the boat is for? If we have an emergency, we can leave by paddling to the mainland." Ella pointed to the left and in the distance, only miles away, she saw the outline of the Alaskan coast.

"I'm stashing the boat bag in the bushes. Since this isn't Grand Central Station, I don't think a thief will be walking around and stumble upon it, but I like to be prepared for emergencies."

"We could have brought one of David's SAR satellite phones."

Josiah leaned close and placed his forefinger over his mouth. "Shh. I didn't want Alex getting distracted with business. This is for her as much as Robbie. Besides, if someone goes missing, David would need the few he has for a search and rescue operation." He dragged the duffel bag to the thick brush at the edge of the spruce forest lining the beach. "This will be a perfect place for the boat."

"So no rivers to go down?" Ella asked, anxious but excited about this new experience.

"Nope." He arranged the branches to hide the green bag. "Only a few streams. I have a place in mind to set up camp, and then we can explore from there."

"Mom, are you ready? Alex has been here before, and she's going to be the leader."

"I'll be right behind you." Ella adjusted her backpack, glad the temperature was quickly nearing sixty degrees. Perfect hiking weather.

"And I'll take up the rear," Josiah whispered into her ear.

A shiver streaked down her neck and spine. The idea he was right behind her sent her heart beating faster.

Ella followed her son into the woods off the shore, the light dimming from the dense foliage surrounding her. As she hiked, the scent of the trees and vegetation infused the air, and the sounds of the birds calling echoed through the forest. As she inhaled the fresh smells and drank in her peaceful surroundings, serenity flowed through her. She hadn't felt this in years, not since she was a child. She might not be a good camper, but she was glad she'd come. She needed this.

Two hours later, in an open area at the base of a mountain, Josiah stopped, sliding his backpack off his shoulders. "This will be home for the next couple of days." He pointed toward the rock face behind him. "On the other side of the ridge is a waterfall that feeds a pond. Farther down the south side is a lighthouse on the cliff."

As her son listened to Josiah talk about the island and what to expect to see, especially the animals, Alex said, "He should be a guide leading groups into the backcountry. I'm surprised he ever left Alaska. It's in his blood."

"It's home. I can understand that, even though I've only been here four years."

"I don't know if I could ever leave here."

"What made Josiah?"

"He wanted to serve his country. Harry was a big influence on him as he grew up, so after he finished college, he enlisted in the military. But the man who came back to Alaska was a changed person," Alex whispered almost to herself, surprise flittering across her expression. She turned, wide-eyed, to Ella. "I shouldn't have said anything. He doesn't talk about his time in the Marines much. All our lives we've been close except for those ten years he was gone. Please don't say anything to him."

"I won't," Ella said. "If he doesn't want to talk about his past, that's his prerogative." But that didn't mean she had to stay around, waiting for something that wasn't going to happen.

Forcing someone to do something would never work in the long run. Keith had used force with her all the time, and finally she'd managed to escape. She knew the situations were different, but after the camping trip, she had to find a way to look at Josiah as only a friend. If not, she'd need to cut her ties completely. She was falling in love with him in spite of trying not to. The very thought sent a bolt of fear through her as all the peace she'd been feeling fled under the memories of her first marriage, based on secrets and lies from the beginning.

"Let's give them some time to bond. Let's put up our tent, then I want to show you a place I loved when I last came."

"I'm glad we decided the guys should share a tent and we girls bunk together. Two tents to carry in are better than three."

"I heard Josiah had to curtail what you were bringing."

As she and Alex worked, Ella said, "I packed my backpack and still had half of the items scattered around me on the floor. Necessary things like a flashlight, insect repellant that I didn't have room for in the bag. I quickly got a lesson on what was essential and what wasn't. I finally convinced him that my moisturizer was important because it was also a sunblock."

"One of the hardest things for me to leave behind was my cell phone. I feel lost without a connection to the outside world. Josiah insisted I not even bring it in the car, so it's sitting on the dresser in my bedroom." Alex chuckled. "I have it bad. But in my defense I run a big business and have a lot of employees."

Ella wished she'd had a sister like Alex, but she'd grown up an only child. She didn't want Robbie growing up like that.

As Alex and she finished erecting the tent, Robbie came over to her. "You did good, Mom. Josiah is gonna let me put up ours and only help if I need it."

Ella ruffled her son's hair. "Ask for help if you need it. That's what you're here for—to learn, so when we go by ourselves we'll know what to do."

He looked at her in all seriousness. "I'm here to have fun. That's what Josiah said."

"Then have fun putting up the tent. Alex and I are going to do some exploring. We'll be back in a little while."

Josiah approached. "Where are you two going?"

Ella nodded her head toward Alex, who was laying the canvas floor down and crawling out of the tent. "She knows. I'm just tagging along."

Alex rose, dusted off her jeans and glanced at her brother. "Overlooking the stream. You know where. Join us when you're through if you all want."

As Robbie went to retrieve the tent, Josiah said in a low voice, "Don't forget to take your gun."

Alex grinned. "Have I ever?"

"Should I bring my revolver, too? It's in my back-pack." Ella glanced at her belongings.

"I thought you were leaving that at your house. Alex and I have our rifles. That should be enough. There haven't been any problems with the bears on this island. The weapons are more a precaution."

"Just so you two know, I'm capable of using a weapon. I learned after I divorced my husband."

With her binoculars hanging around her neck, Alex slung her rifle over her shoulder, plopped her hat on her head and said, "Let's go. Bring your camera instead. You should get some great wildlife pictures."

Ella grabbed her camera and water and quickly followed Alex. "We'll see you all in a while."

Forty minutes later, after hiking up a trail that led to an overhang that overlooked a stream, Ella collapsed on a rock perch. "I thought it was a short walk."

"By distance it is. It's the terrain that makes it longer."

"Yeah, climbing up a small mountain for a gal who sits behind a desk most days is a bit of a challenge. How do you keep in shape? You have a desk job, too."

"I work out when I can, and in the winter cross-country skiing keeps me fit. I sometimes ski to work."

"That's something I could do, but not to work. Twice this winter I had to pick up Robbie unexpectedly from school because he was sick."

"You have a terrific kid, Ella. Having him in the house a couple of weeks ago made me realize I'd love to be a mother one day. I suppose I could look at adopting."

"Or marrying again."

Alex stared at the treetops of the forest across the stream. "No, my husband was my high school sweetheart. Since I was a sophomore, I knew I would marry him. I had five fabulous years with Cade. I can't see myself finding anyone to fill his shoes in my life."

"You never know."

Alex slanted a look at Ella. "How about you? You're a great mother to Robbie. Don't you want more children?"

"I'd love to, but for different reasons I don't see myself marrying again, either."

Alex opened her mouth, but instead of saying anything snapped it closed.

A noise behind Ella drew her around. Robbie appeared on the trail with Josiah right behind him. "What took you all so long?"

"We got some wood for a fire after setting up our tent. So now all you two have to do is fix dinner. Both of us—" Josiah pointed at Robbie then himself "—are hungry. We worked up an appetite."

"First, I'm going to take some photos." Ella lifted her camera to her face. "I'll cook if you agree to clean up."

A black-tailed deer came down to the water about ten yards upstream. She took several pictures as two more joined the first one.

She gestured toward the animals when a fawn moved out of the foliage. "Robbie, a baby deer. Do you see it?"

Robbie sat near her. "It's so cute. I hope no bears are around."

"So do I." Josiah stood behind her son.

Alex passed the binoculars to Robbie. "Take a look through these. You can see the black tails better and the spots on the fawn."

Ella rose to move closer to the ledge. As long as she wasn't at the very edge, she was all right with the height. She wanted to see if anything was on this side of the water. Suddenly all the deer looked up, then raced back into the forest. *What scared them? A bear?* She scanned up and down the stream. The sunlight glinted off something for a second, then disappeared.

"Can I have the binoculars, Robbie, for a minute?"

Her son held them up for her. She took them, then swung around to locate the dense vegetation across the water downstream where she thought she'd seen something—some*one*. It couldn't have been a bear. Then, in the midst of the thick undergrowth, she spied an individual, almost totally camouflaged, with binoculars directed toward them.

"We have company."

TWELVE

When Ella moved nearer to the ledge, keeping the binoculars fixed on the same spot, Josiah closed the space between them. "Found something interesting?"

She turned her head toward him, sliding a glance toward Robbie, then passing the binoculars to Josiah. "I saw someone in that brush down there." She pointed downstream about fifty feet.

He followed the direction she indicated, but he didn't see anyone. "Whoever it was is gone now. Although not many people live on this island, it does get some campers, hunters and hikers. We'll probably run into some while hiking tomorrow. Could be someone looking for deer. It's hunting season."

Suddenly the noise of a gunshot split the air. Ella jerked back, brushing up against Josiah, her hand splaying across her chest.

Josiah clasped her upper arms. "You okay?"

"That stopped my heart. I hope the guy missed, if he's a hunter."

"Mom, Alex and I are heading to camp, but you should stay and take a few more pictures. Maybe you'll get one of a bear."

Ella's eyes narrowed. "I get the feeling those two are conspiring."

Josiah laughed. "When I moved over here to see what you were looking at, they kept exchanging glances, so I'd say you're right."

Another shot rang out. Ella tensed. "You'd think I'd be used to hearing gunfire since I practice at the shooting range. But coming out of the blue like that…"

He leaned close to her ear and lowered his voice. "We'll hear that occasionally this weekend. You'll learn to tune it out."

"Never. Even on the shooting range, I'm aware of every shot fired. When my ex took me there, Keith liked to demonstrate his 'gift,' as he put it. But what it was really was another intimidation technique."

Josiah squeezed her arm gently. "Don't think about him. He's not here, so don't let him ruin your vacation."

She looked back at him. "I know, but no matter how much I try to put him out of my mind, at odd moments he intrudes."

"Don't let him win. You lived in fear for four years. You don't have to now."

She rotated toward him. "How about you? Something has happened to you. By all accounts, I've heard you aren't the same person you were when you went into the Marines. I know you served several tours of duty in the war zone. I also know you don't like to talk about it. I was like that, too. Confiding in you was one of the best things I've ever done. Of course, I can't go around telling the world, since I'm in hiding, but having one person know is enough. I felt a burden lifted from my shoulders. Let me help you, Josiah. And if not me, at least talk to Alex."

"She knows some of it." He stepped away.

"But not all?"

He pursed his lips and averted his gaze. "I can't. I..." He felt as though he was on the side of a cliff, ready to rappel down the rock face, and yet he couldn't make that first move and step off. He wanted to, but something held him back. The memories were buried deep, where he wanted to keep them, and yet...

She started for the path down the mountain.

"Ella."

She turned to him, expectation on her face.

"Wait up. I'll hike down with you."

A mask fell over her features, but not before he saw the hurt in her gaze. She'd given him a part of herself when she'd told him about her husband, but the words inside him were dammed up behind a protective wall.

"That's okay. I'd rather be alone." An impregnable expression met his appraisal. "We're friends, but that's all. I know that, but as a friend, I wanted to help. Now I know my boundaries."

Although her look didn't reveal much, her voice cracked on the last sentence. She swung around and marched down the trail. He'd give her a minute and follow her, staying back a hundred yards. But he wanted to keep an eye on her. He had a rifle; she didn't.

As she descended the mountain, she called over her shoulder, "What part of *alone* do you not understand? I figured you knew that definition well."

He sucked in a breath and slowed his pace, catching sight of her every minute or so on the winding path.

Lord, why can't I talk about it?

As he came into camp, he knew the answer. If he acknowledged out loud the brutality he'd endured, it would be real. It was bad enough that the memories dwelled in his mind. All he wanted to do was swipe them clean from his thoughts. Hatred toward his captors jammed his throat, and when his sister asked him a question about dinner, he couldn't answer.

A fist rose above Ella's head and came crashing down on her, pounding her over and over while Josiah watched, his arms held behind him by an unseen force. He screamed out to her to hold on and struggled with his invisible bonds.

Ella tried to bolt up, but something trapped her to the ground. She clawed at it. Her eyes flew open, a faint light streaming through the tent flaps, as she wrestled with her sleeping bag. Her breath came out in short pants, her chest rising and falling rapidly. Slowly she orientated herself to her surroundings.

Alex still slept soundly two feet away from her. She was camping with Robbie. Josiah. The thought of him broke her heart. He was unreachable. She couldn't fall in love with a man who kept his life hidden from her. She'd shared her dark past and felt better that she finally had because she'd trusted Josiah with her secret.

But he didn't trust her.

She slid her eyes closed for a long moment, trying to compose herself before getting up. After her dream, she wasn't going back to sleep even if the time was only—she glanced at her watch—5:15 a.m. At least it was daylight. She could check the food supplies and plan what she would make for breakfast. Put on a pot of coffee. She needed it to stay awake.

She walked to the edge of the campsite and yanked on the rope that held their food in a tarp off the ground.

It wasn't nearly as heavy as she thought it would be. She brought it to the ground and moved to pick the items she would need. When she flipped the canvas top away, she gasped. All she found were rocks.

All the food was gone.

For a long moment, she knelt on the tarp, stunned.

She heard a movement behind her. She swiveled around, wishing she had her gun with her.

Yawning, Josiah approached. "What's wrong?"

"Our food has been stolen, and not by bears." She leaned to the side so he could see.

His eyes grew huge, and a thunderous expression chased all sleepiness from his face. "Is this how you found it? On the ground?"

She pushed the cover totally off the rocks. "No, it was hanging in the air with these in it. Someone deliberately stole our food and left us rocks."

"This has got to be a joke. Alex has played some on me in the past."

"Like this?"

"Well, not exactly." He strode to her tent and stuck his head inside.

Not a minute later, Alex emerged and charged over to the tarp to inspect what happened. "I'd never do this. I love my food more than you do."

"I wish Buddy was here. I'd like to track down who did this." His scowl evened out a little, and he pulled the tarp off the ground. "I might be able to follow the tracks." He looked at the forest around them and headed back to his tent.

When he came out with a flashlight, probably to use in the dimly lit forest, Robbie was right behind him, rubbing his eyes. Josiah grabbed his rifle and held it in one hand as if he were ready to use it at a second's notice.

"I'll be back."

"Can I come with you?" Robbie asked, starting to follow Josiah.

He turned to her son, clasping his shoulder. "You need to stay here. Help your mom and Alex. I'll be back in a little while. Okay?"

Robbie nodded.

As he left, Alex put one hand on her waist. "We need to start looking for something to eat. I saw some berries not far up the trail. Let's start there, then we can pull out our poles and try to catch some fish when Josiah comes back."

"That'll be a healthy breakfast."

"But, Mom, I hate fish."

Josiah found boot prints that led to the stream, but as he stood on the edge of the flowing water, he was afraid the trail had ended. In many places, the stream wasn't deeper than his thighs, so someone could go ashore in countless places. The freezing water numbed his legs as he started downstream first, not even sure if the thief had crossed to the other side or only used the water as a means to throw him off his trail. Finally, an hour later, he made his way back to the camp, not wanting to be gone any longer.

Ella saw him first and hurried over. "Did you find anything?"

"He used the stream to cover his tracks. I didn't see where he came out, but there were places he could have found stones. I saw footprints but not like the ones I found going away from our camp. To be honest, the guy could have taken his boots off. I figure we should forget about him and enjoy ourselves. He didn't get our bottled water at least."

"We found some berries, and Alex is ready to go fishing. Robbie is all excited. He feels as if he's living off the land like a survivalist."

"Leave it to a child to turn our thinking around. It's a challenge, but one we can deal with. We had a big dinner last night. We have clean water and a stream with fish in it. And to top it off, we can have dessert—berries."

"And we have each other—*friends* enjoying a weekend away from the rat race."

The emphasis on *friends* didn't miss the mark with Josiah. After last night at the bluff, he knew he would always remain broken, and there was no way he would ever enter into a relationship with a woman, especially one with a child, when part of him couldn't shake the hate that kept him locked in a prison of his own making. He wanted to see all of his captors rot in a cell until they breathed their last breath. That realization stunned him. He hadn't known how deep his anger went until now.

"Josiah, are you all right?" Ella touched his arm.

The feel of her fingers on his skin shocked him from his thoughts. He blinked, trying to tamp down the emotions reeling through him. He'd never have a full life without finding a way to forgive his captors. He didn't know what to say to Ella.

She looked long and hard at him, then went to Alex and Robbie to help them with the fishing equipment.

For a moment he watched them, unable to move, to think beyond what he'd discovered about himself. Had

Ella forgiven her ex-husband? Or was she stuck in limbo like him? Unable to move forward with his life?

"Josiah, we're ready," Robbie called out.

"I'm coming," he finally said, shutting his past back into the dark recesses of his mind. He was going to have fun right now, and examine his life later when he was back in Anchorage. "I'm hungry. Let's go get some breakfast."

Later, Ella stuck the trash in a plastic bag to take with them when they left the island. "Robbie, did you get enough food?"

Her son swiped the back of his hand across his mouth. "I'm stuffed. Josiah, the salmon was great."

"This from a boy who less than twenty-four hours ago declared he hated fish. Obviously when you're starving, you'll eat anything." Ella finished cleaning up their used paper products. "Who wants to walk with me to the stream to wash our pan out?"

"I will," Josiah said before anyone else. "Alex and Robbie can get more firewood."

"I think we got the raw end of this deal." Alex stood. "C'mon, Robbie, let's get it so we can sit around relaxing. I promised to tell you about my first search and rescue with Sadie."

Ella had purposefully stayed away from Josiah all day while they'd fished, hiked and gathered a few edible items to complement the salmon. Now she was stuck walking with him. She started toward the stream. He snatched his rifle and hurried after her.

"Wait up. I'm supposed to be your guard."

"In case the thief comes back to steal our skillet?"

"He could. Or a bear could be fishing for salmon.

A better place for fishing is farther upstream, but you never know."

"Sheesh, thanks. Now I'm going to be on pins and needles the whole time."

"Right now, the bears are focused on eating all the salmon they can before winter."

Ella kept walking, concentrating on each step she took rather than the man to the left and slightly behind her. The sound of the water rushing over the rocks lured her closer and closer to the stream. She'd wash the pan and quickly return to camp.

If there had been a way to leave the island, she would have. But she had less than a day before David picked them up. She'd have to deal with being in close confines with Josiah until then, but once she returned to Anchorage, she would keep her distance. She realized she was falling in love with Josiah, but this morning, when she'd tried once more to reach out to him, he'd rejected her. She'd seen that look of pain and vulnerability on his face right before going fishing. But all she'd met was a wall of silence.

"Ella, could you slow down? We don't have to jog to the stream." Josiah's request cut through her thoughts.

"Why? I want to wash this—" she waved the skillet "—and get back to camp. It's been a long day, and I'm ready to sleep."

"It's not even eight o'clock and still bright outside."

She came to an abrupt halt and swirled around. "What do you want from me? You've been sending me mixed messages all day. I can't keep doing this." The words exploded from her as if she'd released the built-up pressure in a carbonated drink.

"To talk."

"Now?" Her gaze drilled into him. She tried desperately to read in his expression what was behind that request. But he was too good at hiding his emotions.

"Yes. I've angered you, and I think we should talk about it."

"Just go back to camp. Leave me alone."

She charged toward the stream at a fast clip. She wasn't going to argue with him. At the creek, she knelt by the edge, dipped her skillet in the water and swished it around, letting the rapid current wash the bits of food away.

Josiah squatted next to her and covered his hand over hers, grasping the pan. He took it and placed it on the ground, then drew her around. "Please hear me out."

The soft plea in his eyes was her undoing. She nodded.

He rose and tugged her away from the rushing stream to a pile of smooth stones. Taking a seat on one, he patted the rock next to him. When she sat, he clasped her hand and turned toward her. Her heartbeat sped like the flowing water.

He inhaled a deep breath and let it out slowly. "I'm not even sure where to begin. I've only shared part of what I'm going to tell you with two people—my sister and the counselor I saw for a year. It isn't common knowledge that I was a prisoner of war for months because my mission was a secret one behind enemy lines. I can't talk about it even now."

"You were a POW?" She'd known he must have gone through some horrific situations while in the Marines, but not that.

"Yes. I was captured and beaten for the details of my mission. When I finally broke, I was thrown into a cell only three feet by three feet. I hated myself for breaking down and tried to console myself with the fact that, by that time, the information I'd given them didn't mean anything. All I wanted at first was for them to kill me. End my pain."

Ella had once thought that herself, after her husband had pushed her down the stairs and she'd broken both arms. Then she'd remembered Robbie, who'd only been three at that time, and knew she had to protect him. She'd begun fighting back then and making secret plans to get away. She cupped her other hand on top of their clasped ones.

"I can tell you every gory detail of captivity if you really want to know."

Tears filling her eyes, she shook her head. "No, there's no need. The fact that you would is all I care about. My relationship with Keith was full of secrets and lies. I care so much for you, Josiah. I didn't want anything to stand between us, or I would never have told you about my ex-husband."

He captured her chin and caressed the tears away with his thumb. "After a while I turned to the Lord, begging Him to end my suffering. He didn't. Instead, slowly I felt my fighting spirit return. I thought of Alex. I thought of my fiancée, Lori, who I was going to marry when I returned from the mission. Suddenly what they did to me didn't mean anything anymore. I had a goal—to escape. To return home. And the Lord would help me."

Like I did. The power of God overwhelmed her. She couldn't stop the flow of tears running down her face, splashing onto their entwined fingers.

"The Lord was with me in that cell. Lately I've forgotten that. I was letting the traumatic past haunt me, letting it drive a wedge between me and God. But not anymore. I know what I have to do. I have to forgive my captors."

She wanted to hold him, but she was afraid that would be a distraction. His greatest need at the moment was to talk about his past. "How did you escape?"

"I could tell something was going on in the camp. A flurry of activity. Many days went by when I never saw my jailer. On the day I made my escape, a young boy brought me water and food." He stared off into space as though he was seeing it all again in his mind.

She stroked her thumb over the curve of his hand. "What happened next?"

His gaze returned to hers, awe in the depths of his crystal-blue eyes. "There was a commotion outside the cave. The boy hurriedly left, and I guess he didn't lock the door correctly. After I ate, I went to the door to see if I could hear anything. That's when I discovered it was unlocked. Without a second thought, I left my prison and managed to sneak away."

"How long did it take before you made it to safety?"

"Just hours. The commotion was a force of our men drawing near their cave hideout. The terrorists were trying to get away."

"Did they?"

"Some did. Others were killed or captured. At least that's what I heard. Our troops called for help when they found me at the bottom of the mountain. A helicopter took me back to the base. Then my journey to healing began."

"And look where you are now. Helping others. Me." She tugged him toward her and wrapped her arms around him. "I'm so sorry for what happened to you. I wish I could erase that part of your past."

He pulled slightly away and framed her face. "And I wish I could erase parts of yours. Have you been able to forgive Keith? Because I don't know how to take that step. If I don't forgive my captors, I'll never be whole again."

She closed her eyes, wishing she could help him. "I haven't forgiven Keith yet. I've prayed to God to help me, but so far I'm still as angry as I was after I managed to get away from him."

"Do you think we have a chance to be more than friends?" The feel of his thumb as it whispered across her cheek tempted her. But she couldn't. "I don't know. I'm afraid our pasts will always be there as a barrier to the true, loving relationship we deserve. I don't know if I can ever let go of the fear and mistrust I have because of Keith."

His hands slipped away from her face. He clenched them, and the strong, tense set to his jawline shouted he felt that way about his situation, too. "The reason I have Buddy is because he was—really still is—a service dog for a person with post-traumatic stress disorder. I still occasionally have nightmares and panic attacks. Not often, but enough to remind me I'm still far from healed. When I came home, I desperately wanted what happened to me to go away as if it had never occurred. When I got out of the hospital, I went to see Lori. I didn't want anyone to tell her I was home until I could see her myself. I didn't want her to see me in the hospital."

"When you love someone, that shouldn't matter."

He looked into her eyes, his stiff posture relaxing

slightly, but tension still poured off him. "I know. In the end it didn't really matter. She'd already moved on and was in love with another man. Thoughts of a life with her were one of the ways I kept myself going while a prisoner, but I realize I've forgiven Lori. I wasn't in any shape to be in a relationship when I returned to the States anyway."

Her throat swelled with emotions. Ella fought the tears rising inside. She couldn't stop them.

He took her into his embrace and pressed her against his chest. The pounding of his heart beneath her ear finally calmed the tears to a whimper. "We are quite a pair," she murmured. "What are we going to do?"

"Maybe when we get back to Anchorage, we should spend some time apart. We both need to figure out what we really want for ourselves and find a way to make it happen."

She leaned away and stared into his eyes, realizing these past weeks she had been fighting the feelings that had developed in spite of her trying to avoid an emotional involvement. In spite of her fear, she'd make the same mistake as she had with Keith. "I love you, Josiah, but I'm not sure that's enough. I can't make a mistake about this because it doesn't just affect me. I have Robbie to consider, too."

Josiah bent forward and kissed her lightly, but before he could deepen it, he put some space between them. "I agree. I never want him to be hurt."

"Then what do we tell him when you suddenly stop coming around?"

"I'll think of something, but for the time being let's just enjoy each other's company for the rest of this trip. Going camping was important to Robbie."

"I can do that." On overload with all that had transpired, Ella rose from the rock. "Are you ready to go back? They're probably wondering what's keeping us."

"Yes." He stood, taking her hand.

When she glanced upstream, she gasped and froze. Three brown bears were in the water catching salmon. "Have they been there the whole time?"

"Yes, but I was keeping an eye on them."

She'd been so focused on Josiah she hadn't even been aware of the huge animals only a football field away. Josiah did that to her. And yet, he also protected her.

As Ella strolled back to camp, she kept glancing over her shoulder. Although she'd lived here four years, it wasn't a common occurrence for her to see three brown bears at one time. But she saw no sign of them being bothered by her and Josiah. As she neared their campsite, she began to relax.

"What are we going to do tomorrow?" she asked, finally breaking the silence between them.

"There's a place we can sit on the shore and watch for whales. I can't guarantee we'll see them, but we can try. I think Robbie will get a big kick out of that."

"He certainly was excited about seeing the bald eagle in the tree today."

"That excited me. A majestic bird. Being around Robbie has renewed the awe I used to have while growing up here. You have a special son."

Suddenly a gunshot reverberated through the woods. Coming to a sudden stop, Ella tensed. "That was close."

Another blast rang out.

"It's coming from the direction of our campsite," Josiah said, grasping his rifle with both of his hands as he set out in a jog.

THIRTEEN

The pounding of Ella's footsteps matched his as Josiah raced toward the camp. As he came closer, he slowed, the beating of his heart thundering in his ears.

On the outskirts, he crept forward, Ella mirroring him. Alex stood with Robbie in front of a rocky facade, a piece of paper stuck on a small tree limb. She was demonstrating how to handle a rifle. A look of deep concentration was on the boy's face.

Ella moved around him, headed toward the pair across the campsite and said with a laugh, "You should warn me before you start target practice."

Robbie whirled toward her. "Alex was showing me how good she is. I drew a bull's-eye on the paper. She hit it twice. I want to learn. Can I, Mom?"

Alex faced Ella and Josiah. "We got bored waiting for you two to come back. Robbie wanted to know about my gun. I was pointing out how it worked and why we carry it when we go into the backcountry."

Ella turned to Robbie, a solemn expression on her face. "When you're older. Until then, you aren't to handle one. I imagine from Alex's demonstration you see how dangerous a weapon can be in the wrong hands or with someone who doesn't know what he's doing. Okay?"

With an equally somber expression, Robbie nodded.

"If we had our food, right about now, we'd be roasting marshmallows and making s'mores," Josiah said to lighten the moment of seriousness. "But we have some berries left instead. Anybody up for finishing them off with me?"

Robbie giggled. "What about breakfast tomorrow morning?"

"We'll need much more than berries tomorrow." Josiah drew the boy toward the fire ring. "We have over an hour's hike to a place I want to show you. We'll need to leave early, so I'm going to get up at the crack of dawn and go fishing. Want to come with me?"

"If you're gonna tell me where we're going to hike."

"Hopefully to see whales."

As Robbie sat near the dying fire, his eyes grew huge. "Really?"

"Maybe seals, some more eagles, too."

Robbie clapped. "Yes!"

Ella joined Josiah and Robbie, taking a seat next to her son. "I gather you're going fishing, then."

Robbie twisted toward her with his solemn expression on his face. "If we're gonna have breakfast, I have to. I'm the one who caught the most fish today."

"I think you threw down the gauntlet, Robbie." Ella's eyes twinkled.

"Gauntlet? What's that?" her son asked.

"A glove. In olden times when someone did that, it meant they were challenging another person to something." Ella glanced toward Josiah.

He smiled. "And I take up that challenge. I'm going

to catch more fish than you by seven o'clock. Deal?" Josiah held out his hand.

Her son shook it. "Deal."

"While you two battle it out at the stream, Alex and I will sleep in and have a blazing fire going by the time you come back in anticipation of all the fish you're going to catch. Now, I wonder who can top me in telling the tallest tale."

Josiah lounged back on his elbows as first his sister and then Robbie took up the dare. Around the fire, with the sun going down, the leaves rustling in the cool breeze and the sound of insects and birds filling the air, he thought about what he had told Ella at the stream. As he'd gone through the details of his ordeal, he'd always thought it would send him into a panic attack. It had when he'd first talked with his counselor. It had when he'd shared some of it with Alex. Would his nightmare return tonight with Buddy at home?

Josiah caught Ella staring at him, her warm brown eyes probing, as though trying to reach into his mind. He averted his gaze. He didn't want to let her go, but he didn't think he was good for her.

The next morning Ella woke up, snuggled comfortably in her sleeping bag. She'd gotten a good night's rest and was ready for the day of hiking before David came at six to pick them up. This weekend had been a revelation—from Josiah, but also inside her. Somewhere deep within her, she needed to find a way to let go of her anger toward Keith and move on completely. Josiah was right. She could never truly embrace the rest of her life if she didn't.

Sitting up, Ella stretched the kinks out of her body,

which wasn't used to sleeping on the hard ground. Even as she crawled from the tent, she continued to work out the stiffness from her muscles. She spied Alex sitting on the ground, her eyes closed, her body relaxed. She'd learned when living at the estate that Alex always meditated first thing in the morning if possible. It was her special time with God. Ella liked that idea, but she found the end of the day worked best for her.

When Ella stood, Alex opened her eyes. Ella quickly said, "I'm gathering the firewood we need. Go back to what you're doing."

Ella hurried into the wooded area near the campsite as Alex slid her eyelids closed again. She'd slept so well she hadn't heard Josiah or Robbie leaving at sunrise to fish. Glancing at her watch, she knew the guys would be back in about twenty minutes, ready to cook the fish. Bending over, she began picking up stray tree limbs until her arms were loaded with firewood.

She heard an owl in an upper branch of one of the trees and stopped, trying to determine where he was perched. Another hoot echoed through the woods. Suddenly she thought about what had started all of this—falling in love with a man who wasn't ready for a relationship. It had been weeks ago when Robbie and his friends went in search of an owl. Something good had come out of the incident with Foster. Maybe sometime later, Josiah and she would have a chance.

I hope so.

All she had to do was let go of the hold Keith had on her. Somehow she would do that because she and Robbie deserved more. She leaned over to grab one more piece of wood before heading back to camp. She straightened and swung around to retrace her steps when she saw him.

The collected firewood tumbled to the ground about her feet.

Keith.

With a rifle pointed at her.

"I won. I won." Robbie danced around in circles at the stream.

Josiah laughed at the glee on the boy's face. "You're a natural outdoorsman. The skills will come as you get older. That doesn't have anything to do with being a natural."

Robbie puffed out his chest. "Can I learn how to cook these salmon you filleted?"

"Sure. Let's go." Josiah washed his hands in the stream, grabbed the fish he'd prepared and headed toward the campsite.

"Thanks, Josiah, for showing me all these things this weekend. Mom isn't too big on camping, but when I get older, I'll be able to go with friends."

"Until then, you can go with me again, if you like," Josiah said, before he realized Ella probably wouldn't want that. Yesterday evening, they had agreed to put some distance between them.

"I'd love that."

They walked through the woods in silence for a while, then Robbie asked, "Do you like my mom?"

Josiah could answer many questions about Alaska, dogs and camping, but that question left him speechless. He couldn't lie to the boy, but he didn't want to give him false hope concerning him and Ella. "I think your mom is very special," he finally said, praying that would satisfy Robbie.

"Would you ever consider being my dad?"

Stunned, Josiah came to a halt. He opened his mouth to say something, but couldn't think of a reply.

The child stopped, too. "I know you two haven't dated long—"

"We haven't really dated at all."

"Well, you have my permission to date my mom." Robbie started again for the campsite.

It took a moment for Josiah to gather his wits. What was he going to say to Ella about this? Then the thought of being the child's father began to worm its way into his mind. He finally trailed a few feet behind the boy, thinking of the prospect of having a child—children. Yesterday that thought would have scared him, but now it didn't sound quite as far-fetched.

When they entered the camp, Alex had her gun in hand and was starting for the forest on the left.

"Where are you going?"

"Ella has been gone too long. She left to collect the firewood we needed. That was over half an hour ago."

Josiah walked to her and gave her the fillets. "Get these ready. I'll track her and bring her back."

As he headed into the trees, he stamped down the gut feeling something had happened. She might have gotten turned around in the woods, especially if she'd wandered too far away.

Ella is all right.

He kept repeating that as he followed her tracks.

Shocked and frozen, Ella stared into the diamond-hard eyes of her ex-husband, boring into hers with such hatred. No words came to mind. Her heartbeat began to hammer against her rib cage at such a rapid pace she thought it would burst from her chest.

"I've been searching for you for four years." His gaze raked down her length. "Finally I get to pay you back for turning me in."

How had he found her? Fear choked her throat, making it impossible to say anything. All her past nightmares came crashing down on her.

"I'm going to kill you slowly, then take *my son* and raise him to be a man."

Robbie. No, he can't. She tamped down the terror threatening to make her useless. Her son's life was at stake. *Lord, I can't do this without You.*

"What? You have nothing to say to your husband?"

"No." It wouldn't do any good.

He tossed her a set of handcuffs. "Put these on. And make it fast."

They fell at her feet. She glared at him.

"If you don't cooperate with me, I'll make Robbie's life worse than you could ever imagine."

Begrudgingly she bent over and snatched the handcuffs, then snapped them on.

"That's a good little wife. No piece of paper will change that fact." Keith slung the rifle over his shoulder and took out a handgun. "Let's go. I have a nice secluded spot for a special celebration between us."

She shuddered at the sneer in his voice, the evil on his face. How had she ever thought she was in love with this man? Because he had been a master at putting up just the right facade for people—at least for a short time. Then his true nature always came out.

He approached her, gripped her arm and dragged her

in front of him. He leaned close to her ear and whispered, "I've been thinking for years about what I would do with you when I finally found you. When you were splashed across the news, you made it so easy for me. You might look different, but Robbie looks just like me." He yanked her long hair tied in a ponytail. "I like this blond color much better than that mousy brown you had. Let's go."

The glee in his voice left her stone-cold. He had to shove her to get her to move. He rammed the barrel into her back and kept prodding her forward through the undergrowth until he came to an animal trail. She knew that Josiah could track, but she wanted to make it as easy as possible. The only thing she had access to was a beaded bracelet Robbie had made her at camp.

As she trudged before Keith, she managed to slip the piece of jewelry off her wrist. She pulled it apart until she held a handful of small beads. Were they large enough for Josiah to see?

Following the set of tracks from the area Alex had indicated, Josiah reached a small clearing and homed in on some scattered branches lying on the ground near a set of her footprints. What had happened here? Why had she dropped the firewood? Had an animal scared her?

He studied the surroundings, taking in the boot prints—similar to the ones he'd tracked after their food had been taken. The tracks stopped right in front of hers. Then they both moved off to the northeast.

His gut twisted and knotted. Ella had been taken. It didn't matter why. He just had to get her back and protect the others. She wouldn't have gone off willingly without letting Alex know.

He raced to the campsite and motioned for Alex to come to him. When she did, he lowered his voice, keeping an eye on Robbie so he wouldn't hear, and said, "Someone took Ella. A large man, by the size of the boot print. I think it's the same man who stole our food. Leave everything, take Robbie and use the inflatable boat to get help on the mainland. The man is taking her northeast."

When she nodded, Josiah snatched up his backpack with binoculars, rope and a flashlight, waved to Robbie, then whirled around and hurried after Ella and her kidnapper. When he reached the small clearing, he began the slow tracking process until he found a yellow bead in the dirt. About twenty yards away, he saw another one—blue.

Ella's legs protested with each step she took. Sweat rolled down her face. Her eyes stung from the saltiness. The constant poking of the gun into her back had become an irritant that made her want to scream out in frustration and fear.

Ahead, a rocky path started to slant upward. She craned her neck at the direction Keith was taking her. She didn't know if she had the energy to go twenty feet up the slope, let alone climb a mountain. But the worst part was how scared she was of heights.

Lord, what do I do?

She slowed her pace at the bottom of the incline. Keith plowed into her.

She fell forward, her knees taking the brunt of the fall onto the stones. Pain shot up her body, and she bit her lower lip to keep from crying out.

"If I have to, I'll drag you up there. Get up. Now."

She placed her fists, one that still clenched the few remaining beads, on the hard surface and pushed herself to her shaky legs. God was with her. She could do this.

"This is for every day I've feared for my life. For my lousy life in the witness security program trying to live on a measly amount of money. But I'm taking my life back. I'm gonna take care of you. Then I'm getting Robbie and leaving the country."

Taunting words filled her mind, but she gritted her teeth to keep them to herself. He'd never be free of the organization he'd worked for because he'd betrayed them. She could only imagine the horrors of what they'd do to a traitor. Even halfway around the world. Somehow she had to find a way to prevent him from getting her son. She wouldn't let Robbie live a life on the run from men bent on murdering Keith.

He shoved her forward, but she managed to keep her balance and tramped up the rocks.

Please, Lord, protect Robbie from Keith. Get him to safety.

She prayed with each step she took up the mountain, her body shaking. She kept her gaze focused on the ground in front of her, not on how far she had come up the incline. She dropped the few beads she had left at the halfway mark of the sixty-degree slope. Part of their ascent was hidden by trees, and she knew they were on the other side of the range from where they had camped.

I'm in Your hands, Lord.

About a hundred yards from the top, Keith propelled her around a large boulder and into a cave in the stone facade. Dark and musky with only one way out, and Keith blocked it, towering over her with a fierce countenance.

His eyes became black pinpoints. "Now we're far enough away from anybody else that even if you screamed no one would hear." He waved his revolver at her. "I have a little place set up just for you. Get up and get moving." Keith gestured toward the black hole that led deeper into the cave.

The last bead Josiah found was a fourth of the way up the side of a mountain. But nothing since. Had he missed the direction Ella and her kidnapper had gone? On a small ledge, he used the binoculars and scanned above him then to the left and right before he surveyed the area below him. Either Ella and her kidnapper had already made it to the top, or they were hiding somewhere on this face of the mountain.

Sweat drenched him. At the moment the only choice he had was to continue straight up and pray the Lord showed him where Ella was. He hoped Alex had gotten Robbie off the island by now. At least Ella's son would be safe.

Since he didn't want to miss Ella and the man who'd taken her, he stopped periodically and panned his surroundings. For the third time he came up empty-handed, and frustration ate at him.

On the fourth survey from the small outcropping where he stood, he sidled carefully to the right, wanting to check out a boulder on a ledge a hundred feet away. Was that an opening? Creeping as far as he could, he held on to a small bush growing out of the side of the mountain to lean as far away from the rock wall as he could.

The second he figured out that the hole in the stone wasn't just a crevice but a cave, the brush pulled away from the rocks. He teetered on the edge, flapping his arms to get his balance.

Deeper in the cave, Ella spied a faint glow up ahead of her; the only light guiding her way was the one Keith wore strapped to his head.

"We aren't far from the cavern I've prepared for us."

They turned a corner, and the faint glow was gone. She couldn't hold her arms out to feel the side of the cave as he did. She took another cautious step, and her foot twisted as it came down between two rocks.

She cried out as she went down, her left arm colliding with a jutting piece of the wall. She fought the tears that welled into her eyes, making what little she could see blurry, and she averted her head before he saw. He'd loved to see her cry and beg. She wouldn't give him the satisfaction.

"Get up." Keith kicked her leg, now pinned between two stones.

Rising anger vied with her fear as she finally yanked her foot free.

"Now."

"I am! If you'd give me a light, I could see where I'm going" were the first words she spoke since he'd asked her if she had anything to say to him.

"Ah, she finally speaks." Mockery laced each of his words.

She struggled to stand, keeping her back to him while she blinked the last of her tears. Her fury was taking over. She wouldn't give up the fight until she drew her last breath.

"As usual, you think you're a big man because you *think* you can cow a woman a foot shorter than you."

He snorted. "I haven't even begun toying with you. To even the playing field a little, I'll give you a head start. I'll count to one hundred while you try to get away from me. I suppose it's possible you could find a hiding place. Who knows? But the only way you can escape is into the mountain."

She finally glanced over her shoulder. The bright light nearly blinded her. The only thing she could see was him holding the gun aimed at her.

"One, two, three. You better get going."

She started forward.

"Four, five, six."

She brought her left arm across her chest so she could run her hands along the side of the wet, cold cave. She tried to block his counting from her mind.

But she couldn't.

"Twenty, twenty-one, twenty-two."

Using the wall as a guide wasn't working well. She gave it up and lifted her arms out in front, then increased her pace. The cave curved to the right, and the glare of his headlamp no longer lit her way, even vaguely. Darkness shrouded her, but she kept going. She needed to find somewhere to hide.

"One hundred. Here I come."

FOURTEEN

Josiah lost his balance and slipped from the ledge. He began to fall down the slope, his arms flailing for a handhold. A stone jutting out from the outcropping grazed his fingers, and he grasped it, stopping his descent down the side of the mountain. He swung his other hand around the rock while his legs dangled in the air. Willing all his strength into his arms, he slowly pulled himself back up to the shelf, his muscles twitching with the strain.

He lay on the rough surface and dragged oxygen into his lungs. He couldn't stay here. He needed to get to that cave and see if Ella was in there. Otherwise she and her kidnapper were already on the ridge, and it would take him a while to pick up their trail. Cautiously he made his way to the right and up.

When he reached the cave's entrance, he checked the ground for any sign Ella was in there. In the dirt just inside the opening, he glimpsed footprints like the ones he'd been tracking. He took a step toward them and halted. Sweat popped out on his forehead. His heartbeat thumped against his chest, and his pulse raced.

Suddenly he was thrust back into the past when he

was kept prisoner in a cage in a cave. His legs refused to move forward into the waiting darkness, as though he'd been flash frozen.

Ella groped around another turn, moving away from the glow she'd spied earlier. She wouldn't put it past Keith to have set it up as a lure, knowing he was going to do something like this. The longer she kept Keith away from Robbie, the better the chance her son would get away. Alex and Josiah would know something was wrong by now and go for help.

You're not alone in this. She felt those words deep in her heart. This wasn't the same as before with Keith when she'd become so cut off from friends and family. When Keith found her, he would discover she wasn't the same docile woman he'd terrorized. If she didn't leave this cave, neither would he.

She glanced back and noticed a light coming closer to the turnoff she'd taken. Twisting forward again, she picked up speed, going several yards when her left foot slammed against a rock. Even in her boots, pain zipped up her leg. She stumbled and went down, using her arms to break her fall. At the same time the collision with the wall knocked the breath from her. She labored to sit up and tried to stand. She crumpled to the rock surface, back against the side of the tunnel.

Before trying to rise again, she patted the area around her. She had to hide. Watching the light growing brighter as Keith stalked her, she hoisted herself to her knees and checked the evenness of the floor in front of her. She encountered another rocky obstacle. She crawled forward to see if there were more. For the next twenty feet she painstakingly made her way from one stone obstruction to another. The path ahead grew narrower.

Until she came to a drop-off. Trapped.

Josiah lifted his foot and moved forward into the cave's entrance. His body shook. His past captors were not going to control him. The anger he always experienced when thinking about them flooded him, making the next step even more difficult.

Lord, help me. Please. Ella needs me.

But the panic threatened to immobilize him. He quaked even more. His breathing became shallow inhalations that left his lungs starving for oxygen-rich air.

Let it go. Forgive.

The conversation he had with Ella took over his thoughts. *As long as I hate them, what they did to me will influence all aspects of my life. Will dominate my actions.*

No! I won't let them.

Time was running out. Every second could be Ella's last. He gritted his teeth and focused on eradicating his hatred, on washing his mind clean, as though he'd been baptized again.

He raised another foot and put it down in front of him. Then another. A faint light ahead drew him in a little farther. Sweat stung his eyes. He swiped the back of his hand across his forehead and pictured Ella's smiling face, her eyes bright with the gleam of mischief.

Then the illumination drawing him into the cave vanished. He halted.

Ella lay flat on the cave floor, inched forward and felt to see if she could figure out how deep the drop-off was. Reaching down as far as she could, she couldn't touch the bottom.

"I will find you, Ella. You won't escape me this time. Never again."

Keith's words echoed through the cavern, chilling her to the bone.

With a quick glance back, she watched the brightness grow nearer. Although it lit that last bend she'd taken, it wasn't enough to illuminate her surroundings. She began exploring them with her hands, searching for anywhere to conceal herself from Keith. To the side was a large stone. Maybe she could hide behind it and pray he didn't know she'd gone this way.

She crawled behind the rock and curled into the smallest ball she could, sending up her prayers to be saved.

His headlamp washed the area in brightness as though a spotlight was pointing to her hiding place. Her heartbeat pounded against her skull. Her body ached all over, and she couldn't seem to breathe enough.

"Come out. Come out. Wherever you are."

She couldn't even cover her ears to keep from hearing Keith's taunting words. They bombarded her as though he was hammering his fists into her body.

The light came closer. The sound of his breathing seemed to resonate against the rocky walls, drowning out her own thundering heartbeat.

"Gotcha."

Claws grabbed her upper arms and yanked her from her hiding place, which in the glow barely blocked her from his view. He hoisted her into the air, his bright light glaring in her eyes. Squinting, she peered down.

Her legs dangled a few feet off the stone ground. He edged toward the dark drop-off.

"I wonder what's down there, how deep it is."

He held her over the hole. She refused to look and instead stared at his waist.

"Mmm. I can't see the bottom."

He'd put his rifle down and had stuffed his revolver in his belt because his two hands were busy gripping her. As he finally stepped back from the ledge, Ella decided it was now or never.

She shrieked and swung her legs toward him.

A high-pitched blood-curdling cry vibrated through the tunnel. Josiah's grasp on his flashlight tightened. The sound chilled him. He increased his pace. In his gut he knew that was Ella, and she was in trouble.

He rushed around the bend in the cave where the glow had disappeared to a faint then nonexistent illumination. He stumbled over the uneven surface and caught himself before going down. Noises drifted to him. A fight? Although the ground was rugged, with large cracks, he accelerated even more.

"I'm gonna kill you," a gruff masculine voice shouted.

Then the blast of a gunshot, the sound ricocheting off the stone walls in deafening waves. Then another gun went off—different, though. A revolver?

Click. Click. Click, followed by an explosion of words that scorched Josiah's ears. Had the gun stopped working?

He flew over the rough terrain, readying his rifle the best he could one-handed since he held the flashlight in the other. As he neared another curve in the tunnel, he slowed because light shone as though it came from somewhere nearby. He flattened himself against the wall and peeked around the wall into the corridor.

The first thing he saw was Ella racing toward him, a revolver clasped in her handcuffed hands. Then he glimpsed a large, muscular man with blond hair charging Ella, holding a rifle like a club, his face red with rage.

Ella rounded the curve. She spied him and slowed her pace. When she was safe behind him, Josiah thrust the flashlight into her hand, then stepped out into the corridor.

"Stop! Drop your gun," Josiah said, and raised his rifle.

But before he could line up a shot, the tall man kept coming, swinging his gun toward Josiah's head. He crouched and barreled into the blond giant, driving both of them deeper into the tunnel. The man's rifle came down on Josiah's back. Josiah rammed him into the wall. Once. Twice. Until the rifle clattered to the ground.

The giant wrapped his arms around Josiah's torso instead and squeezed so tight that pain stabbed into his chest as if his bruised rib hadn't healed. Josiah brought his hands up and hit the man's ears, hoping to throw him off balance so he would loosen his grip. His arms slackened enough that Josiah broke his hold. Then quickly he moved in and punched one fist into the man's nose and the other into his throat.

The guy staggered back, gasping for air while blood ran down his face. His left foot came down on the edge of a drop-off. He flapped his arms, trying to regain his balance, but before Josiah could reach him, he fell backward. The giant's scream echoed through the cave, followed by a thumping sound.

Panting, Josiah peered down into the hole. The man's light still shone, illuminating his broken body at the bottom of a deep pit.

"Is he dead?" Ella's voice quavered behind him.

Josiah swung around, took one glance at her pale features and wide eyes and drew her away from the drop-off. Then he retrieved the flashlight from her and checked the bottom of the pit again to reassure her that it was over.

When he returned to her, he tugged her against him, trying to absorb the tremors that racked her body. "Yes, he's dead. You're safe now."

"That was Keith. He was going to kill me," she murmured against his chest in a monotone as though she was going into shock.

"Let's get out of here. Into the sunshine. He can't hurt you ever again."

"Are you sure?" A sob tore through her.

"He fell sixty or seventy feet onto a rocky surface, and by the pool of blood around his head, I'm positive."

"Is Robbie all right? He was going to take him." She shuddered.

"He's safe. My sister is guarding him."

When he brought Ella into the sunlight, he sat her down on the ledge and pulled her into the crook of his arm. "When you're ready, we'll hike to the beach to be picked up. Alex and Robbie left in the boat to get help. Then when Keith's body is recovered, you'll have to ID him, and the medical examiner can confirm he's dead."

Ella stood at her living room window as Alex parked her car, hopped out and walked toward her house. For the past two days, since returning from the island, Ella had gone through the motions of living, but a part of her was numb as though she was still in the cave with Keith, listening to him telling her how he was going to kill her.

Earlier she'd talked with her minister, but didn't really think she was free from her ex-husband. She'd thought she was before and he'd found her.

He's dead. Everyone has told me that.

She'd repeated that so many times in the past forty-eight hours she would have thought it would finally sink in. But for so long she had lived in terror, and it wasn't that easy to shake it off.

Maybe when she finally identified his body, she'd be free. No more nightmares for her or Robbie. Was that even possible?

Then her minister's words repeated themselves in her mind. *You won't be free until you forgive Keith. You can't let go while holding on to that kind of hatred.*

Alex rang the doorbell. Ella headed to the foyer to answer it, knowing she had to find the power to forgive.

She forced a smile on her face and greeted Alex. "I'm glad you could take Robbie while I go to ID Keith."

"Sadie is waiting for him to come visit. We'll have fun. Don't hurry to come pick him up. You and Josiah should talk. You haven't had much of a chance since all this happened."

"Do you know if they found Keith's campsite?"

"Yes, I got a call when Josiah landed at the airport. They found it and a stash of firepower that could wipe out a lot of people. Josiah said it looked as though he was planning a small war."

Ella hugged her arms. "A US Marshal came to see me this morning to find out what happened. Apparently my husband left their protection and in the process killed a man. He obviously was very determined to get to me."

"He can't anymore."

"I'm trying to realize that, but he's been such a big part of my life for so long. It's hard to think I'm really free." *Am I really until I finally say that I've forgiven Keith and mean it?*

"Sam and I are ready to go, Alex," Robbie said behind Ella.

"That's great. Sadie's in the car waiting." To Ella she added, "We're going to the park before going to my house. Don't worry about the time you pick him up." Alex looked pointedly at her. "Take care of *all* your business."

"I will."

Robbie threw his arms around Ella. "I love you, Mom."

She ruffled his hair. "I love you, too."

Ella stood in the entrance and watched her son lead his twelve-week-old puppy to Alex's car. She was right about talking with Josiah. She needed to. Once they'd walked out of the woods onto the beach, they hadn't been alone in the midst of Josiah helping with the recovery of Keith's body and the search for his campsite. She'd had her hands full with reassuring Robbie they would be all right and then being interviewed by the authorities about what had happened. A whirlwind forty-eight hours. She desperately wanted her life to return to normal, or rather settle into a new normal. She knew where she would go before she went to ID Keith and see Josiah.

Emotionally and physically drained, Josiah entered the State Medical Examiner's building. He didn't see

Ella's Jeep out in the parking lot, so he would wait for her in the lobby. Thomas would be here soon, too.

As he stared out the double glass doors, he realized that now that he'd had time to think, he wanted to move on in his life. Seeing what Ella had gone through for years, all he wanted to do was be there for her and give her a life that would erase her ex-husband from her memories. He'd seen firsthand what anger could do to a person if left to fester and grow. He didn't want that for his life.

As he'd accompanied Thomas and trudged all over the island with Buddy looking for the campsite, they had talked. He'd finally shared his captivity with his best friend. Through Thomas's guidance, he'd given his rage at his captors to the Lord. He never wanted to hate someone so much that he ended up consumed like Keith.

He caught sight of Ella. He held one of the doors open for her, and she entered the building. When she turned toward him, he sucked in a deep breath. She was beautiful inside and out. She gave him hope for the future.

"Are you ready to ID him?" he asked, clasping her hand.

She nodded. "Let's get this over with."

When she saw Keith's face, all she said to the ME was "Yes."

Thomas came into the room as she turned away.

"Thomas, you look as tired as Josiah."

"I've hiked miles the past two days, and I'm ready for a rest. Sorry I'm late. I was turning in the evidence we found at Keith's campsite."

"All Keith said to me was I should have realized I

would never escape him completely. He mentioned the story about Seth's rescue at Eagle River and said that I should quit worrying about people besides myself."

"We found a copy of the story written in the newspaper with a photo where you appeared in the background. Not the same one that was on the TV channel. But that had to be how he discovered where you were." Josiah settled his arm on her shoulders.

Thomas frowned. "He bribed an airport employee for David's flight plan that day you all left for the island."

Ella tensed. "Is the employee still alive?"

Thomas's eyes hardened. "Barely. He was left for dead."

Beneath Josiah's arm, she relaxed the tightness in her shoulders. "I'll pray he makes it. Keith liked to tie up loose ends, and I'm glad he didn't succeed here."

"Your ex-husband's death has been ruled an accident. He'll be buried tomorrow. Everything is over, Ella." Thomas smiled. "Now you two can get on with your lives."

His best friend zeroed in on Josiah's face, his look practically shouting what he meant, especially when he looked back and forth between Ella and Josiah.

"We're leaving," Josiah said. With Ella beside him, he walked into the hallway.

Out in the parking lot, he grasped both of Ella's hands to stop her from getting into her Jeep. "You're a sight for sore eyes, and I really mean sore. I didn't sleep an hour last night. I couldn't rest until any danger of Keith's weapons being found by someone and being used illegally was taken care of." He inched closer. "Now you and I need to talk about our future."

He half expected her to say, "What future?" but she

grinned, her eyes bright. She cupped his cheek. "I like the sound of that. I was a little late because I went to church to pray and ask God to help me let go of my anger toward Keith. By the time I left, I felt it lifted from me. He paid the price for his evil. I won't give him the satisfaction of influencing my life for one more second. I want to spend that life with you. I love you."

He brushed his lips over hers and whispered against them, "I love you, too, with all my heart."

Ella wound her arms around him and deepened the kiss. When she finally pulled away, she said, "I'm here for you. I know with help you can move on—"

He pressed his fingers over her lips. "I came to that conclusion when I saw the extremes a person can go to for revenge. It takes over your life and destroys it as much as you want to destroy the other person."

"No matter what, you would never turn into Keith. You aren't capable of that. You want to help others. He wanted to harm them. You two are worlds apart, and I know that now. For a long time I doubted my ability to really know a person. I thought I did with Keith, and look what happened."

He kissed the tip of her nose. "I want to marry you. We can wait as long as you need, though."

"I don't want to wait any longer. I've been waiting a lifetime for someone like you."

He lifted her against him and swung her around, laughter pouring from him. "Then we aren't waiting anymore. Let's go let Alex and Robbie know to prepare for a wedding soon."

EPILOGUE

Two months later

Josiah put his arm around Ella and approached the elegant restaurant. "We're finally having that special dinner I promised you at Celeste's."

She looked at him, a smile deep in her eyes. "*Special* is the right word. This was the perfect place to have our wedding reception, but you didn't have to buy out the whole place for the night."

"Yes, I did. We have a lot of people who care about us."

When they entered, a sea of familiar faces greeted them with a round of applause and a few loud whistles.

Robbie broke away from Ella's parents, who had come to Alaska for the wedding, and hurried to his mom and hugged her. Then Robbie threw his arms around Josiah. "What took you all so long?"

"You couldn't have been here long. You left the church with your grandparents ten minutes before us." Josiah clasped his shoulder. "Are you going to be all right for a week with your grandparents while your mom and I are away on our honeymoon?"

Robbie grinned. "Yes, I'm going with them to show

them the sights of Alaska. I warned them about seeing bears and moose. It didn't seem to bother Grandpa, but Nana isn't so sure about the trip now. Grandpa said that she'd change her mind."

"It's hard to come to Alaska and not see the wonders. I think she'll come around, too."

Robbie signaled for Josiah to lean down, then whispered in a serious voice, "Can I call you Dad now?"

The question stunned Josiah. He'd hoped Robbie would want to one day, but he hadn't expected it so soon. "I'd be honored if you would."

"Thanks, Dad."

"Josiah, we need to greet our guests." Ella touched his arm, the elated look on her face indicating she'd heard what her son had said.

In front of two hundred people, Josiah couldn't resist kissing his wife of an hour. He drew her into his arms and kissed his bride for a second time that night before an audience.

* * * * *

"I have your new identities." US marshal Jonathan Mast sat across the table from Julia in the hotel where she and her children had been holed up for the last five days.

The Luchadors wanted to kill William so he wouldn't testify against their leader. As much as Julia didn't trust law enforcement, she had to rely on the US Marshals and their witness protection program to keep her family safe. No wonder her nerves were stretched thin.

"We're ready to transport you and the children," Jonathan Mast continued. "We'll fly into Kansas City tonight, then drive to Topeka and north to Yoder."

"What's in Kansas?"

Jonathan pulled out his phone and accessed a photograph. He handed the cell to Julia. "Abraham King will watch over you in Kansas."

Julia studied the picture. The man looked to be in his midthirties with a square face and deep-set eyes beneath dark brows. His nose appeared a bit off center, as if it had been broken. Lips pulled tight and no hint of a smile on his angular face.

"Mr. King doesn't look happy."

Jonathan shrugged. "Law enforcement photos are never flattering."

Her stomach tightened. "He's a cop?"

"Past tense. He left the force three years ago."

Once a cop, always a cop. Her ex had been a police officer. He'd protected others but failed to show that same sense of concern when it came to his own family. The marshal seemed oblivious to her unease.

"Abe is an old friend," Jonathan continued. "A widower from my police-force days who owns a farm and has a spare house on his property. He lives in a rural Amish community."

"Amish?"

"That's right."

"Bonnets and buggies?" she asked.

He smiled weakly. "You'll be off the grid, Mrs. Bradford. No one will look for you there."

Don't miss
Amish Safe House *by Debby Giusti,*
available February 2019 wherever
Love Inspired® Suspense books and ebooks are sold.

www.LoveInspired.com

Save $1.00

on the purchase of ANY

Love Inspired® book.

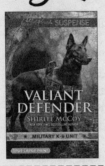

Available wherever books are sold, including most bookstores, supermarkets, drugstores and discount stores.

Save $1.00

on the purchase of ANY Love Inspired® book.

Coupon valid until March 31, 2019.
Redeemable at participating retail outlets in the U.S. and Canada only.
Limit one coupon per customer.

52616176

Canadian Retailers: Harlequin Enterprises Limited will pay the face value of this coupon plus 10.25¢ if submitted by customer for this product only. Any other use constitutes fraud. Coupon is nonassignable. Void if taxed, prohibited or restricted by law. Consumer must pay any government taxes. Void if copied. Inmar Promotional Services ("IPS") customers submit coupons and proof of sales to Harlequin Enterprises Limited, P.O. Box 31000, Scarborough, ON M1R 0E7, Canada. Non-IPS retailer—for reimbursement submit coupons and proof of sales directly to Harlequin Enterprises Limited, Retail Marketing Department, 22 Adelaide St. West, 40th Floor, Toronto, Ontario M5H 4E3, Canada.

U.S. Retailers: Harlequin Enterprises Limited will pay the face value of this coupon plus 8¢ if submitted by customer for this product only. Any other use constitutes fraud. Coupon is nonassignable. Void if taxed, prohibited or restricted by law. Consumer must pay any government taxes. Void if copied. For reimbursement submit coupons and proof of sales directly to Harlequin Enterprises, Ltd 482, NCH Marketing Services, P.O. Box 880001, El Paso, TX 88588-0001, U.S.A. Cash value 1/100 cents.

5 65373 00076 2   (8100)0 12404

® and ™ are trademarks owned and used by the trademark owner and/or its licensee.

© 2019 Harlequin Enterprises Limited

LISCOUP08184